CREDIBLE DAGGER

A World War II Thriller

GREGORY M. ACUÑA

FREE BOOK

For My Family

Inspired By True Events

Author's Footnotes

It has been a life-long passion to write a World War II spy thriller. That is why I decided to write *Credible Dagger* as my second novel, instead of the sequel to *The Balkan Network*.

Credible Dagger is the story about the early lives of four characters I introduced in *The Balkan Network*: Harold Mattingly, Josef Kostinic, Penelope Walsh, and Yuri Pavol (codename "Preacher"). It explains the significance of why the Defense Intelligence Agency picked three aging men to lead the 1999 operation into Serbia.

This is a work of fiction; with the exception of historical figures, all characters portrayed in this novel are fictitious or figments of my imagination. However, *Credible Dagger* is based on real events and real people. As such, I have included footnotes within the text to emphasize historical information or clarification. Normally, this is not done in a novel. However, as an avid reader of this genre myself, I have often come across something in my readings that I've wanted more information on, especially if it was significant or of a historical nature. Many times, I had to put the book down and research the topic until I found the answer. It is my hope, that you, the reader will find these embedded footnotes helpful.

Prologue

It was a beautiful Sunday morning in August of 1947. A thin layer of wispy, white clouds lightly covered the hills of Palo Alto, California. The young couple, Josef and Celeste Kostinic, approached the small cottage along Junipero Serra Boulevard near the Stanford University campus. Celeste held the small piece of paper with the address, "Right here, this is it, 624 Junipero Serra Boulevard. He should be home at this hour of the day."

Josef and Celeste were living in Berkeley, just across the bay, from Palo Alto. Josef had gotten a job as an assistant professor teaching geography at the University of California. After the war, Celeste, a former British secret agent, spent several months trying to locate US Army SHAEF assistant and OSS analyst, Harold "Hal" Mattingly, and finally found him. It seemed that when the war ended, SHAEF closed down immediately and General Eisenhower and his staff were dispersed to various locations throughout the United States. Josef stayed in Europe as a representative for Allied forces, tracking down war criminals. Celeste and Josef were desperate to find Mattingly, because they had crucial information about his fiancée, Penelope Walsh. He needed to be informed.

"Should I ring or knock?" she asked Josef.

"Go ahead and knock. The latest information we have is that he has a live-in housekeeper and he may still be asleep."

Celeste acknowledged and knocked gently on the door. A few minutes later, she heard the sounds of little footsteps, giggles behind the door, and a young child speaking French. Then she heard larger footsteps, followed by a voice in broken English with a strong French accent, "Who is it?"

Celeste recognized the French and responded, *"Mon nom est Celeste Kostinic. Je suis une amie de Penelope Walsh. Je viens pour vous, Monsieur Mattingly."*

The woman didn't answer, obviously surprised someone spoke in her native tongue, and the door cracked opened slightly. A small, elderly woman with white hair, wearing a large apron greeted the two visitors; she continued in French, "I have all the proper immigration papers. What is it that you want?"

Celeste continued in French, "No, it's nothing like that. We've come to see Mr. Mattingly with important information about his fiancée. Can we please step in?"

The woman opened the door fully and motioned the couple to enter, "Have a seat in the living room while I get Mr. Mattingly. Can I bring you coffee or tea?"

"Tea, black, for both of us, please," Celeste responded as the couple entered the cottage and took a seat on the sofa.

The woman nodded her head and disappeared into the kitchen where the young child hid curiously behind a swinging door. Celeste heard the older woman speaking

French, telling the child it was not the police, but friends of her father.

She gave Josef a curious look because he did not hear the conversation between the woman and child, "I didn't know Hal had a child?"

"I didn't, either, but a lot of things can happen in three years after the war. He could have moved on, got married, and started a family."

Ten minutes later, Hal Mattingly walked into the small living room. He still looked much the same to Celeste as she remembered back in 1943, tall, lean, with dark-brown hair, and a thin mustache. He was already showered, dressed, and ready for the day. He wore a corduroy coat, blue jeans, and loafers. He seemed much like any other twenty-four-year old, Stanford University student. He recognized Celeste immediately. The last time they had seen each other was in London, on the night he proposed to Penelope, "Well, I'll be damn, you're the last person on earth, I expected to see at my front door. It's good to see you, Celeste."

She gave Mattingly a big hug, "It's good to see you, too, Hal. This is my husband, Josef Kostinic. You remember. We were in the war together. We talked that night in London, about our mission into Yugoslavia. Josef and I were married in a barn."

Josef stood and greeted Mattingly. Hal extended his hand out to Josef, "Ah, yes, I remember now. You had an ox and pig as your attendants—pleased to meet you." He then yelled out in French for his housekeeper to bring a cup of coffee as he sat himself down on a recliner. "So, what brings the two of you to Palo Alto so early in the morning?"

Now Josef spoke, "We're sorry to bother you on a Sunday, but we thought this was the best time to catch you at home. I heard you're working on your master's degree and knew you'd be busy during the week."

"Compliments of the GI Bill, I've already secured a teaching job here at the university, thanks to my contacts with Eisenhower. What about you?"

"Right across the bay. I was offered a position as an assistant professor. The University of California had no trouble locating anyone associated with OSS. I'm surprised they didn't find you."

Celeste interrupted the pleasantries and got right to the point, "We've come with information about Penelope."

Hal sank into his recliner as he heard Celeste speak her name, "I was told by the British war department that the Americans attempted a rescue operation while she was being held prisoner of the Gestapo, but it was too late. The SS had already sent her to Jasenovic concentration camp."

Tess added, "That's only part of the story. Josef and I have a lot of information to pass on to you about your beloved fiancée. Are you prepared to hear what we have to say?" Mattingly let out a sigh, but nodded his head in acknowledgment.

Painful memories were still vivid in everyone's minds. Josef took a seat on the sofa. He placed his teacup down on the small coffee table and leaned closer to Hal, "Very well then. *I,* was the strike team leader for that failed rescue operation. Celeste and I pieced together her entire story from personal interviews, military records, eyewitness accounts, and war crimes depositions. It all began eight years ago. I was a twenty-three-year-old student from Pittsburg, Pennsylvania beginning my second year of studies. I was introduced to the Serbian National Federation by my boyhood friend, Dick Vojvoda. Dick was already in his third year at Belgrade University *supposedly* studying engineering. The Federation was a group organized by immigrants from Serbia, offering scholarships for young Americans to go back to Yugoslavia and study, along with transportation across the Atlantic. They also included a small stipend of twenty-five dollars per month which was a real incentive for me back then. You have to realize, Hal, that the equivalent of twenty-five US dollars a month could buy you a small fortune in Yugoslavia in 1939 . . ."

Part I

THE EARLY YEARS

Chapter 1

BELGRADE

It was August 25, 1939, Josef Kostinic, a second-year college student, stepped off the train and onto the platform at Belgrade's, Zeleznicka train station. Josef was not a tall man at five-foot, six with a short, stocky build and thick, black curly hair. He had difficulty seeing over the taller men at Zeleznicka station, where he searched for his good friend, Dick Vojvoda. Dick was instrumental in convincing him of the great opportunity to study abroad in Yugoslavia. He had written to him practically every month reminding him of the opportunity. As the steam from the locomotive cleared, Josef could make out the tall features of his friend.

"Josef, I'm over here!" Dick waved and shouted out to his friend in English.

Josef clutched his suitcase and overcoat and made his way through the crowd at the busy station. Dick, now in a full sprint, raced to Josef and gave him a bear hug, "How was the trip across the Atlantic? Did you come onboard the *Majestic* like I did?"

"Unfortunately not, it was a smaller ship. I was sick

most of the time until we reached Cherbourg. After that, I felt better once we rode the train to and from Paris."

"Well, I'm glad you've finally made it here, old friend. I'll drive you to the dormitory where you'll be staying. Once you've settled in for the semester, you can move off-campus into an apartment. Your salary will more than cover anything downtown."

"Did you say you were going to drive me to campus?"

"My Packard's parked out front. I'm afraid it's a small piece of information I neglected to pass on to you while you were still back in the States. Most of the American and British students here drive Packards or Rolls-Royces. You'll learn all about that later."

Dick was a contrasting figure to Josef. He was tall, at six-foot, four, with a strong, chiseled chin and speckles of gray mixed with his thick, black hair which gave him an older, distinguished look. He spoke with a deep baritone voice. He put Josef's bags in the back of the trunk and then unlocked the side door for him. "Let me give you a tour of the city before we head over to campus. Not only is this a great place to finish your degree, but you'll be exposed to many different cultures and nationalities. Most of the foreign students you'll meet are from either the United States or the United Kingdom, but the student body is composed of many nationalities from all over Europe."

By September of 1939, the young American students were enjoying a carefree collegiate lifestyle in Belgrade. Flush with cash and few worries, Josef and Dick enjoyed most evenings in bars, restaurants, or cafés where they spent their money. They drank, sang, and listened to live music. The bars were also filled with young, beautiful women.

One of these places was the British-American Club on

campus. It was where Josef and Dick spent a lot of their free time. It was also where Dick, being the womanizer, introduced Josef to two women, Celeste Bowman and Penelope Mitchell. Both young women were British students from the university. Celeste and Penelope played the piano and sang duets at the club.

Celeste worked part-time as a teacher's aide. Penelope worked part-time at the British Embassy. No one really knew what Penelope's job was at the embassy because she never talked about it. Dick believed she did some sort of translation work because he heard a broadcast on the BBC one night and he was positive the voice on the air was that of Penelope Mitchell.

Like Dick and Josef, Penelope and Celeste also became close friends, and the two women had the opportunity to practice their French and Serbo-Croatian, since both of them spoke the languages very well. Celeste was a beautiful, young, twenty-year-old with long, black hair and blue eyes. She was petite with a girlish figure and quite reserved. Penelope, on the other hand, was a classmate of Dick's and was studying to be a nurse. At twenty-three and more mature than most women her age, she did not fall for any of Dick's womanizing. She liked him anyway, mainly because he was indeed a lot of fun to be around. Penelope came from a working-class family who lived in south London. Penelope was petite in build at five-feet, three. She had short, blond hair and hazel eyes. Her father was an Englishman, but her mother was Serbian. That's the reason she also took advantage of a Serbian scholarship fund for British students.

The first time Josef saw Celeste at the British-American Club, he was instantly attracted to her. In fact, he couldn't take his eyes off her. She was wearing a light-blue dress with yellow flowers. He told Dick, "She's the most beautiful woman I've ever seen in my life."

Dick said, "Well, we need to do something about it."

So, he arranged an afternoon picnic one weekend with Penelope. He invited Josef to come along and of course, Penelope asked Celeste to join them. It was love at first sight for Josef and Celeste. Neither of the two could be separated that Sunday afternoon at Kalemegdan Park in Belgrade.

The first semester at Belgrade University, Josef was totally committed to his studies. He no longer went out with Dick to bars or Kafanas. Unlike most of the British and American students, he didn't squander his stipend. Instead, he kept to a modest, frugal lifestyle, living in the dormitory on campus and spending his free time with "Tess" as he now called her. To save money further, he elected not to purchase a fancy, American sports car like the other students. Instead, he used public transportation or rode his bicycle.

By the end of the second semester in May 1940, Josef moved off-campus into a small flat downtown, mainly because the dormitories closed for the summer. The move gave him the opportunity to be closer to Tess and spend more time with her, since he didn't waste time riding his bicycle or taking the streetcars. Josef fell deeply in love with Tess and he considered his next course of action.

One night at Tess and Penelope's apartment, Josef spoke about their future, "I told my parents about you. They seem very pleased I met someone with a similar background. What about you? Have you told your parents about us?"

"Good heavens no. Things are still old-fashioned at home. We go about things differently than you do in the States. Naturally, they would want to meet you before we dated—even get their permission to take me out. I haven't told them anything about us. I think it's best I don't mention it for now. The time will come soon enough."

"Tess, I want you to have this." He passed her a crumbled piece of paper with his hometown address and telephone number. "This is where you can reach me should I have to leave you unexpectedly. I want you to have it. Promise me that you'll contact me if we should ever be separated."

Tess was surprised to hear this even though she had heard about the terrible events in other parts of Europe. "Nothing's going to happen. We're far from the events in the rest of Europe. Besides, I have a British passport. I can leave anytime I want, just like you can with your US passport."

"I'm not so sure about that. Take a look at what's around you. Tensions are high in the city right now—we're surrounded. The Fascist Italians are to the west and the Nazis already occupy Hungary and parts of Bulgaria. Jewish citizens have already been identified for deportation. It's only a matter of time before the Nazi war machine reaches the streets of Belgrade, and they'll seal off the exits. In fact, for your safety, you should consider going back to England this summer instead of returning next semester."

"That's out of the question. I'm almost finished with my studies. My French and Serbo-Croatian are getting better and better all the time, thanks to you and Penelope. I'll graduate next year and with the war going on back home in England, I'll most certainly get a job with the war department. Besides, Penelope has already been told by her supervisor that she and I can get jobs doing *special employment* whatever that means, back in England."

"That reminds me about something. Why is she so

secretive about her job? What exactly does she do at the British Embassy?"

"I'm not supposed to tell you, but since you asked, and you'll find out sooner or later, I'll tell you. I hear she broadcasts over BBC airwaves. Not glamorous work, but the pay is good and the hours flexible for her studies. More importantly, she's made several contacts at the embassy that can help her get a job when she returns home. She doesn't have a problem talking to men much older than her, especially with *her* looks."

Josef finished his cup of tea and got up from the kitchen table, "I best be getting home now. It's late and Penelope will be home shortly. She'll want to get some rest after a long day." Josef left Tess's apartment and never again questioned her about the work Penelope did at the embassy.

That summer, before school started again, Josef and Tess lived a carefree life with little concern except each other. The events in Europe in 1940 seemed far away and it was hard to imagine that war would interrupt a wonderful time in their lives.

By the beginning of his second term in late August of 1940, Josef decided to major in cultural geography with an emphasis on Eastern Europe and the Balkans instead of history. Belgrade University had an excellent geography department and encouraged students to take excursions deep into the heart of the country to explore the vast religious and language differences. This gave Josef and Tess the opportunity to travel during the weekends, but in reality was another excuse for the couple to get away by themselves. A favorite destination was the Fruska Gora

National Park located a short, one-hour, train ride from Belgrade. Here, they rented bicycles or hiked to the numerous orthodox monasteries located in the area. One of the monasteries, Jazak, even opened their doors and allowed the couple free access to the entire facility. The other was the Ravna Gora region of Serbia with its high mountains and dense forests where they hiked and picnicked. There was never any more talk about leaving Yugoslavia until world events suddenly changed.

Chapter 2

OPERATION PUNISHMENT

Eight months later, on the morning of April 6, 1941, just after sunrise, the first of Field Marshal Hermann Göring's Luftwaffe bombers appeared over Belgrade in *Operation Punishment*. The explosions knocked Josef out of bed just after six in his small apartment. His initial reaction was to get under the bed and take cover as he crawled along the floor, keeping his head down and away from the tiny window in the kitchen. Then he realized that his apartment was located not more than a few blocks from the main rail station and surely targeted by Nazi dive-bombers. He raced downstairs to the basement, still in his pajamas, taking cover with the rest of the occupants of the building. Luftwaffe bombs dropped all around them, each time with a thunderous explosion that shook the building. After two hours of continuous bombardment, the planes disappeared over the horizon and returned to their bases.

For the time being, it looked as if he was lucky. His apartment was still standing. However, most of the surrounding buildings were either bombed to rubble or on fire. Josef made his way up to the lobby floor where the telephone was located. He called Tess's number first, followed by Dick's, only to discover the telephone lines were down. Josef thought to himself, they probably targeted the telephone exchange on the first wave. He had no choice; he would have to go on foot to see if Tess was all right. Tess and Penelope's apartment was located several blocks away to the west and he was not even sure she was still alive. He went back upstairs to his apartment, grabbed his passport, bank records, and all the cash on hand. Next, he changed clothes and packed a light suitcase in the event his apartment was bombed on the next wave. Fully dressed and clutching his small suitcase, he clambered downstairs to the streets below.

Josef was stunned by what he encountered on the streets of Belgrade. Buildings were on fire, streetcars and other vehicles were blown to pieces, men, women, and children wandered around dazed. Body parts and pieces were strung about. He ran through the panic-stricken people and debris to Tess's apartment. All the time his heart was pounding; he wondered whether she was even still alive. Remarkably, when he arrived at her apartment, it was in one piece. He made his way inside and climbed the stairs yelling, "Tess! Tess! Are you all right?"

To his amazement, Tess was standing at the top of the stairway, still in a state of shock. The couple embraced and tears dripped down her cheeks as Josef spoke, "We can't stay here in the city. I knew this was going to happen sooner or later. We don't have much time. In an hour or two, the Luftwaffe will send in their second wave. German troops will be in the streets by noon. We need to take refuge in the countryside."

Tess wiped the tears from her eyes, "I was worried about you. I thought you were killed. I was watching from the window and all I could see were bombs dropping around the train station."

"The telephone lines are down. I tried calling you and Dick, but the lines are all dead. He's got a car. Maybe we could use it to take refuge."

Just as he said this, Dick's Packard pulled up in front of Tess's apartment. Dick ran from the driver's seat with Penelope in the front. She had just gotten off work at the embassy as the first bombs fell on the city. Luckily, Dick had had the foresight to get out of bed and move his car well before the attack was under way. He figured the embassies would not be targeted and had driven the car there as quickly as he could to get Penelope. He was able to pick her up and take her to one of the nearby bomb shelters. He parked his car inside the embassy compound and then he and Penelope waited out the attack underground.

Upon seeing both Josef and Tess still alive, Dick commanded in his baritone voice, "We don't have a moment to lose. There'll be another wave within the hour. We need to get out of the city before pandemonium sets in." He grabbed Tess by the shoulders and looked her in the eyes, "Get your passport and all the cash you have. Penelope knows what to do. She'll help you pack a light suitcase. We need to leave in fifteen minutes!"

Twenty minutes later, the four companions were on the road heading southwest from Belgrade toward the city of Sabac. There, the four friends met up with another contingent of British and American students. Several of the young men had been planning for such a possible scenario and already were getting reports about a British cruiser that would come to a coastal village and take anyone who wanted to evacuate to Greece. The problem was that it would be difficult to travel all the way to the coast by automobile. Armed refugees might commandeer the vehicles and they could be stranded or fuel supplies could be exhausted. Worst yet, Nazi aircraft might strafe any vehicle leaving the cities as targets of opportunity. The four students decided their best way to escape was by train. The trains were still running on schedule, for the most part, but it would take about one full day to travel to the Montenegrin port city of Bar, the nearest coastal city with direct rail service.

At nine in the morning, the train station at Sabac was already crowded with refugees waiting for the train to arrive from Novi-Sad. It appeared that German aircraft had not targeted Novi-Sad on the initial wave and thus trains were still leaving on schedule that morning. That could all change as the day progressed. The four students bought first-class tickets to Bar. The station café was open and remarkably, the four found a table and decided to eat something before departing. Penelope spoke up first because everyone was still in a state of shock and she seemed the most level-headed, "I need to find a telephone. There's someone I need to talk to."

Dick lit a cigarette and blew the smoke over everyone's heads, "Most of the phone lines are down. You'll never get through."

"Yes, I know that. I don't need a regular phone line. Usually the stationmaster has communication links to stations down the line with their internal network. Let me see if I can charm the man into using it." She got up from the table and disappeared into the stationmaster's office.

Dick continued, "It won't be long before the country is occupied, which means foreigners will have a difficult time moving, especially our Jewish friends. They might even arrest us just for being British or American citizens. We've got to get out of the country now. It's our only way to survive."

The waiter arrived and brought the young students their breakfasts, which consisted of tomato omelets with goat cheese and coffee ersatz. Penelope came back to the table and the four devoured their meals. A few minutes later, an announcement was made over the loudspeaker, that the train to Bar was arriving early and would depart *ahead* of schedule. The four companions finished their breakfast and gathered their luggage just as the train pulled into the station. Dick straggled behind the others as they made their way to the first-class coaches.

"Dick, hurry up, so we can get a seat!" yelled Josef. Dick ignored him, continued to slow down, and then came to a complete stop.

Penelope saw Dick stop dead in his tracks and spoke up next, "What the bloody hell has gotten into you? What are you waiting for?"

"You three go along. I'll take a later train. I've got to do something about my car."

Josef yelled out frantically, "Have you lost your mind, Dick? Leave the damn thing here! You can't take it with you, anyway!"

"I might need it to go after more students leaving the city. I've got several friends at the Jewish house who'll need to get out."

Penelope grabbed hold of Tess's arm and moved her along, "Go with Josef on board the train. Let me see if I can try to talk some sense into him." Tess and Josef climbed aboard the train while Penelope came back to Dick and spoke into his ear, so he could hear over the sound of the locomotive, "What the bloody hell has gotten into you? You know you can't stay here, you said it yourself. Listen to me, you big oaf. I was able to use the railway telephone. I got a call off to London through the embassy switchboard. I can confirm there *is* a British cruiser making way to the coast. They'll pick us up and take us to Greece. From there, we can all get back home."

"You three go ahead. I've got to get some more students out of Belgrade before it's occupied. Get back on the train before I pick your ass up and carry you."

The train whistle blew and Penelope had no choice but to board. She waved to Dick and blew him a kiss, then thought to herself, He's either very brave or very stupid.

Back aboard the train, Penelope found Josef and Tess and took a seat in the first-class compartment as the train started moving.

"Where's Dick?" asked Josef.

"He's not coming. He said he wanted to get more students out of Belgrade before it fell. Knowing Dick, it's probably another woman who's motivating him."

Josef leaned across Tess toward the window and got a look at Dick, still on the platform, running to keep up with the departing train. He tried to yell, but his voice went nowhere. He did, however, see Dick give a final wave. Penelope leaned toward Josef and said, "He knows what he's doing. Let him go. Somehow I get the feeling this won't be the last time we see Dick Vojvoda."

Josef sat back in his seat while Tess placed her hands over her face. Josef put his arms around her and thought to himself, it's up to me to get us home. "None of us can worry about Dick." He closed his eyes and began formulating a plan then he spoke in French to the girls, "There's a lot of foreigners on the train just like us. We're lucky to get this far. Let's keep to French because I don't want everyone listening to our plan. If it's true what some of the British students said, we don't want thousands of refugees following us."

Penelope spoke next in French, "I agree—here's what I found out back at the station. The British Navy does indeed have a cruiser heading toward the coast. At this point, I don't know exactly where they'll be offshore. It could be anywhere along the coast, even as far north as Split, no one knows. I'll have to make another call in twelve hours. By then, the British Admiralty will know more."

Josef quickly looked over his train schedule, "It'll take us a full day to get to Bar by train, maybe longer if we come under attack. This train crosses over two-hundred tunnels and trestles on this route. If the Luftwaffe tries to attack a train in motion, it'll be a difficult shot. Dick was right about one thing. The train is the safest way to the coast."

Tess gradually came to her senses asked, "How much will it cost to get aboard the cruiser?"

Josef answered, "It's not the cruiser that I'm worried about. It's the ride *out* to the cruiser that worries me. Once news gets out that refugees need passage to sea, everyone and anyone who owns a boat will take advantage of the situation and it could cost an enormous amount. How much hard currency do you girls have?"

"A couple a hundred pounds between the two of us," replied Penelope.

"I've got at least one-hundred American dollars on me. Between the three of us, that's more than enough for all of us. I also have a few kunas[1] and dinars. When the train stops again, we can buy food for the trip, but only enough to last us a few days. We don't want to squander all our cash."

The three students closed their eyes and tried to rest for a few hours as the train traveled south along the narrow rail line. By noon, the train stopped at Uzice. The platform was already crowded with passengers and refugees waiting to leave. After a brief stop for water and fuel, the train was on its way again. As the train made its way up and down the mountains and tunnels, the three started to nibble on the bread and cheese they bought at the station and then the train made a sudden acceleration. Conductors frantically yelled, telling everyone to get down below their seats. The three students dove for cover, the bread and cheese went flying in all directions. They felt the train rock with vibration. A German ME-109 was attempting to strafe the rear cars with its 20 mm cannons. Luckily, most of the Messerschmitt 20 mm cannon shells fired from the nose prop spinner missed the train and exploded harmlessly alongside causing minimal damage, but they shook the ground and tracks. The locomotive engineer desperately tried to make his way to the next tunnel for cover as more shells exploded outside the cars. Josef grabbed hold of Tess and covered her with his body as the ME-109 made its final pass.

The Yugoslav National Railroad train pulled into the small Montenegrin coastal town of Bar, at dawn. By now, most of the passenger cars were empty as people had gotten off the train at some of the smaller towns and villages in the mountains near Jasenovo and Podgorica. Josef, Tess, and Penelope were still exhausted from the stressful, full-day trip. News got out to them that all of Yugoslavia was now under German occupation. All assets of the former Yugoslavia were in possession of the Third Reich. If chance was on their side, they'd have another two or three days before the coastal cities and towns were occupied by German forces. That was still plenty of time to make it out to the cruiser if they could get a boat.

Josef took all the luggage and he and Tess walked off the train and into the small station. Posters were hanging inside the station. The SS informed passengers that all movements were strictly controlled by the Gestapo. Penelope calmly went directly to the stationmaster's office to try to use a telephone. Josef and Tess waited in the small station lobby. Visibly shaken, Tess began to show signs of emotional breakdown and said in English, "Where's she going now at a time like this?"

Josef composed himself and replied in French, remembering their plan of escape, "She needs to use a telephone," as he placed his arms around her. "I think it's only a short walk to the city. From there, we can take a bus or taxi up the coast to the next town or further north where we can get a boat out to sea. We're almost home. Just hang on a little longer."

Josef succeeding in calming Tess's worries and she again resumed her French, "You know I'm not totally sure what her job was back at the British Embassy, but she seems to know a lot of people connected to the government, probably, as high up as the prime minister's office. She never talked about her work very much."

Josef now understood the reasons for Penelope's surreptitious behavior, even admired her courage, "By now she should have more information about the cruiser. It's only a question if she can make a telephone or telegraph connection."

A few minutes later, Penelope calmly walked into the station lobby and spoke French, "I found what we're looking for. We need to make a stop at the bakery first. They should be open now."

The three young students gathered their belongings. Josef and Tess followed Penelope out of the station and walked the short distance into town. The streets were paved with cobblestones and the women had difficulty walking in the shoes they were wearing. They needed to change into something that was more suited for the journey along the coast; otherwise, they would quickly build up blisters on their feet which would make walking extremely difficult.

The small town of Bar was bustling with activity despite the early hour. News probably had spread that the country had fallen to the Nazis. Penelope confidently walked three feet ahead of Josef and Tess and seemed to know instinctively where to go. She turned right on one street, then left on another without hesitation, and before the three knew it, they were inside the bakery. Penelope spoke to the woman behind the counter, presumably the baker's wife, in Serbo-Croatian, "I hear you make the best croissants outside of Paris?"

The woman replied in French, "Only at the beginning of the week."

This time Penelope replied in French, "I only need three."

The woman hesitated for a brief moment as she pondered her response, nodded her head, and then continued in French, "Come with me," and led them to the back room. Here, a man, probably her husband, was busy mixing a batch of dough. The woman spoke again in French to the man, "These three young people are looking for croissants. Do we have any left?"

The man stopped kneading the dough and wiped his hands with a towel. He scrutinized the three students up and down, and then spoke in French, "You're a little inexperienced for this sort of work, judging from the way you're dressed. Why are you in need of my croissants?"

Penelope spoke, still in French, "We're foreign students from the University of Belgrade. The city was attacked the day before yesterday. Obviously, we're not going back to our studies under German occupation. I was told you could possibly help."

The man answered, still in French, "The situation is

very dangerous in these parts. The Italians have already taken control of the roads along the coast. The Germans will be here shortly, perhaps as early as today."

"We have money. We can pay you."

The man replied, "If the Gestapo finds out we've been helping people like you three, they'll take my shop and kill us all." He went back to kneading his dough. There was silence in the room for several minutes and then he spoke without looking at the three, young students. "I have a scheduled delivery this morning. My truck leaves in fifteen minutes. We're already late. The driver is my son. You do not need to know his name. He will take you to Tivat. From there, we have a small boat that we use to make deliveries across the bay. You can ride with them to Lepetane. It saves us an hour drive along the coast, very important in our business. Once you get to Lepetane, you're on your own. That's the best we can do."

"You've been very kind. How much do we owe you?"

"You owe us nothing. The only thing that can help you is quick feet and a good pair of walking shoes. Not like the ones you have on your feet. My son will be waiting for you out back. Please do not speak to him. The less he knows the better."

"I understand," replied Penelope.

Josef and Tess watched in amazement as Penelope talked her way through the stressful and difficult situation in a profound, confident manner, almost as if she'd been trained to do so. Josef was beginning to wonder if she did have ties to the intelligence community back at the British Embassy. A basic twenty-three-year-old college student would not have come up with this plan by herself. Josef finally spoke. "How far up the coast do we need to go?" he asked Penelope.

"Luckily not far. The ship is anchored offshore from the Bay of Kotor."

By mid-morning, the three college students were at the Bay of Kotor, walking along the busy coastal road. Tess and Penelope had changed into shoes more comfortable and suitable for walking. Many cars, trucks, vans, ox-carts, and horses crowded with refugees were heading north along the coast, obviously knowing some sort of transport was waiting offshore. Many people were in a state of panic as motorists jockeyed for position in line on the highway. One of those vehicles was a Packard loaded with passengers. The young student driver did a double take as he noticed the two beautiful, young women walking alongside the road carrying their luggage. The driver put the brakes on and came screeching to a halt.

"Do you girls need a lift?"

Penelope replied, "Yes, me and my two friends."

Penelope climbed into the front seat next to two other young men while Josef and Tess moved into the crowed back seat. The drive to Kotor took over an hour with bumper-to-bumper traffic on the road. Once there, the team of students was shocked to see that the small town was already overcrowded with refugees. As anticipated, anyone who could get a boat booked passage for the trip out to sea. But it might take several days before they would be able to take all refugees. By that time, the Nazis would have sealed off the coastline and the chances of escape would be nearly impossible. Some of the British and American refugees were already making alternative plans.

Josef, Tess, and Penelope elected to stay in Kotor and take their chances with whatever transport they could acquire for the trip out to sea. Any boat would do. After several hours of haggling and bargaining, the three students, again thanks to Penelope, managed to book passage on a small fishing vessel. Unfortunately, they had to wait until the next evening for their turn out to sea. The small town of Kotor was overcrowded with refugees and supplies quickly diminished. The prospects for a successful escape by sea were not looking good. The three elected to spend the night in a makeshift campsite constructed by some of the college students outside the city limits. Everyone felt it was safer in numbers as opposed to trying to find a place to sleep in the town. The three friends curled up on the ground and fell asleep by the campfire.

The next morning, Josef woke up to the sounds of automatic gunfire. He quickly grabbed hold of Tess and Penelope and told them, "Stay low and still." More gunshots sounded off in the distance, near the seaside.

Penelope whispered, "It could be the Germans have already arrived or pandemonium has set in among the fleeing refugees."

Josef spoke softly, "Let's stay here in the campsite, as long as we can. It could be far more dangerous if we go into town."

"I agree," replied Penelope. "There's the possibility we may not make it out tonight anyway."

As the day progressed, most of the college students and other refugees in the campsite left. The automatic gunfire they had heard earlier were the shots fired by panic-stricken refugees. Josef, Tess, and Penelope stayed busy repacking their suitcases or cleaning their clothes. Some of the students abandoned their cars loaded with fuel believing they would not come back. Josef found an old, beat-up Packard with the keys still in the ignition. The three students used it as a shelter to lie down and rest for the day. As the day progressed, it appeared that some of the refugees were getting out because there was indeed less traffic on the highway. One car heading in the opposite direction out of town stopped at the campsite and told Josef there would be no more boats going to sea. It appeared the Italian fighter aircraft had strafed the escape boats as they approached the cruiser. The ship had no choice but to head back out to sea and all escape craft were returning to Kotor.

"We're stuck! What will we do now?" cried Tess.

Penelope let out a sigh and said to Josef, "I need to speak to you. Can we take a walk?"

"Tess, you stay here in the car, Penelope and I need to clear our heads and come up with another plan."

Josef and Penelope took a short walk along the hiking trail, parallel to the main road. Once safely away from any students and refugees, Penelope said, "When we were in Bar yesterday, I was able to use the phone. I used a special number that connected me to the British Embassy in Cairo. They informed me of the possibility we wouldn't make it to the ship, so they gave me an alternate plan. I didn't want to say anything earlier because it's extremely risky and there are certain conditions. I wanted to see if we could all make it out on the cruiser, first." She took a deep breath and continued, "There's a British *submarine* that will surface off the coast of Brac at oh three-hundred hours tomorrow morning. They'll take us, but the one condition is they can only take Tess and me. I'm afraid you can't go along."

Josef stood back and absorbed what he'd just heard, "Wow, you're talking about a rescue operation for British military and government personnel. Just what exactly do you do at the embassy?"

"I work for an organization called GSI. It mostly involves monitoring German troop movements and translation work, but they also work closely with MI-6, the British Secret Intelligence Service. It would appear that I know too much, and if the Germans should capture me, the information in my little head would be of great value to the Third Reich. The submarine is to evacuate all essential government personnel. I had difficulty convincing them to let Tess go with me. I said she was essential to the war effort."

"Does she know your connection to MI-6?"

"I haven't told anyone, except for you. Dick doesn't even know." Penelope changed the subject and moved on to their escape plan. "Luckily, we have the car. We have to leave immediately if we're going to make it all the way to Brac by three in the morning. Once all those boats come back to shore, it'll be impossible to get out of here. At this point, the less Tess knows the better. It's going to be heartbreaking enough when she realizes you're not getting on the sub with her. I suggest we wait until we're almost ready to board the sub before we break the news to her."

"Agreed, what else can you tell me? Do the Americans have anything in place for an evacuation?"

"I'm afraid not. You're on your own. You've got a US passport. Hopefully, that'll get you out of the country, maybe through Bulgaria or Turkey."

"Bulgaria? How do I get there? I'll be out of cash by then and I'm miles from the border. By the time I get there, the Germans will have complete control of the Balkans."

"I heard there is a resistance movement. You saw some of the rudimentary elements the other morning. Try to find someone who can help you. Get back to one of the major cities nearby, maybe Mostar or Sarajevo. Those cities will be dangerous, but they have more opportunities for freedom. Maybe Dick knew something we didn't all along; that's why he stayed behind."

Josef was silent as he pondered his fate, "If you get

back to London, contact my parents. Let them know my situation. Tess has my address back in the States."

"I'll do that, you have my word." She placed her hand on his shoulder, "I'm really sorry, Josef. I tried to get them to take you out, but they insisted on only essential British personnel. Now, I need your help with the next phase. What's the best way to get out to Brac?"

Josef's geography of Yugoslavia was very good in his studies back at the university, "Let's have a look at the map, shall we?" Penelope nodded her head in agreement.

Josef unfolded his map of the country, "Our best bet is Makarska or Podgora. Both cities have small fishing fleets. I suggest Makarska first because it's closer to the island of Brac. Once we get to Makarska, we need to find another boat to take us out to sea. I don't think we'll have the same problems up there as we did down here. It's just a matter of cost for the boat."

"We'd better get going before all those boats come ashore."

The drive along the coastal highway was long and tedious. There were still many refugees fleeing the interior sections of the country. Many on the road felt that the resort city of Dubrovnik would be the safest place since the Germans probably wouldn't bomb the ancient city[2]. The three continued on past Dubrovnik along the coastal road. Josef drove with Penelope in the front and Tess in the back. Penelope explained the plan to evacuate as they drove during the night. There was silence in the car as they pulled into the small fishing village of Makarska around eleven at night; the car was nearly empty of fuel. They found the docks and looked for the closest pub that was still open. Here they found what they were looking for. Several fishermen were more than willing to take anyone out to sea for a price. After haggling over the cost, Josef found a young, anchovy fisherman who would take them for fifty dinars apiece and the keys to the car, "We'll leave at one in the morning. Meet on the promenade. I'll have the boat ready," said the young man.

As the late evening passed into early-morning hours, the three college students passed the time parked in the old Packard alongside the docks. There was an eerie silence in the air as the people of Croatia waited for their fate in the tiny seaside community. The only sounds were the small waves crashing against the rocks below. Josef held Tess's hand, "We'll be leaving shortly. When we get on the boat, it should take us no more than a couple of hours to travel out to Brac. We'll wait for the sub to surface on the western side of the island."

At exactly oh one-hundred hours, as promised, the young fisherman approached the docks. He was dressed in wool pants, rubber boots, and a stocking cap. He didn't speak, but motioned them forward with his hand. The three students followed the young fisherman to the far side of the dock. There, bobbing in the water was a small fishing craft with a covered wheelhouse, "Get in and take a seat below deck."

Penelope approached the man. He was about Josef's age with dark, leathered skin and a long beard. Penelope held out a piece of paper with detailed instructions, "Here's the coordinates for the rendezvous."

The fisherman took the lantern and placed it closer to the paper Penelope had scribbled on. He took out his nautical chart and marked the distance. "If we hurry, we should make it by three. Stay below deck. It will be warmer and drier."

The trip out to Brac took over an hour and a half. The seas were calm, so they made good time. As the fishing boat approached the southwest side of the tiny island, they could already see the silhouette of a vessel on the surface. As they approached, a small spotlight shined in their direction. The submarine surfaced completely and the fishing boat made its way toward the craft. Josef could see men on deck of the sub dressed with yellow life vests. They were waving. They shined a bright light on the fishing boat and the fisherman maneuvered his craft alongside the sub. Two sailors threw a line to the boat as Josef reached out and caught it, then secured it to the vessel. Two more sailors appeared with Sten submachine guns and pointed them at the small vessel. Once the boat was secured, an officer came in sight and shouted using a megaphone, "We have authorization to pick up two passengers, Penelope Mitchell and Celeste Bowmen. Please prepare to show your British passports."

Josef looked at Tess and said, "This is where I must leave you. The British have authorization to take out you and Penelope, only."

Tess cried out, "No please, I'm not going without you!"

"I'm sorry, Tess. It's for your safety. Penelope will look after you. You're going home. I promise I'll see you again. You have my word."

Penelope placed a hand on Tess's shoulder, "I knew since yesterday about the sub. The Admiralty generated this mission solely for the purposes of rescuing you and me. We have to go. If we both don't get onboard that sub, they have orders to sink the fishing boat."

Tess cried out again, as she knew Penelope was right, "Josef, isn't there anything you can do?"

"No, I'm afraid not. Now get onboard the sub. I promise I'll see you again. Please go before it's too late. The sub can only surface for a few minutes and then they need to submerge."

Penelope grabbed Tess's hand and hoisted her on to

the sub as two British sailors helped them to the gangway. Josef looked on as the two women disappeared below deck. The young fisherman spoke, "They're very lucky to escape. There's already talk the Italian Air Force is patrolling the skies along the entire Adriatic coastline. They're not letting anyone out to sea."

"Yes, I know. We were in Montenegro yesterday when we heard about the air strikes."

The two men watched in the darkness as the submarine disappeared below the surface. "Come,

my friend," said the fisherman. "You'll have to work with me until daybreak just in case the authorities secure the docks and start asking questions. I'll show you how to fish for anchovies."

For the rest of the morning, Josef helped the young fisherman drop his nets and fish the seas of the Adriatic. When daylight approached and the vessel headed to shore, the fisherman said, "I hear there is a resistance movement. They may be able to help you. You should make your way to the hills near Mostar. Try to hook up with the Chetniks. They control the highlands. Ask for a man named Mihailovich. Stay away from anyone who wears a red star emblem."

"Thank you, my friend. You have been very helpful."

---

1. Kunas were the local currency of Croatia at that time. Serbia and Bosnia-Herzegovina used the dinars. After World
   War II, Yugoslavia went back to using all dinars. In 1995, Croatia switched back to the kuna when they declared their independence from Yugoslavia. In July 2013, they expect to be a full member of the European Union.
2. Ironically, fifty years later, it was the Serbs, not the Nazis who shelled the beautiful, old city of Dubrovnik in October, 1991.

Chapter 3

THREE DESPERADOS

It was now the morning of April 10, 1941. Once back on shore, Josef saw German and Italian forces, patrolling the streets of Makarska. They were not letting anyone out to sea, not even the fishermen. Penelope and Tess were indeed, very lucky and probably the last to leave by sea.

Josef took his tattered suitcase and walked toward the bus terminal. There he found a bus leaving for Sarajevo. He bought a ticket for Mostar. Surprisingly, there were few people wanting to go into the interior sections. By mid-day, Josef was in the town of Mostar, Bosnia-Herzegovina. He was completely exhausted from the whole ordeal and this was as far he dared to go into the interior for the time being. He found a small inn not far from the bus terminal and the ancient arched bridge. As he walked into the lobby, he saw a man in civilian clothes standing near the front desk, "Good afternoon," Josef said to the man.

The man could smell fish and salt water on Josef's clothes, "I represent the local authorities. What's your business here in Mostar?"

"I'm an American student. I've just come from

Belgrade by way of the Adriatic. The Germans bombed the city a few days ago. I'm trying to get out of the country, but I need some rest before I continue."

"Let me see your passport."

Josef handed the man his passport and he examined it carefully then handed it back to Josef. "There have been several people claiming to be foreigners without passports. If you didn't have a passport, I would have to arrest you for being a spy. However, since your passport is in order you may stay here for one night, and one night only, then you must leave."

"I'll only need one night anyway—to clean up."

"Go up to the desk and ring the bell. The hotel clerk with be with you shortly."

Josef went up to the counter, rang the bell, and the hotel clerk appeared from the back room.

"One room for one night, please." Josef asked.

The clerk, a tall, thin, elderly, Bosnian-Muslim mumbled, "I only have one room with bathroom down the hall. That will be twelve dinars, please."

"Twelve dinars! I don't think I have that much."

Upon hearing this, the man in civilian clothes approached the desk and listened.

Josef realized he'd spent most of his kunas and dinars securing passage out to sea. The only cash he had left was in US dollars, "I only have dollars. Will you take that?"

Before the clerk could answer, the inquisitive man said, "What are you doing with American dollars?"

"As I told you, I'm an American, a college student studying at Belgrade University. I should say *was* studying at Belgrade University. I don't have dinars, only the American dollars I came here with when I arrived from the United States."

"Having foreign currency, especially American dollars is suspicious. I'll have to take you in for questioning."

The hotel clerk interrupted in Josef's defense, "This is a tourist city. We have foreigners all the time with different currencies. He can exchange the dollars for dinars at the bus station. It's only a short walk. He can be there and back in less than fifteen minutes at the most."

The inquisitive man contemplated his response. He looked at Josef then said, "Open your suitcase and let's have a look inside."

Josef opened the suitcase, and the inquisitive man examined the contents. Once satisfied there was nothing hidden inside he said, "Be back in fifteen minutes or I'll have the local Gestapo agents look for you. They are not as cooperative as I am."

Josef nodded his head and sprinted out the door. Ten minutes later, he was back at the hotel desk, winded, and with Yugoslavian dinars in his possession. He paid the hotel clerk and received the key to his room.

"Check out time is eleven o'clock in the morning. Would you like breakfast in your room?"

"That will be fine. You can bring it up at seven. I'll be awake by then."

"Leave your clothes outside of your room. I'll have them laundered for you."

The next morning Josef woke at sunrise. He hadn't slept well that night. His thoughts were on Tess and Penelope and he wondered if they would get back to England and not be torpedoed by a German U-boat. He also thought about Dick Vojvoda and wondered if he was safe. Then a knock on the door interrupted his thoughts. "Yes?"

The hotel clerk answered, "I have your breakfast and clean clothes ready. Can I come in?"

Josef opened the door and let the man in. He placed

the tray on the small nightstand then handed Josef the bundle of clean clothes, "I brought you some coffee, Turkish style, of course."

Josef closed the door behind the man and locked it.

The hotel clerk continued, "The man you met downstairs yesterday is a member of the Croatian Ustaša, a resistance movement that has taken sides with the Nazis. The Ustaša agents, for the time being, have taken control of all security matters in occupied areas of Croatia and Bosnia. Some say they are more ruthless than the Nazis. You must trust no one."

"How can I be sure that you're not one of them?"

"I wouldn't have told you about changing your money at the bus station. I could have let him take you away to the local Gestapo station."

"Yes, I suppose you're right, thank you."

"I brought your breakfast to your room because I can talk freely with you. The Ustaša agent hasn't figured this out yet. He stays downstairs in the lobby and monitors the movements of my paying guests. I did have my people follow that man after you checked-in yesterday. He went straight to the Gestapo and told them about you. They will be here at check-out time, probably with several men and weapons to arrest you. The fishy smell on your clothes may have had something to do with it. It was too suspicious to overlook."

Josef ate his breakfast while telling the man the whole story, of how he fled Belgrade and secured passage out to sea for the two women. Then he said, "I was told by the fisherman in Croatia to seek help from a group calling themselves the Chetniks, specifically a person by the name of Mihailovich."

Upon hearing that name, the hotel clerk was suddenly startled, "You know of this man?"

"I was simply told to seek him out specifically and ask for help. I was told that he might be able to get me out of the country."

"What else do you know about resistance movements?"

"Avoid anyone wearing or displaying a red star emblem."

"Mostar is a dangerous place, young man. You cannot travel on the main highways or railroads. Your best chance for survival is to use the countryside." The hotel clerk rubbed his chin in thought then continued, "I cannot help you, but I know some people who can. Before you check out this morning, do not go to the lobby or the front desk. Instead, go to the kitchen at nine-thirty. There, someone will meet you who can help. The front entrance will, of course, be covered by the Ustaša agent. That is all I can do. Good luck, my friend."

Just before nine that morning, Josef repacked his suitcase and put on the now clean clothes he'd been wearing for the past several days before walking downstairs to the kitchen. Just as the hotel clerk advised, there were two men with burly beards and long hair waiting in the kitchen drinking strong coffee. Both men were dressed in heavy woolen clothes and the sight looked like a scene from the biblical ages. Then one of them spoke. He was the younger of the two, slightly older than Josef, with strong muscular arms and hands.

"You are American, yes?" Josef nodded his head. "My name is Rudko. I am a Chetnik guerrilla fighter. I'll be your guide. This is my brother, Stefan. You must pack your belongings in this," and he tossed Josef a worn leather knapsack. "That suitcase will never make the journey you are about to undertake. Listen to me. We don't have much time. The Ustaša agent will be here shortly to arrest you. I hear you need safe passage?"

Josef acknowledged with a simple nod of his head.

"We can get you to Chetnik headquarters located across the Drina River. We have a link to Allied forces in Cairo. They may be able to help you. It will be a long journey across rough terrain. We will pass through Partisan as well as Nazi-occupied territory. You may not make it, but this is your best chance for escape out of the country."

"I was told to seek a person by the name of Mihailovich? Is he the one who can help me?"

Rudko replied, "Do not mention that name again! It would put us all at great risk. We have enemies everywhere. Not only the Germans, but from other resistance groups who would like to see him dead. From now on, if you must reference the man, call him, The General. Now, hurry and repack your belongings. We will be back shortly to take you away."

Josef did as instructed; the two men disappeared out the back entrance as the hotel clerk came into the kitchen, "I'm going to run an errand. The less I know the better. When it is time for you to leave, wait in the lobby. Your two guides will meet you there," then he departed.

A few minutes before eleven in the morning, Josef grabbed his leather backpack and took a seat in the lobby. He took out his now worn map of Yugoslavia and tried to figure how they were going to make the trip over the rugged terrain when the front door burst open and the Ustaša agent appeared holding a pistol; luckily, he was alone.

"I see you are still here."

"I was just getting ready to leave."

"I'm sorry to tell you this, but the Gestapo has insisted you come with me to headquarters. They have a few questions for you."

While Josef was getting up to leave, the two Chetnik

fighters appeared from behind the Ustaša agent. They moved as quietly as a fox. The Ustaša man never knew what hit him as Stefan inserted a dagger into the man's throat. He collapsed to the floor, blood gushing from the side of his neck as he bled to death. Josef was stunned as he witnessed the sight.

Rudko shouted, "Quickly, before the Gestapo gets here! We have horses out back. I hope you know how to ride." Josef didn't bother answering the question and followed the two fighters out the back door to the waiting horses. He took the smallest of the three animals and the three men galloped away, like three desperados.

Chapter 4

DRAMA MIHAILOVICH

For the next three weeks, Josef traveled with the two guerrilla fighters across the rugged countryside using a combination of horses, mules, ox carts, and on foot. They avoided German patrols by crossing rivers, mountains, and valleys. They stopped at several villages along the way, taking shelter in the small, thatched homes of peasants and ate what little food they offered.

One night, as the three were sleeping, they woke to the sounds of automatic gunfire. Immediately, Josef assumed the Germans were on to them when Rudko and Stefan grabbed him by the arm, shoved him to the floor, and told him that Partisan guerrillas were attacking them. The three escaped the firefight and fled across the Drina River into Serbia. From there, they moved to Pranjane near the city of Cacak. This was deep in Chetnik territory. Exhausted, hungry, twenty pounds lighter and filthy, Josef finally made his way into General Mihailovich's camp.

Rudko led Josef into a small house, where several men were sitting on the floor talking, smoking, and drinking *slivovitz*. Rudko made his way to the man in the center. He whispered something into his ear then left. Josef was all alone in the room with these humble men sitting on the floor talking amongst themselves. He tried to make out their conversations, but the fire, crackling in the fireplace, muffled their sounds. Finally, the man in the center, the one Rudko walked up to originally, motioned for Josef to come forward. He was dressed in the military uniform of King Paul. His face was covered with a long beard and he wore round spectacles. He appeared more like a university professor than a guerrilla fighter. He spoke with a well-educated voice, "Come forward, young man." Josef moved closer. "Have a seat and let me have a closer look at you."

Josef followed the instructions and sat on the ground just like the other men. The bearded man continued, "My name is Draza Mihailovich. You must be the young American student. I've heard about your ordeals and attempted escape by sea. You've already earned quite the reputation in this country. Tell me young man, what is your name?"

"Josef Kostinic, sir. Both my parents are Serbian from Novi-Sad." Josef recanted his entire escape story and his ordeals of the past several weeks.

"You've come a long way from the Adriatic coast. How can we help you?"

"I was told you might be able to help me get out of the country."

Mihailovich handed Josef a cup of slivovitz, "Have a sip. You must be tired because of your long journey."

Josef took the cup, gulped the plum brandy down, and remained speechless.

Mihailovich continued, "What can you give me in return if I help you get out of the country?"

Josef considered his response then said, "I know someone who works for the British government. She was the one who escaped aboard the submarine. I can contact her and maybe she can do something to help your cause, perhaps equipment, and supplies?"

Josef could tell the General was already thinking strategically and waited for his response. "As you can see young Josef, we don't have a lot of contacts with the outside world, as of yet. However, you are correct. We could use a few things against the Nazis. Do you smoke?" the General offered a cigarette.

Josef shook his head as the General continued, "We are not only at war with the Axis powers, but there is also an internal, civil struggle, specifically between the Communist Partisans led by Broz[1] and me. The Partisans would kill you, being an American, just as easily as they would a German soldier. So, you were fortunate to fall into our hands and not the communists." Mihailovich took a long drag from his cigarette and continued. "Believe it or not, your best chance of escape is to get back to Belgrade. My sources tell me that the easiest way of getting out of the country if you have a passport is simply fly out on a regularly scheduled flight to Sofia. The Bulgarians are not officially at war yet. You can still move about freely there. Once inside Bulgaria, get yourself to the Turkish border at Matochina. From there you can easily cross the border into Turkey. The train is still the best mode of travel inside Bulgaria. Once you cross into Turkey, you can get back to the United States by way of Istanbul. The problem I see is you'll never get on the flight. There are thousands of people already waiting to get on the one or two seats available. You'll have to buy a ticket in Reichsmarks and you could wait several weeks, if not months, to get out. By that time, the political situation could change and they may not even run the flight."

"Any other suggestions?"

"You can go around the long way, but it will keep you

moving. My men can take you north to the Sava River. From there, they'll help you board an oil barge. The Germans will do anything to keep their Romanian oil moving freely into the Third Reich. If you're working on the barge, they'll let you in and out of the city with no problems. The oil barges continue on the Danube River all the way to Ruse. Get off at Ruse and take the train south to Radovets and Matochina. That is the latest information I have on safe passage."

"I still have some money in the bank along with my bank records. If the Germans haven't destroyed the banks, I can get the last of my remaining funds and convert them to marks."

Mihailovich began to rise from the ground. Everyone in the room stood. Josef joined in and then Mihailovich continued, "Come with me, Josef. Let's go for a walk, just you and me."

The two men left the hut and walked around the small village as Mihailovich spoke, "I'm giving you this information because if you make it out, please tell the US government we have a strong and organized force to fight against the Nazis, but we need communications equipment, weapons, and supplies. At the moment, we can only transmit messages by unsecure telegram to the embassies. It would be nice if we had a two-way radio to communicate directly with Cairo."

"If what you said is true about getting out on the oil barge, you have my word."

The trip to Belgrade on the barge was uneventful. Josef was surprised that most of Belgrade was not pulverized to the ground, but largely intact, despite the bombing raids. He even found his bank, closed out the account, and withdrew all the remaining funds, which weren't much, but enough to get him out of the country and back to the United States.

He stayed in Belgrade for the night before continuing on. He spent that night sleeping aboard the vessel. No one at the docks or in the city questioned him about his status as an American student leaving the country. Josef used the day in Belgrade to try to find any information about Dick, but with no luck. His apartment was abandoned and the proprietor said she had not seen Vojvoda since the first days of the attack.

After the one day wait, Josef cast off from the docks on the oil barge grateful and relieved. While onboard the barge, Josef continued to think about the fate of his friends and wondered where they would be by now. It had been over three weeks since their initial escape from the city. Tess and Penelope should, at the very least, be in Allied territory, possibly Gibraltar.

Josef worked on the barge for the next week as they made their way down the river toward Romania and Bulgaria. On the second day of the trip, the Captain told Josef they were in Bulgaria, near Vidin. For the time being, Josef was out of Yugoslavia. Mihailovich's sources were correct. He didn't experience any problems crossing the border into Bulgaria. On the seventh day, he arrived in Ruse where he disembarked. The city was not yet in full Nazi occupation and he could more or less move about freely, as Mihailovich foretold. He had to stay in Ruse for two more days over the weekend, so he could change more money at the bank. Luckily, the small hotel he stayed at allowed him to pay in US dollars. On Monday morning, bright and early, he took the train to Matochina. This was a small village on the Turkish-Bulgarian border with no more than a dozen little houses. Josef discovered there was no running water or flush toilets, but Mihailovich was right in that the town was the only way to get from Bulgaria into Turkey safely. The locals had found an area around the manned, border checkpoints and for a small fee would show you the way.

Once Josef was ready to cross the border, the locals took him to the strip of land and pointed out the safe route marked by green strips. The villagers made it clear that he must stay between the markings. Josef handed over the equivalent of twenty-five dollars for the safe passage. Then he began his trek across the hundred yards of no man's land from Bulgaria to Turkey, taking his time and placing his steps between the strips. After walking for about fifteen minutes, he got to the end of the path. There, Turkish border officials were waiting for him in a small truck with big grins on their faces. One of the officers took Josef's passport, looked it over, handed it back and said in English, "Welcome to Turkey, young man! Continue to follow the path ahead until it ends by a small grove of trees. There is someone waiting to meet you."

Josef was surprised to hear this piece of information and couldn't imagine who would be waiting for him, but did as instructed. He continued to walk the remaining distance along the trail to a clump of shady trees. There, waiting inside a rusty, old vehicle at the end of the path, with his feet sticking out from a window, smoking a cigarette was none other than Dick Vojvoda. Josef could not believe what he was seeing. Josef slapped his hand on the top of the roof, "How the hell did you get here and how did you know I was arriving at this very moment?"

Dick blew cigarette smoke out of his mouth and casually said, "I have my sources. I knew about the escape route through Bulgaria. That's why I couldn't go with you on the train in Sabac. There were over one hundred Jewish students, still in Belgrade who needed to escape. So, I stayed behind and coordinated the trip to Turkey. Some got out by train, others by car or plane. Most made it, but a few were impatient and were killed or deported en route."

---

1. Josef Tito.

Chapter 5

LIEUTENANT WALSH

About the same time Josef was crossing the Turkish border, Penelope and Tess disembarked from a tiny Belgian freighter on the docks of Falmouth. The trip aboard the submarine had taken them across the Mediterranean Sea to Gibraltar. From there, they were taken ashore to a waiting Belgian freighter for the trip to England. Even though the two girls were now safely in England, the skies overhead were not much safer than the skies over Yugoslavia. The battle of Britain had begun in early 1940, German dive bombers, and V-1 rockets were a constant threat. London, in particular, was a much different city than when the girls left it in 1939. Sand bags, air raid shelters, ration coupons, and military personnel were everywhere. Tess took the train directly to Oxford, her home, located thirty miles to the northwest of London. There, her family owned a small inn. Her mother worked running the inn while her father worked as a railway worker.

Penelope, on the other hand, lived in South Lambeth, in the heart of London. She caught the first train to Southampton, then on to London, arriving at Victoria

Station. She took the Tube to Stockwell Station and walked the three blocks to her flat, arriving late in the evening, but before curfew. She rang the doorbell then waited several minutes and gazed upon the neighborhood streets. There, she could see the blackout curtains and paper covering the windows. Searchlights streaked the skies looking for enemy aircraft. She rang the bell a second time; this time, she could hear her mother, Aleks Mitchell.

"Just a minute, love, I'm on my way." The door opened slowly, "Oh my God—it's you!" She hugged Penelope and spoke in Serbo-Croatian, "Come in, dear. What a pleasant surprise. We got word from the war department that you got out of Belgrade, but we had no idea when you'd come home."

Penelope made the switch to English, "Good to see you, Mum, everything's all right. I'm just so happy to be home. We've had a very difficult and long journey."

"Well, I couldn't imagine. Come in, dear and let me get the kettle going. Dad will be down shortly. He's on duty tonight as an air raid warden."

Penelope spent all night talking with her mother, retelling the story of how the four college students left Yugoslavia. She also mentioned that she could not bring one of them back on the submarine and he was probably still behind, somewhere in Yugoslavia.

"My dear, I'm just so happy to have you back. You know, you can finish your studies when the war's over."

"Yes, Mum, that's my plan, but for the time being, nothing would please me more than a nice warm bath and a cup of hot chocolate."

Several days passed as Penelope stayed with her mother. Her father was busy as a factory worker and air raid warden, so Penelope used the time to reacquaint with her mother and to help around the flat. One afternoon in early May of 1941, the doorbell rang. Penelope raced downstairs, "I'll get it!"

She opened the door and standing outside was a young naval officer in his mid-twenties. He was tall and slender with a thick head of brown hair ducked neatly under his white cap, "Good afternoon, miss. I'm Lieutenant Tony Walsh. I'm with the war department. I'm looking for a Miss Penelope Mitchell."

"That's me, won't you come in?"

"Yes, thank you, miss. I'm here to summon you to the war department for debriefing. I know you've just recently come back from abroad, but the London office needs information on the evacuations."

"Yes, I suppose they'll need something, after all, they did arrange for my escape."

"I'm sorry for the rush, but it's vitally important to the war effort that they know the latest information coming in from the field."

Penelope thought about her job at the embassy back in Belgrade, "I see. Well, there isn't much to tell. Could I just give you the details here and now and be done with it?"

"I'm afraid not, miss. Here's the address. They'll be expecting you tomorrow morning at nine hundred hours sharp." Tony handed her a slip of paper with directions to Whitehall and a meeting with a Mr. Hugh Shellworth.

"In that case, I'll be there. Good day, Lieutenant," and she escorted him out.

The next morning Penelope made her way to the address Tony Walsh provided. To her amazement, the address was not at Whitehall, but rather on the third floor at the St. Ermins Hotel on Caxton Street in the heart of Westminster. As she approached the St. Ermins, she noticed several men from all branches of the service running about. Some claimed to be from the Admiralty others from the Army or Air Ministry, either way the St. Ermins was indeed a very busy place. "I'm here to see a Mr. Shellworth," she asked politely to the hotel staff member behind the front desk.

"Yes miss, third floor, room 301. You can take the lift to your left."

"Thank you, sir."

Penelope waited in the small foyer of room 301. It was a basic suite, with one table and one chair placed in the middle of the room. There were maps and drawings strewn about and the smell of tobacco and cigarette smoke filled the air. Then she recognized a familiar face. Lieutenant Walsh appeared from the adjoining room.

"Good morning, Miss Mitchell. Lord Shellworth will be with you shortly." He escorted her inside the adjoining room. Tony pointed to another small wooden chair in the middle of the room, "Come have a seat." Another man in his late fifties was on the phone talking with his back to Tony and Penelope. He seemed entrenched in conversation with the person on the other end of the line. He was tall, with silver hair, a thin mustache, and was dressed in a dark suit in contrast to a military uniform, worn by the other men in the hotel. After several minutes talking on the phone, Lord Hugh Shellworth, head of the British Special Operations Executive[1] (SOE) secured the telephone receiver, turned around, and addressed Penelope.

"Good morning, Miss Mitchell. Thank you for coming."

Penelope stood and shook Shellworth's hand. He had a firm grip and had a look of determination in his eyes. "It's a pleasure to meet you, sir. I'm sorry to tell you, but I don't have much to debrief you about my escape from the Balkans."

"Have a seat, young lady." Shellworth talked on his feet

and continued the dialog as if speaking to no one in particular. "This meeting is not about debriefing your escape by submarine. We already have most of that information anyway. I'll be quick and to the point. I've asked you here because we believe you can provide us something very useful in the war effort."

Penelope thought for a moment and could not believe what she could possibly have that the war department needed. Shellworth continued, "You made contacts with resistance movements in Yugoslavia, and I might add, you did a very good job indeed. I was told you had a certain air of confidence about you."

"I believe what you're referring to is my meeting with the baker and his wife in Montenegro. He was very helpful in getting us a ride to Kotor."

"I was also told that you speak good German, but your French and Serbo-Croatian are excellent. Also, that you worked with the embassy in Belgrade."

"Yes, but it was mainly doing translation work and broadcasting on the BBC."

"The organization you worked for no longer exists, Miss Mitchell. Most of their assets are now incorporated into MI-6. However, I and Lieutenant Walsh here, work for an entirely different department, separate from MI-6 or MI-5. We answer only to the office of the prime minister. In fact, that was the PM on the phone just now. The work is very dangerous and the Germans don't like what we're doing, but it's extremely important in the war effort and has to be done if we're to win."

Penelope looked down at her feet and deduced what he was asking her to do, then, Shellworth continued, "I suppose you're wondering about your parents?"

"Yes, Mother is all by herself most of the day with Dad

working days and nights. She's taking a liking to having me home full-time now."

"And your studies? I understand you were about to graduate with a nursing degree."

"I'll continue my studies after the war is over."

"Your young, attractive, and play the piano, too."

"I don't see what I could possibly do that is so important to the war effort unless you're referring to . . . *special employment?*"

"Then you *are* familiar with the term and what it implies, so there's no need to go into specifics."

Penelope looked at Tony, who was standing beside her, and realized the significance of the interview, "I'll have to give it some thought, of course."

"Very well, you don't have to decide at the moment. Lieutenant Walsh will be in contact with you, should you reach a decision. In the meantime, you must tell no one about this interview, not even your parents or closest friends. You must never mention my name or this meeting place to anyone. Do you understand?"

"Yes, of course."

"Good. If and when the time comes you decide and wish to join us, simply refer to 'special employment' in all correspondences."

"Thank you, sir, you have been very kind."

"Good day, Miss Mitchell, Lieutenant Walsh will show you out."

Tony walked Penelope out of the St. Ermins Hotel and could not help but notice her looks. She was small and slim, with short, curly, blond hair and lovely hazel eyes. Even though she was only in her early twenties, she seemed much more grown-up. There was something rather sexy about her and Tony, being unmarried, couldn't resist any longer, "Can I take you out for lunch? I know of a quiet, little pub just around the corner that serves up some hearty grub and they say the suds are good, too."

Penelope smiled and said, "Aren't you supposed to be on-duty or something like that?"

"One has to eat sometime you know."

In war-torn London in 1941, with no money in her purse and hungry, she took him up on his offer. They ate and laughed and talked about many things and generally enjoyed the afternoon with each other.

----

1. Winston Churchill created a separate, war-time intelligence agency, completely apart from MI-6 to conduct sabotage and insurgency operations behind enemy lines. Thus, SOE was created to Set Europe Ablaze.

Part II

CALL TO DUTY

Chapter 6

IN THE ARMY NOW

It was June of 1942 in Horning, Pennsylvania, almost a year since Josef left Yugoslavia. Josef found a job working in a nearby steel factory. He managed to get back to the United States thanks to the help of Dick Vojvoda. How Dick managed to get out of Yugoslavia himself and get to the Turkish border remained a mystery. All Dick would tell him in letters he wrote was that he was offered a job with an oil company and he had connections in the Middle East. With the United States now entered in World War II, Dick knew that if he went back to the United States, he would surely be drafted, so he took the offer to work for the oil company out of the Middle East section.

Josef, on the other hand, made the trans-Atlantic voyage back to the United States by way of Istanbul. He managed to finish out his degree at the University of Pittsburg. Despite the war going on in Europe, Josef had all his transcripts sent over from Belgrade. It turned out his hard work and discipline paid off. He had enough credits to earn a double bachelor of arts degree, one in geography, the other in Serbo-Croatian, but it was a matter of time before he was drafted into the military.

It had been almost a year and he still had no contact with Tess. Each day he went to the mailbox and each day he was disappointed because there was no letter. At night, as he lay in bed, he thought about her and her life back in England. If she had made it out alive, she must be living a difficult life in war-torn London.

Two weeks later, after he was about to give up on his beloved sweetheart, he found a letter in the mailbox in a powder-blue, tattered envelope addressed to him. It was from Tess, but with a return address he didn't recognize.

Assistant Section Leader Celeste Bowmen, WAAF, WAAF Number 34 Group, RAF Bomber Command, Edinburgh, Scotland.

He was so excited he could barely open the envelope. The letter read:

Dear Josef,

I hope you receive this letter. If you do, it means you made it back to the States. I am so sorry it's taken me this long to write. I misplaced your contact information. Luckily, you gave it to Penelope as well and I was finally able to get it from her. More about her later. The war in Europe has taken its toll on all of us.

After I returned to England, I came home to Oxford and worked at my parents' inn. Dad was busy working on the railroad and Mum needed the help. Oxford is thirty miles northwest of London, but that has not stopped German aircraft from dropping bombs outside our city. London is nothing like I remembered when I left almost four years ago. The city is in near ruins and fires burn every night. I couldn't stand the death and destruction and all our brave boys being killed overseas. Each night as we lay in our beds, I heard the sounds of explosions from Luftwaffe bombers. They reminded me of Belgrade and our time together. With the sound of each explosion, I couldn't help but think about you and wondered if you made it safely out. That's one of the reasons why I joined the WAAF. It stands for the Women Auxiliary Air Force. We do noncombat-related work that would normally be done by our brave young men. I'm training to be a radio operator. They said I have the fingers because I play the piano.

Penelope went back to live with her parents in South Lambeth. She wasn't home for more than a few weeks when she was summoned to the war department for debriefing. There, she met a young naval officer named Tony Walsh. The two fell in love and he asked her to marry her after the third date! Can you believe that? She must have been the love of his life because she accepted his proposal and the couple married shortly thereafter. Naturally, I attended the wedding as her maid of honor. Tony worked for the war department, and through his connections, got her a job at Whitehall doing special employment. I'm still not sure what that entails; remember she always said she could get a job back in England doing that kind of work. Anyway, Penelope and Tony wanted a family right away, despite the war and difficulties living in London; she became pregnant immediately.

Unfortunately, Tony was killed in a night bombing raid that destroyed Farrington Station where he took refuge one night, thus leaving a widow and young child. The good news from all this is Penelope gave birth to a healthy baby girl, named Sarah. The loss of her husband was terrible, but she managed and thinks nothing, but caring for her young daughter. She also decided to join the FANYs (First Aid Nursing Yeomanry) to do her part to support the war. The last I heard, she was driving ambulances and carrying stretchers.

Now that I've brought you up to date, please write to the above address and let me know if you made it out safely. I've grown up now and there is no need to keep our relationship away from Mother and

Dad. My dear Josef, I can't wait to see you. Just remember that I will love you always.

Your beloved,

Tess

Josef was so ecstatic with joy that he began to shed tears. It was through these teary eyes he caught sight of another letter addressed to him in the stack of mail. It was from the war department. He was being drafted into the army with a report date of July 26, 1942.

WHEN JOSEF REPORTED for boot camp at Fort Ord, California in July 1942, his drill instructor, Sergeant Drake, discovered he held multiple degrees and spoke numerous languages. Thus, he was singled out, in particular, to perform the most unpopular and laborious additional duties for the platoon. He was given the job of kitchen help, peeling potatoes for thousands of recruits at three in the morning, cleaning latrines, and scrubbing floors.

One afternoon while Josef and two other recruits were out scrubbing huge pots and pans behind the mess hall, Josef noticed the most beautiful peach tree teaming with fruit. Josef loved fresh fruit and it was something that was almost nonexistent in the military. The army's answer to fresh fruit came in the form of canned, fruit cocktail. Josef couldn't stand it any longer, watching this beautiful tree drop ripened peaches to the ground. So, he made his way over to the tree and picked several. They were the tastiest peaches he'd ever eaten in his life. As he was sitting in the shade enjoying the fruit, his drill instructor, Sergeant Drake, saw him sitting down in the shade enjoying his tasty snack and began shouting, "What the hell do you think you're doing? Get the hell back to the mess hall and start working like a real soldier! You're not some smart-ass that thinks he can sand-bag it all day! No, wait, I've got a better idea. Come with me."

Josef got up from the shade and followed Drake back to the mess hall where the other two recruits were still busy scrubbing pots and pans, and he yelled to them, "Get inside and help. Kostinic is going to work outside from now on!"

The two recruits hurried back into the kitchen while Josef stood at attention in the sun. Drake took out a toothbrush from his pocket and said, "I want you to use this and scrub this entire loading dock from top to bottom! I want it done by sixteen hundred hours just in time for PT. After that, you'll run two additional miles."

"Yes, sir. I'll get on it right away."

"Don't call me sir! I work for a living, remember!"

As Josef went to fill up a pail with soapy water, he saw an army Jeep pull up to the loading dock and stop in front of Drake. It must have been an officer driving because Sergeant Drake snapped to attention and pointed toward Josef. The officer then drove the Jeep closer to Josef and came to a stop in a cloud of dust.

"Are you Private Josef Kostinic?" a young, baby-faced Second Lieutenant asked.

Josef saluted the young Lieutenant, "Yes sir, that's me."

"I want you to come with me. There's someone from Washington who wants to speak with you. By the way, what are you doing with that bucket and toothbrush?"

"Sergeant Drake ordered me to scrub the loading dock with it."

"He did?"

"Yes sir, and he wants it done by sixteen hours, so I

hope the man from Washington won't keep me too long. I've got two more miles to run tonight, as well."

"It doesn't matter if it takes us all day and all night. Let me have that bail and brush," and he marched back over to where Sergeant Drake was still standing and handed it to him. The young Second Lieutenant decided to demonstrate his authority and ordered, "I want *you* to clean the dock before sixteen hours! This private is coming with me and he could be with us until midnight. Now, *you* get to work!"

The Lieutenant came back to Josef, "Hop in, Private." Josef took a seat as the Jeep drove away in a cloud of dust. As they passed the mess hall, Josef took a final look over his shoulder and saw Drake on his hands and knees scrubbing the loading dock with his toothbrush. Josef reached into his pocket, took out a fresh peach, and bit down deeply, enjoying the sweet, tasty fruit.

Back at Post Headquarters, Josef was ushered into a small office where he was to be interviewed by a man dressed in civilian clothes. When Josef entered the room, the man stood and introduced himself, "I'm Howard O'Donnell, from the Office of Strategic Service in Washington. I've come here to ask you a few questions. Please take a seat." O'Donnell was in his early fifties with short-cropped hair, a square jaw, and medium height.

Josef did as instructed and tried to get comfortable in the hard, wooden chair.

The man from Washington continued, "I see from your records you speak several languages and you spent time in Yugoslavia. In fact, I see you had a difficult time getting out of the country."

Josef trembled as he heard the words, "I studied at Belgrade University for two years before the German invasion. There were many students from all over Europe.

Some of my best friends spoke several languages. Once you learn one language, it's easy to learn another. As far as getting out of the country, I was fortunate to get help from the local resistance."

"Let me get to the point, Private Kostinic," replied O'Donnell as he continued the conversation in Serbo-Croatian without skipping a beat. "Our office is looking for bright young men like you, who spent time in Europe and speak foreign languages. The job involves work overseas and could be dangerous. Our country is at war now and there is nothing short of total victory over the Axis nations, which means we have to pull out all the stops, using conventional and unconventional warfare. Do you think this line of work will interest you?"

Josef didn't have to think about a reply and didn't even notice that O'Donnell spoke in Serbo-Croatian. As soon as O'Donnell said the job involved work overseas, he immediately thought of Tess and that this might be his way of getting to England, "Yes sir, without question!" Then Josef realized O'Donnell had coerced him into speaking Serbo-Croatian as a way of evaluating him, but didn't mind.

O'Donnell seemed unaffected and unemotional by the switch in languages and continued in English, "You do realize that this line of work is strictly voluntary. If you feel you're not up to this line of work or if you don't think you'll handle the specific training, you can back out now with no repercussions against your record."

"I understand. When do I report for duty?"

"First line of business, if you agree to the terms, then I'd like you to sign your orders." He passed the written orders across the desk. After reading, Josef signed the Official Secrets Act and directive, ordering him to the Office of Strategic Service upon completion of basic training, even though he had no idea what the OSS was. Then O'Donnell spoke, "You'll complete basic training, then go to Fort Benning, Georgia for parachute school, an abbreviated one, of course. After that, you'll be reassigned to formal OSS training schools in Washington and elsewhere to learn the craft. If all goes well, we should be able to use you in the field sometime in the spring of next year. Do you have any questions for me?"

"You mentioned work overseas. Is there a possibility of going to England or Yugoslavia?"

"Maybe, but we won't know until you've completed your training. After that, mission requirements dictate when and where you'll be sent."

Josef was overjoyed. At last, he had found a way to get to England. He felt in his heart that things were finally starting to turn around. He also thought about what he had said to Mihailovich and the promise he made for helping him escape, "By the way, Mr. O'Donnell, when I was in Yugoslavia, I met a resistance leader by the name of Draza Mihailovich. Does that name mean anything to you?"

O'Donnell raised a single, curious eyebrow then replied, "Only from what I've read in *Time* magazine. The boys in Virginia will know more. For now, you must concentrate on boot camp. You must also realize that this meeting must be kept confidential. Do you understand?"

"Yes, I understand. You can count on me."

"Should someone from your platoon ask why you were summoned here, you can tell them you talked to someone about follow-on assignments. Welcome to the Office of Strategic Service, *Mister* Kostinic." O'Donnell stood up and offered his hand, "I look forward to working with you."

Chapter 7

SPECIALLY EMPLOYED

In August of 1942, Tess was at her radio station monitoring traffic from Bomber Command. Most of the young RAF trainees were learning to fly the Lancaster bomber. These RAF aircraft were returning to bases in Scotland from their training sorties over the North Sea when Tess received a cable from London. She had applied for a commission in the WAAF and so far, had heard nothing up until now. In the cable, it stated she was scheduled for an interview in two days with a Mr. Potter in room 238 at the Hotel Victoria on Northumberland Avenue at 1100 hours. The subject of the meeting was to discuss details of her commission. She was to wear civilian attire. Tess thought she could take the evening train out and spend the night at Penelope's flat, then catch the Tube to Embankment Station the next morning. The hotel was just a few feet from the station. She was overjoyed at finally receiving positive news about her commission.

Tess arrived at Penelope's flat in South Lambeth late in the evening before curfew. She knocked on the door and could hear footsteps coming down the stairs. Penelope opened the door and saw Tess, worn and tired, but otherwise in good spirits, "How great it is to see you. This is a surprise."

"It was a short notice order. I finally received news about my commission and I've been summoned here to London to discuss the details. I thought I could spend the night with you."

"Of course, come in."

"How's the baby?"

"She's doing great. Looks like her father with those big, blue eyes. She's asleep now."

"I know it's been difficult on you, with the war and losing your husband, but what a blessing you have."

"I'll remember that the next time she cries in the middle of the night and wants to be fed. Come have a seat. We've got so much to catch up on. Have you heard from Josef?"

"He's in the Army now, drafted as a private, not an officer."

Penelope led Tess inside to the parlor on the first floor, took her suitcase, and then rushed into the kitchen to make a pot of tea. A few minutes passed when she came back into the parlor with a tray of tea and biscuits. "Have you been able to write to him much?"

"I've only been able to send him one or two letters, but he sends me a postcard or letter every week."

"How long will you be in London?"

"Just for the day. After my commissioning appointment, I'm to return to Scotland via the fastest means available. By the way, how's life in the FANYs?"

"The usual boring things, driving Lorries, talking to wounded soldiers, that sort of lot. I did get a promotion. They must have felt sorry for me because of Sarah. I'm working as a secretary at Orchard Court. Perhaps we could ride together on the Tube. I have an excellent provider who takes care of Sarah when I'm at work. We can have a cuppa before your meeting. By the way, where is your appointment tomorrow morning?"

"The Hotel Victoria, off Embankment."

"That won't work. I'll be in Mayfair, off Baker Street. Maybe some other time?"

"What kinds of questions do you suppose they'll ask?" inquired Tess.

"From my limited experience, I'm sure they'll ask you about your time in Belgrade. Should they ask, remember don't tell them too much about how we escaped?"

"What do you mean?"

"Let's just say that it's probably best you don't say anything about me talking with British intelligence or contacting local resistance leaders, that sort of thing."

"Good God, I'd almost forgotten about that. Yes, I suppose you're right. The less they know the better. Besides, it's none of their business anyway."

After tea and chatting until two in the morning, Tess finally fell asleep on the sofa. Penelope went upstairs to her bedroom. Before she went to sleep however, she thought, *looks like they got my recommendation.*

The next morning, just after ten o'clock, Tess stepped out of the Embankment Tube station and walked the two blocks to the Hotel Victoria. The streets were crowded with pedestrians walking up and down Northumberland Avenue. One could easily see the aftermath from aerial attacks everywhere. Some buildings were still smoldering, firefighters desperately working throughout the night. Sandbags were stacked up, eight to ten feet high in front of all the buildings all along Embankment and Whitehall. There were soldiers everywhere, busy coming and going to various offices and buildings. Finally, she found the entrance to the hotel. A butler wearing a steel helmet was at the door.

"Good morning, miss. Can I help you?"

"Yes, I'm here to see a Mr. Potter."

"Right, upstairs to the second floor, at the end of the hallway. You'll have to use the stairs because the lift is out. You'll need this," and he handed her a piece of paper, which served as a building pass.

On the second floor, Tess found room 238 at the end of the hallway with the door open. She approached the door and was greeted by a young man in his thirties, dressed in a plaid, wool suit, smoking a pipe, "You must be Miss Bowmen. We've been expecting you. Thank you for coming early, I'm Potter, please come in."

Tess could hardly believe her eyes. The room was completely empty except for a table, two chairs, and a lamp. All the bedroom furniture was removed. As Potter closed the door behind them, the room darkened and he switched on the lone lamp on the desk. "Please have a seat," he said as he offered her a cigarette.

"No thanks, I don't smoke," she replied as she tried to get comfortable.

Potter continued, "You've been assigned to Bomber Command in Scotland. Are they treating you well?"

"As good as expected under the circumstances. It's cold during the winter and hot in the summer."

"I see you play the piano. How long have you been playing?"

"I've played since I was eleven."

"You've already received training in Morse code?" Tess nodded her head. "You've studied abroad at the University of Belgrade and you speak French, German, and Serbo-Croatian. Am I correct?"

"Yes, but I can explain all of this."

Pottered interrupted again, "And you're a good athlete. I see you did remarkably well on your physical fitness tests."

Tess was confused with the questioning and finally uttered, "Mr. Potter, what on earth is all this got to do with my commission?"

Potter walked over to the windows where the curtains were drawn, making the room dark in appearance, and reached into his coat pocket for a match to light his pipe, contemplating a response. He then placed the unlit pipe into his mouth and said, "There's a reason for all this secrecy. My name is not really Potter. I'm Captain Jepson and I work for an entirely different department in the war office. I'll get right to the point. We believe you have certain skills that could be beneficial for the war effort, specifically, clandestine wireless radio. We're in need of highly skilled radio operators who can transmit under difficult conditions. I must also inform you at this time that the work is extremely dangerous. You could be captured by the enemy, if not killed. In the event of capture, you would be interrogated by the Gestapo—a thing no human being could withstand with anything but terror."

"Mr. Potter, what sort of work are you referring to?"

"You would be working with local resistance fighters in occupied countries relaying their requests and information back to headquarters. You see, Miss Bowmen, the Germans don't like what we're doing and they've become very good about homing in on our radio operators. As a woman, you stand a much better chance of survival. You'll blend in better with the local population with your language skills and you could avoid detection and capture easier as a woman. I know this is all very difficult for you to grasp at the moment."

"Yes, indeed it is, but isn't there someone else more qualified than I am?"

"There are probably people out there with your same abilities, age, sex, qualifications, and so forth, but you were difficult to find as it was. We found you by accident and by a recommendation."

Potter sat in the chair by his desk, "You don't have to make a decision at the moment. You can think about it for a few weeks, and then get back with me. As far as your commission, if you agree to join us, you will be assigned the rank of Flight Officer in the Royal Air Force. We just need to know your decision so we can move on."

Tess thought for a moment about what he said and wondered who could have recommended her for such an assignment, and then she said, "How *did* you find out about me?"

"I'm sorry, I'm not at liberty to discuss that, but I can say that you came highly recommended."

"Then I should think it over and get back with you, Mr. Potter, or excuse me, Captain Jepson."

"That is all one can ask. I'll give you a fortnight to think about it. Here's my contact information." He signed her hall pass and then escorted her out the room.

As Tess walked outside the Hotel Victoria, she couldn't help but remember Mr. Potter saying she had been recommended from a highly reliable source. She didn't know who that person could be except for Penelope Walsh. Tess remembered Penelope said she worked as a secretary at Orchard Court just off Baker Street. It was not far. She decided to pay her one last visit before she left for Scotland. She took the bus and got off at Portman Square. Across the street, she saw the entrance to Orchard Court covered with sandbags and guarded by armed sentries. She crossed the street and walked up to the entrance. A bellman was stationed out front just like at the Hotel Victoria, but this one wasn't wearing a steel helmet.

"I'm here to see Penelope Walsh. I do believe she works as a secretary here."

"There is no one here by that name that I'm aware of. You'll have to enquire at 64 Baker Street, just up the road."

As she was about to walk up Baker Street, Tess saw a figure at Portman Square across the street. It was Penelope, dressed in civilian clothes and not her khaki FANY uniform. Quickly she darted through traffic across the street and thought, *she's got a lot of explaining to do.*

THE BRITISH SUBMARINE surfaced at 0200 hours off the Dalmatian Coast. On board was a three-man insertion team led by British Captain Niki Potok and two Canadians, Peter Pavloc and Andre Simac. All three men were assigned to the Special Operations Executive and their mission was to establish another communications link between Tito's Partisan headquarters in Brac and British SOE Cairo. All three men knew the area well from their childhoods and none expected any difficulty establishing a communications link. Pavloc was the courier for the team and Simac was the radio operator. Simac had in his possession the Marconi Mark II wireless radio used by SOE for clandestine radio transmissions. The devise weighed approximately thirty-five pounds and fit inside a small suitcase. The previous night Tito's Partisans received a BBC broadcast over the entertainment program that said, "Tea will be served for breakfast." These were the code words telling them to prepare for the arriving agents by sea.

The submarine would only be on the surface for five minutes. During this time, the agents had to make their way to a waiting rubber raft, where they would board, and then paddle to shore and then be picked up by Partisans. The three men climbed down the gangway and into the raft. Two sailors tossed their equipment sacks and radio equipment into the raft and then went below deck. The sub vanished below the surface as Potok, Pavloc, and Simac paddled away. It was a beautiful August night in 1942, with clear skies and warm temperatures. The fresh air felt good to the men compared to the musty, oily smell of the sub as they paddled toward land, which was now clearly visible.

"There should be a small beach ahead," shouted Pavloc. "We'll head right for the middle."

As the three men paddled closer and closer to shore, it became obvious that something was terribly wrong. First, they were supposed to be off the island of Brac, but on closer scrutiny, the land was linear and stretched several miles to the north and south. Second, the men could see lights and traffic moving along the coast. Their landing location on the island of Brac was supposed to be uninhabited.

"Bloody hell, mate. Do you see what I see?" said Simac.

"There's no way this is an island. It looks like the coastline to me," replied Potok.

"I was thinking the same thing. Do you think we should paddle off to the side? Maybe there's a place near the rocks where we could land."

Pavloc quickened his pace and said, "I can't believe the Royal Navy is that stupid. They dropped us in the wrong place. No wonder we're losing the war."

The waves were getting rougher as the men paddled to shore. The little rubber raft struggled with each swell. Harder and faster, the men paddled until they eventually made it to the surf and shoreline, but they encountered rocks everywhere. They steered the raft to an area where they saw the least white foam and prayed. The raft hit a pile of rocks and the raft tipped over, capsizing into the sea. Fortunately, the water was shallow and the men could stand. They pulled the raft and their cargo ashore and the three men tumbled to the sand completely exhausted.

When they caught their breath Pavloc said, "We need to get off the beach and up the hill, find a place to dry off, and send a radio message that we were dropped off at the wrong spot. How about up there?" he said as he pointed to a clump of trees.

Simic answered, "Looks good to me, my radio should be dry, packed in the watertight bag."

Simac grabbed his radio bag and equipment and started walking up the hill, Potok and Pavloc came behind, carrying the remaining equipment. As they got to the top of the hill, they stumbled onto a roadway where a truck with three men was off to the side of the road. They were not German soldiers but civilians. The British agents had no choice, their presence was compromised; they would have to engage the men. Potok, still winded and wet, said in Serbo-Croatian, "Greetings, my friends. We had an accident at sea with our boat and we had to bail out overboard. Do you think we could have a lift into town?"

One of the men holding an oil lantern moved forward from the darkness and spoke, "We have been here all night patrolling the coast. We did not see a boat in trouble. We did however see your raft as you paddled from the sea." The man removed a pistol from his holster and said, "What's in the bags?"

Pavloc tried to fire a shot from his revolver, but it was useless. As soon as he made a move for his weapon, one of the men fired his pistol, hitting Pavloc between the eyes, and he dropped to the ground.

Potok and Simac raised their hands and said in Serbo-Croatian, "Don't shoot! We're unarmed."

Potok asked, "We're looking for Partisans. Can you take us to Tito's headquarters?"

The three civilian men started laughing, then grabbed Simac and Potok and shoved them to the ground. Another picked up Simac's radio sack and opened it, "Let's see what was so important in the bag." He tore open the watertight sack and saw the suitcase. He opened the suitcase and saw the Mark II radio, "What splendid luck. This will bring us a handsome reward."

The two British officers were the first Allied agents captured behind enemy lines in Yugoslavia. They had stumbled unfortunately not into Tito's Partisans, but rather onto a Croatian resistance movement called the Ustaša, who pledged allegiance to the Nazis. The two British officers were transported by military rail to Gestapo Headquarters in Belgrade for further interrogation.

Part III

BEHIND ENEMY LINES

Chapter 8

SHANGRI-LA

In early September of 1943, Josef Kostinic finished his six-month OSS Formal Training School in Virginia known as, *The Farm*. Once there, his instructors discovered his talents and put him through a longer course that involved not only Special Operations (SO) training, but also Special Intelligence (SI). He also completed another parachute-jumping course, a mini-course on covert communications, and wireless radio operation. He even spent time at a rail yard where he learned to power-up and unpower locomotives. At the end of his training, he was officially a member of the OSS and promoted to First Lieutenant. It was during this time that Josef received word about his next assignment. He was just getting ready to go to the OSS canteen for a light snack when two men whom he never seen before approached him and said, "Josef Kostinic, would you please come with us?"

The two men escorted Josef to a Ford sedan painted olive-green with white star. He was taken to a secluded, wooded area approximately sixty miles outside Washington, DC. OSS personnel unofficially called this area,

Shangri-La[1]. It was around suppertime when he arrived and the Ford sedan parked in front of a small cabin. There, the two men ushered him to the front door where a naval officer was waiting, "Welcome to Shangri-La, Mr. Kostinic. Everyone's here, they've been expecting you. You can go right on in." The officer opened the front door and gestured with his hand for him to enter.

Inside the main living room, a huge stone fireplace took up most of the space. Seated in large comfortable arm chairs were three men: an older man with short-cropped, thin, gray hair, Howard O'Donnell, and a familiar face, Dick Vojvoda. The three men stood up from their chairs as Josef entered and O'Donnell spoke first, "Ah, there you are, Kostinic. We've been expecting you. Come in and join us."

Josef walked into the living room and stood before the three men. O'Donnell, now wearing the rank of Lieutenant Colonel instead of his civilian clothes continued, "I'd like to introduce you to our boss, General William Donovan, Commander of the Office of Strategic Service."

Major General William Joseph Donovan was a stocky, gray-haired man of fifty-eight. He was a Hoover Republican, Irish Catholic, World War I, Medal of Honor hero, millionaire, Wall Street lawyer and hand-picked by President Roosevelt himself to head the newly formed, American spy agency.

Josef extended a hand to Donovan, "It's a pleasure to meet you, sir. I've heard your name for the past several months and now I finally get to meet you in person."

O'Donnell continued, "I do believe you already know Captain Vojvoda. He's one of our Air Movements Officers."

Josef, in disbelief at seeing his old friend, uttered, "I

can't believe it's you again, Dick. What are *you* doing here?"

Vojvoda, stood in his army uniform sporting the rank of Captain, holding a glass of Scotch and smoking a cigarette said, "I've come to pay you a special visit. I'm back in the States, at least for the time being, no more drilling and barn-storming in the Middle East."

Josef, still in a state of disbelief upon seeing his old friend said, "Dick, you're full of surprises and never cease to amaze me. The last time I saw you, we were in Turkey. By the way, how *did* you get out of Turkey after you arranged my passage out of Istanbul?"

"Yes, well that's part of the whole story, my friend."

"Dick, why don't you tell him about it," said O'Donnell.

Dick placed his glass of Scotch down, "After I helped you get to Istanbul, I ran into a former acquaintance of mine. He's an older gentleman who works for an oil company in the Middle East. I told him I'd studied engineering at Belgrade University before the Nazi occupation, but had to leave my studies. It turns out that my friend was in Turkey recruiting engineers to come work for his firm and he offered me a job on the spot. Naturally, being unemployed at that time, I accepted his offer. It turned out that I didn't do much oil work. Once my employer discovered I spoke foreign languages, they put me to work as an interpreter. I also worked in their aviation department. I scheduled and coordinated air movements of our employees back and forth from the United States and the Middle East. Then war broke out. After Pearl Harbor, I came back to the States, where I was asked to join the OSS. They were looking for people who spoke Serbo-Croatian and other languages with experience in air movements. The job reported directly to the president and I was offered a commission. Of course, with the war going on, I accepted the commission and agreed to work with General Donovan and the OSS instead of going to the infantry."

A young Philippine steward entered the living room, "Sorry to interrupt gentlemen, but dinner is ready."

Donovan finally spoke up, "I don't know about the rest of you boys, but I'm absolutely starving. What do you say we continue this discussion in the dining room? There, we can discuss the reasons why we asked young Kostinic to join us this evening."

Everyone took his cue and proceeded to the dining room, which was located in the adjacent room. The four men took seats around the small, round table. No one spoke during dinner, only the occasional request for more Scotch, which all the men, except Josef, drank feverously. When the dishes were cleared and the cigars and brandy flowed, Donovan spoke, "Howard, why don't we start with you, since you're head of the Balkan Section Field Office."

O'Donnell sipped his brandy and said, "Josef, we've read your training reports, saw your debriefing on escaping Yugoslavia and have had a chance to hear your Serbo-Croatian. In a nutshell, we like what we see. You could do extremely well with our next phase of operations in the Balkans."

Donovan added, "We've joined forces with the British in establishing an Allied post with resistance fighters in Yugoslavia. British SOE has already been operating there since the early part of 1942. They've sent in several teams already, mostly to Partisan territories. The information so far is inconclusive as to which resistance unit is the most effective fighting the enemy. The president is ready to extend support, both militarily and monetarily, to those resistance fighters killing the most Germans. We can't extend that support, unless we know which ones are doing the greatest amount for the war effort. There're too many tax dollars at stake and we want to make sure we spend those dollars wisely."

O'Donnell picked up where Donovan left off. "That's why we need you. Since they're supposedly the self-proclaimed experts, the British insist on taking the lead in all clandestine operations in the Balkans, but as the General pointed out, we're getting conflicting information. We want to send *you* as the American representative for the next infiltration into Yugoslavia to sort through the mess and give it to us straight. You'll drop in ahead of our SOE counterparts as a three-man team. They'll provide the team organizer and radio operator. You'll go as courier and second-in-command."

Now it was Dick's turn to talk, "The British have the operational plan, so we won't discuss the details here and now. I can tell you that you'll be going to London, SOE Headquarters, and be given all the specifics about the operation at that time. I'll coordinate air movements to and from London, so naturally I'll accompany you there, as well as on to Cairo."

Donovan continued, "We've been getting reports that Mihailovich is helping some of our downed airmen who were fortunate to parachute into Chetnik territory after attacking the Astra Romana oil fields in Ploesti. The British missions and Partisan resistance fighters led by Tito dispute those actions and actually report Mihailovich is openly *assisting* the Germans. We can't make any sense of the matter. All we know is that upon debriefing those coming back *most, if not all,* of our airmen were returned to us with assistance from Mihailovich and his Chetnik fighters, not from Tito and his Partisans."

"I did manage to meet with Mihailovich during my escape in forty-one. I gave him my word that I'd do whatever I could to help him with his resistance movement if he helped me escape. The information he gave me from his informants was accurate and I did get out of the country. I don't see any reason why he wouldn't help us again," said Josef.

"That's why I want you back in Mihailovich's territory," replied Donovan. "You've already made contact with him once before. He'll recognize you. Maybe he'll even trust you as you gave him your word. You did give him your word that you'd help?"

"That's correct, sir," replied Josef. "You've obviously read my debriefing. He asked for supplies, weapons, and especially a radio."

"We're prepared to give him whatever he wants as long as he's killing Germans and helping our boys get back home. We just have to make sure that's still the case," added O'Donnell.

"All right, it's settled then," said Donovan. "Josef, you and Dick will leave for London tomorrow by B-24. After your briefing from SOE, you'll be flown to our Cairo headquarters. There you'll be given your insertion instructions." Donovan stood, obviously determining that the meeting and the dinner were over. All three men stood in unison, "I have a driver waiting to take you back to Washington." Donovan reached his hand out to Josef and said, "Best of luck, young man. Colonel O'Donnell will be your OSS case officer starting as of now and throughout your mission."

Dick and Josef were in the back seat of Donovan's chauffeur-driven, Ford, touring car, heading back to Washington. Neither said a word until they had crossed the Potomac River and then Dick broke the silence, "I didn't say anything in front of Wild Bill about Tess. As far as the OSS is concerned, they don't need to know about her or

Penelope, for that matter. I know you must be excited about finally getting a chance to see her. You held it in extremely well."

"Thanks Dick, you're right, I thought about saying something, but better judgment said otherwise."

"When we get to London, we won't have a lot time. They're already expecting us and Colin Gubbins, the new head of SOE doesn't want to be kept waiting. We'll do what we can in the short amount of time we're there. I can't promise anything, but it's the least I can do, as your friend."

* * *

SS OBERSTURMBANNFÜHRER, Hans Flosberg of the Sicherheitsdienst (SD),[2] along with his technical assistant, Ernst Gerhert, walked down the tiny steps of the Gestapo prison to the cellblock. Both men were dressed in civilian clothes. Flosberg held the SS equivalent rank of Lieutenant Colonel. At forty-five years of age, he was tall, lean, and handsome with brown hair and blue eyes. Before the war, Flosberg was a criminal investigator for the Hamburg police department. When war broke out in Germany in 1939, the SS took all the brightest and successful civil servants and inducted them into the military. Flosberg was the lead homicide investigator for the Hamburg police department so the SS gave him the rank and responsibility of handling all internal security matters for Yugoslavia. He commanded thousands of Gestapo and SS personal inside the country. His word was final when it came to internal security matters in the occupied country. Gerhert was a civil servant and former English teacher before the war, thus he needed no military uniform. Flosberg however, felt that as a police investigator he could accomplish more by not wearing one. In fact, he was rarely seen in his SS uniform.

This section of the prison, unlike the rest of the facility, housed political prisoners. It was here that Flosberg held his most valuable assets and did his interrogations. The SD was the German Security Service of the Third Reich responsible for gathering information for the SS. Flosberg's primary job was counterespionage, mainly by turning captured Allied agents. Flosberg knew that the basic Allied plan was to tie up as many German forces as they could, so they could not be deployed to the Western front. In addition, he knew British intelligence was sending in numerous teams to assist the resistance movements, further tying up German counter-intelligence assets. That plan also had it weaknesses and Flosberg knew it because he could also tie up British intelligence assets by diverting attention away from the occupied territories. Thus, the German plan was to turn captured British agents and feed false information back to the Allies using captured radio sets. This operation was known as *Funk Spiel* or Radio Game.

The two captured British agents were being held in separate, small rooms toward the front of the cellblock. Each room had a small glass window covered by iron bars which could be opened or closed depending upon weather conditions. In addition, there was a small bed with a mattress, chair, table lamp and table. These facilities were considered luxurious compared to the rest of the facility. The two British officers made up the first segment of Flosberg's counter deception and counterintelligence operation designed to penetrate Allied intelligence operations in the Balkans. Flosberg was trying to duplicate the highly successful SD counterintelligence operations of Belgium and France by playing back captured Allied wireless radios to London.

As the two SD men reached the bottom of the stairs, Flosberg said to the uniformed Gestapo guard, "Bring the radio operator to my office at once. And make sure he doesn't smell like a rat." Then he turned to Gerhert, "He's had enough time to think about his fate. After all, he's heard the cries from the other prisoners held in Gestapo cells." Flosberg turned on his heels and climbed back up the stairs, Gerhert in tow.

---

1. This area is now known as Camp David, Maryland, the presidential retreat.
2. During the war, the term Gestapo could be used to identify three, separate intelligence agencies; the Abwehr; the German military intelligence service; The Geheime Staatspolizei or Gestapo and finally, the Sicherheitsdienst or SD, the SS RSHA counterintelligence service. Regardless, the Allies treated them as one and the same, the Gestapo.

Chapter 9

SOE HEADQUARTERS, LONDON

Dick and Josef were dropped off at the front of SOE headquarters by a special car. They had just arrived from their flight from the States. Both men were dressed in their army uniforms and were completely exhausted from the long journey; nevertheless, they had a meeting scheduled that afternoon with SOE. As Dick and Josef walked up the stairs to Gubbins' office, Dick could not help but notice the amount of FANY women in the facility.

"This place is teeming with women. I don't think I've ever seen so many in one spot. You know, if I have time, I'll do some searching, to see if I might be able to find Tess or Penelope. At the very least, someone might know of them and tell us where we might be able to locate them."

"I'm not getting my hopes up. The last letter I received from Tess, she told me she was stationed on the south coast, doing some sort of advanced training."

"It's worth a shot anyway. Besides, we don't leave for Cairo until tomorrow morning. Once your meeting ends with Gubbins, we have the rest of the day and night to try and find them."

The two men walked into Gubbins' office at 64 Baker Street and removed their hats. Seated at the front desk was another FANY in uniform working the phones, one in each hand. She looked up from her tasks and said, "Excuse me gentlemen, I'll be right with you." She ended her conversations on the lines and said, "I'm terribly sorry. You two Yanks are early. We were not expecting you for another hour. Colonel Hueron is already here, talking with Gubbins. Which one of you is Kostinic?"

Josef raised his hand, "That would be me, ma'am."

"Your friend will have to wait out here. You may go in now, Lieutenant."

Dick grabbed Josef's hat to hold while he was in the meeting, "I'll be fine, maybe the nice lady can show me the canteen?"

Josef entered Gubbins' office. Standing in front of a large map of Yugoslavia were three men. Josef recognized Gubbins from photographs he'd seen, but was unfamiliar with the other two. All men were dressed in civilian attire. One of the men turned around and spoke to Josef.

"You must be Kostinic. I'm Colonel Stevens, head of the Yugoslav section. I've come all the way from Cairo to brief you on your assignment. This is Colonel William Hueron and of course, no introduction is needed for Brigadier Gubbins." Colin Gubbins, the new chief of SOE, was in his late forties with thinning, brown hair and a mustache.

Josef extended his hand, "Pleased to meet you, gentlemen."

"Won't you take a seat?" replied Stevens.

Josef took a seat at the conference table and the other men followed. Gubbins spoke next,

"Lieutenant Kostinic, I'd like to welcome you as the first American to join our team. I've already spoken to

Donovan and he speaks highly of you. He assured me you're the best man for the job."

"Thank you, sir. I'll do my best."

"With that, let me start off by telling you that Colonel Stevens is in charge of our Yugoslav section all the way from Cairo. He'll coordinate activities and information from there. Colonel Hueron here will join you as team leader and organizer. He's been to Yugoslavia before, but to Partisan territory. He knows the area and will be a great asset to the team."

Colonel William Hueron was in his thirties with black hair and broad shoulders. The tall, powerfully built man and former civil engineer said, "Please to meet you, Lieutenant. I've read your file from OSS. I could use a good man."

Gubbins continued, "You'll also have a wireless radio operator who at the moment is still in training. You'll be the first combined team of British and American officers dropped into Chetnik territory to make contact with Draza Mihailovich, codename Credible Dagger. We already have a team in Partisan territory who has been in contact with Tito, codename, Credible Sword. Your team will be called Team Hueron named after, of course, Colonel Hueron. Your mission will be to determine the true credibility of Draza Mihailovich and his Chetnik forces. We need to find out which resistance group is best suited to receive Allied support to fight the Germans. Basically, we want to find out who's killing or capable of killing the most Germans. Colonel Stevens, will you take over and brief the operation?"

Stevens rose and approached the map of Yugoslavia, "The situation is extremely complex. The Chetniks and Partisans have control of the hills and mountains in Yugoslavia. The Germans frankly don't have the manpower or the resources to counter them. They've concentrated their resources into the major cities and towns. We're confident we can drop your team into Chetnik territory without many difficulties. Once your team is in place, you'll be our eyes and ears on the ground. You'll limit your activities to observation. This is an intelligence-gathering mission, not a sabotage mission. We don't want you doing any hostilities outside of self-defense. Also, the Americans want an unbiased view. That's why they're sending you in with our people."

Josef asked, "Can you show me where Mihailovich has his headquarters now?"

"At the moment, we don't have the precise location. You'll get that in Cairo before you leave. But, our latest estimate is that he's somewhere near Loznica in the surrounding hills," he said as he pointed to the area on the map.

Josef stood up and approached the map, "Do you mind if I take a look?"

"Sure, go right ahead."

Josef looked closer at the location, "I do believe this is the same area I was at when I first met Mihailovich over two years ago. He moves frequently and covers vast distances on horseback. He might not be in this same spot when we're dropped."

Stevens responded, "That reminds me. When the time comes to insert the team, we can't afford to drop everyone in all at once. We'd be doing a blind drop. Therefore, we've decided to send you in alone first; make contact with Mihailovich's forces, secure a landing zone for the rest of the team and equipment, and the rest of the team will follow."

"In other words, I'm expendable?"

Gubbins interrupted, "No, just cautious. There's too

much at stake on this mission. We don't want to drop the whole team right into the hands of the Gestapo."

"One last thing before you go," said Stevens. "The Germans are very good at monitoring and tracking our radio transmissions. Once your team is in place and starts transmitting, the Germans will be pointing all their direction-finding (DF) equipment on you. The good news is that you'll be operating in remote areas and the Germans will have a difficult time getting to your locations once they triangulate. Just to be on the safe side, though, you'll adhere to strict radio discipline and only transmit for brief moments. That's another reason why we have the radio operator in an advanced training course right now so he'll be absolutely proficient when the operation begins."

Gubbins rose, "You'll get your final briefing in Cairo before you leave, for now, that about wraps it up for this meeting. We have a flat down the street where you'll spend the night before going to Cairo. My assistant out front will have more when you leave. Good luck to you, Kostinic. I'm looking forward to hearing your reports from the field."

Dick was still waiting outside Gubbins' office when Josef exited. He had just returned from the canteen. "That didn't take long. They serve wonderful sandwiches, coffee, and tea downstairs, not to mention an assortment of FANYs."

Gubbins' assistant interrupted Dick's words, "You two gentlemen will be staying the night at our Norwegian flat down the street. Check in with the butler at the front door. Here's your billeting slips," she said as she handed one to each of them. "Our driver will give you a lift. Enjoy your limited stay here in London."

As Dick and Josef rode the short distance down Baker Street to the Norwegian section, Dick spoke, "While I was at the canteen, I met a nice young FANY who gave me some very good information on the possible whereabouts of our friend, Penelope. It appears she's quite well known within all departments at SOE. Evidently, she's special assistant to the vice commander of the French section, another female by the name of Vivian Tate." Dick moved forward from the rear seat and asked the driver, "How far is the French section from where we'll be staying tonight?"

The driver, under strict orders to use discretion in communicating with anyone coming out of SOE headquarters, gave a muffled grunt, "Not far," then continued driving.

Dick moved back into his seat, "He's a big help."

"You're next door, so-to-speak," replied the driver. "F" section, as they're officially known around here, has their headquarters at Orchard Court. But if you're looking for someone in particular, maybe I can help you."

Dick responded, "Well, go ahead, we've only got till tomorrow morning."

"The young lady you're referring to is working right now as we speak. In fact, I just gave the young lady and Miss Tate a ride back to headquarters. You can't meet her today; she has a very busy schedule. A lot going on today at F section so don't go near Orchard Court."

Dick wasn't satisfied and decided to pursue further, "What about *after* hours. She does go home at night?"

The driver replied, "I'm not at liberty to give you that information, but I can tell you that a lot of staff members stop off at the Studio Club on their way home. It's located in Knightsbridge. Any cab driver will know of it and can give you a lift. I'm afraid that's the best I can do."

Josef answered back, "Thank you, driver, that helps us tremendously," and handed him one quid. He looked at his watch, "It's one-thirty right now. I need to get some rest for a few hours. Why don't we try tonight, say around six-thirty? That will give Penelope enough time to get there, assuming she does stop off, on her way home."

"Don't worry, she'll be there," replied the driver.

The Studio Club was located in a quiet, residential section of Knightsbridge a few blocks off Brompton Road on Herbert Crescent. There were no signs or markings on the outside and one would never know of the place simply walking by. Just as the SOE driver mentioned, the cab driver knew exactly where the place was and dropped Josef and Dick off at the front door. The curtains were drawn on the front windows, probably in preparation for blackout hours. They could hear music and laughter coming from inside the building, but on first observation, it appeared the place was unmarked and uninhabited on the first floor. There was only a single number eight marked on the black door. They rang the doorbell and waited. After several rings, the door finally opened and two British officers exited. One of them, seeing Dick and Josef in their US Army uniforms with their intelligence insignia on their lapels, spoke, "Can I help you boys?"

Dick answered, "Were looking for the Studio Club?"

"You've come to the right spot, but I'm afraid you can't go in unless you're escorted."

Josef asked, "What do you mean, escorted?"

"You've got to *know* someone. This is a private club."

Dick started to lose patience with the British mentality, "Now look here, we're both American officers on special assignment with your country's war department. We don't have all the time in the world. We're leaving tomorrow morning for Cairo. We were told this is the place where the FANYs hang out. We're looking for a friend of ours. We went to school together in Yugoslavia. Perhaps you know of her, Penelope Walsh?"

The two British officers looked at each other, obviously

recognizing the name, "We know her. In fact, she's here. We were just talking to her before we left."

"Then could you do us a favor and tell her that Dick and Josef are out front waiting to come in?" asked Josef.

"We're in a hurry, you know," said one of the men. "We have another engagement this evening and we're already late."

Dick said, "Look, buddy, I'll buy you a drink if you just let Penelope know we're here. It shouldn't take you more than three minutes to go back in and tell her, assuming she is in fact here, like you said."

British pride obviously got in the way when the two men reversed course and reentered the Studio Club, closing the door behind, leaving Dick and Josef out on the doorstep.

"Maybe we could scale the fence out back," said Josef.

Then they heard a female voice scream out loudly, "No bloody way!" and heavy footsteps pounded down the stairs from inside the club and then the big black door was flung open. "Oh my God! It *is* you. I thought those two blokes were joking, but no one knows your first names other than me, so I knew it must be true. Come in. Let's have a drink on me," replied Penelope Walsh.

The three friends danced and drank until closing. They talked about many things: Yugoslavia, the war, family, and friends. As they were about to be kicked out of the club, Josef asked, "Have you heard from Tess?"

"Haven't seen or talked to her in several months. Last time we talked, she told me about your letters and getting drafted into the army. She's still very much in love with you, but I'm afraid the war has kept her away from me as well. She's been in high demand these days with the RAF. Seems they can't launch their bombers without her. She's in the south somewhere doing special training for her next assignment."

"We don't have the time to go looking all over the United Kingdom for her, either," replied Dick. "We're leaving tomorrow morning. Or should I say, later this morning for Cairo."

"I won't ask what you'll be doing there. Just be safe and return home. Don't worry, when I do see Tess I'll tell her you came looking for her all the way from the States."

The three friends kissed each other good-bye for the evening; Dick, Josef, and Penelope said their farewells once again.

Chapter 10

OSS HEADQUARTERS, CAIRO

Forty-six hours later, Lt. Col. Howard O'Donnell was seated behind his desk in Cairo. O'Donnell was the chief of the Balkan section field office. He was a Balkan specialist from the University of Michigan. Before the war, he was a professor of history and geography for the region. He spoke fluent Serbo-Croatian and was considered by both Roosevelt and Churchill as the most qualified intelligence officer, British or American, on matters pertaining to Yugoslavia. He had just finished reading the latest report on Chetnik activity against German forces when Josef Kostinic entered his office.

"Sorry for being late, sir, but it was a long flight from England. The plane made stops in Algeria and Alexandria before arriving in Cairo late last night."

"No apology needed, young man, just got here myself. Anyway, I'm glad you made it in one piece." O'Donnell lit another cigarette, "I was reading over the latest reports from the field. Let me ask you something?" O'Donnell held up a copy of a cable in his hand, "Do you think we can trust him?"

"I'm assuming you're referring to Mihailovich?" O'Donnell dropped the cable onto his desk and slowly nodded his head in agreement.

"I can only tell you that when I met him back in forty-one, we had a lengthy conversation. He appeared to be evaluating me as much as I was evaluating him. Based on what I saw and experienced from his network, he is a force to be reckoned with. His network stretched to Bosnia and Croatia as well as all of Serbia and portions of Montenegro. His Chetnik forces personally escorted me from Mostar all the way to his headquarters in Ravna Gora. I'd estimate his strength to be several thousand fighters. He did give me valuable information that got me in and out of the country. He didn't have to provide that information to me. So, yes, I'd say I can trust the man with my life."

"The reports I'm getting from the field are that he's been known to actively collaborate with both the Germans and Italians. Also, his intelligence network, as you just mentioned, is quite good and extensive. He has informants everywhere; maybe he's a little *too* cozy with the Axis Alliance."

"He may be doing it as a way of getting supplies. If I'm not mistaken, he's still short of weapons, food, and medicine, thanks to our British *friends*."

O'Donnell moved on to another subject, "Hueron is a good man. SOE finally picked someone who knows what they're doing, unlike some of the other knuckleheads running their country sections. He's been to Yugoslavia before, but never made contact with Chetnik forces. OSS has an advantage over SOE in that you've met Mihailovich and spent time with him. I want you to keep an eye on the British as much as Mihailovich. Your SOE controller for Team Hueron, here in Cairo, will be a Major Tobe

McAdams. He's the deputy chief of SOE Yugoslav section. All information transmitted from your team will go directly to him first and then passed on to SOE London, finally to me. I don't like the son-of-a-bitch, personally. He's an open communist. I met him once before at Cambridge University, when I was a fellow there. He was the student body president for the Communist Youth League. Now he's practically running SOE Cairo because Stevens spends all his time shuttling back and forth to London." O'Donnell picked up a pack of cigarettes and offered one to Josef. Kostinic shook his head, indicating he didn't smoke. O'Donnell flipped one out and placed it between his lips without lighting it, then continued with the cigarette dangling as he talked. "If you think they're at all sending wrong or conflicting information, I want to know about it immediately. That's why I want you to have your own radio."

"Will the British go along with it?"

"They're not going to know about it." O'Donnell picked up his phone and made a call. "We're ready now. Send him in," then he placed the receiver down on the cradle. A few minutes later, the office door flung open and a young private came in carrying a small suitcase and placed it on O'Donnell's desk.

"Thank you private, you can leave it here," then the young man left the room. O'Donnell opened the suitcase and presented the SSTR-1 wireless transmitter, used by OSS personnel, "The British plan calls for a blind drop without a transmitter. They want you to establish contact with SOE Cairo via unsecured telegram from Mihailovich's headquarters to the Cairo embassy, announce your arrival, and secure the drop zone for the rest of your team. It's a well-known fact the Gestapo has already penetrated several SOE cells and they're using captured radio sets. They've become very good at playing back the sets, contributing to more captures of Allied agents. I don't want you walking into a trap with the Gestapo waiting on the other end. In addition, I don't want that son-of-a-bitch McAdams to pass any crucial information to the communists. So, that's why you're going in with this."

Josef scrutinized the strange-looking contraption inside the small suitcase, "I don't know much about wireless radios nor am I skilled at sending and receiving messages. Back at the Farm, I was only given bits and pieces. Most of that was on codes and ciphers."

"We've taken that into consideration. You'll be given an accelerated course on how to use the set along with the basic codes and ciphers. All wireless transmissions are first coded, then transmitted in the hopes they won't be intercepted by the Krauts. Therefore, you'll only be given enough information to transmit your arrival messages. After that, you won't need the set because by then the entire team will be in place, including the radio operator, and I might add, *his* radio. You'll continue your mission from that point on, using standard operating procedures and British radios. This is my back-up plan, sort of an insurance policy. I want you to use this device exclusively on three occasions. Put on your thinking cap, because I'm only going to say this once, so you better get it right. First, to communicate your arrival *after* you've cabled Cairo; second, when you believe your messages are getting improperly transmitted to the British or if you're in trouble. Then I'll know something's up by the use of this radio."

"That does make sense, now that you've explained it."

"That's two, there's one more time—listen carefully. Once you've cabled SOE Cairo via telegram, I want you to transmit the exact same message to me, using the SSTR-1 radio set. Eighth Army will supply the air assets for the rest of the British team. I'll get a copy of the tasking orders from SOE. If the drop coordinates don't match what you've transmitted, I'll know McAdams is up to something. I'm not leaving you there at the hands of the Gestapo or Partisan bandits. There's one last piece of information that ties everything together. You need to listen to the BBC broadcast on the night of the drop. If the mission is cancelled or scrubbed, the code phrase is, *Alice in Wonderland*. It could be in French, English, or Serbo-Croatian. Frankly, I don't know what language they'll use, so you'll have to listen very carefully. Now you know why I wanted you to put on that thinking cap of yours."

O'Donnell rose from the desk, "You'll leave for Yugoslavia on the next full moon. They'll drop you in via parachute near Mihailovich's headquarters. You'll make your way on foot to his camp. If my hunch is correct, Mihailovich's fighters should pick you up well before you get to his headquarters. Unfortunately, if I'm wrong and you find yourself in Partisan hands, try to contact the British MI-6 missions embedded with the Partisans. We'll get you out from there. If, on the other hand, you're met by the Gestapo, you're well-trained; you'll know what to do."

"I understand, sir. If they drop me in the correct location, I should make contact with Chetnick forces within minutes after landing."

"Best of luck, my young friend. I'll be monitoring your progress throughout the mission. SOE will take over from here."

* * *

HANS FLOSBERG WAS SEATED behind his desk at

Gestapo Headquarters in the Hotel Palace, Belgrade. Behind him was his technical assistant and interpreter, Ernst Gerhert. Both men were once again dressed in civilian clothes. Flosberg preferred wearing tailor-made suits from Paris. Gerhert preferred casual clothing without coat or tie. The twice daily interrogation sessions were routine. Each day, at nine in the morning, before breakfast, the prisoners were brought to Flosberg and again at nine in the evening, before supper. How the prisoners responded determined the status of their meal selections. If they provided the information requested, then they were rewarded with better than normal rations. On the other hand, if they chose to say nothing or give useless information, they were provided the usual meager sustenance.

Thus far, the two British agents captured from the submarine had provided very little information. Their resistance was admirable. Flosberg considered himself a professional. He did not believe in the ruthless tactics used by his Gestapo or SS counterparts sharing the same building. Flosberg's responsibility was counterintelligence and turning captured agents, not murdering them. None of his prisoners received torture unlike so many others held in captivity by the Gestapo.

Seated in front of the two Germans was Lieutenant Andre Simac. Thus far, he had not revealed much information. In particular, Flosberg and Gerhert were looking for his true check and bluff radio checks. Gerhert had already used Simac's radio and transmitted several, urgent distress messages, informing SOE Cairo that his team had landed, but had sustained injuries during the insertion. Gerhert informed SOE that their team's courier, Peter Pavloc, had drowned during the maritime landing and that their radio sustained severe water damage, and they desperately needed another radio and crystals. The message was transmitted duplicating the urgency of the situation, but with the omission of both security checks. Flosberg and Gerhert knew that British code masters would consider this an "undecipherable" message and at best, would assume the team was under stress and therefore, unable to transmit the proper security checks. Gerhert, using Simac's captured radio, again transmitted a second message stating that he and Potok were both being chased by the Gestapo and were unable to establish a scheduled transmission (SCHED) and again requested a new crystal. Two days later, a message came back from Cairo on Simac's radio informing him that a new radio and crystals would be dropped on the next moon and indicated the precise drop-zone coordinates. They also informed Simac that he had omitted his security checks and in the future, requested he attach both his *true check* and *bluff check*.[1] The radio and crystal were dropped, as promised, by the British. Now, Flosberg and Gerhert were in possession of a new radio and crystal unique to Andre Simac. All they had to do now was to establish a schedule and transmit from the captured radio. Flosberg lit a cigarette, blew the smoke in a cloud over his head, and spoke in his perfect, fluent English, "How are you today, Andre?"

Simac said nothing and continued to stare at the two Germans. Flosberg continued, "Andre, it's pointless to resist. In fact, you could be putting more of your fellow compatriots at risk. We've already used your radio and coordinated the drop of another special operations team to follow up on your mission. We have their schedule on the next moon and their location. They'll be dropped right into our hands. We have some of our best SS divisions committed to the capture of your fellow countrymen. All they have to do is wait for my orders. The SS troops and their Gestapo henchmen are not professionals like Ernst here and me. They're cutthroats. They'll just as easily kill them for sheer sport. Andre, just tell me your security checks, and I'll make sure that my colleague here takes charge of the arrests, and no harm will come to any of your countrymen."

Simac continued to stare away from his two captors then Flosberg put out the cigarette in the ashtray, "Andre, we already know everything. We know how and where you were trained, how you were inserted. We know where you grew up in Canada and where you went to school. We even have someone *inside* Baker Street and in Cairo. Why do you think the submarine dropped you in the wrong place?"

Simac could not believe the words he was hearing, especially the part about having someone inside the Cairo station. Thus far, his Nazi interrogators had not told him about this. He was starting to believe it could be true, given the fact the submarine did indeed drop them in the wrong place and could explain why they were so far off-course. He still said nothing.

Flosberg, as professional as ever, said to Gerhert in English so Simac would understand, "Ernst, I think it's time for breakfast. I haven't eaten yet, have you?"

Gerhert responded, "No, now that you mention it; I haven't either. Would you like me to call down for something?"

"I think that's a splendid idea. After all, we've got all morning, especially since our friend, Andre here, is not telling us anything."

Gerhert picked up the telephone on the desk and made a call to the kitchen downstairs. Speaking in German he said, "I'd like breakfast for two please, coffee, tea, all the trimmings and the usual, please. Thank you.

Have it sent up immediately." Then he hung up the phone.

Flosberg picked up another cigarette from the case on his desk and tapped it several times, "*English* cigarettes— from the last shipment that was dropped into our hands, thanks to our man in Cairo." Simac continued to stare off into space. "Look Andre, how about this? Forget about the security checks, why don't you just *transmit* on the radio? Tell them anything you want."

Finally, Simac spoke, "Why should I transmit for you? You'll just use it against us."

"We must be getting somewhere. That's the first time you've spoken in weeks." There was a knock on the door, then Flosberg said, "Ah, just in time. I think we could all use a break."

"Can I go now?"

"Absolutely not," said Flosberg. "You can wait right here until we finish our meal."

Gerhert opened the door for the porter, an older Serb woman, "Set it there on the desk," he said to her in Serbo-Croatian as she placed the tray in front of Flosberg. The aroma of fresh coffee was already filling the air as well as the smell of scrambled eggs and bacon. Flosberg opened the coffee carafe and poured himself a cup. Next, he reached for a small jar containing real sugar. "Would you like one or two lumps, Ernst?"

"I prefer my coffee extra sweet in the morning, Hans, how about three."

"Three it is," he said as he dropped three huge, brown lumps into a cup and poured. Then he dropped two lumps into his cup. "Would you care for cream?"

"Please, but only a little, just to make it amber."

The aroma of real coffee in the air affected Simac as he fidgeted on his chair. He hadn't had a cup of real coffee since he had left England and the heavily sweetened, black goo they served in Cairo as an excuse for coffee didn't count.

Flosberg lifted the silver covers off the plates of scrambled eggs, bacon, and sausage, each man helping himself to generous proportions. Simac continued to stare with his mouth gaping open. Flosberg and Gerhert sat down, eating in silence, only occasionally asking one another for another helping from the tray that held enough food for at least six men. Finally, after two helpings of eggs and bacon and two cups of coffee each, Flosberg spoke, "You know Andre, it's standard procedure around here that anything left has to be given to the dogs. God forbid if anything left-over goes to feed hungry Yugoslav citizens."

Simac cried tears of pain, "They won't be listening."

"What did you say?" asked Gerhert.

"I said, they won't be listening. The wireless radio specialists don't even show up for duty until fifteen-hundred hours, local Cairo time. Nobody is even monitoring the radios this time of day."

"Ernst, I do believe we're getting somewhere. Do you think we can spare just a little? After all, the dogs can't possibly be hungry after all the prime rib they had last night. No, you'd better take the tray down now."

"Wait! Please don't do that! I can transmit for you. All I ask is a small portion."

Flosberg picked up a plate and proceeded to dish out a huge, generous portion.

* * *

IT WAS a desolate airfield on the outskirts of Cairo. The small briefing room located next to the flight line was quiet and empty. The flight crews had finished their supper and were getting a few hours of sleep, before the all-night flight to Yugoslavia. Josef Kostinic and his escorting officer, Dick Vojvoda, were in the staging area going over last-minute details. "You'll be going in as an inserted military officer attached to the British mission, so there's no need for a cover story or dress. Your code name is Alum. You're embedded, so you'll be dropped in with whatever military uniform you so desire."

"I've already selected a comfortable khaki outfit with standard US Infantry insignia[2] on the collars."

"That should work just fine. Next, I'll give you your weapons. Argentine Lama and this," he then handed Josef a small 9 mm submachine gun. "This is the weapon of choice for OSS personnel dropped into the field. It's a Merlin submachine gun with two, twelve-round box magazines attached side-by-side, upside down for a total of twenty-four 9 mm rounds. The Lama is a Colt 45 clone except it uses standard 9 mm rounds instead of 45s. Therefore, the ammo is interchangeable with both weapons. The Merlin gives you enough fire-power without fumbling around for another magazine and is almost five pounds lighter than the Thompson." Dick took out a cigarette from his pocket and lit it using a gold Zippo lighter, then gave the lighter to Josef. "Solid twenty-four-karat gold, a personal gift from General Donovan himself. You may need it, even though you don't smoke."

Neither spoke for a few minutes as Dick finished his cigarette, and continued, "The wireless radio and your supplies will be dropped separately before you go out of the aircraft. I don't need to tell you how important that piece of equipment is. Don't let anything happen to it. If it should be damaged during the landing, send word via telegram immediately so we can send another one along with the proper crystals. Use the code words *request winter clothing* in your cable."

Josef pulled out a small map made from silk and showed it to Dick, "I've selected the landing zone myself. It's a small field; just enough cover to hide until I can retrieve the supplies and radio set. Hopefully by that time, Chetnik fighters will be on the scene to assist me."

"Josef, the drop is the most dangerous part of the mission. It's essentially a blind drop. You could be met by Partisans, Ustaša, SS, or Gestapo, but given your background, it's a risk we're willing to take. Just to be on the safe side, I want you to have this." He handed him a packet with a small, white tablet. "This is your L pill. If you think it's hopeless or suspect the Germans will torture you beyond human endurance, take it."

Josef held up his hand. "No thanks, Dick, I won't be needing that. If I'm captured and I'm sure that's not the case, I can withstand anything they try to do to me, at least for the first forty-eight hours. After that, I'll just have to tell them anything."

"Suit yourself. If it were me, I'd take it just for good luck." Dick changed the subject, mainly to put himself at ease because Josef seemed quite calm. "O'Donnell knows Yugoslavia and their politics better than anyone at OSS or the State Department, for that matter. He'll be monitoring your transmissions and reports. If the situation dictates, we could have you extracted out of there and leave the British to fend for themselves."

"Again, I don't think that's going to happen. Mihailovich is a good man. I know we can trust him. It's my job to make sure Churchill understands this." He extended his hand out to Dick. "I'll see you when the war's over."

* * *

AT THE SAME TIME, in his small office at the Hotel Palace, Ernst Gerhert, lead technical advisor to SS Obersturmbannführer Hans Flosberg, removed his headphones from the Mark II wireless radio set from around his head. He had successfully duplicated Andre Simac's fist[3] and was both receiving and transmitting messages to British Intelligence. The SD had successfully played- back his radio and penetrated one of the British missions in Yugoslavia. He had just received a message from SOE Cairo and was decoding the message when Flosberg entered the room.

"Another message asking who your sister is married to?"

"No, this is quite different. The message is specifically addressed to Simac using his codename, Beacon. I'm just finishing up the decoding. Here it is now," he said as he penciled the last words and handed the written copy to Flosberg.

FOR BEACON

MAKE CONTACT WITH ALUM-STOP

DROP COORDINATES AS FOLLOWS-STOP

5KM N/NW OF KRUPANJ-STOP

DROP TIME 0400 TOMORROW-END

"It would appear the British have confidence their man is still in place. Do you believe it's legitimate?"

"It's the first message we've received with actual code names, words, and drop coordinates. I'm afraid we don't have a choice. We'll have to follow up on it."

"I'll alert the SS division at Sabac for tomorrow morning at oh four-hundred hours for a possible airdrop. They are our closest assets. If they drop in an agent or another team, they'll be waiting for them."

1. The Germans discovered there was a security check system in place. Agents then carried a double security check system. If home station deciphering staff saw 'Bluff check present, true check omitted' it mean the agent had been captured or was under duress.
2. OSS agents operating in the field wore as little military uniforms as possible. Usually collar rank and some sort of insignia were consistent, along with jump wings, British or American. Agents dropped into Yugoslavia usually wore their respective rank on their right collar and US Army Infantry muskets on the left, signifying a member of the US Armed Forces.
3. All wireless radio operators had a unique signature when they tapped out Morse coded messages. This was called a fist. The signature was unique to a specific individual much like a fingerprint. However, in time, a skilled radio technician could easily mimic that signature.

Chapter 11

DROPPING INTO SERBIA

The US Army Air Corps blackened B-24 Liberator designed for night, clandestine operations lumbered along slowly at twenty-four thousand feet. Josef Kostinic was suited up in his specially designed camouflage jumpsuit. He was the only passenger on board this aircraft. Underneath his jumpsuit, he was dressed in standard-issue army khakis with a brown leather flight jacket, a gift from his good friend and air movements officer, Dick Vojvoda. The leather flight jacket contained another added feature of an OSS field agent, the blood chit. This consisted of an American flag sewn inside the silk lining with letters written in both Serbian Cyrillic and Latin Serbo-Croatian, identifying the owner as a US military officer. This chit contained a message offering anyone a monetary reward for the safe return of the individual. Clutched in his gloved hands was his Merlin submachine gun. The flight from Cairo had been uneventful, up until now. The jumpmaster shouted into Josef's ear that a flight of enemy fighters was closing in on the aircraft and that the crew would have to prepare for engagement.

This version of the B-24 only had the top gun turret installed. The lower ball turret was removed to allow parachutists to drop from the opening, known as a "Joe Hole." If his calculations were correct, they were only forty-five minutes from the drop zone. If the pilots took evasive action and threw the aircraft off-course, the navigator might not be able to get back on course, and the mission would have to be scrubbed. Josef took up his position behind a steel plate attached to the floor for just such an occasion. The B-24 continued on track and altitude for several terrifying minutes when the flight engineer came down from the cockpit and gave everyone the thumbs-up signal. He motioned Josef to come forward, "The aircraft commander and the navigator want to speak to you right away, sir" said the young, baby-faced staff sergeant. Josef unbuckled his seat belt and came forward as instructed.

Inside the darkened cockpit at his duty station, the navigator was busy making calculations on his chart. Josef came closer to the dimly lit table as the navigator spoke, "Two Me-109s came at us nose-to-nose but for some reason, then kept going. We're not sure if they saw us, or they were after someone else. In any case, Lieutenant, we're still on course to the drop zone."

Josef reached into his jumpsuit and pulled out his small, silk map marked with the drop zone coordinates. This was completely different from the ones he had supplied to SOE (5km W/NW of Krupanj). He wanted to make sure he landed safely and in order to do that, he needed a landing zone that was known only to himself and OSS. That's why he and O'Donnell chose a different landing zone (3km N of Osecina). It was nearly twenty-five miles due east from the SOE coordinates, but would be closer to Mihailovich's headquarters. He leaned toward the navigator and shouted, "I want to make sure you drop me here," and pointed to the location on the map. "It's got to be this location or nothing! If there's any uncertainty on your part, I'll have to abort the mission and return to base. I'm going in blind and I don't want to be dropped into an area surrounded by Germans."

"I'll make certain of it, Lieutenant," and he gave Josef a pat on the shoulder. "The jumpmaster will let you know when we're approaching the new DZ." Josef nodded his head and went back to the troop compartment, leaving his map with the navigator. He did not need it or a compass for that matter. Everything was inside his head. All he had to do when he landed was take off his jumpsuit, find his radio, and head east for Chetnik territory.

The tallest terrain over the drop zone was fifty-three hundred feet above sea level. The B-24 dropped down to an altitude of six-thousand feet, roughly eight-hundred feet above the ground. Josef Kostinic dropped through the opening in the bottom of the Liberator, after his supply canister and radio. The parachute opened up automatically and the white canopy blossomed with air and slowed his descent. The early, September full moon lit up the terrain like daylight below and he had no trouble finding a place to land and monitored the canister as it drifted to earth . It was ironic how tranquil the descent was after the all-night flight in the vibrating bomber. He saw a small clearing and maneuvered his parachute in that direction. The landing was hard, but he tumbled over on his right shoulder, absorbing the impact in a classic, parachute-landing fall; he unfastened the harness and disconnected the parachute. Next, he slung his Merlin submachine gun over his shoulder, gathered the parachute, and headed for a clump of poplars surrounding the drop zone. He caught his breath and listened for any approaching adversaries. He heard nothing, so he climbed out of his protective jumpsuit and used a small shovel to bury the suit and para-chute in a crude hole. Then he went looking for the supply canister.

The canister had come down less than fifty yards away and was hung up in an oak tree. The wind was blowing slightly and the parachute was fluttering in the wind, ready to take the canister on another ride. He had to move quickly or he'd never see his radio and supplies again. He raced to the base of the tree and saw it hanging ten feet above the ground. "*Psovati*," he said outloud in Serbo-Croatian. He would have to climb the tree in order to free the device. He took off his small backpack, dropped his Merlin, and proceeded to scale the tree when he heard a voice speak out in Serbo-Croatian, "Don't move, or we'll blow your head off! Come down with your hands up!"

Josef crawled down slowly and dropped to the ground, raising his hands. He couldn't see anyone, so he replied back in Serbo-Croatian, "I'm an American military officer. I've come to see the General."

A lone man emerged from the shadows and came forward, looking Josef over. He was young, perhaps eighteen, or nineteen, holding a German MP-5 submachine gun, "Are you a flyer?" he asked.

"No, I'm here on a special mission to contact General Mihailovich. He's expecting me. I'm going to lower my hands and give you something. Is it all right?"

The young man could now see Josef clearly dressed in his US Army uniform, but was still not convinced he was a friendly, "Turn around, while I tie your hands together."

Josef did as instructed; the young man tied a piece of rope around his hands then said, "Come with me."

"Don't you want the supplies I brought with me?" Josef asked as the young man realized the supply canister was still suspended from the tree above and in danger of being whisked off.

"Sit on the ground and don't move. I'll get it down."

The young man scaled the tree with the skill of a monkey and cut the canister down, then whistled into the darkness. Two more men came from the cover of the trees holding bolt-action rifles. One of the men, sporting a long beard and Chetnik cap, stopped in his tracks as he noticed Josef sitting on the ground. The man scratched his head in disbelief.

"Josef, is that you?" he asked.

Upon hearing the man's voice, Josef immediately recognized him. He was one of his escorts who had brought him out of Bosnia-Herzegovina some two years earlier.

"Rudko! Yes, it's me, Josef Kostinic. I promised I'd come back. Call off your goons and help me get these supplies to the General's headquarters."

Rudko gave a double whistle from his mouth and a team of Chetnik fighters emerged from the shadows. There must have been over a hundred fighters cleverly hidden in the grass and trees. Josef could hardly believe what he was seeing. He had not been more than twenty feet from the men the entire time, but they never gave away their positions. This was a classic move by a well-trained and disciplined, guerilla fighting force.

Josef asked Rudko, "How many are there?"

"It's hard to say. At last count, we had over a hundred fighters on patrol tonight. Come my friend, you can ride on one of the horses."

The trek back to Mihailovich's headquarters was slow in the moonlight. The patrol had to stop several times along the way because of German patrols. Even though the Chetnik fighters outnumbered the enemy in the area, they still did not want to take the chance of engaging for fear of reprisals against the local villages. At dawn, they arrived at Mihailovich's camp. Several men confronted the patrol with rifles drawn, then upon seeing the weary and familiar faces, put down their weapons.

Rudko said, "Stay with me until I get you inside the General's hut."

Josef nodded in acknowledgment. The men in Mihailovich's hut were just waking up for the day. One of the fighters noticed Josef in his clean US Army uniform and immediately called to Mihailovich.

"We have company, sir. I think your Allied officers have arrived."

At about the same time as Josef was entering Mihailovich's camp, a detachment of SS troopers was waiting near the original drop zone (5KM N/NW of Krupanj) supplied by SOE. This location was provided to them by the local counterintelligence service headed by Obersturmbannführer Hans Flosberg. They had been waiting since four in the morning. That was the time given to them when an Allied aircraft was scheduled to make a drop. No one in the detachment saw parachutes or aircraft in the skies above Krupanj. They did, however, hear a large aircraft several miles away, but could not tell if it dropped anything. It was out of sight. The detachment boarded their half-tracks and headed back to base. They would have to tell the Gestapo they came up empty-handed.

Draza Mihailovich was washing his face when Josef entered his small hut. Josef could see that Mihailovich recognized him once he put on his signature round glasses and motioned at him to come forward.

"This is a pleasant surprise. I wasn't expecting to see a

familiar face. I see you made it safely out of Belgrade. Did you experience any problems on the escape route?"

"No, sir. Everything worked just as you said it would. It did take me well over a week to finally get to the Turkish border. I made you a promise, if I ever got out of here alive, I'd help your cause and so, I've come back to pay my gratitude."

Mihailovich wiped his face dry, "I received a cable from Cairo that an American officer was making a blind drop to coordinate the arrival of the rest of the team. We feared the worst because all the normal drop zones are covered by the Germans."

"I didn't use the normal landing zones. I changed them at the last minute."

Mihailovich cracked a smile, "That was very clever of you, my young friend. Had you dropped into the normal landing zone, you wouldn't be here right now. My sources told me the Gestapo had all their men tailing the drop zone. Now come, let's have some breakfast."

During breakfast, Josef briefed Mihailovich on the welcoming plan according to O'Donnell. He was to send word back to Cairo by telegram first, then transmit on the radio. Once OSS Cairo received the message, they would send coordinates and times for dropping the rest of the team.

Josef continued, "We're expecting a British officer and his wireless radio operator. We have strict orders not to engage in paramilitary activities, but rather simply report on what we observe. When the British arrive and start sending their reports, British Intelligence could change the mission parameters and do more. We'll just have to take it one day at a time."

Mihailovich replied, "I was hoping for a lot more support from the Allies."

"I've been told you'll get support from the Americans. To show our commitment to your cause, let me share with you what I have brought with me. Could you have my supply canister brought here?"

Mihailovich nodded his head and two men disappeared outside. A few minutes later, they came back carrying the metal supply canister and dropped it before him.

Josef got up, opened the canister, and produced the SSTR-1 wireless radio, "I do believe you need one of these. After I make my first radio transmissions, the set it yours, along with the ciphers." Next, he opened up one of the sealed packages and presented Mihailovich with a stash

of American cigarettes and a small amount of cash, mostly in Reichsmarks, "Compliments of my friends back at OSS Cairo." Then he opened another package with coffee, food, and medicine, "I'm afraid this was all I could take on my first drop. If everything goes as planned, you'll receive more humanitarian and military shipments, but for now, I must ask you to help me transmit my arrival message."

THE ARMY CLERK ran down the corridor to O'Donnell's office. O'Donnell was busy reading his daily reports from the field when the young corporal came in.

"Sorry to disturb you, sir, but this just came in off the teleprint. It's an "eyes only" message for you."

"Thank you, soldier, let me know if you receive any more," then the young man left the room.

The message was a single line written in code. O'Donnell already knew the code; he had assigned it to Kostinic before he left on the mission. It was to let him know that he had arrived safely at Chetnik headquarters. The message, when decoded, simply read *the apples are fresh*. O' Donnell reached into his pocket and took out his Zippo lighter and put the flame on the message, then dropped it into the ashtray. Next, he picked up the phone and called Vojvoda.

"Get your ass down to my office right away."

"Is there a problem, sir?"

"Only if you're with SOE Yugoslav section!"

* * *

AT THE HOTEL PALACE, Belgrade, Hans Flosberg had two more captured British officers in his possession. They were captured trying to flee his pursuing SS troops, who intercepted their wireless transmissions. Unlike his counterparts in occupied France and Belgium, his enemy transmitted in remote locations and not the cities. He did not have access to the sophisticated DF vans that roamed the streets and searched for wireless signals. His section had to rely on specially modified aircraft that patrolled the remote areas during times of transmission. Once the wireless radio operators came on the air, all the aircrews had to do was place their DF antennas on the emission, then call for a fighter strike to strafe the area. It was that simple. Once the enemy agents discovered they were compromised, the only thing they could do was retreat further up to the mountains. That's when the SD called in their special hit squads to pursue the agents. The results were the agents could not flee without discarding their equipment along the way to lighten their loads. Eventually, the fleeing agents would give themselves up. This was the case for the two captured British agents. Not only did they capture the agents, but they also were successful in retrieving their radio sets and ciphers as well.

The two British officers were brought to Belgrade by prison railcar, very similar to the ones the SS used to transport victims to concentration camps except these cars were more civilized. The windows could actually be opened to allow in fresh air.

Chapter 12

A MAN CALLED MATTINGLY A WOMAN CALLED TATE

At six in the morning, Penelope entered F section at Orchard Court. She arrived early that morning because she wanted to analyze the first reports coming in from the field. As she entered the office to make coffee, she noticed the lights were on and there was already a strong pot of coffee steaming on the hot plate. Next, she heard light footsteps walking toward her from the hallway and she knew immediately whom they belonged too. Penelope had never feared anyone, man or woman, until she met her supervisor, F section vice-commander, Vivian Tate. In fact, one of the reasons Penelope worked for her was because Tate had a hard time keeping assistants. Many of the young girls simply could not stand to work for her for very long. They felt Miss Tate was too harsh. Penelope was the only exception.

Vivian Tate entered the canteen holding a cigarette and an empty coffee mug. Miss Tate as she was officially addressed within F section, was in her early thirties, with black hair cut short, blue eyes, an extraordinary mind, and steady resolve. Yet she had a will of iron. Recruited by

British Intelligence at the young age of twenty-three, she was the only *non-amateur* in SOE. Vivian Tate had conducted two perilous espionage missions inside the Third Reich for MI-6 before the war. Some said she was captured, interrogated, and tortured by the Germans, but not before she pulled off a daring escape right from under their noses. Supposedly, she slipped out of a washroom after demanding a bath, then climbed out the window totally naked and onto the rooftops, where she fled into the streets of Berlin.

When war broke out in 1939, Vivian's fierce intellect, courage, and knowledge of several foreign languages quickly propelled her into the Special Operations Executive and the leadership echelon. She was always well-dressed with high heels and silk stockings[1]. She also wore her skirt lengths two inches shorter than most, showing off her shapely legs. She was only five-foot, three, but the shorter skirts and heels gave her the appearance of being much taller, thus giving off a commanding presence to her younger, female assistants. Despite all this, in the flesh, she was ruthless. She hardly ever smiled or laughed. She was all business.

"I'm glad you're here, young lady," she finally said. "We've been up all night. I'm afraid there's been some bad news from the field. Grab a notepad and follow me." Penelope knew this was bad. Vivian never stayed all night. Although she was notorious for not being an early riser, however, she made up for it by staying late into the evenings, sometimes well after midnight. This was going beyond that.

"Yes, ma'am, I'll be right along. Do you want me to fill that?" as she reached out for Vivian's empty coffee mug.

"Make it black. This one's for Mac. I'm afraid it's a

rather heated discussion right now. They needed a little space." Then she turned and walked back down the hall.

Colin Gubbins, Commander of SOE, Jacques MacAlister, head of F section along with Vivian Tate were standing looking over a map of France on the wall, in heated conversation as Penelope entered the briefing room. The code master, Henry Parks, was also present, standing off to the side and shaking his head in utter disbelief. Penelope could hear Parks utter to no one in particular, "We must assume the worst and concede the entire circuit is compromised. We have no alternative."

Gubbins nodded his head, "I agree. There's no point in trying to salvage what's left over. We have to start again from scratch."

MacAlister seemed the only opposition. "He could be injured, like they said."

"Don't be ridiculous," shouted Parks. "It's obvious they're playing-back the god damn radios!"

Gubbins finally noticed Penelope had entered holding the coffee mug, "Ah, there you are. It's not good at all. Please take a seat. Miss Tate will bring you up to date on our French operations."

Vivian briefed Penelope on the latest disaster in occupied France, "Several agents were arrested in the Scientist and Donkey circuits; one of which was the radio operator. Now, all communications from the field should be considered compromised." She continued, "It doesn't look good in the Balkans, either. Yugoslav sections report similar arrests in the field, but they have a slight advantage over us because they operate in remote areas. We'll have to build all our circuits back up again from scratch."

Penelope said without thinking, "You can send me in. I'm a trained radio operator, don't forget."

"That's out of the question. You're much too valuable

here," replied Gubbins. "We need you to help decode the undecipherable ones. In fact, you were the first to predict the Germans were playing back the radios."

"I'm in agreement," said Vivian. "We'll have to send in replacements as they come available out of training."

Later that morning, after the disastrous meeting, Vivian confronted Penelope, "There must be no more talk about what happened this morning. It's essential we continue our operations as planned. Tonight, at the Savoy Hotel, there is a reception to honor General de Gaulle and his "Puke" section[2]. Everyone who's anyone will be there. We can't give the slightest indication that something's gone wrong. I want you to accompany me as my escort. Help me keep an eye on things just to make sure no one has any loose lips. I expect there'll be plenty of champagne and who knows what one will say. General Eisenhower and several Allied officers from SHAFE Headquarters will also be present. Wear something elegant, not too formal. You *do* have something, don't you?"

"Yes, ma'am, I know just the thing."

"Good, I'll have the car swing by your place and pick you up at six. We'll go to the Savoy together from there."

The Savoy Hotel was beautifully decorated for London's wartime standards. The grand ballroom where the reception took place was spectacular, with tri-color tablecloths and linens. The band played classical French music and the air was filled with arrogant personalities and tobacco smoke. Vivian Tate wore a long, black evening gown. Penelope had on a simple grey-colored gown, with thin shoulder straps. British, French, and American officers were everywhere. Some were there to honor de Gaulle; others were there simply because there was nowhere else to go. Many of the young, junior American officers were already drunk from the free-flowing, French champagne.

Penelope did her duties that night as Vivian's escort, which consisted of staying by her side and holding her handbag, listening very carefully. When dinner was finished and the accolades said, the dance floor was opened. What few women attended were quickly swooped up on the dance floor by Allied officers. Penelope was one of the first on the floor, obviously the topic for many of the young men in the hotel that evening. She danced with several partners as each one cut in on the other. More songs played, one after another, and she was beginning to get tired. One British officer cut in on a young Canadian, while Penelope said, "I think I've had enough for now. Will you please excuse me, gentlemen?" Another American officer, obviously drunk with slurred speech, tried to cut in as well when she finally said, "I really do think I've had enough. My superior officer is looking at me now."

"Where is that son-of-a-bitch? I'll tell him a thing or two," shouted the American.

"He's a she, and *she* can be very persuasive, not to mention ruthless." Penelope was extremely tired at this point from having a very, long day that was still, officially ongoing, "If you boys will kindly excuse me, I think I need a bit of fresh air!" she said as she ran off the dance floor and out of the ballroom.

She headed for the exit, but not before Vivian Tate saw her and asked, "Is everything all right, dear?"

"Everything's a snafu, ma'am, I only need a bit of fresh air and a smoke. I'll be back in a jiffy."

Penelope moved quickly through the crowed hotel to the main entrance. Outside, there was a stream of military vehicles parked on both sides of the street. Some had their drivers still in the front seat waiting. Others were standing on the sidewalk smoking or talking. She couldn't stand it any longer. She needed to get away from all of them. She had had enough arrogance and stupidity for one night, as she made her way down the street where there were just a few cars parked and unoccupied. This will do, she thought. She took out a cigarette and began to light it when it starting raining. The rain came down in buckets and she had no umbrella. "Damn, can't I have one bloody smoke in peace!" she cried out loud.

Then a voice from the darkness, "I have an umbrella, ma'am. You could use mine."

It's a pleasant voice. Perhaps it was another officer out having a smoke as well, she thought.

Then the voice said again, "If you'd like, ma'am, you could have one in the car. It will definitely be drier inside." A tall lean figure emerged from the shadows dressed in a US Army uniform holding a very large, green, umbrella, "I promise I won't bite."

Penelope took him up on the offer because now it was pouring down and she was getting completely soaked, "I don't mind if I do. Thank you," she said as she came closer to the Ford sedan and confronted the young man. He was rather nice-looking with a thick head of black hair and sporting a thin mustache over his lip.

He held out his hand and bowed slightly, "Private Harold Mattingly, at your service—driver extraordinaire, chauffeur, and all around clerk and handyman for General Eisenhower himself."

Penelope did not know what to make of the handsome, young man. He seemed pleasant, but had a shy look on his face as if he were not used to talking to young women. "Well, are you going to let me in?" she finally said.

Mattingly grabbed hold of her hand, opened the door, and moved her to the front seat while he went around to the driver's side. He held out a dry cigarette and lighter for her as she took a seat. "Penelope Walsh," she finally said, "It's a pleasure to meet you."

"Busy night tonight. Did you attend the reception?" as he handed her a small, green towel to wipe and dry herself.

"I'm afraid so, too many egos and hot tempers for one night, not to mention champagne. I've had just about all I can take. By the way, did you say you were Eisenhower's driver? I didn't see him tonight. Was he there?"

"No, he wasn't. He sent his aide; security is a bit tight in a situation like this."

"Yes, I suppose so."

"By the way, ma'am, it's none of my business, but you're dressed rather nicely tonight. Can I ask what a beautiful young woman like you, is doing at a place like this?" as he motioned to the Savoy Hotel and loosened up his tie.

"Yes, I do seem out of place at the moment, but I can assure you, it's not what you think. I'm here with my supervisor. She's the one who's attracting all the attention in there. I'm her escort for tonight. You know, carrying her handbag and making mental notes from all the dignitaries she meets."

"Ah, so she's another woman. I'll bet not just *any* woman. Most women who attend these kinds of functions are either senior officer's wives or work for specific departments with the British government."

Penelope gave Mattingly a curious stare and said, "You seem rather observant for a clerk and driver."

"Well, that's my job, ma'am. I couldn't be much help as a courier if I wasn't. I see all kinds of people from different lifestyles. Some from other countries, some from different parts of the United Kingdom You, my pretty lady, are quite different. You're definitely English; specifically, a local girl from London, judging by your accent. I can see that you've travelled abroad or spent time overseas. And you probably also speak a number of languages."

Penelope was becoming quite fascinated by this young stranger. Not since Tony had she met someone as extraordinary; maybe even more so. He seemed very mature and much older than he probably was. "All right, I can tell you that I work as a FANY. Have you ever heard of that organization before?"

Mattingly started to laugh uncontrollably and Penelope followed, though she didn't know what in the world he was laughing about. Then Mattingly said, "First Aid Nursing Yeomanry[3]. I knew there was something about you. That stuff about the FANYS might have worked on some of the blokes inside, but I'm afraid you don't seem like the type who goes around driving ambulances and changing bedpans. It's okay, your secret is safe with me. I won't ask another question about your employment."

"That's mighty kind of you, Harold."

"Please, call me Hal."

"Only if you stop calling me, ma'am. It's Penelope. Please call me Penelope." The two broke out again in uncontrollable laughter. She also realized they were both speaking in French and she had no idea at what point in the conversation the switch was made. "You tricked me! Your French is excellent," she said in English and shoved Mattingly on the shoulder.

"I was taught by my French housekeeper. My father died at a young age, so my mother had to raise me as a single parent. Naturally, she needed the help, so she hired Sonia to help around the house."

"Where are you from in the States, Hal?"

"California, a small town called Palo Alto. Have you heard of it?"

"I'm afraid not."

"It's a university town, just south of San Francisco. I'd like to see you again, if it's all right. I'm off this weekend. Perhaps you could show me the sights of London. I'm still rather new in this city. I've only been here a few months."

Penelope finished her cigarette and stamped it out in the ashtray as she gave the question some thought. She thought of her daughter, Sarah, and wondered how this fine, young man would take the news. She opened up her handbag and took out a fountain pen, "All right, do you have something I can write on?"

Mattingly fumbled in his coat pocket and produced a small notepad, "Here you go, will this work?"

Penelope grabbed the notepad out of his hand and scribbled her telephone number, "The best time to reach me is after eight in the evening. I'm usually home by then and things have generally calmed down for the night." She handed back the notepad with her telephone number. "Give me a call and we'll set something up. Now, I'd best be getting back inside. The rain's lightened up a bit for now."

Mattingly quickly got out from the vehicle, opened up the large umbrella, walked around to the passenger side, and opened the door for Penelope, "You can be assured I'll call you this week. Let me walk you back to the hotel."

The two strolled in silence as Mattingly held the umbrella high over Penelope's head. Penelope didn't say it, but she was actually looking forward to meeting her newfound, young, gentleman friend.

"Good night, Hal," she said as they reached the entrance of the Savoy. Then she blew him a kiss.

---

1. Silk stockings were hard to get during the war. Most of the time if you found them, you had to make the purchases with cash instead of ration coupons.

2. SOE operated a separate French Section called RF headed by Charles de Gaulle in exile. This section was geographically located on Duke Street instead of Baker Street. Those who worked at SOE F section at Orchard Court often referred to RF as Puke section.

3. Some female SOE agents used the cover of the FANYs, mainly because of the ability to move about freely and not arouse suspicion in war-time England. Others used the WAAF with the same results.

Chapter 13

THE WELCOMING COMMITTEE

At Chetnik headquarters, Mihailovich, his senior officers, and Kostinic were sitting on the ground going over a map. Several locations were circled as possible drop zones.

"What about this place?" Josef said as he pointed to a circle.

Mihailovich took a puff from one of the cigarettes Josef supplied, "It's not too far from here. There's plenty of foliage, so we can easily cover the zone. I can have my men positioned in several locations. Rudko can take the road leading up to the area. Most importantly, we have not seen any German patrols in that area."

Josef wrote the coordinates down on his notepad, "How much time do you need to secure the drop zone?"

"My men can have it done by tomorrow."

"The rest of the Allied team is ready for the airdrop and waiting for my message." Josef looked at his watch that had the day and date, "Three nights from tonight at three in the morning."

The next morning, after Josef telegraphed his message

to Cairo he showed Mihailovich how to set up and use the SSTR-1wireless radio. He had two Chetnik fighters crank the accumulator to supply power to the system. His radio work was simple. The message was already coded. All he had to do was transmit. He was on the radio for less than three minutes then shut off the system.

It was determined that morning as well that the joint British/American mission was too important to be stationed alongside Mihailovich's forces. Instead, the mission was to take up positions in nearby villages in close proximity to Mihailovich's camp. Since Mihailovich moved frequently, it was also determined that the mission would subsequently move to a different village frequently, further enhancing security of the team. Josef was unrolling his sleeping bag in the hayloft of a farmhouse when he thought about Tess. She was constantly on his mind when he was alone and he wondered when he would ever see her again.

Early the next evening, in preparation for the drop, Josef was listening to the BBC broadcast for any last-minute changes in the plan. He blew a sigh of relief when at the end of the broadcast, there were no messages indicating a change in operations. The BBC broadcast that evening was in Serbo-Croatian and there was no reference to *Alice in Wonderland*. Everything was pre-planned and pre-arranged. Colonel Hueron, along with his radio operator, would drop by parachute. Kostinic and Mihailovich's forces would secure the drop zone and prepare to receive them. Josef packed a bag with his change of clothes for the night operation and saddled up on a horse given to him by Rudko.

At 0200 hours, Josef waited in the cover of darkness near the drop zone. He had on his green uniform instead of his summer khakis and a black, knitted stocking cap over his head. It was almost frightening that evening as everything was going like clockwork. Josef estimated that Mihailovich had nearly five-hundred men stationed on-site in preparation for the air drop. There were over one-hundred and fifty alone stationed with Rudko to protect the road leading up to the drop zone. Another one-hundred near the drop zone itself and fifty more were covering the hills above. Most importantly, no one saw any German patrols that evening. The skies above were perfectly clear. Josef glanced at his watch; in another hour, the specially modified, black, B-24 Liberator would be overhead. If the drop zone was clear, he was to signal the B-24 that the welcoming committee was ready to receive them by flashing his high-intensity flashlight[1] three times. The B-24 would acknowledge with one steady, red light. His thoughts were interrupted by the sounds of gunfire coming from the hills surrounding the drop zone. He turned to one of his Chetnik fighters, "What the hell? I thought this area was supposed to be free of German patrols."

The young man, about Josef's age, replied, "We've been scouting this place for nights. There are no Germans here. It could be Partisans! Stay here. I'll try to find out what's happening." He whistled like a bird and two more fighters joined him as the three vanished into the darkness.

Gunshots still rang out in the night; Josef could not believe what was happening. Everything was going too well. Another fifty-five minutes and the B-24 would be overhead. He had to secure the zone or he would have to call off the airdrop. All he could do now was grab hold of his Merlin sub-machine gun and wait.

It was dark and cold inside the B-24. All the interior

lights had been turned off hours earlier so the two parachutists could adjust their night vision. Colonel Hueron and his radio operator were making their final preparations for the airdrop. Each one was dressed in dark, green jumpsuits with foam jump hats to protect their heads. Their faces could barely be seen. Hueron could tell his young radio operator was nervous by the sight of shaking hands. The lower B-24 ball turret gun was removed to provide an opening for the parachutists. The jumpmaster came up to Hueron and shouted in his ear, "We'll be over the drop zone in twenty minutes—time to take your positions." Then he patted him on the back. Hueron looked at his young radio operator, gave a thumbs-up signal, and removed the cover over the opening, "We'll be dropping soon, get ready!" he shouted.

The gunshots were more intense now as Josef could hear screams in the distance. Another ten minutes and he would have to call off the airdrop. Then a noise in the bushes caught his attention. Two of the Chetnik fighters returned with news on the firefight.

"It's just like I thought. A patrol of Partisan fighters stumbled upon some of our men. They had no choice but to return fire. We outnumber them, ten to one; it should be over in a few minutes."

The unmistakable sound of a single B-24 could be heard in the distance. Josef looked at his watch. He thought to himself, they'll be over the zone in minutes. He had to decide right away. He still heard a few sporadic gunshots, but in the distance. He hoped the crew onboard the B-24 did not see the muzzle flashes and call off the drop themselves. He had to take a chance. It was now or never. He took out his high-intensity flashlight and signaled the B-24.

The navigator onboard the B-24 was already training

his eyes on the drop zone looking for any signs from the welcoming committee. He was surprised to see the flashing, white light coming from the trees. At first, he thought it might be muzzle flashes, but then he saw the signal again. It was unmistakable. It was the correct signal for a safe drop. He flashed his red light three times indicating acknowledgement. A single steady light was returned from the welcoming committee. They were ready for the drop.

Josef secured his high-intensity light and told the Chetnik fighters, "Keep the perimeter of the drop zone secure. I'll wait here until they land. We don't want to give up our positions until they've landed. There could be more Partisans bandits waiting for us to make our move."

Josef saw the B-24 as it descended to drop altitude, then two objects dropped from the bomber, followed by two more. All four canopies opened and fell to the ground. Josef could see two figures release their parachute harnesses and one went over to assist the other. Then the two gathered their parachutes. It appeared the drop was a success. Josef gave a signal with his hand and three Chetnik fighters emerged from the trees to assist the parachutists with their supply canisters. Once the parachutists were secure from their harnesses, Josef sprang to his feet and raced to their location, holding his Merlin submachine gun.

As he approached the two parachutists, one of them said, "I'm Hueron. This is my radio operator, Flight Officer Bowman."

The two British agents removed their jump hats and Josef could now clearly see their faces. He was stunned as he looked into the eyes of the young radio operator to see his long-lost and almost forgotten sweetheart, standing in front of him. They were together again at last.

"Tess, is that you?" he asked.

"Oh my God, I should be asking you the same thing! The last I heard, you were going overseas."

"You two know each other?" asked Hueron.

Tess answered, "Know each other? We were practically married. He's the one I told you about, but I never expected him to be *the* OSS agent."

Shots fired, in the distance, interrupting their excitement. Everyone ducked for cover on the ground as several rounds passed over their heads.

Hueron shouted, "What the devil is going on here? I thought the drop zone was supposed to be secure."

"It *is* secure of German patrols. Earlier, a group of Partisan bandits attacked us just before you dropped. This must be what's left of them. Our Chetnik forces can take care of them. We've got over three hundred men protecting the area."

More bursts of gunfire came from the trees as the party realized they were pinned down in the open by Partisan gunmen. Josef crawled slowly on the ground with his Merlin and tried to return fire, but was unable to get off a shot. The accompanying Chetniks fired their weapons, but quickly ran out of what little ammunition they had. Then Josef heard the sound of automatic weapons from his rear. Hueron and Tess were firing their Sten guns, sending the Partisans for cover. Josef fired his Merlin in the direction of the Partisan activity. Then, more shots fired from the surrounding areas. The Chetniks protecting the drop zone took out the last of the remaining Partisans. The area was now safe and secure.

* * *

"DON'T FORGET, you're a widow, think of your child.

What will she think when she starts seeing young men appear all the time?"

"Oh Mum, I'm not a child anymore. Besides, I can't spend the rest of my life in mourning. And you won't see young men here all the time. It's just one man."

"You don't know a lot about this young Yank. He's probably no different than all the rest of the half-million of them, over here."

"He's not like that, Mum. He's intelligent, witty, speaks excellent French and best of all, very handsome. I told him I'd like to see him again. I do say, he has his hopes up, and I don't want to disappoint the young man."

"Where are you going tonight? You know there's a curfew after eleven."

"Yes Mum, I'm quite aware of the curfew. He should be calling any minute now. I told him the best time to reach me was after eight."

A few seconds later, the telephone rang. It was a minute past eight o'clock. Penelope sprang to her feet and went to the telephone. "Hello, this is Penelope."

"So, you didn't give me a bogus number after all. I prepared myself all day, not wanting to get my hopes up."

"I told you the best time to reach me was after eight. I do say you are very astute. You know it's only two minutes after the hour."

"Like I told you, I've been looking forward to this all week. By the way, how was your week?"

"Very busy as usual, I'm sorry. I can't talk about it much over the phone."

"Understand, thinking the same thing myself. Perhaps dinner tonight? Nothing fancy, just a good meal and maybe a pint or two."

"I know just the place. It's a small pub around the corner. How soon can you be here?"

"That, my dear lady, depends upon where you live. If it's not too far, I can drive a car."

Penelope gave him the address and the directions after which time Mattingly said, "I can be there in less than an hour. Will that work?"

"That will do. I'll be ready when you arrive."

Hal pulled up to Penelope's flat an hour later. He was driving the big, Ford sedan used for transporting Allied officers. He parked the car out front and walked up the steps to her door. Before he could knock or ring the doorbell, Penelope opened the door. Hal was dressed in his army uniform, sporting his new rank of corporal.

"You look dashing this evening. Won't you come in for a minute?"

Hal removed his cap and walked into the small foyer. Penelope's mother was there to greet the young stranger.

Penelope made the introductions, "Harold, I'd like you to meet my mother, Aleks Mitchell."

"Pleasure to me you, ma'am. Please call me Hal. I can assure you that I have the utmost respect for your daughter, and I will be back before the curfew."

"Dad's not here tonight. I'm afraid he's got warden duty, but there is someone else I'd like you to meet." She grabbed hold of his hand and led him upstairs to the bedroom. Penelope's young child was asleep in her room. She opened the door quietly and said, "I'd like you to meet my daughter, Sarah."

"What a beautiful child. How old is she?"

"Two, she'll be three this summer. Her father was killed during a V-1 attack almost three years ago. He never got to see her. He was a naval officer, and yes, I'm a widow."

"I'm sorry to hear that. He was a lucky man, having you two."

"I didn't have to tell you about her, but if you're to get

to know me, I thought it best to know everything up front. That way, you know where we stand."

---

1. This was the method used before it was discovered white flashlights could be mistaken for muzzle flashes, thus prone to friendly-fire accidents. Today, they use green flashlights for the same purpose.

Chapter 14
CODES AND CODE BREAKERS

It was mid-morning on the day of the airdrop. Hueron, Tess, and Josef were standing in a circle around General Mihailovich. There was a small celebration from the local town's people. The three Allied officers were given wreaths of flowers welcoming them. Josef still could not believe Tess was actually with him again, in flesh and blood. She was much more attractive now than when he had left her over two years earlier. The young female student had blossomed into a beautiful woman quite different from the simple college student he knew when they first met. Her appearance was more refined now. She looked very *English* with her FANY cut and dark eyes and eyebrows that were actually trimmed and plucked. She told Josef she learned to make herself up from the other girls while she was in training with the WAAF.

Mihailovich then spoke to the gathering, a mixture of farmers and Chetnik fighters, "The time has finally come when our British and American allies have come to support our cause. Protect them and watch over them.

Provide them with any assistance they so desire. In return, they will provide for us."

Then it was Hueron's turn to speak. His Serbo-Croatian was excellent, "Men and women of Serbia, I have come here at the request of Prime Minister Winston Churchill himself. He has asked me to provide him information on your strengths as well as weaknesses. We know you have a fine and credible fighting force, which seeks nothing but an end to this occupation and tyranny. With your help, we will defeat the Nazis and restore your country to peace and prosperity once more." Then he turned to Josef and Tess, "These two officers are working with me. Take a good look at them. Make sure they are kept safe."

When the celebration was complete, accompanied by lots of music and slivovitz, Team Hueron met again at their temporary headquarters in a tent outside Mihailovich's camp. They were gathered around a small table and stove, heating a kettle to plan their strategy. The first order of business was for Tess to transmit her arrival message back to Cairo. The scheduled transmission was at 1600 hours that afternoon. What was foremost on Josef's mind was how Partisan forces just happened to know the exact time and location of the airdrop. It could not have been a coincidence. His thoughts went back to what O'Donnell told him with regards to McAdams, a known communist sympathizer. They could be battling enemies on several fronts, the Nazis, the Partisans, *and* the communists.

Josef addressed his new commander, "Not only do we have to worry about the Germans, but we have to consider the Partisans as well. Approximately seventy-two hours passed since I cabled Cairo about the drop last night. That's plenty of time to pass that information on to the

Partisans. We know two things aside from being a coincidence as of right now. One: it could have been Chetnik forces sympathetic to the Partisans who passed that information. Or two: that information was deliberately passed on to the communist Partisans directly from Cairo."

Hueron scratched his stubble, contemplating a response, "You transmitted that report via telegram, which could have been intercepted commercially."

Josef had left out the part of retransmitting a different, secure message via his SSTR-1 radio set.

Hueron continued, "We have our own radios now. For the time being, we'll have to assume the Partisan ambush was a coincidence. The important thing to remember is that we're all safe on the ground. We'll continue our mission as originally planned."

Josef responded, "All right, if that's the case, then I suggest we use a more secure location to transmit our messages, away from any Chetnik forces deep in the mountains. We can establish that area as a base of operations for further transmission. Once we transmit, we can move back down closer to Mihailovich. This will accomplish two things—First, we'll be by ourselves, away from Chetnik forces. Second, we'll be deeper in the mountains and further from German DF aircraft."

"Agreed," replied Hueron. "Do you have an area in mind?"

Kostinic unfolded his map and spread it across the table, "Mihailovich moves frequently, but stays in the same general area," as he circled the location on his map. "The mountains just above Sabac will do."

Team Hueron spent the rest of the day searching the mountains for a base of operations. They hauled their transmitter, battery, and foot-driven generator with them. They settled on an area cut deep into the side of a mountain protected by large trees and boulders, which gave them high ground to spot anyone coming up the mountainside. Once satisfied with the location, Hueron and Kostinic coded their respective messages. Tess stood by, ready to transmit her report. Tess connected the aerial to the Mark II transmitter and connected the leads to the accumulator. Josef pedaled the foot generator as Tess began transmitting her first report from the field, known now as "Post Celeste." The time was exactly 1600 hours.

Back at SOE Cairo, the radio technician received the first of Tess's transmission. Her fist and radio checks all agreed. Her message read as follows: Team Hueron in place. Successful contact with Credible Dagger. Sizable fighting force in place. Requesting arms, explosives, ammunition, and medicine. Standing by for instructions and scheds.

At the Hotel Palace in Belgrade, SS Obersturmbannführer Flosberg received a report from the field detailing a Partisan ambush on Chetnik forces the previous night. Several casualties were reported on both sides. Preliminary assessment was an Allied, clandestine landing. What he could not determine was whether the landing was successful and to whom the Allies were supporting. Gerhert was seated next to him with his radio headphones on over his head; he was monitoring the airways. Scheduled radio transmissions were being broadcast at the predetermined time of 1600 hours throughout many parts of Yugoslavia. Gerhert was monitoring several radio sets in Bosnia and Serbia. One, in particular, caught his attention. The fist was unrecognizable. It was from a different radio operator. It was new on the air. He had never heard the signature before. The Morse code tapping was flawless and precise. He switched on the recording devise to record the transmission.

"Someone new is on the air, Herr Flosberg. I've never heard this before. Usually the coding has flaws and inconsistencies. This one flows smoothly." Just as Flosberg was about to put on a headset so he could listen, the new transmission stopped. It was on the airwaves for less than three minutes. Not nearly enough time to get a DF fix from the Stutka aircraft.

"What was different about it from the others?"

"It was soft to the touch and very accurate. The operator is very skilled. We could have a difficult time with this one."

"Can you give me a general location?"

"I would venture to guess as being very close to the location of the Partisan/Chetnik ambush last night."

"That's right in the middle of Mihailovich's forces." Flosberg picked up his phone and contacted the SS regional command in Sabac.

A young Lieutenant answered the phone. "Geheime Staatspolizei, Sabac," replied the Lieutenant.

"This is Obersturmbannführer Flosberg, SD Belgrade. Are you working the tasking tonight?"

"Yes sir, what can I help you with?"

"We've picked up a new signal tonight in the Cer mountains near Loznica. I'd like you to deploy your forces there. I'll follow up with written orders via telegram."

Hueron and Kostinic secured their transmission site for the day and headed back down the hill for the night. They settled on the farm and barn Josef had secured earlier in the week. This was to be their base of operations, for the time being, in Chetnik territory. Tess was in the main farmhouse cleaning up in the small washroom. She had warm water brought to her by an elderly, Chetnik woman who befriended her. This gave Hueron and Kostinic time in the barn by themselves without Tess being with them.

"I trust your personal life will not interfere with our mission. I know she means a great deal to you, but you must remember we have a very important job to do out here. Had I known you two were acquainted, I would have never agreed to bring her on this mission."

"I understand, sir, you have my word. It's just that I haven't seen her since I put her on a sub over two years ago." Josef gave Hueron a brief recap on how they escaped from the German occupation in April 1941.

"Well, that explains her strong desire to come back. Baker Street told me she volunteered for this assignment. She specifically requested not to go into Partisan territory. You know she's the best radio operator in all of England. We had a difficult time getting her assigned to Yugoslav section. French section wanted her badly, too, but the situation there has become extremely dangerous and we felt she could be better used here, instead of France or Belgium."

"Before we go to bed tonight, do you mind if she and I have a little private talk? There's still a lot of things we have to catch up on."

"Why not, have a good night. I'll see you two tomorrow morning for breakfast. We've got a full day."

Josef walked down the path to the farmhouse where Tess was billeted. She had just finished cleaning up for the night. It was actually a beautiful night in the Serbian countryside with a clear sky and bright starlight illuminating the ground. Josef knocked on the door of the farmhouse and the elderly woman opened it. Most of the farmhouses all looked the same, usually made of stone, plastered, and whitewashed or painted white. The roofs were either red tiles or weathered shakes. A brick or stone, Dutch oven was in the back right corner that provided both room heat and an oven for baking. There was a narrow, wooden bench attached to the walls around the perimeter of the room and stove. To the far left, a shrine, usually holding a plaster figure of the Holy Mother. To the left of the entry was the main room (usually semi-private), normally reserved for the husband and wife. Tonight, however, the woman was by herself. Her husband was on a Chetnik raiding party gathering food and supplies from the Germans. Josef removed his Chetnik hat as he entered the cottage and spoke to the woman, "I've come to talk to her. May I come in?"

The Chetnik woman grunted something that even Josef couldn't fully understand as she raised her arm and pointed to the side bedroom. Josef proceeded delicately, not wanting to offend the woman in her house. He knocked on the sturdy wooden door, "Tess, can I come in? I need to talk to you away from Hueron."

Tess slowly opened the door. She was dressed in a long, woolen gown. Josef could see her naked body underneath the thin material. Her firm nipples protruded outward and the dark-brown patch between her legs stood out in the dim light of the room. Her short, brown FANY cut hair was still damp from the sponge bath. She was happy to see him and she immediately put her arms around him.

"I was hoping for a bit more than that," he said. Then she reached up and kissed him gently on the lips.

"It's been a very long time, my love. Sorry for being such a prude, but I have to maintain my composure in the field."

"The Colonel said it was all right for me to come down. I told him about our escape out of Yugoslavia. He seemed very impressed."

"I did leave out that part during my training back at Beaulieu[1]. They never asked, so I didn't volunteer to give them that information."

"Tess, I left you once and it tore my heart out when I had to put you on that sub. I'm not leaving you ever again.

No matter what the circumstances are on this mission, I'm staying with you until the end."

"The mission is supposed to last eight weeks. After which, they should have enough information on how best to supply the Chetniks. You may not have a choice in the matter. Don't forget, you're with OSS. Hueron and I can be recalled anytime. By the way, what is it that you wanted to talk to me about in private, away from Hueron?"

"From your training back at Beaulieu, what can you tell me about German counterintelligence matters?"

"Specifically, what would you like to know?"

"How likely is it that the Gestapo has already intercepted your transmissions?"

Tess gave him an overview of the codes and radio checks and assured him that their transmissions thus far were safe. It would be very difficult for the Germans to break their codes this early in the game. They would have to record her transmissions and then play them back several times before they could duplicate her fist. After which, they would still need her decodes. It would take another month or longer to do that and only if they captured another agent with the key pads.

"Let me ask you another question," said Josef. "When you transmit to Cairo, can you transmit simultaneously to OSS?"

"No, not on the Mark II sets; I've been told that your OSS radios and radio operators have that capability and are trained to do just that. Why do you ask?"

"Nothing, it was just something that crossed my mind." Josef started to unbutton his shirt and take off his boots. Then Tess said, "The straw mattress is infested with lice. If you think I'm hitting the sack with you after I just took a bath, you're out of your mind."

* * *

PENELOPE WALKED BRISKLY along Baker Street near Portman Square holding onto her FANY mackintosh to keep it closed. The strong wind and rains from a summer storm were pounding the London streets. Her face was wet and she was walking into the wind. She had just come from a meeting at Orchard Court. There was confirmation the Belgium section was rounded up by the Gestapo. Several circuits were penetrated and everyone arrested. SOE would have to rebuild the Belgium section from scratch; sending in new agents. Vivian Tate put Penelope on notice that she could be transferred to "N" section. Vivian, up until now, was successful in keeping Penelope safe in F section as the records keeper, but she could not guarantee that for now. N section would be looking for anybody to fill the gaps for the captured agents and radio operators.

Penelope thought how she would break the news to her family if she were sent into the field. In particular, how was she going to break the news to Mattingly? The two had become inseparable the past two weeks; Hal, made the trip into the city daily after his shift. The two would meet at Penelope's flat, Hyde Park, Kensington Gardens, The Studio Club, or anywhere in between. Tonight, she made her way to the Baker Street, Tube station where she would transfer to the Circle line and on to Paddington Station, where they were to meet. He was due to arrive on the five o'clock train, from Haines Lodge. The two never discussed each other's work. It was understood that the two were involved in highly sensitive positions and neither talked about their jobs during the day. Instead, the two concentrated their time on each other, each wanting to know more about the other rather than shop talk. Tonight, however, could be a different story. Penelope had to put

Hal on notice that she could be leaving very suddenly and if that were to happen, she needed to discuss the possible implications with Sarah.

The five o'clock train arrived at 5:15 p.m. As the train came to a stop and the steam cleared the platform, Penelope saw Mattingly standing out above the rest of the passengers. At six-foot, three, Hal seemed like a giant compared to the rest of the sullen passengers. She waved her hand as Mattingly immediately recognized her in the crowd.

"My dear lady, how are you tonight? You look absolutely ravishing," he said as he took hold of her thin waist with his strong hands and kissed her affectionately on the lips. After what seemed like an eternity, the two separated.

"I've had a rough day, but it's already getting better. Where would you like to go tonight?" she asked.

"I'd like nothing more than to accompany you back to your flat where we'll sit in your living room and I can stare at you all night until I have to leave."

"That sounds wonderful. I'm not in the mood myself for crowds tonight. Maybe I can fix you something to eat at home. But remember, Mother has Sarah there."

"Yes, all the more reason to go back to your place."

"You like her, don't you?"

"I'm afraid so. She's a lovely child. She reminds me so much of you every time I see her."

"We can talk about her later. Let's get a move on."

Penelope and her mother were in the kitchen fixing dinner while Hal was in the living room playing with Sarah on the floor, acting like a horse, "He's grown quite fond of her, hasn't he?" asked Aleks.

"Yes he has, very much so, unlike a man of his age. He was an only child and raised by his mother and a French housekeeper. His father died unexpectedly from a heart attack at a young age."

When dinner was over, Aleks took Sarah to bed. It was after ten. The curfew would be in effect, shortly. This gave Penelope and Hal time to be together downstairs in the living room. The two had tea. Hal was sitting in a chair while Penelope was sitting on the floor with her arms over his knees.

"Thank you for dinner tonight. It was lovely. Your mother is a great cook."

"She had a bit of trouble getting the meat, but I was able to use some of my ration coupons and picked it up the other day at the office commissary."

"It must be nice having your own personal, grocery store, conveniently located at work. I'm afraid all I get is what's being served in the mess hall."

"Hal, while we're on the subject of work. Can I talk to you about something?"

"Sure, go right ahead."

"No, this is serious. We've never spoken much before about our jobs, but there's something I need to say to you." Hal straightened up in the chair and put down his teacup, she continued. "I'm afraid even Mother doesn't know what I fully do at the war office. I don't know how to begin, so let me just say it up front. But please, you must never mention what I'm about to say to you ever again, to anyone, not even to Mother."

"All right, dear, you have my word. My lips are sealed. Now, what is it?"

"That stuff about the FANYs. You seem to know a little about it."

"Yes, go on."

"To be specific, I work for the Special Operations Executive, otherwise known as SOE."

"Yes, I've heard of it. I made several trips to Baker Street myself."

"Then you know what goes on in there?" Hal nodded his head, giving her a concerned look.

"I work down the street at Orchard Court at the French section. Our section is responsible for infiltrating agents into occupied France. My job's officially called the F section Records Keeper; F Recs for short, but I'm the special assistant to the number two man at F section who happens to be a *woman* and a very powerful one indeed. She's the one I told you about the night we first met."

"Yes, I remember."

"Her name is Vivian Tate. That name in itself is an official, state secret because it's not even her real name. Between you and me, she's really the one running the section. Anyway, I do all kinds of tasks for her and I don't want to go into specifics, but some of the things she asked me to do are very sensitive to national security."

Hal reached down, picked her up from the floor, and placed her on his lap. "So what, you're a secret agent. I can accept that. What is it that you really wanted to talk to me about?"

"One of my jobs is reading undecipherable codes from agents in the field. I can usually make sense out of some of the transmissions. Because I speak French, I also read undecipherable codes coming in from Belgium. Today, Miss Tate informed me the entire Belgium section was rounded up and arrested by the Gestapo from top to bottom. SOE is going to have to replace the captured agents as quickly as possible. Miss Tate told me today that I could be transferred to Belgium section and be used in the field. In other words, because I'm already a trained radio operator, I could be dropped behind enemy lines somewhere near the French/Belgium border should they determine I'm needed."

Hal was stunned to hear this piece of information. Mainly, because of the sensitive nature of the information, she just gave him, "Wow, nothing like taking me from the blind side."

"I'm telling you this now because I honestly don't know how long I can stay safely in F section as their *records keeper.* If I'm needed, they'll send me out with little notice, and I'll have no way of contacting you. You'd assume I just packed up and left you for some other man. Nothing could be farther from the truth and I wanted to let you know."

"What are the chances they'll actually send you in?"

"I honestly don't know. That's why I'm telling you this. It could happen tomorrow for all I know. Miss Tate tells me I'm too valuable in F section and she'll do what she can to keep me there, for as long as she can. But, even she has her limitations." Tears began rolling down her cheeks.

Hal wiped away her tears with the back of his hand and gently kissed her saying, "I'm so much in love with you that the thought of losing you would crush me forever."

"There's more. If something should ever happen to me, and I shant return, I want you to take care of Sarah. Can you do that for me?"

"Shouldn't she be with your mother?"

"Mother's getting old now and if something should ever happen to me, she might not be in the condition to look after her. Besides, I want her to go back to America in case the war doesn't turn out in our favor."

"Yes, of course, I can do that for you, but nothing's going to happen. Besides, you haven't even left yet or been ordered out."

She began kissing him affectionately on the lips. He slipped his tongue inside her mouth. They began caressing each other and then slowly he slipped his hands under her blouse. She began to moan, "Try not to make too much noise. It's the right time of the month."

They made love on the living room floor for the first time that night. Mattingly exploded inside of her, not holding anything back. After it was all over, Penelope got up, still naked, and walked to the kitchen to make some more tea. When she returned, she sat back down on the floor.

"I love seeing you naked. Don't you know that a man likes seeing the woman he loves naked, no matter what the circumstances?"

"We can't stay like this all night and morning. Sooner or later, Mother or Sarah is going to come down." Penelope slipped on her dress and smoked a cigarette. She then told Hal the entire story about her time and escape from Yugoslavia. When she finished, the curfew was over. It was six o'clock in the morning. She was due back at Baker Street in less than two hours.

* * *

IT WAS STILL dark outside when Josef and Tess were awakened by pounding on the door. The two slept naked on the dirt floor, in sleeping bags and military blankets instead of the lice-infested straw mattress. One of Mihailovich's officers was calling for them. Josef looked at his watch. It was only five in the morning. They quickly got dressed and opened the door. A Chetnik fighter was standing in the dim light of the cottage breathing heavily. He said, "The General needs to move out. He wants you to move with him. There's been another ambush by Partisan forces. Several men were killed last night. The woman's husband was one of them. We must go now."

Hueron, Josef, and Tess were seated around a small campfire at Mihailovich's headquarters. He had a team of horses already assembled and loaded for the redeployment. He spoke with a concerned voice, "I don't even have the arms and ammunition to fight off the Germans, let alone the Partisans. If we had automatic weapons, it would have been over in minutes. As it turned out, my men only had one or two rounds apiece, from bolt-action rifles. The Partisans had machine-guns, grenades, and mortars. I'm moving closer to Sabac. There, we can stage hit-and-run attacks on German supply columns. They have the guns and ammunition we need. It's important we strike while the iron's hot. The Germans know the Partisans were attacking in this area last night. If we attack now, they'll think the Partisans did it. The Germans will then counter with their own attack on Partisan positions."

Hueron said, "I've asked for more supplies, but so far I have not received any replies from Cairo. We'll try again tonight, but I'll send the report with a greater sense of urgency."

Josef interrupted, "We need something to send with the report. I'll volunteer to go with them on the attack, strictly as an observer, not a saboteur. That way, I'll have firsthand knowledge that we can send with our request. Can you hit something big, General?" asked Josef.

"I only have a small amount of TNT; not enough to take out a bridge or railway line. The only thing we can hit is the fuel depot at Sabac. The explosion will set off a secondary explosion. That is all I can do until you get us more plastic."

"Go for the fuel depot," said Hueron.

That night, Chetnik forces hit the fuel depot at Sabac. The facility was totally destroyed mainly due to the addition of plastic explosives Josef donated from his supply, which was to be used for destroying his radio equipment should they be overrun or captured. All members of the raiding party returned safely to Chetnik headquarters. No one was happier to see the motley crew ride up on horseback than Tess. Josef and Hueron immediately sat down and began composing their message to SOE Cairo.

* * *

BACK IN CAIRO, Major Tobe McAdams received the wireless radio report as soon as it was decoded. McAdams was not a tall man at five-feet, four inches tall. Contrary to military regulations, he always wore his RAF flight cap indoors, to give the appearance of added height. He was in his early thirties with thinning hair, wore large, round spectacles too big for his face, making him look more like an accountant than an intelligence agent. McAdams took the message, placed it in a classified folder, and went back to his office. Once inside his office, he closed and locked the door and then seated himself at his desk. He took out a cigarette and lit it as he opened the file. The message was from Team Hueron and Post Celeste:

TO HOME STATION:

ALUM EYE REPORT-STOP

ATTACK ON FUEL DEPOT SABAC LAST NIGHT-STOP

EXTEME ENEMY SETBACK-STOP

SEND FOOD AMMO AUTOMATIC WEAPONS AND PLASTIC-STOP

OTHER RAIDS POSSIBLE BUT ONLY WITH ADDITIONAL SUPPLIES-STOP

REPLY ON SCHED-STOP

POST CELESTE

McAdams took the report and held it over the astray.

He flicked on his lighter and placed the flame to the edge. The report went up in flames. Next, he opened his desk drawer and took out a half-sheet of paper similar to the one the report was typed on. He placed the paper in his typewriter and began to type:

TO HOME STATION:
EYES ONLY REPORT FROM ALUM-STOP
ATTACK ON FUEL DEPOT FAILED-STOP
ALUM REPORTS NO FURTHER ATTACKS PLANNED-STOP
FEARFUL OF GERMAN REPRISALS-STOP
CREDIBLE DAGGER UNRELIABLE-STOP
SEND UPDATE WITH NEXT SCHED-STOP
POST CELESTE

He placed the half-sheet of paper in the classified envelope and began to draft his response message to Hueron.

TO HUERON:
UNABLE PLASTIC-STOP
WILL DROP SUPPLIES AND WEAPONS-STOP
EXPECT SHIPMENT ON NEXT DROP-STOP
SEND COORDINATES ON NEXT SHED-STOP
HOME STATION

Meanwhile, back at Gestapo Headquarters in Belgrade, Gerhert and Flosberg were analyzing the wireless radio transmissions from the previous night. Gerhert listened to the sounds intently over his headset. It was definitely the same radio operator who had the unmistakable fist. They would have a difficult time triangulating their position. Gerhert turned on the recording device to record the transmission. He would have to analyze it repeatedly.

* * *

FOR THE NEXT FOUR WEEKS, it was always the same.

Team Hueron would send their messages to Cairo and each day their reply would be that more supplies were coming. Yet, when they coordinated the drops at great risk to themselves and Chetnick forces, all the canisters were filled with simple tokens of food, mostly crackers, undersize shoes, small coats, small amounts of ammunition, and no explosives. It was becoming very frustrating. Hueron and Kostinic continued to accompany Chetnik guerrilla fighters on hit-and-run attacks on German positions. They hit another fuel depot outside Cacak and a supply column along the Sava. They sent messages back to Cairo saying the Chetniks were indeed a formidable guerrilla fighting force and were worthy of more Allied support. However, it appeared to Hueron and Kostinic that all their efforts were in vain. Hueron was becoming very frustrated. Mihailovich was losing patience. The Germans were taking severe reprisals on Chetnik villages, oftentimes razing a complete village to the ground in retaliation for some of these attacks. The General could have none of this without more Allied support.

All the while, Team Hueron did their best to support Chetnik forces. As an added security measure, they changed positions and moved around frequently in the countryside. Each day they set up camp in close proximity to the General's headquarters. Each day they monitored Chetnik guerrilla activities. They set up the radio and transmitted their messages and then quickly broke them down to avoid German DF equipment. Tess was becoming a very skilled radio operator. Thus far, Team Hueron had avoided Stutka dive bomber patrols in hot pursuit. The Gestapo knew that the Allies were transmitting wireless transmission each day at 1600 hours. Every day the Germans sent in their Stutka divebombers. Sometimes, they watched the bombers dropping bombs in close proximity to their location; however, it was obvious the Germans still had not pinpointed their exact location. The situation was becoming very tense.

On the night of October 1, 1943, Hueron transmitted a final report to Cairo indicating that if nothing was done to resupply Chetnik forces, their mission to Chetnik territory was indeed over. Nothing more could be done. It was all up to London now and the Allied command to determine if the Chetniks were a credible fighting force. To make matters worse, they were beginning to receive reports that several Allied airmen were being held in Chetnik territory. Team Hueron had already assisted several of these downed crewmembers with safe passage via the Adriatic.

Josef, Tess, and Hueron were sitting around the table of a farmhouse contemplating their next move. Thus far, they were successful in avoiding any severe engagements with enemy forces. Most of their activity was observation, but on a few occasions, they were actually attacked by Partisan forces and were lucky to escape. On the previous night, they were hit by Partisan guerrilla fighters. They were awakened in the middle of the night with the sounds of automatic weapons. Two Chetnik fighters awakened them and asked them to leave quickly. They gathered their belongings and wireless radio and hurriedly made their escape through the back of a farmhouse, running for several miles. Several Chetnik fighters lost their lives. These attacks were disturbing to Team Hueron because the Partisan attacks upon the Chetnik forces were conducted using weapons provided by the Allies. Joseph picked up a Sten gun and a US M-1 carbine rifle from two fallen Partisans.

"I can't understand why the Allies aren't listening to us," said Hueron. "We've transmitted several messages and reports favorable to Mihailovich and Chetnik forces. They are indeed a brave and credible fighting force. What's sad is they lack Allied support to fight effectively. Something is definitely wrong back in Cairo. Either they're not getting our reports or somehow our reports and transmissions are not being passed to the appropriate agencies."

"Sir, may I make a suggestion or offer a possible explanation," said Josef.

Hueron nodded his head. "Go ahead, I'm all ears."

"I was briefed by OSS commanders back in Cairo before deploying that there was a real possibility SOE had been infiltrated by the communists. In particular, SOE Yugoslav vice- commander, Tobe McAdams is a possible collaborator. Colonel O'Donnell specifically briefed me that the communists could betray us. O'Donnell knew McAdams before the war while at Cambridge. McAdams was the president of the Communist Youth League at Cambridge University and now he's the number two man for SOE Yugoslav section. If there's a breakdown in the system, I would say it's with our messages themselves being transmitted directly to SOE. We might be able to salvage our operation, or at least test the waters, so to speak, if we could somehow transmit our reports to OSS rather than to SOE and copy the reports to SOE. McAdams will have no choice but to honor our reports and to provide the requested supplies because OSS will know about them *first*. In other words, there's no way McAdams can manipulate our reports."

"We don't have that authority nor is it technically possible."

"If I can find a way, do I have your authorization to proceed?"

"What are you suggesting?"

"Before I was dropped in, O'Donnell gave me an American SSTR-1 wireless radio set in case I had trouble cabling Cairo. It was also a back-up if we lost or damaged the Mark II, or if I was in distress. The simple fact that I transmit on the radio will alert O'Donnell that something's gone wrong on the mission. Once I made contact back to OSS successfully to coordinate your initial airdrop, I had no use for the radio, so I left it safely with Mihailovich, as per my instructions from OSS."

"You mean he's had that thing all this time?"

"Yes, I'm afraid so, sir. But it's in the safest location. He travels with it. Wherever he goes, the wireless goes with him."

"I'll be a son-of-a-bitch. Why didn't you tell me this earlier?"

"Because it was not an SOE operation at the time. I was still under OSS command. They issued me the orders prior to dropping in."

"How difficult is it to get the radio back from Mihailovich?"

"All I have to do is ask. And I may point out that if we can send our reports to OSS with another special request to assist downed Allied airmen, we can almost be assured we'll get our supplies to Mihailovich."

"Tess, can we make it work?" asked Hueron.

"I was told that the SSTR-1 has the capability to transmit to two separate stations. The Americans use the same codes, so I shouldn't have trouble sending the message. They could suspect the set was captured and that the Germans are using the radio because the Americans don't have my security checks."

Josef interrupted, "They can use mine. They know I have the radio. All we have to do is transmit the report with my security checks. They'll decipher your fist from the transmissions and verify with my security checks."

"All right, one final thought," said Hueron. "If we get

through to OSS with the request for more supplies and the British find out about it, they might not approve the drop."

"OSS already thought about that, sir. Remember, the Americans control the air movements. I can almost assure you that my contacts back in Cairo will approve the air movements, if I transmit on the SSTR-1 radio."

"All right, let's get it done on the next SCHED."

Josef and Hueron rode back to Mihailovich's camp on horseback. There, they had a meeting with the General and discussed the plan. He was all in favor of anything that would help his cause. The radio was exactly where Josef had left it, safely with Credible Dagger. Tess stayed behind under the watchful guard of three Chetnik fighters. This was an added security measure taken so that if the team were overrun, Tess and her radio would not fall into German hands.

Also added to the sense of urgency, two more American crewmembers, shot down returning from Ploesti, were brought before Hueron and Kostinic. They were both in bad shape with leg and ankle injuries and in no condition to travel. It would be difficult in itself to get these men to safety. It was agreed that if a message could get back to OSS Cairo, that these men were being harbored safely in Chetnik territory, then that could add to the seriousness of the situation. They might even land an aircraft to medevac the men out. Josef asked one of the flyers, First Lieutenant Oliver Thomas, a B-24 navigator from Toledo, Ohio if he could be available to authenticate his identity. The man agreed, but could not travel with Hueron and Kostinic back to their encampment on horseback.

Mihailovich spoke, "I've received word from my sources that the Gestapo has focused their counterintelligence efforts on clandestine radio transmissions. They're getting very good at triangulating the signals. It's believed they're already reading Partisan radio traffic. We can't take the chance transmitting from here. You'll have to move to a much safer location. I'll arrange for the movement. In the meantime, I'll get you the radio so you can start working on the message. Go back to your camp. I'll send for you when we have the new location. In the meantime, the two flyers will stay here."

* * *

IT WAS JUST after sundown in Cairo. The scorching heat of the day was finally starting to cool down, but only by a few degrees. O'Donnell and Vojvoda walked rather than take a vehicle to the officer's mess on the Allied compound. The shade from the few palm trees lining the dusty street provided little relief from the searing heat. The two men could talk openly because there was no one around them.

"What can you tell me about Alum and his network?" asked Vojvoda.

"I can only tell you what the British told me. He's been operating in the field for over a month now and thus far reported the Chetniks have not displayed any credible activity. They've hit a few soft targets, but nothing of any importance."

"What about supply drops?"

"Minimal thus far. I have not seen his reports from the field. I only get briefed once a week from Force 399[2]." O'Donnell took out a cigarette. He organized his thoughts before he spoke again, "I should have never agreed with McAdams to send Kostinic in without direct contact with OSS. For all I know, he could be dead now and I'd have no idea. I was expecting a lot more activity from Mihailovich's forces. He seems less aggressive than we originally thought."

"There's been some talk within 9[th]Air Force that a lot of their crews are bailing out over Mihailovich's territory. They say they have eyewitness reports of several chutes opening up and falling to the ground safely. What can you tell me?"

"That's news to me. The only reports I've seen about Allied airmen are coming from Partisan territory. So far, there's been nothing to indicate that our boys are with the Chetniks."

Dick changed the subject and continued his quarrying, "I'm not supposed to be talking with you about this. I'm officially only to discuss air movements, but he's a personal friend. If it wasn't for Mihailovich, Kostinic would have never gotten out in 1941. Do you think the reports are valid? I guess what I'm saying is, do you think the Germans have captured the team and are playing back the radio?"

"I thought about that myself, but thus far, all the security checks from the British radio operator are in order. I agree with you. I think something is out of the ordinary. I have a scheduled meeting tomorrow with SOE. I'll do what I can. In the meantime, I need a stiff drink."

* * *

HUERON and Kostinic rode on horseback to their camp with the American SSTR-1 radio set. Tess met the two men as they rode into camp. Several Chetnik fighters helped unload the horses and the equipment, then the team quickly went inside one of the village huts and proceeded to take out the SSTR-1 radio set. Josef connected the power leads to the fully charged battery. However, Josef decided to use the hand crank to keep the battery fully charged while they worked on the set. They did not want any uneven current flow in order to send a clear transmission. "We don't have much time if we're to get the radio modified before scheduled transmission time this afternoon. I was given minimal training back at Cairo. I was only given enough information to authenticate my fist and transmit my initial arrival report. On the first transmission, I can establish the link using my security checks. After that, Tess can start tapping out our message."

Tess looked over the radio set to familiarize herself with the dials, controls, and indicators, "This is a very simple set; I should have no problem using it," she said as she moved each dial and switch. "The crystals are already in place. I assume they're yours?" she asked Josef.

"It's already channelized to broadcast to OSS Cairo."

"Okay, I understand the system now. Once I transmit to OSS, there is a frequency selector switch here," she said as she pointed to the dial. "All I have to do to broadcast to SOE Cairo station is dial in our frequency, switch crystals, and they'll receive the message."

"Great," said Hueron. "This is turning out easier than I thought."

Tess continued, "There's one thing to be concerned about. The Germans will easily pick up our signal because it's very distinct from the British radios in use at the moment. We'll have to keep our message short. To be on the safe side, I would suggest being on the air for less than two minutes. After that, the Gestapo listeners will pick up my fist."

Hueron grabbed a pad of paper, "All right, let's get the message coded so you can practice tapping it out. We'll time you and adjust accordingly."

Hueron and Josef worked together and wrote out their specific message, keeping in mind that the actual transmission would alert O'Donnell that Josef was in distress. After which, Josef coded the message using his poem code. They worked back and forth several times before Tess could tap the message out in less than two minutes:

TO MICHIGAN:

DAGGER CREDIBLE-STOP

CONTRADICTING REPORTS-STOP

NEGATIVE SUPPLIES DROPPED AS REQUESTED-STOP

SEVERAL US FLYERS NEED SAFE PASSAGE-STOP

SEND SUPPLIES, WEAPONS, MEDS FOR DAGGER-STOP

NO UK INVOLVEMENT-STOP

REPLY NEXT SCHED-STOP

ALUM

POST CELESTE

When she was finished, she switched radios and transmitted using the Mark II radio to SOE Cairo. Her message was as follows:

STILL NEED SUPPLIES AND PLASTIC-STOP

WAITING FOR NEXT TASKING-STOP

CREDIBLE DAGGER FORCE STRONG-STOP

POST CELESTE

At 1600 hours at Gestapo Headquarters, Belgrade, SD listening specialists monitored the daily schedules from the field. An entirely different signature was on the air. Ernst Gerhert was alerted to the transmission and immediately switched on the recording device. The fist was recognizable, but coming from a different frequency band, not British, but one used by the Americans. He was sure it was the same radio operator who had eluded them thus far. He immediately contacted Luftwaffe command and ordered a Stutka aircraft in the vicinity to monitor the transmission. It was too late. The system went dead and the operator was off the air. Then, to his surprise, another transmission came on the air almost immediately. Similar to the one he just heard, but this time coming from a British frequency band. He recognized the signature fist again. It was the same radio operator; on the air for less than thirty seconds, then off again. There was no way to trace the two signals. He pounded his fist on his desk and shouted to himself, "Son-of-a-bitch. I almost had him. Another twenty seconds and we could have had him!"

He took off his radio headset and threw it on the floor in frustration. He took a drag from his cigarette and blew the smoke out forcefully through his nose and mouth. This is no ordinary radio operator, he thought to himself. I've got to think of something. He placed his headset on and played back the recording. It was definitely the elusive radio operator he'd been tracking, transmitting on two different radio sets. The light tapping sounded as if he was playing a musical instrument. Then the thought occurred to him, That's it! It has to be a woman. No one else could duplicate that fist like a woman. Not just *any* woman, someone young, petite, very intelligent, who played musical instruments.

He picked up the office phone and called Flosberg. "I need to speak with you. I'll be up to your office in five minutes. Clear your schedule for the next hour. I think I may have something."

Gerhert tossed the transcripts on the desk, "They're using two different radio sets. There's no other explanation. I've listened to the recordings several times. I know the fist by heart. I can recognize it in my sleep. And I'm almost positive it's a woman."

"If they're using two sets, one British, one American, then it must be a joint operation in Chetnik territory."

"Yes, I believe so. If we could capture that team, we'd

have access to both British and American radio traffic. This could be the bonanza we've been hoping for."

"The scheduled transmission is tomorrow night at sixteen hundred hours. If they've sent an urgent message, then they'll be expecting a reply. I'll have all DF assets airborne waiting for them to come on the air. If it's that urgent, then they'll be replies back and forth. This will put them on the air longer than the two minutes they've done in the past. Let's let them run with it for a while. I'll deploy added aircraft from Partisan territory, so we can add to the accuracy of the DF."

* * *

ON THE SAME day at 1730 hours back in Cairo, OSS signal operators monitoring scheduled radio transmissions picked up an urgent call from the field. The address was from a radio set belonging to a Lieutenant Kostinic, assigned to Force 399. He looked through his tasking sheet and saw that this radio message was to be forwarded, *Eyes Only*, to Lt. Col. Howard O'Donnell (codename Michigan), Balkan section Field Chief, immediately. The young private tore off the message from the teletype and handed it to his supervisor. He called OSS Headquarters and asked for O'Donnell. Luckily, O'Donnell was still in his office and took the call personally.

"This is O'Donnell."

"Sir, this is Sergeant Knox, at Cairo Com Center. We've got an urgent message for you, Eyes only. How soon can you get over here?"

"I'm on my way."

The Com Center was located several blocks away from OSS Headquarters. O'Donnell didn't wait for the car and driver. At fifty years of age, he walked the distance despite the heat and sun of the October evening in Cairo. When he got to the Com Center, all hot and sweaty and read the message from Kostinic, he was stunned. Just as he and Vojvoda suspected. There was a mix-up in the message traffic. Kostinic was reporting that SOE never got his requested supplies. No United Kingdom involvement meant Kostinic suspected McAdams had something to do with it. The downed flyers added urgency and confirmed Vojvoda's reports. "Sergeant, I need to make an important call. Get me a phone line."

The young sergeant showed O'Donnell to the telephone. He called Vojvoda, but there was no answer at his office. He suspected he'd gone home for the day. Next, he contacted OSS Headquarters and talked to the duty officer. "I want a runner sent out to look for Captain Vojvoda. He's probably at the Officer's Club. Tell him I need him back at my office immediately. I don't care if you have to scour the entire streets of Cairo, but find him tonight!"

THAT NIGHT AFTER SUNDOWN, Team Hueron moved further southeast and set up a new camp near Koceljevo. Here the terrain afforded better protection and there were many places where they could coordinate airdrops. They set up encampment in another farmhouse all too familiar now. Hueron and Kostinic slept in the barn while Tess stayed inside the main cottage. The two crewmembers were brought on ox cart and stayed with Hueron and Kostinic inside the barn. They used an oil lantern for light and made a small table using one of the milking stools. Hueron spoke to the two airmen, "We need to prepare our message tonight so we can transmit tomorrow afternoon. It's extremely important we get the message in as few words as possible. We've informed the Allies back at Cairo that we have you safe in our protection. They may want us to authenticate your identities further."

Kostinic interrupted, "What the Colonel is suggesting is that Cairo may want more information on your identities, so you'll have to stay close to us during the radio transmissions." Kostinic took out his tablet and pencil. "Try to give me information that only you would know about."

Lieutenant Thomas, the B-24 navigator spoke up, "Our call sign was Banjo Nine."

"No, that's too easy. The Germans could have gotten that information simply by monitoring radio frequencies. What else do you have?"

"I was assigned to the 459 Bomb group out of Tripoli. My aircraft was a replacement, so we didn't have a nose mascot like some of the others in our attack formation. All of our aircraft except mine had sharks' teeth painted on the nose."

Josef jotted down some notes then asked, "Did you have a name for your crew tent back at Tripoli?"

"Why yes, we called it Rat Flat."

"That'll do for now." Just then, Tess walked into the barn. The two flyers instantly dove to the ground. She was dressed in a white cotton dress and had just taken a bath. She smelled like sweet roses and cherries. The scent filled the musty barn as she walked in. She was carrying a tray of goat meat, cheese, black bread mixed with straw[3], and wine.

"Get up, you two," said Hueron. "This is Flight Officer Celeste Bowmen; she's an officer in the Royal Air Force and our radio operator. If you want to be rescued, I'd suggest you give her the respect she deserves."

The two men got themselves up from the floor and dusted off their pants. Lt. Thomas spoke up, "I'm sorry, miss. I wasn't expecting the radio operator to be a woman."

Tess sat the tray on the small, improvised table, "I have supper for everyone. They don't have much, but it's probably better than what they've been eating."

As the two American flyers ate, Josef and Tess continued composing their message, intermixing the message with coding on the two Americans. Next, Tess practiced transmitting, using the key pad while Josef and Hueron timed her with their watches. Their message was as follows:

LOCATION 15 SW KOCELJEVO-STOP

TWO FLYERS FROM SHARK SQUADRON-STOP

RAT FLAT PLUS ONE-STOP

COORDINATE RESCUE AND SEND SUPPLIES TO N44.06.312.2 E20.09.21.2- STOP

WILL STAY ON AIR-STOP

ALUM

POST CELESTE

It was 2200 hours back in Cairo. Dick Vojvoda and O'Donnell were peering over maps and aerial photos of Team Hueron's location in the small office. The cigarette smoke in the room was so thick they could barely see each other. The two men had been working since after seven that night when Dick received the message from the runner.

O'Donnell said, "This is the major reason why we have our own man embedded with the British. Donovan wants positive proof that Mihailovich can be trusted. Kostinic was very clever in transmitting his message using our radio set. This next SCHED is extremely important. We've got to make sure he's not in enemy hands, playing back the radio. When he transmits tomorrow, I want to get confirmation he's the real thing. That's why I want you there with me for the SCHED tomorrow."

"I agree. They'll have to keep the radio on as we make contact."

"Yes, I know that. I'm willing to take the risk. The Germans can't track them when they receive transmissions. They can only track them while they're transmitting. If everything checks out, I want to get him to a telephone where he can contact me directly. You know the area. What's the best way to do that?"

Vojvoda looked over the map and photos, "If he's operating in this area, we'll have to get him to the town of Koceljevo. There's a railway station and a small inn. That's the best place," he said as he pointed to the location on the map. "It'll mean him coming down from the safety of the mountains, but he'll know what to do."

"All right, it's agreed. Our objective tomorrow is as follows: First, we confirm his identity; second, we coordinate the air drop; finally, I want him on the telephone."

Just before 1600 hours on the night of October 14, 1943 Team Hueron, along with the two US Army Air Corps flyers, were ready for the transmission. Captain Rudko and his brother, Stefan, stood guard outside the village farmhouse. Three-hundred Chetnik fighters were stationed along the outskirts of the small village scouting for German patrols. The horses were packed and ready to move the team on short notice in case of a German air strike. Josef adjusted his feet on the foot pedals of the hand-cranked generator. The SSTR-1 radio was ready. Hueron, holding his watch, counted down the time to transmission. At exactly 1600 hours, Hueron nodded his head and hacked his watch. Tess began tapping out her transmission authentication. Then she proceeded with her message. Two minutes later, she finished tapping and Hueron stopped his watch.

"One minute fifty-two seconds. That's got to be a record. There's no way the Germans can trace that."

Tess turned up the volume of the set, so they could all monitor. After several minutes, the SSTR-1 radio came to life. Beeps and dashes came over the air waves and Hueron and Tess copied them down. Josef continued to pedal the hand-crank with his feet while writing down the codes. They compared notes. They had all copied the same thing. Hueron nodded his head while Tess decoded the message. She wrote it down and then handed it to him. He looked at the note and read it several times and finally said, "They've got it. Josef, they're asking you one question. They want to know who accompanied you to dinner that night at Shangri-La?"

Josef couldn't believe it, not only was he positive they had received their urgent message, but it appeared that two of the men present that night were sitting in the same room asking the questions.

"There are only four men alive who know that answer. Two of them are present back at Cairo. The answer is Howard O'Donnell, Dick Vojvoda, and William F. Donovan."

"Tess, code the response and prepare for transmission," said Hueron, then he stepped outside and asked one of the Chetnik guards, "How does it look?"

"Very quiet, sir, nothing in the air at all." Hueron returned inside as Tess finished the encoding and was ready for transmissions. They began the process once more. This time Tess was on and off the air in seconds. The response message from Cairo was equally swift in return. They decoded the message once more as a team. Everyone jumped for joy with excitement. The message said to expect the supplies the following night at the drop zone coordinates specified. The final request was for Josef to make telephone contact within forty-eight hours.

Thirty miles away, Gerhert was in a mobile DF van outside the city of Valjevo. Flosberg had this specially modified van shipped in from France in order to help track the elusive radio operator. Valjevo was the largest city in the area. He moved closer to the probable transmission site to be in a better position to direct SS forces in the event of a DF lock-on. Tonight, he picked up the elusive radio operator's signal very quickly; however she was on the air only seconds. A short time later, he picked up inbound radio traffic, then another outbound message. Although, she was on the air only a few seconds, this time he was waiting for her. He already had his listening device pointed in the right direction. Her signal was strong, her tapping precise. He got her location. He was able to get the DF lock-on with help from airborne Stutkas in the vicinity. They were transmitting in a heavily guarded Chetnik location. In addition, he was becoming more skilled at reading Allied radio transmissions. Some of the codes he had actually broken. One word in particular was received over the airways that he recorded and recognized. The word was "Celeste" and it appeared several times during transmissions from Cairo. He could not be sure of the meaning, possibly a code name, but he knew one thing. They would have the whole mountainside surrounded by SS troops by morning. He immediately called back to Flosberg with the wonderful news.

"I'll call in the airstrike tomorrow morning," said Flosberg. "The Allied agents won't be expecting an attack that late after their transmission. We'll catch them off-guard and hopefully get them to give up."

On the morning of October 15, 1943, Team Hueron

woke to the sounds of aircraft in the skies. ME-109 and Stutka dive-bombers were everywhere. The planes made strafing runs on the entire village. Women and children ran everywhere. Farm animals, houses, barns, and chapels were blown to pieces. Hueron and Rudko came running out of the farmhouse; Josef behind shouted to the two other men over the loud sounds of the dive-bombers. "I've got to find Tess. Where is she?"

Rudko, running out of breath and gasping for air said, "She's already gone up the hillside. She took the radios with her. Stefan is waiting with her. We've got horses and men standing by."

Hueron, seeing the attack from all directions, told Josef, "Go after her. I'll stay here with the two airmen and coordinate the airdrop. We've got to get that shipment of supplies tonight or we'll lose the support of Mihailovich. Get to a telephone as instructed. Contact your OSS superiors. Find out what they want so urgently by phone. Meet me at the General's headquarters in three days. I'll be all right."

Josef extended his hand, "Good luck to you, sir. I'll see you back at Ravna Gora." Josef turned and quickly ran up the mountainside, ducking for cover every time he heard an aircraft. He jumped into a ditch as he watched a Stutka bomber drop its load on a house. The structure was pulverized to pieces. He continued and followed the fleeing villagers up the hill, hiding behind trees and boulders as he made his way up the mountainside. In a thick wooded area, Josef heard a whistle from Stefan. He motioned him over to a clump of boulders and several horses already saddled up. Tess was sitting on top of a brown mare. All she had on was her green army blouse and a pair of woolen trousers. She had been lucky to get out of the farmhouse alive. Gasping for breath, Josef said, "We've got to go further up into the mountains. Hueron is staying behind to coordinate the airdrop. Are you all right?" he asked Tess.

"We've been through an airstrike before. *Dobre Beche*[4]. This time I didn't wait. Now, get on the horse, you fool."

Stefan, Josef, and Tess, along with three Chetnik fighters, made their way safely to higher ground. From this location, they continued to watch the attack. Wave after wave of fighter aircraft continued to strafe the small village. Women and children fled in all directions. Horses, cattle, and farm animals were blown to pieces. It was obvious to Josef as he watched the carnage below that the Germans had fixed onto their position last night. Even though Tess was a skilled radio operator and she had transmitted her messages swiftly, the Germans had somehow locked onto their position. They had probably been tracking them for several days. It would be a miracle if Hueron made it out alive. In the meantime, they had to continue. He had to get to a telephone to make contact with Cairo. It was obviously a very urgent request. O'Donnell probably wanted to speak to him personally about something. Maybe he didn't trust Hueron or any of the British. Maybe McAdams was intercepting the radio transmissions himself and didn't want to take the chance of jeopardizing the mission. Either way, they had to find a telephone. Josef dismounted from the horse, "Let's take a break, everyone. I think we're safe from any aircraft patrols, for the moment. There's a lot of cover from the trees. They'll be shooting blindly if they appear at all."

Stefan said, "There will be more Chetnik fighters ahead. We can meet up with them. They can assist us. Enemy patrols have already surrounded the hillsides. We must make it to higher ground. I know of a small village up there. We can take refuge there until we formulate a plan."

Once they caught their breath, they mounted their horses once again and proceeded up the hill. It was a slow process as more German aircraft continued to patrol the skies, mostly observation aircraft on the lookout for people fleeing the attack. It was about two in the afternoon before they reached the safety of the small village. Stefan went to a farmhouse and asked if they could stay for the night. The man and his wife agreed, but warned him that Partisan forces had been there the previous day. If they found out they were harboring Chetniks there could be severe reprisals against them. Stefan informed the man that he had two Allied officers under his protection. He was under direct orders from General Mihailovich himself to protect them. If they were killed or captured, regardless if it was done by Germans or Partisans, the repercussions would be the same; the General would hold them equally responsible.

Tess came off her horse and approached the couple in her polite, Serbo-Croatian voice, "We mean no harm. All we ask is a place to stay for the night. We have our own food and water. We can sleep in the barn. No one will know we're here." The couple agreed.

As they entered the barn, Stefan placed another man on guard while they planned their next move. Josef unfolded his map and began to formulate his plan. "The nearest telephone is probably located in Koceljevo. The Germans will have it surrounded by the end of the day. There's no way we can get to the railway station or hotel without being questioned. What's the next best thing?" he asked Stefan.

"We can tap into the lines directly, but we'll have to

attack a German communications unit to get access to the equipment needed for the job."

"That's too risky without more Chetnik support and we don't have the time to scour the entire mountainside looking for them."

They heard footsteps outside and one of the guards went to the door with his rifle ready. The woman cried out, "Can I come in? I have something for you."

Josef nodded his head and Stefan opened the door slowly in case it was a trap. The woman entered. She was middle-aged with black hair and strong, working hands. She came over to Tess, "You're a very beautiful young woman. You looked like you could use some things, so I brought you these." She handed her a bundle of clothes, "They belonged to my daughter. She was killed last summer by the Partisans."

Tess reached for the bundle and said, "I'm sorry for your loss. Thank you, you've been very kind." Tess opened the bundle and saw the clothes were very beautiful. They were not peasant clothes, but rather very dressy clothes probably purchased in Belgrade. Upon seeing the clothes, Josef was struck with an idea.

"We won't stay here for the night. The Germans will probably send up more aircraft first thing in the morning hoping to catch us. I would also expect a platoon to follow up on foot. We need to move out at night. We could be down the mountain and inside the township by early morning, while it's still dark. Tess and I can dress up. We can make it to a hotel and check in. We can say we've traveled all night and need a place to stay. The Germans won't be out that early in the morning. We can avoid any patrols checking travel documents. Once we get to the hotel, I can make the call. We'll stay there until normal hours, and then work our way out."

1. Beaulieu Manor was a stately manor in Hampshire, Southern England where British secret agents received their final training before going into the field. This facility is now the home to the UK National Motor Museum.
2. At some point during the war, SOE Yugoslav section changed their name to Force 399.
3. They ground the straw to a fine pulp and mixed it with what little flour they had. It's very similar to adding chicory to coffee during the war except chicory tastes a lot better.
4. "Things will get better" in Serbo-Croatian. It was a common phrase during the war by Chetnik fighters.

Chapter 15
THE STREETS OF KOCELJEVO

At 0400 hours the next morning, Josef and Tess walked in the streets of Koceljevo in total darkness. As expected, the town was completely deserted. A German patrol was camped outside the city limits. Tess had on the clothes given to her by the peasant woman. Josef had on a knitted blue coat over his army khakis and Chetnik hat. They found a small hotel two blocks from the train station. They knocked on the door. Several minutes passed before they heard a slight voice from an elderly man, "Just a minute, just a minute." Then they heard the door unlock from the inside and the man asked, "What do you want at an hour like this?"

Tess spoke up first, "We've come all night from Belgrade. We're very tired. Do you have a room we could use to rest and freshen up?"

The door opened and an older man still in a night-gown and cap and holding an oil lantern said, "It's not wise to be out and about this time at night. There's a curfew 'til six you know."

"Yes, I know, that's why we need shelter. My husband is with me. Can we please come in?"

"All right, just a minute," he said as he opened the door fully and allowed the couple to enter. The inn was a small, stone, two-story structure. The main living quarters were downstairs and the guest rooms were upstairs. "I'm afraid the inn's full. German SS officers have taken the place over. They've been here for several days. They have their encampment set up outside the city."

"There must be some place you can let us stay for a while. We don't need a full night, just enough time to rest. We'll be on the next train out of here."

"That could be several days. Trains never run on time around here. You're better off taking refuge on foot. How did you get here, anyway?"

Before he could ask another question, Josef emerged, "We have money," he said as he held out a wad of dinars.

"We only accept Reichsmarks, I'm afraid, been that way since the occupation. I could let you stay in the barn, but it will cost you ten marks for the two of you."

"Ten marks! That's outrageous for a bed of straw," said Josef.

Tess reached into her handbag and counted out ten marks, "Do you have a telephone by any chance? I need to make a call to Belgrade."

"That'll cost you ten more. The SS officers use it all the time and never pay me for it. I've got to make up for it somehow."

"I understand. That won't be a problem," she said and she counted out another ten marks. "Here you go. Now, could you show us the way? My husband and I have been up all night."

"Yes, of course, follow me."

They walked around the back to a small stone structure

with a heavy wooden door, "Be careful with the ox. He's not used to strangers."

As they entered the barn, Josef could see that along with the ox, a small wagon with sturdy wheels was parked inside. A large hayloft with plenty of straw was to the back, "This will work. When can we use the telephone?"

"The phone's inside, behind the front desk. The guests are all asleep. This bunch are not early risers plus they had a lot to drink last night. You should use the phone *now*."

Josef put down his pack, "All right, give us a few minutes to unpack and we'll be right there."

The man turned to leave, but not before he said, "Come in through the back door by the kitchen." Josef nodded his head in acknowledgement as the man turned and walked away briskly.

Tess spoke with a concerned voice, "There's no way we'll pull this off without getting everyone killed. What if the Germans get up and see us using the phone and start asking questions? What if the Germans intercept your call?"

"We'll have to be quick about it. It could take a while for German signals staff to piece the information together and pass it on to the Gestapo. It's a risk worth taking." Josef took out his Merlin and placed it inside the small duffle bag he'd been carrying, "Hand me your Sten." Tess reached into her handbag and took out the Sten gun with silencer, "You'll have to cover me as I make the call." She nodded her head.

"Please be careful."

"I liked it when you called me your husband," he said as he gently touched the side of her cheek. "I haven't let you down yet. We'll be out of here before those drunken idiots wake up."

Together, Josef and Tess walked to the back entrance

of the inn. They carried all their belongings, in case they had to make a quick getaway. Tess opened the door slowly as she saw the innkeeper putting a kettle on the stove. There was no one inside the kitchen other than the man. He held his finger to his lips for them to be quiet and then motioned for them to enter.

"They're still asleep. No sound at all from upstairs. You'll have somewhat of an advanced notice if they wake up and make their way downstairs. You'll hear the noise easily from down here." The innkeeper brought the phone into the kitchen. Luckily it was attached to a long line. Josef pulled out his Merlin submachine gun and Tess readied her Sten gun. Then Josef spoke quietly to the innkeeper, "Listen to me carefully. We're not going to hurt you. We're Allied officers working behind enemy lines. We've got to make contact with our people back in Cairo. Get me an outside line."

The man did as instructed as Tess stood covering the door with her Sten gun ready. After several minutes, they got through to the overseas operator. A short time later, Josef was on the line with OSS Cairo.

He spoke in English very quietly, "Get me through to Colonel O'Donnell, of the Cairo station immediately!" He was put on hold for another ten minutes, which seemed like an eternity. Tess continued to hold her Sten gun firmly on the hotel clerk and the doorway.

"You know you're going to get us all killed," the man said. "The Germans monitor the phones. They're not that stupid."

Josef replied, "We've planned this out thoroughly, that's why we'll be out of here just as soon as I make the call."

"They'll never believe me."

"I know, that's why you're leaving with us. I'll guarantee your safety."

The Cairo switchboard finally got through to O'Donnell who took the call immediately. A relieved Josef spoke in Serbo-Croatian and gave O'Donnell a detailed briefing on his mission thus far. He told him about Mihailovich's forces and numbers and the attacks on German supply depots and columns. He detailed his reports on Chetnik forces in Bosnia, Montenegro, and Macedonia and that all forces in these republics cast their support to Mihailovich, bringing the total Chetnik guerrilla force to over ten thousand. O'Donnell was not surprised by these reports. He had been expecting more Chetnik activity and Josef's report from the field confirm his expectations. He also instructed Josef to continue to send routine reports to SOE via the Mark II radio. All logistical support requests, including supply drops to Mihailovich however, would be transmitted by the SSTR-1 radio set from now on.

O'Donnell spoke over the phone, "Also, keep me informed on Chetnik activity using your radio set, not the Mark II. I'm sending Donavon your full report. I'm sure McAdams will manipulate the numbers in favor of the Partisans."

"Is there anything else, sir?"

"The British are in control of the mission. When McAdams finds out about your reports, he's going to go ape shit and squeal to London. They could pull Hueron and his radio operator out and insist we recall you. If that's the case, I'll send you somewhere else. We still need reliable assets in the field. I don't trust anyone but you at the moment."

"There's one more thing. The innkeeper, he risked his life and is in grave danger if he stays behind. I've guaranteed him his safety."

"Show him your blood chit and bring him out if you can. He'll have the full support of the US government."

Josef hung up the phone. It was five-thirty in the morning. He could hear movements upstairs as the Germans began to awaken, "Quickly get what you need and come with us. You heard me. We'll guarantee your safety."

"I can't. This is my life. There is nowhere else I could go. My wife was killed by the Nazis, my sons by the Partisans."

"All right, that's your choice. I don't have time to argue. Sit down here," he said as Josef tied the man to a kitchen chair and then placed a rag into the man's mouth. Next, Josef hit the man on the side of the head with the butt of his Merlin. He then stuffed several marks into a tea can in the cupboard, "If you survive the war, I will never forget you."

"Now, can we get out of here?" Tess asked as she held the back kitchen door open, mission accomplished.

It was just after six in the morning and they were hiding in the dense trees on the hills, overlooking Koceljevo. The day was just beginning; Stefan and three other Chetnik fighters were monitoring the streets with their binoculars. They took up positions in range of their rifles to provide sniper cover in the event they needed it. They could see the streets were still mostly empty. There were a few farmers making deliveries to local businesses billeting German soldiers riding ox-driven carts. Stefan could plainly see Josef and Tess walking casually hand-in-hand down the street, heading outside the city. The few German patrols riding motorcycles and sidecars did not even slow down or notice them. The plan was proceeding on schedule. As he was previously briefed, if they found a telephone and used it successfully, they were to walk away hand-in-hand. All Josef and Tess had to do now was make it to the outskirts of town and then hike up the hillside to safety. The couple did not pay particular attention to the utility van moving along the streets at a steady speed. It looked much like any other utility vehicle on the roads at this time of morning. Inside the van however, were SD radio specialists, Ernst Gerhert, along with two other SD radio operators monitoring Allied radio transmission. Gerhert decided very early that morning to move out of Valjevo and position his DF equipment to Koceljevo in order to get a better radio triangulation. He did not pay much attention to the local citizens walking about the city until he saw the young, ordinary-looking Serbian couple walking briskly along the street together.

"Slow down a little," he told his driver and then he continued to gaze upon the couple. "Something doesn't look right."

The driver, a young SS corporal happy to be away from the Russian front said, "What is it, Herr Gerhert?"

"There's something unusual about those two. I can't be certain, but something doesn't seem right about them."

The SS corporal slowed the DF utility van and looked across the street as the two young Serbians walked into an alleyway, "They looked ordinary to me. Probably just another local farmer making deliveries in town. The man did seem to be wearing a nice pair of boots, though."

"That's it! He's wearing US Army-issue jump boots. I knew there was something unusual about him. Turn the van around." The SS corporal turned the van around quickly and headed back toward the small alley. The street narrowed too much for the van to get through. It did not make any difference. The young couple was nowhere in sight.

Josef held Tess against the corner of a building, hiding them from incoming traffic, "I'm almost certain they turned around. They must have seen or suspected something was wrong about us as we passed on the road."

"We're out in the open. We can't stay here all day long. If we move out, they'll see us and surely come after us."

"See if you can get down on the ground and take a closer look. I'll cover for you. Let me know what we're up against."

Tess dropped to the street on her knees and slowly peeked around the corner then ducked back behind the safety of the building, "I don't think they saw me, but I saw two men dressed in civilian clothes; one older, the other younger in the driver seat. They're about twenty feet away. The van had a strange-looking contraption on top of the roof. The two men inside the cab appeared to be discussing the situation."

"It's a DF van used by the Gestapo to trace wireless radio transmissions. They travel without a military escort to disguise their operation. They could have two or three other men in the back working to triangulate. They'll all be armed. The only reason they haven't come down the alley is because the van won't fit. Obviously, they don't want to be put at a tactical disadvantage if we engage them."

Josef reached into his utility bag and took out his Merlin machine gun then looked up toward the mountains, "We'd be exposed for at least a hundred meters if we make a break for it now."

Tess unbuttoned her jacket and took out a British fragmentation grenade, "Can we use this?" she asked.

"Where did you get that thing?"

"Hueron gave it to me before we left Algiers. He said I might need it."

"If they come out of the van, we won't stand a chance. I have an idea. Give me the grenade."

Tess handed the grenade to Josef while she took out her Sten gun and unscrewed the silencer for maximum efficiency. Josef pulled the pin on the grenade, "I'm going to roll the grenade on the street and under the van. When it goes off, I want you to open up on the van with your Sten gun."

Tess closed her eyes, "Whatever you say, I'll be ready."

"If there was another way I'd do it, but I'm afraid we're trapped. After we empty our rounds, we'll make a dash up the hillside to Stefan and the rest of the men."

Tess nodded her head, "All right, I'm ready. We trained for this back at Beaulieu. I know what to do."

"Good girl." Josef released the grenade and rolled it around the corner. The men in the vehicle never saw him. The grenade exploded under the left side of the van igniting the gasoline. They could hear men screaming in agony. Josef and Tess emerged from the alleyway and began firing into the vehicle. Their rounds, however, did little damage, as it was obvious the van was re-enforced. When their magazines were empty, Josef and Tess turned up the alley and ran for the hillside. As they were climbing the steep hill, Josef looked back and could see one of the men emerging from the passenger side. They made eye contact and then he fell to the ground and rolled just as the van exploded in a fireball.

Occupying the high ground, watching the two operatives make their escape, Stefan and his men were ready to open fire upon the DF van. Stefan shouted, "Hold your fire, men! If we shoot, they'll have a fix on our position and call in support. Let the couple make it up the hill into the cover. We'll all have a better chance of escape."

Chapter 16

BELGIUM SECTION

Penelope, on her way to work, emerged from the Baker Street Tube station right after six in the morning. It was raining and there was little traffic on the streets. She could feel the cold, wet air coming through her FANY mackintosh. She tried to raise the collar to keep out the dampness as she walked two more blocks before coming to a stop at a crosswalk. A big, green, Ford sedan with tinted windows came to a stop just beside her. The door flung open from the inside. Penelope heard the distinct voice of Vivian Tate, "Get in."

Penelope obeyed the harsh command from her supervisor, "Yes, ma'am," and climbed inside the cab as the car sped away.

It was warm and dry inside the smoky sedan. Vivian was seated with a cigarette dangling from her lip. Penelope shivered in the back seat next to her, not sure if it was because of the cold rain or the presence of her supervisor.

"You're going with me to the airfield this morning. The Belgium section chief was evacuated last night. He arrived earlier this morning by Hudson aircraft at Tempsford

Field. We're going to debrief him. Everyone is waiting for us. He was lucky to get out alive."

"How bad is it, Miss Tate?" asked Penelope referring to the penetration.

"Disastrous—the Gestapo penetrated all circuits. There isn't one circuit that wasn't affected in some way or another. We'll know more once we're debriefed. Baker Street is running out of options, young lady, I'm afraid you may be going in on this moon period."

The two SOE women rode in the car to the secret airfield in Bedfordshire. Penelope was at a loss for words and still shivering. The car journey was completed in near silence as Vivian looked out the window at the passing countryside, her mind wandering in a multitude of directions. She remembered Penelope was the first to reveal the possibility that the Gestapo were playing back F section radio sets, even though MacAlister did not or would not believe it for himself and continued to send agents into the field.

They drove to a large, attractive, country house near Sandy. The house was an eighteenth-century mansion a few miles from the secret airfield at Tempsford. The house stood well back from the road, hidden from view in a wooded section. The big, green sedan screeched to a stop outside the cottage on the uneven gravel driveway. Vivian did not wait for the driver. She opened the door herself, placed another cigarette between her lips, and then stepped out. "Don't do like you did last time. Whatever you do, don't utter a *peep* until I tell you. Do you understand?"

"Yes, as you wish, ma'am."

Then Penelope shadowed Vivian in her footsteps as she stomped toward the cottage, obviously familiar with the surroundings. Once inside, Penelope caught sight of a large lounge complete with a long bar on the first floor.

There were also a few tables set up in the dining room next to the bar. In the dining room were a number of men, commandos, RAF pilots, and Special Forces officers going about various matters. There was an air of tension in the smoke-filled room as the two women entered the dining room. Upon seeing the two women, an RAF officer approached Vivian and said, "They're waiting for you in the briefing room. Moon Squadron has cleared everything off their schedule for the morning; you shall not be interrupted. Right this way, Miss Tate," he said as he led them to an adjoining room and then closed the door, leaving the two women with the other occupants.

Inside the briefing room, seated at the large oak table, was Colin Gubbins, commander of SOE. Seated across from him, dressed in grey slacks, a leather jacket, and beret and looking very continental was another man. The two men rose from their seats upon the entrance of Vivian and Penelope.

"Ah, Miss Tate, there you are. How was the drive in from the city?" asked Gubbins.

"It was, shall we say, very quiet. I had a lot to think about."

"And rightfully so. Please, be seated you two. This is Peter Newman. He just flew in by Hudson from Belgium. We flew him out to give us an assessment of the damage. I'm afraid it doesn't look good."

Newman was tall and slender in build, in his mid-thirties with dark hair and pale skin.

"Peter, this is Miss Tate from F section and her assistant, Miss Walsh. No need to bring Miss Tate up to speed. Let's get right into it. Miss Tate practically runs F Section. We can formulate a plan as we debrief from here."

Newman put out his cigarette and unrolled a map that

was on the table. He secured the top end with an ashtray and the bottom with a large mug of coffee heavily laden with cream and sugar that was still steaming hot. Penelope and Vivian took seats at the table as Gubbins motioned with his hand for the appropriate seats. Newman began.

"It was a complete roundup. The radio sets were captured here and here," he said as he pointed to a location along the Belgium coast and the French border. "Once the sets were in enemy hands, it was very easy to close in on the rest of the group. All they had to do was play the radios back. I've learned the Gestapo broke the codes as early as six months ago. They've been monitoring the radios for some time. They were just waiting for the right moment to strike."

Newman sat back down at the table and took out another cigarette. "I'll give you my honest assessment. It is my belief we still have time to reestablish the network before the invasion. We desperately need the northern flank to protect the invasion force. The only surviving member of the Belgium section has moved across the border to Lille. He's being harbored in a safe house awaiting my orders. Juggler circuit in northern France will coordinate movements for Belgium until we get our own radios back in the field. I believe that if we can get a trusted radio operator and a new set of codes, I can reestablish and organize the resistance. Nevertheless, we have to act quickly. We can't afford to wait several weeks for N to send in another team. I've got to pick up the pieces from what I have left and then go from there. That's why I need you, Miss Tate."

Vivian nodded her head. She turned to Penelope, looking her in the eyes. Penelope was now the subject of the discussion, "She is a trained radio operator and knows the code work. Officially, she's our records keeper, but in reality, she's our expert in deciphering the undecipherables. If she leaves, it will mean F section will be affected as well."

"We've taken that into consideration, too, Miss Tate. I think it will only be a matter of weeks at the most, during the moon period, of course. You'll still have Henry Parks, the code master to decode your undecipherables, if needed," added Gubbins.

Newman also voiced his concerns, "Yes, I can understand your concern, Miss Tate, but I'll only need the radio operator to accompany me on the clandestine landing and coordinate from Lille. Once we establish a secure foothold, your radio operator can return on the next moon flight. We won't need her to go on from there. During this period, N can take the time it needs to send in additional assets."

Gubbins coughed out loud, indicating it was his turn to speak, "Miss Walsh, you can see the seriousness of the situation. They could use your expertise."

Vivian spoke, giving Penelope permission to speak, "It's your choice, my dear. We don't want you going in the field unless you're up to it."

Penelope sat upright in her seat with confidence, "Yes, of course I'll go in. When do we leave?"

"That's settled then," said Gubbins. "As soon as Belgium section can work out the details, we'll send her in with the rest of the team on the moon flight. We'll go in using the Lysander out of Tangmere. Thank you, Miss Tate, Miss Walsh. You've been a great help."

After leaving Tempsford Field and their detailed debriefing, Penelope and Vivian returned to London in the big, green sedan. When they arrived at Baker Street, Vivian told Penelope to meet her at the Orchard Court office. There, Vivian briefed Penelope on preparations.

"Effective tonight, young lady, you'll be officially

assigned to N[1]. As we've previously discussed, I don't need to tell you about the seriousness of the situation and the importance to the invasion. You've already gone through the entire SOE training course. Therefore, you'll leave tomorrow morning, for Beaulieu Manor. There, you'll receive up-to-date training and instructions on your mission into France." Vivian looked on her desk where she kept a large desktop calendar with the moon periods depicted, "I would say they'll probably send you in by the end of the week. Of course, it's up to N section to pick the day. They're calling the shots now. Is there anything you want to update on your emergency data card?"

"No, ma'am, everything is current. I've left Sarah in good hands. If anything should happen to me, I want Mr. Mattingly to take custody on Sarah's behalf. It's all there on the card." She added, "But nothing's going to happen, like Newman said. I'll be back at the end of the moon period."

"Very well, my dear. I'll send your card up the street to Norgeby House. They'll handle your affairs until you return. You're free to go. Take some time off and be with your family. I won't be there to send you off when the time comes, N section will, of course, supply their own escorting officers. You are free to stop by here any time before your departure, if you care to."

"That won't be necessary. Thank you, Miss Tate for everything you've done. I'll see you when I get back. You can save your *merde*[2] for my return." With that, Penelope gathered her belongings and left Orchard Court for the last time.

* * *

HAL MATTINGLY CALLED several times at Penelope's flat

looking for her, but each time Mrs. Mitchell said she had no idea where she was, "She came home from work early one afternoon and started packing."

Hal changed into his best civilian clothes; a sport coat with silk tie and he borrowed a car from the motor pool. He had to know for sure if she had gone overseas. An hour and a half later, he was in Knightsbridge. He parked the car alongside the street near Harrods's department store and walked the block and a half to the Studio Club. Every time he'd been there in the past, he was with Penelope. You had to be a member of some special unit in order to be granted entry into the club. The door attendant was very particular on who he allowed into the club. He hoped that he would recognize him from the numerous occasions he was with Penelope. Hal walked up the stairs and knocked on the black door. The door attendant opened it and stood blocking the entrance.

"I'm here to meet Miss Walsh. She told me she'd be here this evening."

"Sorry, old boy, but you must be a member to enter."

"You know me, I've been here before. Just last week, remember?"

"Sorry, like I said, you must be a member. Now be off with you. There are plenty of places for you young Yanks to hang out," he said as he closed the door.

It started to rain slightly then increased in intensity while Hal was still standing on the porch. He turned around to walk back to the car when the door opened and a young officer came out. "I couldn't help but overhear, but were you looking for Penelope Walsh?"

Hal turned around, "Yes, she's my gal. I've been looking for her for the past two days. I was hoping she would be here tonight."

The young man, wearing a British army uniform with

the rank of captain said, "There's a pub around the corner, about a block and a half from here. Not the greatest, but they do have suds. Meet me there in fifteen minutes." Then he turned around and went back into the Studio Club.

Hal had nothing to lose. It was raining steadily now, and he didn't have the big, green umbrella, so he needed to get out of the rain anyway. He walked briskly around the corner. He turned to his right and walked further and then saw the light from the tavern. He walked in and sat at the bar. No sooner had he ordered his first beer than the young Captain came in dry, folding his umbrella.

He did not speak a word, but sat next to Hal and ordered a beer from the bartender. After taking a few sips from his pint, he turned to Hal and said, "Let's have a seat," and motioned to a table at the rear of the tavern. Both men came off their stools and took a seat at the table. The Captain spoke in a light voice so no one would over hear him.

"I've seen you two before at the Studio Club. Several times actually. She's a darling. Most of us would do anything to be in *your* shoes. Judging from the way she looks at you, I would say she's quite in love with you. Anyway, I'm with an SAS parachute regiment. It's not important you know my name. If fact, it might be best that you don't. I'm not at liberty to discuss operational matters, but I can tell you that Miss Walsh won't be back at the Studio Club for some time. She's left on a very important assignment. I'm only telling you this because I don't want you coming back to the Studio Club looking for her and causing a scene. There are certain things we just don't want to cause a lot of attention to, this being one of them."

Hal gulped down his beer, "I understand—you won't

be seeing me around Knightsbridge any more. Thank you for telling me this." Then he got up and started to walk away.

The Captain said, "One more thing, mate, she's extremely faithful and loyal to you. I want you to know that." Hal didn't say anything in response. He placed his hat on his head and walked out.

---

1. SOE assigned occupied countries with a country code. For Belgium and Holland, they used the letter N.
2. The French word, merde was an F section time honored salute of good luck and farewell used during the war. The expression is still commonly used today in many parts of France to express good will.

Chapter 17

SETTLING THE SCORE

The field hospital set up outside Valjeco consisted of a few tents and medical personnel. The Germans here had not seen any real action in these parts for some time. Most of the patients were suffering from small arms wounds inflected by Chetnik or Partisan attacks. The two radio specialists working inside the back of the DF van had been killed in the Chetnik guerrilla attack the previous day; both burned to death as well as the driver. The passenger, however, suffered only second-degree burns on various sections of his body, along with a slight concussion; he was released.

Gerhert was seated on a field bed, his left arm and hand wrapped in dressing to protect the burns. He would fully recover, but would be in pain. Luckily, the burn was to his left hand, which did not affect his wireless radio capabilities. Obersturmbannführer Flosberg made the trip personally from Gestapo Headquarters and was seated next to Gerhert. Aside from the two SD men, there was no one else present inside the field tent.

"What can you tell me about the attackers?" ask Flosberg.

"Typical terrorist cowards, they attacked from the protection of a narrow alleyway. I did not see their faces very well. It was a man and a woman in their early twenties. The woman was small and petite, the man, short, stocky and built like a wrestler, with black hair. He sported Chetnik attire with one exception."

"What's that?"

"His boots—my driver pointed it out. I never noticed them until he mentioned it. The male attacker was wearing an excellent pair of high-quality US military jump boots. That's something no ordinary Chetnik foot soldier would have."

"Then you agree they could be the elusive spies we've been tracking?"

"Yes, it's a very good possibility. I would say it's about a ninety-five percent probability."

"It's time we settled the score. I'm getting impatient with our results thus far. My counterparts in Belgium and France are having tremendous success. I'm taking off the gloves. It's time we go after these bandits with unconventional means. We are in the counter espionage business, are we not?"

Gerhert nodded his head, "What do you have in mind?"

"Abwehr is holding a high-ranking Partisan officer. He was unable to provide any useful intelligence under interrogation simply because the idiot doesn't have anything, plus the Abwehr is run by a bunch of imbeciles. I can secure his release and transfer him over to us. In exchange, I'll turn him to do counterintelligence work for us just like we did to those weak-minded excuses for British officers. The Abwehr's loss is our gain."

"What's the Partisan officer's name?"

"He goes by Sava Crntza, a known, hard-core communist and a Major with the Partisan Fourth Zone in Slovenia."

* * *

JOSEF, Tess, and Stefan, under heavy Chetnik escort, made it back to regional Chetnik headquarters in Rava Gora. Colonel Hueron was there and thankfully still alive. He had had a rough day and a half. They eluded several Partisan ambushes and German attacks. On one occasion, after they narrowly escaped German reprisal attacks, Partisans, using Allied supplied, automatic weapons, ambushed them as well. Two Chetnik boys were taken prisoner. Hueron escaped with his Chetnik escorts, but not before they witnessed the Partisans brutally kill the two Chetnik boys. One Partisan officer pulled out an American Colt .45 automatic pistol and emptied his magazine into the boys at close range while they were lying face down on the ground. Hueron was in shock as he witnessed the ordeal. The two boys were not more than thirteen years old. The three agents met at Mihailovich's camp and discussed their preparations for the first airdrops.

Hueron continued, "I've secured the landing site. We've selected this site because it can be easily defended. The Chetniks can protect all approaches. The Germans, or Partisans, for that matter, will not get within ten miles of this place without being cut to pieces. The Chetniks have a restored American fifty-caliber gun salvaged from a downed B-17." Hueron placed an English cigarette in his mouth, "How did it go on your end?"

Josef gave him a full debriefing and told him about their escape using a grenade on the DF van.

"The DF vans are news to me. Baker Street didn't expect the Gestapo to have them in the Balkans. Thus far, they've been limited to the major cities in other parts of Europe. It looks like they may have become more sophisticated in their electronic gathering techniques."

"There's another thing," added Josef. "The DF vans are heavily armored. Much more so than what I would expect. It's a good thing we used the grenade and it went off *under* the vehicle, which was less protected. If it had gone off on the side, there would have been minimal damage. When Tess and I opened fire, the bullets seemed to do little damage. It's almost as if they just ricocheted off. We might have had a better chance using Thompsons or better yet, a BAR (Browning automatic rifle)."

"We'll request those with the next drop. I'm sure your friends at OSS will have no trouble getting the weapons for us."

Next, Josef and Hueron prepared their transmission request for Tess. That night, Post Celeste transmitted a full request back to OSS Cairo using Josef's SSTR-1 radio and detailed Hueron's report of Partisan atrocities using Allied supplied weapons. The reply came in, to expect a full load from a B-17. Mihailovich would get his supply requests, including three Tommy guns and one BAR.

Tess then connected her Mark II radio and transmitted the exact radio request to SOE Cairo with one exception; the airdrop would be scheduled three hours *after* the OSS drop. She waited a full thirty minutes to transmit and over a different frequency band. That way, Gestapo listeners would have to retriangulate her transmission. The reply came back from SOE almost immediately to expect the airdrop at the requested time and place.

* * *

AT 0800 HOURS the next day in Cairo, Tobe McAdams received the radio reports from Team Hueron. As usual, they requested more arms and explosives. He picked up a pen and made a few notes on the side of the cable. He would authorize the drop request personally. It would consist of minimal amounts of food and no weapons or explosives as Hueron requested. Instead, further shipments would be diverted to the Partisans. After his supply request was finished, he locked his office and walked downstairs to the streets below. He called for a cab to take him to Cairo.

Once inside the city, the waters of the Nile divided to make an island called Gezira. The moorings on the western side of the island were crowded with houseboats rented to visitors with means at their disposal. McAdams knew exactly where to go. He had been to this location several times during the year to meet a young, Russian diplomat known by the name of Fritz. Nobody knew Fritz' real name. That was the only name he was known by. At first glance when you looked at the Russian diplomat in his late twenties, he could have easily been English or even American. He spoke excellent English with a slight American accent.

As McAdams approached the boarding plank, an English-speaking servant stopped him and said, "It's early, the master isn't awake yet, but you can come aboard. I have some coffee ready."

"Wake him up. I don't have all day. I need to get back to the office."

"Please come inside and have a seat. I'll announce your arrival."

The servant escorted McAdams aboard the lavishly furnished houseboat where he took a seat in the kitchen. He could smell the fresh coffee brewing.

"You talked me into it. I'll have one. Lots of cream and sugar, of course."

The servant brought the sweetened coffee to McAdams and placed it before him, "I'll wake the master. He was up very late last night," then he left the room.

McAdams sipped his coffee and looked out from the small window of the kitchen. He could see several boats lined along the waterway. Many of the occupants were just stirring. This was obviously a place where people partied until wee hours of the morning. Before McAdams could finish his cup of coffee, Fritz came in. He was dressed in a silk shirt and white trousers and had obviously freshened-up before meeting McAdams. He was a good-looking fellow with muscular features. He was also the number two man for the Soviet NKVD[1] Cairo and McAdam's Soviet controller.

"What brings you out here at this time of the day? You know you're not supposed to meet me in broad daylight."

"How long do you expect me to keep up this charade? Hueron is asking for more supplies. I've delayed him for too long."

Fritz burst out in an uproar of laughter as he sat down and poured himself a cup of coffee from the carafe, "That all depends on *you,* my friend."

"I don't see the humor in this. What are you talking about?"

Fritz, still chortling with excitement said, "I was up all night with our signals people. In fact, I just recently went to bed." Fritz placed the coffee cup down and leaned closer to McAdams, "You've been outfoxed again. Our signals department intercepted a wireless transmission from the Americans. Your team inside Chetnik territory has sent their requests for more supplies directly to the Americans using their *own* radio set."

* * *

IT WAS ALMOST three in the morning at the drop zone. Josef and Hueron placed the flare pots in preparation for the airdrop. As they finished, they heard the sound of a single aircraft overhead. Everyone ducked for cover and waited. Hueron, with his good eyesight, tried to get visual confirmation on the B-17. It could just as easily be a German Junkers preparing to launch a ground attack on their position. As the noise grew louder, Hueron used his binoculars and saw the outline of the big four-engine aircraft. It dropped down to one thousand feet above the terrain. They flashed the white Morse code letter of B.

"That's them," he yelled to Josef.

Josef took out his Aldus lamp and flashed the coded response letter of W. The B-17 began its circular maneuver and then dropped the canisters. They counted seven large parachutes and three smaller ones. Once the drop was complete, the B-17 reversed course and climbed away. This was the largest airdrop in Chetnik territory thus far during the war. A small army of Chetnik fighters emerged from the poplars and willows and recovered the canisters. Hueron left detailed instructions for the fighters to take the canisters to Mihailovich's headquarters immediately. Once the canisters were secured, everyone waited for the second aircraft to arrive.

Josef took out his flashlight and went over his notes, "Tess says the British code letter for their airdrop is Alpha. We'll respond with X-ray. This came straight from Cairo. There should be no confusion on the code words unless it's done intentionally."

"When they're ready, send the reply," said Hueron.

Two hours later, a British Halifax showed up and circled, but flashed the wrong code letter. Upon seeing this,

Team Hueron was not surprised. They did nothing and after a few minutes, the Halifax left the area. The Halifax crew would simply explain the wrong code letter had been used and the drop canceled.

Hueron extinguished his flare pot, "Let's get back to Mihailovich's camp and see what Uncle Sam brought us."

When they arrived at Mihailovich's headquarters, the General was already waiting with the sealed canisters. Tess was with him inside the small hut, which was by now becoming all too familiar. Tess had changed into her nighttime, clandestine attire, which consisted of a short, black, wool coat, dark-brown corduroy pants and a dark-brown blouse. She was talking to Mihailovich and going over the supply list when Hueron and Kostinic walked in.

"Everything went like clockwork," said Hueron to the General. "Your men did an outstanding job. Unfortunately, as predicted, the British shipment never arrived. The aircraft gave the wrong interrogation signals. Let's go ahead and open the canisters."

Mihailovich motioned to his men and they immediately began the process of opening the canisters. Everything Mihailovich requested was dropped, even the three Thompsons and BAR Josef had requested along with several rounds of ammunition. The supplies were a welcome relief to all the Chetnik forces, especially the one hundred and fifty thousand dinars.

Josef handed Mihailovich the bundle of dinar notes. "That is a small token of appreciation for what you have done for the Allies. I only wish we could have gotten you more and sooner," said Hueron.

Josef took out another package marked with his name and opened it. Along with the package, there was a small note attached, written in code. It was from his good friend,

Dick Vojvoda. Once Josef decoded the message, it read as follows:

I HOPE THIS PACKAGE FINDS YOU IN GOOD SPIRITS. EVERYTHING YOU REQUESTED IS IN THE CANISTERS. ALSO ENCLOSED IS A PORTABLE NAVIGATION DEVICE TO HELP STEER FUTURE AIRCRAFT TO YOUR DROP ZONES ALONG WITH A KLAXON PHONE. DIRECTIONS ARE INCLUDED FOR YOUR CONVENIENCE. PLEASE USE THEM FOR ALL FUTURE OSS AIRDROPS.

REGARDS, DICK

Josef unwrapped the packing material, took out the two pieces of equipment, and then began reading the instructions. Tess moved closer so she could get a better look, "We called them S phones. Directional microwave transceivers that allow air-to-ground communications. They're very effective if both the aircraft and the ground station know how to use them. They work on a very narrow frequency band. I've been told the Gestapo has no means of tracking the transmissions. This could be the wave of the future as far as covert communications are concerned."

"I can see that. It will also put *you* out of business."

* * *

MCADAMS WAS FURIOUS. When he returned to SOE Yugoslav section, he still had not gotten over his rage for what Hueron had done. His orders were clear. All radio transmissions back to SOE home station were to be handled by the British, not the Americans. This was a directive not from SOE, but from Churchill himself. He had no choice. He would have to notify London immediately. Hueron would be recalled. He would insist on that. The only concern was whether London would query him on how he got this information. He already had an explanation. All he had to do was go down the street and confront O'Donnell and blame him. He would deny it, but they would have the air movement orders to disprove otherwise. He picked up the phone, "Get me OSS Balkans, immediately!"

---

1. Soviet State Security service during World War II. The NKVD was later named the KGB.

Chapter 18

DOUBLE EXCHANGE

It was the end of October 1943. Italy had just fallen and the Italians had surrendered to the advancing American forces. The Allies were moving up the Italian peninsula toward Rome. All Italian forces in the Balkans surrendered. This was a terrible setback for the Germans. The Germans could not afford to send any troops from the Russian front to help. Hitler ordered all his forces in Yugoslavia to hold their ground until reenforcements could be brought in from other parts of occupied Europe. Flosberg moved his staff to SS Regional Headquarters at Jazak monastery in the Fruska Gora hills. This area was not in control by the Partisan or Chetnik forces, so it was the likely choice to set up headquarters.

The SD counterintelligence section took over the northeast wing of the structure, which was a fortress in itself. Flosberg sat at his desk with Gerhert behind him. Major Crntza was seated at the front of the desk, facing the two. A week earlier, Flosberg staged an elaborate escape by Crntza, even issuing a press release to all local media outlets that a high-ranking, Partisan officer had escaped from the notorious Gestapo prison at the Hotel Palace in Belgrade. Crntza returned to a hero's welcome to his unit. Instead of providing intelligence to Tito's Partisans about German counterintelligence matters, it was now the other way around. Crntza was supplying Flosberg with information about Tito and his clandestine activities. In addition, Flosberg was able to turn Crntza to use one of his Soviet contacts in Cairo to supply information that was even more valuable. In particular, matters related to Soviet activities within Yugoslavia. Therefore, despite the huge setbacks in the war, Flosberg was now in possession of some of the most sensitive and damaging information on SOE and OSS activity in the Balkans. No one in the Partisan ranks suspected, the Gestapo had turned Crntza.

"You have cooperated fully, Major, but I must remind you that in exchange for letting you return to your Partisan unit, you must provide useful, verifiable counterintelligence, or you will be in breach of our agreement. Do I make myself clear?" said Flosberg.

Crntza was a Montenegrin in his late twenties, of medium height with dark skin and black hair. He nodded his head, "Yes, I'm fully aware."

"We have you on a short leash. You are under constant surveillance. We know your every move as well as those of your family. So, let's pick up where we left off yesterday. What is the latest from your contact in Cairo?"

Crntza began to sweat as the two German men waited for his response. "The British are extremely upset at their man in Chetnik territory."

"You mean Colonel William Hueron, of course?" asked Flosberg.

"Yes, of course that's who I mean. They're recalling

him back to London and sending in a replacement from Vienna."

Flosberg turned to look at Gerhert, raising an eyebrow. "What about the courier and radio operator?"

"They still don't have names. They're using code words. All I can tell you is it's a man and a woman. The man goes by the code name Alum and the woman by Celeste."

Gerhert asked, "When will the exchange take place?"

"I don't know. For all I know, they could have already replaced Hueron."

"All right then," said Flosberg. "Your instructions are to find when this exchange is going to take place and how it will be carried out. I'll have my driver take you back to Belgrade. The place is loaded with communists. We'll meet here again in four nights. This should give you plenty of time to make your contacts."

Flosberg stood and walked to the door and opened it, "I'll have some of the plainclothes men take you back." Crntza rose and moved swiftly out of the room. When he was out of sight and down the hall, Flosberg closed the door and asked Gerhert, "I told you good police work always comes at the right moment. Now what's the latest from the technical side?"

"I was waiting to hear from Crntza to corroborate the information from my listeners. It looks like we have broken the Allied codes working in Chetnik territory. The elusive *pianist* we've been searching for has given us the codes. We can now read all incoming and outgoing messages to her radio. Crntza story confirms what my technicians have already discovered. The radio operator is definitely a woman and she's been recalled along with Hueron. I'm afraid we're running out of time to catch her, but we do have a small window of opportunity if we act quickly. Post Celeste is scheduled to come on the air in fifteen minutes."

Tess's radio came to life at her scheduled transmission time. They were operating, as usual, in a small farmhouse with two rooms. The aerial was placed outside the window in one of the back rooms. It was a long message. Josef peddled the hand-crank and was seated next to her as she wrote the coded message on a piece of paper. Then the Mark II radio went silent. Cairo was finished with their transmission. She began decoding the message.

"This could be a while," said Tess. "Isn't there something that you and Hueron have to do right now?"

"The Colonel is monitoring a Chetnik attack on a German supply column. He won't be back for another two hours."

Tess took off her headset and began coiling up her aerial. She tore out a sheet from her decoding tablet and began her work, "Then you can help me. I want you to write this down as I look up the codes."

As Tess was reading out the code words, Josef could not believe what he was hearing. First, there was a demand from SOE Cairo to break off all contact with OSS. They obviously discovered they were transmitting on the other radio to OSS. Second, and this came from the highest authority (meaning Churchill himself), was that Colonel William Hueron was to be recalled back to London by first available means and his radio operator to follow shortly thereafter. Third, he and Tess would coordinate the replacement officers being transferred in from Vienna. Finally, SOE Cairo was shutting down and moving their entire operations to Brindisi, Italy. From now on, all radio transmissions would be directed to and from Brindisi. Tess handed him the last of the coded messages. It read:

WE HAVE THE INFO WE NEED ABOUT CRED-
IBLE DAGGER-STOP
THANK YOU-STOP
YOU HAVE BEEN MOST HELPFUL-STOP
HOME STATION-CAIRO-STOP

"They're shutting us down, Tess. Right when Mihailovich's forces are doing the most and re-supplied the best, they've ever been. I can't believe they're doing this."

"The OSS radio is scheduled to come on the air in two hours. That's perfect timing for Hueron when he returns. I'm sure he'll be delighted to hear the news."

Josef was in a state of disbelief. He felt strongly that Mihailovich's forces would make a significant contribution to the Allied victory, especially now that the Italians had surrendered.

"You know, Tess, when Mihailovich opened the package with all the money, you know what he did? He called in all his senior officers and asked them to distribute the money to the families who contributed to the resistance. He told them he wanted all those who suffered, compensated. He took no money for himself."

"He's quite the humble man."

"You know what Tito would have done with one hundred and fifty thousand dinars? He would have kept it for himself and built an even larger villa on Hvar."

Two hours later when Hueron returned, he, Josef, and Tess huddled around the SSTR-1 radio set in the farmhouse. They were reading over the latest wireless messages from OSS Cairo. It was true; the Italian victory gave the Allies a foothold closer to the continent to stage wartime activities. In addition, OSS was reporting that Baker Street was extremely upset with them for transmitting wireless radio traffic directly to the Americans. Hueron was being recalled immediately. He would travel to the coast with the retreating Italians forces, where he would meet up with another British mission, and evacuate by sea. Tess and Josef were to stay in the field and wait for their replacements. It was to be a double-exchange. SOE would coordinate the rendezvous. Furthermore, OSS Cairo wanted to contact Josef by S-phone. Scheduled time for transmission was in two nights, at 0300 hours. Josef was indeed looking forward to the call.

Chapter 19

THE RENDEZVOUS

It was the first week of November, 1943. The weather in Yugoslavia was changing. Temperatures were falling and the winter season was rapidly approaching. Hueron was leaving shortly by courier line. Josef and Tess were gathered with him around the small oven inside the farmhouse used as their headquarters. Hueron reflected to his team for a moment.

"We've accomplished our objectives on this mission. Namely, determining the true credibility of Draza Mihailovich and his Chetnik forces. It's unfortunate we're stuck in the middle of an elaborate chess match. I only hope that in time, history will not forget what the Serbs and their Chetnik fighters contributed to the war effort."

"What about you, Colonel? What will they do to you?" asked Josef.

"SOE doesn't let their operatives have a certain amount of discretion in the field as your General Donovan does. I will probably be reassigned to some other insignificant task, back at Baker Street. Home station needs you two to stay here and coordinate the exchange of our

replacements. After that, you'll probably both be transferred to other units."

The next day, Hueron officially received his follow up
orders for himself and the rest of his team. As Josef
already knew, Hueron was to make his way down south, to
Dubrovnik, and escape by sea. Tess and Josef were to meet
the new organizer and his radio operator, code names
Henry and Thomas. Once they escorted the two replacements back to Mihailovich's headquarters, Josef and Tess
would leave on Hueron's same escape route by sea. Josef
and Tess were to meet the replacements at the railway
station buffet in Stremska-Mitrovica in four days. The train
was scheduled to arrive at 1830 hours in the evening.
There, Josef and Tess would introduce themselves with the
code words, "Do you need a hotel?" The response would
be, "Yes, but only for one night." They had no descriptions
of the men other than they were coming in from Vienna
and traveling together.

Hueron told Josef, "You're on your own from this day
forward until you get safely back to Italy. You'll have to
secure the rendezvous point ahead of time. Take whatever
Chetnik forces you need."

"We can take care of it. I'll make sure," said Josef.

"I'll start packing for my trip home."

* * *

BACK AT JAZAK MONASTERY, Flosberg and Gerhert
were going over their counterintelligence activities. What
Allied intelligence didn't know was that by this time in the
war, German counterintelligence efforts had broken all
Allied codes in most of the continent, including the
Balkans. It had taken some time, but Gerhert, and his technical staff were finally able to duplicate Post Celeste's fist

and sent messages to SOE Cairo and received replies. The latest message stated another agent coming in from Vienna along with his radio operator were replacing Hueron and his team. All the Gestapo had to do was question anyone coming in on the train from Vienna who remotely resembled an Allied agent. In time, they would have their men. The British had underestimated the SD and their capabilities. Flosberg and his staff were extremely good in identifying such individuals. Also, they had the exact rendezvous location. All they had to do was slip their people in place. It would be a double operation, successfully penetrating the Serbian cell. Flosberg had a map of Yugoslavia spread out over his desk and pointed to Gerhert as he spoke.

"Once the railway Gestapo make the arrest on the train, I want the two British agents brought before me. We'll extract whatever information we can out of them before we make the swap with our people. I already have people in my department who can easily fill in for the two. The British will never know what hit them. It'll be just like we did in Belgium and France."

"What about the train schedule?"

"It's simple—we'll delay the train and announce over the wires that the train *is* on schedule. With the delay, the two British agents waiting for their replacements will have to honor the schedule at the agreed-upon time. This gives our people enough time to monitor their movements in Stremska-Mitrovica. They'll have no choice but to give up their identities because they'll have to wait for the train to arrive from Vienna. Once the train arrives, our imposters will get off and make contact with the two agents, except, they'll be our men instead of their replacement British agents."

"Can I make a suggestion, Herr Flosberg?" asked Gerhert. "Rather than have the two British agents arrested on the train *before* they get to Stremska-Mitrovica, why don't we let them run. Let them feel their mission was successful. That way, it will further give the Allies a sense of security. That's what SD did in Belgium and it worked. They ended up arresting the entire northern France and Belgium circuits by letting them *run*."

Flosberg took out a cigarette and began to smoke, obviously thinking about his response, "If what you told me is correct as far as the Team Hueron agents go, they don't know the identities of their replacements, because they were only given code names."

"The only risk I see is if one of the agents knew the actual name of one of the agents *prior* to leaving England. That is very unlikely because that's the whole idea of using the code names instead of using their real identities in the clear."

"I like your way of thinking, Herr Gerhert. You'll make an excellent detective once the war is over. We can get more out of them without actually doing any interrogations. We'll let them run."

With Colonel Hueron safely on his way to the Adriatic coast with full Chetnik escort, Josef and Tess could concentrate on the replacement plan back at Mihailovich's headquarters. They had a map of all Yugoslavia spread out on the table in the barn they were now using as a base of operations. Josef detailed and highlighted the map showing the railway lines, roads, telephone and telegraph wires, and the location of the town of Stremska-Mitrovica. "I don't like this location. If it had been up to us to coordinate the rendezvous point, I would have chosen a different city. One that was much more secure. There're too many traps at the rendezvous point. There're not enough places to take cover until the agents emerge from the station. We'll be exposed the whole time."

Tess looked over a map of the city, "The rendezvous is scheduled for six-thirty at night, assuming the train is on schedule. It will be dark by then. We could use the café across the street and pretend we're having a meal and then at the last moment we can emerge."

"That will work, but it will also prevent us from continuously monitoring the site for a possible ambush."

"Well then, how about a picnic? We can spread a blanket out on the square across the street from the train station. We'll eat and enjoy our supper until the last moment."

Josef rubbed the stubble on his chin as he contemplated the possibilities, "That would give us the opportunity to see if the Gestapo is waiting for us."

As he looked closer at the city map of Stremska-Mitrovica, Mihailovich and several of his officers entered the farmhouse. They had just come back from a meeting with highly placed informants in Nazi-occupied Belgrade, "Josef, I must speak with you at once. There have been some very important developments I must pass on to you that we've recently discovered." Mihailovich took a seat on the floor and the two other Chetnik leaders followed. Mihailovich then reached into his tunic, retrieved a large bundle of papers, and unfolded it on the dirt floor. One of the Chetnik officers held a lantern closer to the document to provide additional lighting.

"I've discovered significant developments on German intelligence units inside Yugoslavia. This was probably not known to the Americans or the British before your arrival. I am passing this on to you because it could save your life. At the moment, there is an internal struggle inside the Third Reich between two rival intelligence agencies: The Abwehr and the Sicherheitsdienst. The SD is politically controlled by the SS in Berlin and the Abwehr by the military from Admiral Canaris' office in Hanover. The two are fighting among themselves as to who is ultimately responsible for counterintelligence operations. At the moment, the SD is having huge successes in Belgium, Holland, and France and the Abwehr is trying to make up some of their lost ground here in Yugoslavia."

"This sounds more political than operational. How does this affect our replacement efforts?"

Mihailovich continued, "Stremska-Mitrovica is loaded with Gestapo agents, both Abwehr and SD. They could both be after you with the other not knowing about it. The city is strategically important because it crosses the Sava River and is a major rail junction into and out of Belgrade. You may have a difficult time unless you have my support. Stefan and his men will be no match for the highly trained and battle-hardened SS. You'll need real transportation into and out of the city. I can offer a petro vehicle procured from one of our civic leaders from the surrounding area. He's offered his utility truck. It's not much and doesn't have the speed of the Gestapo vehicles, but it will get you in and out of the city safely and quicker than horses. I can also offer you additional men to help with the rendezvous and help cover your rear."

"All right, where would you suggest we use the vehicle?"

"You'll have to get in and out of the city as inconspicuous as possible which means moving in the cover of darkness and during curfew hours. We can disguise the utility truck using livestock, probably sheep or goats because that's all we have. Get into the city early in the morning before dawn and return to the countryside after ten at night using empty milk cans. The Germans will allow essential workers access during curfew hours. I have a safe house you can stay at before and after the rendezvous.

Here is the address." He handed Josef a small slip of paper, "You'll have to memorize the location as well as the security code words. This is one of our best locations. We do not want it compromised. All we need to do now is come up with the right credentials for you and Tess. The other two British agents without credentials will, of course, have to be concealed in the vehicle until you're safely in the countryside."

"Can you get the credentials to get through curfew hours by rendezvous time?"

"That's not a problem. I can have them for you by tomorrow. All I need is your approval."

"Let's do it. As far as additional men, I'll leave that to your discretion. I don't want to take away from any of your operations." Josef was indeed impressed with Mihailovich's intelligence network. O'Donnell was right about one thing; his network was vast.

* * *

IN THE FALL OF 1943, German counterintelligence was successful in reading most, if not all, of the clandestine wireless radio traffic going into and out of the Balkans. In addition, the Germans realized it was more productive to let the agents "run" for a while instead of arresting them on the spot. This had two advantages: First, by tailing the agents, the Gestapo could find out more about their mission rather than trying to torture the information out of them during interrogation. Second, by letting them run, it gave the agents a false sense of security. This was the case in the fall of 1943. The two agents sent to replace Hueron and Celeste at first followed strict security precautions. The two boarded the train in Graz separately; they were assigned separate compartments. Each time the train was stopped and boarded by the railway Gestapo, they kept their cool and their cover stories. Unknown to the two British agents at the time was the fact that railway Gestapo had identified the two men almost immediately after boarding in Austria because of their poor language skills. This information was passed directly to Flosberg's SD headquarters in Yugoslavia. Flosberg allowed the two British agents to pass on the rail line unopposed. The two men had no difficulty switching trains in Zagreb and continued their journey deeper into occupied Yugoslavia along the Zagreb-Belgrade railway.

It was during this final portion of the train trip that the two agents, after being lured into a false sense of security, abandoned their security precautions and boarded the same compartment. The two even dined together in the dining car for several meals, leaving their suitcases and luggage, along with the wireless radio, unattended in their private compartments. Flosberg's counter-intelligence staff used this opportunity to switch radio crystals altogether along with the radio codes. As a bonus, they found the operational orders detailing their instructions on how they were to make contact with Alum in clear text. Flosberg even had detailed photographs taken of the two British agents without their knowledge. Flosberg was beginning to wonder if Baker Street were staffed by morons. This was too good to be true and the SD decided to take full advantage of the security blunder. They would allow the two British replacement agents to proceed to destination and make contact with Alum and his radio operator. This would give the SD a total of four more enemy agents and possibly information on the Allied invasion of Western Europe, the ultimate prize.

* * *

JOSEF WAS STILL uncomfortable with Mihailovich's overall plan, so he took extra security precautions. He instructed Stefan and his men to discard their Chetnik uniforms, shower, shave, and dress in civilian clothes. Then, well before the rendezvous was to take place, the men would move into town disguised as railway workers and pre-position themselves on the rooftops of all surrounding buildings near the train station. They were equipped with rifles to provide cover for him and Tess. If it looked like a trap and he and Tess were arrested, they were instructed to open fire. In addition, Josef took the wooden stocks off his and Tess's Thompson, sub-machine gun, so they could better conceal them inside the picnic basket. Each of the two Thompsons were fitted with eighty-round, drum magazines to add additional firepower if needed. The added weight of the drum magazine was a challenge for Tess, but it was felt the additional firepower outweighed the difficulties of the weapon. Josef was betting that if the Gestapo were waiting, they would be lightly armed. Josef was also looking forward to talking on the S-phone for the first time. This would clear up many questions he had on his mind.

The principle of the S-phone[1] was simple. Use the small tactical navigation beacon so the onboard navigator could get an exact location of the drop or landing zone. In this case, it was a communication zone since no airdrops or landings were planned. The aircraft, a lone American B-24 Liberator, would arrive overhead, homing in on the beacon in a straight line. Josef, holding the navigation device, would allow the aircraft to fly toward him in a straight line. At the same time, someone onboard the aircraft would attempt contact with Josef using their portion of the S-phone. Josef would answer on his end and in direct and clear communications. It would be easy to identify and confirm because the person in the aircraft would be able to ask Josef a few basic security questions to ensure positive identification.

Tess was holding the navigation beacon. It was the beginning of the moon period for November. There was a slight cloud cover, but it didn't matter on tonight's mission. Josef held the S-phone, which resembled a large walkie-talkie except a headset was connected to the device. This was done more so that the volume could be controlled and adjusted in the event covert communications were necessary. Tess was unable to hear the transmissions from the aircraft so the conversation was extremely private. At the scheduled arrival time, they heard the light rumble of the B-24 Liberator as it approached. Tess held the beacon steady as Josef prepared to authenticate.

"This is Bagger two-four calling Alum," came the words through Josef's headset.

He leaned over and said to Tess, "They're calling now. The transmission is crystal clear. I can hear them as if we were talking on a regular telephone."

Tess, still holding the beacon steady, said, "Just talk in a normal tone of voice. Don't rush. It might distort the transmissions."

Josef nodded his head then spoke into the S-phone, "This is Alum, I read you loud and clear."

"Josef, it's me, Dick."

Josef could not believe it was him, but still wanted to make sure it wasn't a trap. "Dick, glad you could join us tonight. Can you tell me where I met you when I escaped out of the country?"

"It was Turkey, you fool. Don't you think I can't recognize your voice? Now listen up because we can only talk for a few minutes. Hueron's replacement and his radio operator are on their way. Their names are Jonathon

Cochran and Hugh Montgomery. We wanted you to have this information because British home station only gave you their code names. If you suspect a trap, and they don't go by the names of Cochran or Montgomery, abort the mission and get out of there as fast as you can. Do you copy?"

"Roger, I copy. Is that all?"

"When you make your way get back to Mihailovich's headquarters, we want you and Tess to leave the same way as Hueron. There'll be a PT boat to pick the two of you up, when the time comes. Leave your wireless with Mihailovich, just in case we have to contact him. That's all I got, buddy. Good luck to you. I'll see you back home, over and out."

The B-24 made an immediate one-hundred-eighty degree turn then headed back in the direction it came. Josef took off the headset and coiled up the cord around the S-phone.

"That didn't take long. What did you find out?"

"That was Dick Vojvoda, our old friend. OSS was very clever by having him send the message by S-phone. I found out the actual names of Hueron's replacement and his radio operator. Do the names Jonathan Cochran or Hugh Montgomery mean anything to you?"

"Yes, they do. I knew a Major Jon Cochran. We went to demolition school in Scotland together. He spoke German and Hungarian very well, but no Serbo-Croatian as far as I can remember. Is he the one they're sending to replace Hueron?"

"It would appear so. Can you tell me what he looks like?"

"Well, I don't remember much about him. They kept us separate because I was a woman and he was an officer. He was short, rather stocky, with slick, black hair combed over his head. I'd say about thirty-five to forty. Not much of the ladies' man, I'm afraid."

"Well, that will do. It's actually quite a lot to go with. We'll know for sure if it's him or the Gestapo. You don't think by any chance there could be more than one Johnny Cochran in SOE?"

"That would be a very slim chance."

"Do you think you could recognize him from a safe distance?"

"Not a problem. Like I said, I remember him being short and stocky."

* * *

AT ABOUT THE same time Josef was talking on the S-phone, Penelope Walsh, along with her organizer, Peter Newman, took off by Lysander aircraft at Tangmere Airfield near Chichester, for the journey across the English Channel. They began their clandestine flight from Tangmere cottage just opposite the main gates of the Royal Air Force station. The cottage was partially hidden by tall hedges and covered with ivy. After a hearty supper and a light nap in the bedrooms upstairs, the two agents were driven out to the airfield in a dark-green American Ford with the windows blackened. Their escorting officer from Baker Street accompanied them the entire way until they were airborne.

The aircraft was a small, high-winged, monoplane with a single pilot. The passenger compartment located just to the rear of the pilot held Penelope and Newman. They sat facing each other on the hard wooden seats. Their luggage and wireless radio were stowed under their seats for the journey across the Channel. They climbed to eight thousand feet and headed for Cherbourg. Once over France, they continued south past the heavily defended areas of Caen and Le Havre. Once behind the Atlantic defensives, the Lysander made a course change to the northeast, staying to the west of Paris. They dropped down to two thousand feet elevation and continued to fly using only the moon light. By 0300 hours in the morning, they had arrived overhead the airfield. The pilot came on over the interphone, "We're waiting for the signal from the reception committee. If we don't get the correct response, I'm afraid we'll have to turn back. I should know something here in a few minutes."

After circling for ten minutes, they landed in a field near Compiegne, two kilometers, north-northwest of Estrees-St. Denis and were greeted by a French reception committee. It was the first night of Penelope's two-week mission to reestablish the Belgium resistance networks. It was also the first of many clandestine operations she would conduct over the course of the war. However, unlike her fellow SOE radio operators inserted into France, Penelope would not go into any of the major cities, especially Paris. She stayed in the rural areas, transmitting from different locations and often driven in relative safety by car during curfew hours.

---

1. OSS called the S-Phone a Joan-Eleanor or Klaxon phone. The hand held transceiver was codenamed Joan. The airborne transceiver was codenamed Eleanor. For simplicity, the term S-Phone is used throughout.

Chapter 20

ABWEHR VS SICHERHEITSDIENST

The last of Post Celeste's radio transmissions were on the air. Flosberg and his staff already had their DF equipment pointed in her direction. Gerhert by now was in total control of her radio set and would be recording the entire transmission. She was still a very skilled operator and was only on the air for a few minutes. Then her set stopped transmitting. Unfortunately, he could not get an accurate DF on incoming transmissions; only her outgoing transmissions were subject to DF equipment. He could, however, record her transmission from home station and have it decoded back at Gestapo headquarters. This was the situation tonight. His technical staff was already reading her messages from Cairo. What was significant about this transmission was that SOE home station was moving to Brindishi, Italy, and they confirmed the time, date, and location for their rendezvous in Stremska-Mitrovica. Everything was ready for their trap except for one thing. Unknown to the SD, the Abwehr, through their own informants, also had the information about an exchange of British agents, which was to take place in Stremska-Mitrovica. They dispatched two of their top agents to arrest all the British agents during the exchange. Flosberg's counterintelligence operations were in jeopardy. Weeks, if not months, of effort were now at risk.

At dawn, riding in the gasoline powered truck provided by Mihailovich, Stefan and two other Chetnik fighters, along with Josef and Tess, reached the outskirts of Stremska-Mitrovica. Most of the

Germans were still asleep and there was not a lot of activity on the streets of the city. They pulled into a small warehouse used by the local resistance and unloaded the herd of sheep into the back courtyard. Here they prepared for the next and most dangerous phase of the operation. Tess was carrying her radio and Josef carried a bag containing cash and their weapons.

Josef began his briefing, "At first sunlight, Stefan, I want you and your men to leave here and take up positions on the rooftops surrounding the train station and wait for the rendezvous. I don't know how long you'll have to wait, but the sooner you get there the better your chances of going unnoticed. My guess is the Gestapo won't position their surveillance team until just before the train arrives." Josef unfolded a map of the city and spread it on the floor. "As you can see, we're not far from the station. The safe house is on the other side of town. Tess and I will stay there until sixteen hundred hours and then move into the plaza across the street from the station. From there, everyone will be able to monitor the passengers getting off the train. As soon as Tess recognizes our man, we'll make the move to approach them. Remember, if it looks like a trap, don't hesitate to open fire. We'll do the same with our weapons. In either case, we meet back here at twenty hundred hours tonight. That will give us roughly one and a half to two hours, after the train arrives at the station. Does everyone understand?"

Everyone nodded their heads in agreement then Tess began, "We'll be on foot during this last phase of the exchange. Everyone must do their best to get back here after the switch. It will be rush hour in the city so the streets will be busier than what we've experienced so far."

"She's right. If we get into a shootout, get back here the best way you know how. We'll wait for your arrival then."

Stefan and his men nodded their heads, "Understood, my friend," said Stefan.

A little after seven in the morning, Josef and Tess left the warehouse and headed for the safe house. They focused their attention on the side streets and avoided anyone who looked like the Gestapo or SS and found Mihailovich's safe house. It was a small apartment, three blocks from the train station. They knocked at the door and an elderly woman answered.

"Yes, who is it?"

Josef spoke in Serbo-Croatian, "The mayor sent me. We have meat and cheese."

"I'll need more by Sunday."

Both parties used the correct brevity codes and the woman unlocked the door. She motioned to the two to enter, "You're much too young and beautiful to be doing this kind of work," she said to Tess.

"It'll be all right. We won't be here long."

The woman gave Josef and Tess a hearty breakfast of eggs, bread, and smoked pork. Then she told the two agents to use the upstairs bedroom and rest for their time at the safe house. Josef asked the woman, "Before we leave, can we trouble you for something to have a picnic?"

"That I can give you, it's the other essentials I'm lacking, coffee, sugar, flour, meat."

Josef opened his bag and handed her several hundred marks wrapped in brown paper, "It's a gift from General Mihailovich and the US government. We are indeed very grateful for your services. We know you're taking a huge risk."

Upstairs in the bedroom, Josef took off his boots and placed them on the floor while Tess slipped off her dress in preparation for a light nap. She sat at the small vanity and brushed her hair.

"You know, it's been so long living in the field I forgot what it's like to lie down on a clean mattress. I'm used to lying on a pile of straw or hay."

Josef moved behind her and placed his hands around her bare shoulders, "Have I told you recently that I love you?"

Tess turned around and placed her arms around his waist, "No, you haven't."

"If something should happen today and I don't make it out, I want you to know how I feel about you."

Tess was quite calm. She unbuttoned his shirt and moved her hands along his chest, "Don't worry, everything will work out. If I don't see a short, stocky fellow emerge from the train station, we're getting up and walking away. It's as simple as that."

"I only wish I shared your optimism."

Tess glanced back in the mirror and noticed in the reflection something odd in the corner of the bedroom that seemed out of place. She turned around and saw Josef's US army issue boots strewn about. "You remembered everything except one very important item, your boots! If it's a Gestapo trap, that's the first thing they'll notice. I'll see if our hostess can get you something that's not so obvious."

* * *

"BELIEVE it or not the train is actually on schedule. They're due in at six-thirty," said Gerhert. "We can delay the train before they arrive. That'll give us plenty of time to survey the area and see if the enemy agents show themselves."

Flosberg replied, "I don't want to make a scene. The more inconspicuous we are the better our chances of capturing the whole team. As usual, you and I will wear civilian clothes, and I'll take only three uniformed SS men. They'll be out of sight until I whistle for them. You and I will take up positions in the café across the street and wait for the train to arrive. We'll have a Gestapo checkpoint at the station inspecting the credentials of all the passengers except the local railway Gestapo have pictures of the British agents. They've been instructed to let them pass through and act on my orders."

Just after four in the evening, Josef and Tess moved out of the safe house. They carried all their personal belongings, including Tess's wireless radio.[1] Josef carried the picnic basket and bag containing the machine guns. He was also wearing a different pair of shoes that were Serbian manufactured, instead of his combat boots. After the rendezvous was complete, they would head back to the warehouse, bypassing the safe house completely. That way, if they separated, they would not have to go back and retrieve the radio set. Thus far, everything seemed to be working as planned. They arrived at the train station and walked across the street to the plaza. It was getting late and they were running out of daylight, but this didn't matter. If anything, it helped them. They found a place to spread the small blanket on the grass to make their picnic supper. They sat so that either one could look out in front or back to make sure no one was approaching them.

Josef glanced at the rooftop surrounding the courtyard and hoped Stefen and his men were in position, "Let's see what we have for supper," Josef said as he opened the picnic basket. He handed Tess a sausage link and some bread, "The Gestapo have a checkpoint set up in the usual location at the train station. They won't let anyone out of the station until they pass all the security checks. I can also see two men in civilian clothes and two other uniformed Gestapo men with submachine guns. They could be a problem if we get into a firefight."

"Transportation?"

"One vehicle and two motorcycles, standard escort package."

Tess bit down on a piece of sausage and bread and looked on, "There's another car across the street and outside the café, sporting brand new tires; a definite Gestapo give-away."

"Could be back-up or worst yet, a second team. We might already be surrounded."

Across the street in the small café, Flosberg and Gerhert were sipping coffee ersatz. Both men were dressed in business suits with felt hats covering their heads. The two spoke in English. Across the street at the train station, people mingled about in anticipation of the arrival of the long-distance train from Zagreb. Gerhert placed his coffee cup down and lit a cigarette. He took a deep drag then exhaled, "I've delayed the train for thirty minutes, but told the railway dispatcher to post an on-time schedule."

Flosberg stubbed out his cigarette, then lit another, "No one seems out of the ordinary in town, mostly town folk going about their business." He didn't notice the couple across the street having dinner in the courtyard.

Josef and Tess finished their meal and then got up to stretch their legs. Tess did a couple of squats, very unlady-like, to get the blood circulating, "It's six-thirty and the train's still not here. I called from the house before we left and the train was on schedule. They must have been delayed somewhere on the line." Then she put her arms around Josef, "It won't be long. Listen, I can hear something, in the distance."

The train was behind schedule, but making up time fast. It appeared it would arrive at the station within the next few minutes. Josef sat back down on the grass and packed the picnic basket and checked inside the bag with the loaded Thompsons. Stalling for more time in the court-yard, he opened a container, poured some water into his cup, and took one final look around the square.

The train finally pulled into the station at 1850 hours. It was dark now and the lights from the platform illumi-nated the train as it came to a halt. The passengers disem-barked and proceeded to the Gestapo security checkpoint. Most of the passengers moved deliberately with purpose toward the exit. Cochran and Montgomery were some of the first to exit. They came off in the initial wave and moved to the checkpoint before heading to the station cafe-teria. Tess struggled to get a good look and visual confir-mation on Cochran.

"Can you tell if it's him?" asked Josef.

"I believe that's him. We'll know better once and if they clear the Gestapo checkpoint and move to the buffet."

The two British agents reached the head of the check-point and handed their traveling credentials to one of the plainclothes, railway Gestapo agents. He looked at the two men and then checked their paperwork. Satisfied with their identities and credentials, he motioned for them to proceed. Cochran and Montgomery exited the station. Tess got a good look at them and nodded her head, "It's him."

Josef and Tess got up and started to move toward the station. Just as they were about to walk across the street, they heard the sound of screeching rubber coming from around the corner. A black, German sedan came to a stop directly in front of the two British agents. They never had a chance to make a run for it. Two men emerged from the sedan holding pistols and yelled, "Hands up!" The Gestapo men staffing the checkpoint saw the commotion and quickly ran outside the station with guns drawn and yelled at all the men to lay down their weapons. Shots were fired; then automatic weapons opened up from the uniformed Gestapo men. Josef and Tess were caught in the crossfire. Everyone dropped to the ground. Shots fired from behind and upward. A Gestapo man fell to the ground as Stefan and his men obviously opened fire from the rooftops. More shots came from the two men from the German sedan and then everyone started yelling. One Gestapo man with the submachine gun returned fire on the rooftops near Stefan's position.

Josef, seeing what was going on, reached for his Thompson, pulled back on the bolt, and opened fire on the uniformed Gestapo men firing at Stefan. The .45 caliber bullets from the Thompson shattered everything in sight. Tess went for her Thompson and began to fire on the black sedan, rendering it useless by hitting the radiator. Josef saw two men emerge from the café across the street with pistols drawn and one was blowing a whistle. Josef fired on the motorcycles and the other vehicle, taking them out as added insurance. Sniper fire from the rooftops came down on the men from the café and they had to retreat inside to avoid being hit. Josef and

Tess made a run for it and headed away from the station as fast as their legs would take them, firing their weapons toward the café in the process. Bullets shattered the windows to pieces as they turned the corner. They could still hear the sounds from rifles on the rooftops. It was a horrific firefight.

When the shooting stopped, Flosberg's three SS men, riding in sidecars with machine guns drawn, approached. Flosberg and Gerhert reemerged from the café and ran across the street to the station. Four Gestapo men were lying on the pavement, dead from gunshot wounds. The two men from the black sedan were placing handcuffs on the two British agents when Flosberg arrived with his SS support and yelled, "Don't make a move! Who the hell are you and what do you think you're doing?"

The men dropped their weapons when they saw the SS troops in full uniform. One of the men said, "We're Abwehr; we've come to arrest these two British spies."

"You stupid fools! I'm Obersturmbannführer Flosberg of internal security, head of all police and Gestapo units throughout the country. You've just ruined a counterintelligence operation we've been planning for weeks and four of my men are dead because of your stupidity. I should have you two shot on the spot!"

Gerhert, with his pistol still drawn, covered the area around the courtyard. He saw the spot where Josef and Tess had had their picnic supper. The blanket was still on the grass as well as a picnic basket and a suitcase. He bent down and picked up the suitcase. It was heavier than one would expect for packing luggage. It weighed approximately thirty pounds. He undid the latches and saw Tess's Mark II radio and codebook. During the exchange of gunfire, she had abandoned the radio and run for her life. Gerhert closed the case and returned to Flosberg and the fiasco in front of the train station. Flosberg was on the verge of hitting one of the Abwehr men when Gerhert held his arm, "Leave them be. I think you should have a look at this."

Josef and Tess made it back to the warehouse. They quickly closed the large wooden door and fell to the floor completely exhausted. Josef gasped for breath, "I can't believe we made it out alive. Do you have any idea of what just happened back there?"

Tess wiped the sweat from her face, "Not only was it a trap, but I'd say it was a double trap."

"What do you mean?"

"I can't fully explain it, but all I saw were Germans shooting Germans. Luckily, Stefan kept everyone pinned down until we could get out of there."

"They'll have the whole town locked down within the hour. Let's hope and pray Stefan makes it back."

Just then, Josef and Tess were startled by a commotion from the herd of sheep in the back. Stefan and his men entered the warehouse from the rear, winded and bewildered.

"We escaped through the rail yard by pretending to be working on the tracks," said Stefan. "The whole town is blanketed with SS and Gestapo. They'll have all entrances and exits to the city sealed off within the hour. Everyone is looking for you. We best wait here for at least a couple of days until the dust settles."

Josef contemplated their situation, "Under the circumstances, I'd say our mission is over anyway. We never made the exchange. Tess had to leave the radio. We have no way of communicating with home station. At this point, it's a matter of survival." Josef placed his hand on Tess's shoulder, "I'll worry about the escape route to the coast later.

Stefan, what's the best way back to Chetnik territory once we leave here?"

"We're on our own, for the time being. I'd say we attempt to leave as planned using the truck and milk cans, but two days from now. The Gestapo will eventually call off their search and move on to other things if they don't find us. We can slaughter some of the animals for food. There's plenty of water here in the warehouse. This will get us through for a couple of days."

Flosberg commandeered the local police headquarters, holding Cochran and Montgomery along with the two Abwehr men. He didn't know who to interrogate first, the British agents or the two, bumbling Abwehr men. They were using the office of the local Gestapo commander. Gerhert had both captured radio sets open and on the desk. One was from Tess, the other from Montgomery. He then spoke to Flosberg, "Between the two radios we now have in our possession, we have enough to play a serious radio game. We may yet get the information on the invasion."

After his interrogation, Flosberg determined the British agents had no idea who they were supposed to meet for the exchange. All he could get from Cochran and his radio operator was that they were supposed to meet someone. The two Abwehr men were told that two dangerous British agents were on the loose, aboard the train from Zagreb, and were ordered to intercept them en route and arrest them immediately. They even had photographs and detailed descriptions of the two individuals, which explained why they had apprehended them so quickly as they exited the station. This also explained why Flosberg never saw them, because they were in the car watching from a safe distance hidden from view from the entire operation. Flosberg determined that someone within the

Abwehr had received conflicting information or deliberately tried to botch the operation and take credit for the arrests. He was now fighting a battle on two fronts; one against the Allies and the other against his own rival intelligence agency.

* * *

TWO DAYS later after ten at night and during curfew hours, Josef, Tess, and their three Chetnik escorts boarded the truck now loaded with empty milk cans to make their escape. They had just enough petrol to get back to Chetnik territory. The five of them had stayed in the warehouse eating some of the slaughtered sheep. They had kept as quiet as possible while living there. Several German patrols, manned by Hungarians, came knocking on the door, but for fear of their lives, they did not open any doors or make a sound. The patrols eventually moved on to another building, thinking the warehouse was abandoned. Josef and Stefan decided to use the only road south out of the city toward Glusci, Bogatic, and eventually back to Mihailovich's headquarters near Loznica. They felt the closer they got to either of these towns, the more likely they would encounter Chetnik fighters who had anticipated something had come up and could help them get through the security checkpoints, which were still active along the route. Their only guise was to act as essential workers needed for food production to supply the German army. It was also a sure bet the Germans were on the lookout for a young couple traveling on their own leaving the city. It was a chance, and their only one at that, of making a safe getaway.

It was dark on the streets of Stremska-Mitrovica with the curfew and black-out in effect. A light snow was falling over the area. The utility truck they were driving only had one functioning headlight and was in desperate need of a completely new muffler. The noise of the truck could not help but draw the attention to anyone within a quarter a mile. Tess drove the truck while Josef stayed in the passenger seat. His Thompson was partially loaded and concealed under his seat at the ready. Stefan and two men were hidden as best they could, within the empty milk cans. They had abandoned their rifles during their escape from the rooftops. Their only weapon was Tess's Thompson with fifteen rounds left in the drum magazine. They all agreed that if it came down to a firefight, they would only open fire if the odds were in their favor, otherwise they would surrender and hope for the best.

They made it outside the city limits and crossed the Sava River. Here, they encountered their first checkpoint. It was a simple roadblock manned with a few armed soldiers and floodlights. As they approached, the guards motioned them to stop. Josef slowly reached under the seat and placed one hand on the Thompson. Tess slowed the vehicle to a stop. The window did not roll down so she had to open the door. A young soldier approached. Wearing a Bulgarian uniform and holding a submachine gun, he spoke in horrible Serbo-Croatian, "May I see your papers please?" as he held a flashlight into both of their eyes. "Slowly, don't be foolish and let me see your hands," he added in German.

Tess spoke in her sweet voice using her best German, "Of course, I'll need to get them out of my handbag."

The guard obviously did not totally understand her, but he moved his machine gun upwards as if to say, get along with it. Josef could make out the Bulgarian accent and took a chance with his limited language skills and spoke in Bulgarian, "It's been a long day for us. We still have a way to go. I'm going to reach for my travel papers under my seat." Josef was about to grab the Thompson and open fire, but the young guard spoke to him in a friendly voice, "Ah, you speak Bulgarian?"

"Just a little bit. Before the invasion, I was a student studying at Belgrade University. We had several friends from Bulgaria. They invited us to stay with their families during break. I picked up the language from them."

The young Bulgarian continued, "What brings you out after curfew?"

"We have all the proper credentials from the Third Reich. We're farmers providing food for the Wehrmacht. This morning we delivered sheep, goats, and milk to the local field kitchen."

The Bulgarian flashed his torch at the back of the truck and saw the milk cans. Josef interrupted the young man's thoughts, "We bring the empty cans back to be refilled."

"I see now. Well, normally I'm supposed to have you get out of your vehicle and check your cargo and papers, but since you'll be delayed further, I will insist you move on."

"That's very kind of you. I'll be happy to show you my papers." Josef relaxed his grip on the Thompson.

"That won't be necessary. I'll take your word. As you can see, we are not Wehrmacht. We have been conscripted into service for the Germans. The German Twelfth Army is greatly undermanned here in the Balkans. They're spread too thin and don't have the manpower to work these checkpoints after curfew. I was told they only have eight divisions instead of twenty-four as they're leading the Allies to believe. You can move along now. There is another checkpoint further up the road. They're manned by Croat, Ustaša units. They're no different from the

Nazis, maybe even worst. Be careful with them. They've been very trigger happy these last few days, something about an insurgent attack in the city. I don't know all the details, but be careful with them." Then he motioned his hand for them to proceed.

Tess put the truck in gear and moved on past the sentries. A safe distance away and out of sight, they stopped the truck. Josef got out, checked on the three Chetniks, and told them to be ready for possible action at the next checkpoint. They drove on, waiting to see what was in store for them up the road.

"Your Bulgarian wasn't half-bad, what did you tell them?"

Josef recapped what he told to the Bulgarian and then said, "There's more; the Bulgarian just gave us some valuable information that Allied intelligence doesn't know about. He told me the German strength here in the Balkans is only *eight* divisions instead of *twenty-four*. In addition, the Germans are extremely short-handed in the Balkans. They're using foreigners to do some of the work the Wehrmacht would normally do. He also warned us about a Ustaša checkpoint ahead. He said there could be trouble if we're not careful."

In the town of Bogatic, the road split into two directions. One went southwest to Loznica and Mihailovich's headquarters, the other toward Petlovaca and Sabac. The sleepy, Serbian village was darkened for the curfew hours and they made their way through the village without being noticed, despite the lack of muffler. However, as they approached the fork in the road on the outskirts of town, a sentry turned on a floodlight, illuminating the checkpoint. Several men armed with machine pistols quickly emerged from the shadows. Josef could make out from their tattered uniforms that they were Ustaša. He estimated that they were outnumbered. It would be difficult to talk their way out of this one. He turned his head and banged the back of the cab. Stefan came closer to hear Josef.

"What is it?"

"Ustaša—about twenty-five to thirty men. We're outnumbered. Our only chance of survival is to surrender. Hopefully, they'll send us back to Stremska-Mitrovica for interrogation by the Gestapo. I'll take my chances with them. You, on the other hand, may not have that luxury. It's up to you my friend. If you make a run for it now, you might be able to escape before we get closer."

"I know the risks, but I've sworn my life to protect you. We go with you to the end."

"All right, we'll wait until they stop us at the checkpoint ahead and start asking for credentials. At that point, I'll surrender and give ourselves up. Trigger happy or not, they probably won't shoot us on the spot."

They stopped the truck short of the checkpoint. Josef told Tess, "Turn off the engine and let them come to you." She acknowledged and did as he asked. A Ustaša officer came forward pointing a machine pistol at Tess.

"Get out of the truck, young lady."

Josef spoke up, "There's no need to be uncivilized about this. We're the ones you're looking for. I'm an American intelligence officer and the young lady is a British agent. We're surrendering."

The officer, hearing this piece of information, didn't know quite what to do. He stepped back and was about to ask Tess to get out of the truck again when two large German troop-carrier trucks with military markings, came around the corner at full speed heading into the village. They came to a stop and swerved parallel to the checkpoint. The Ustaša officer motioned for them to move on, but the two vehicles held their ground. Then a figure emerged from the back of one of the trucks and flipped the canvas cover open. The other vehicle did the same and exposed two American, 50-caliber machine guns, mounted on the beds. Both machine guns opened fire simultaneously, on the Ustaša checkpoint. Josef and Tess dropped to the floor of their vehicle for cover. They could not see anything, but they could hear the big American guns ripping into the wooden hut and surrounding area. Men screamed as the 50-caliber bullets tore their flesh to pieces. In a few seconds, it was all over.

Then a man shouted in Serbo-Croatian, "You two, get out of the truck and hop aboard. We've got to get out of here!"

Josef did as instructed just as Stefan and his two men jumped over the side of the truck. A young Chetnik fighter about thirteen years old came over to help Tess out of the driver seat, "Come, let me help you. We've been waiting for you for two days."

Josef, bewildered and dazed, came out from the passenger side and approached the vehicle with his hands up, "Who are you?" he asked.

"My name is Aleksander Radivich. They call me Propovjednik[2] because I wanted to be a priest before the war. Now, I'm in charge of this machine gun outfit. We salvaged these 50-calibers from a downed B-17and stole the trucks from the Germans. We use them primarily to cover airdrops, but lately we haven't had any. Come quickly! The General is expecting you."

Josef, Tess, Stefan, and his two Chetnik escorts hopped into the back of one of the German trucks while someone dropped the canvas cover back down. The two German trucks turned around and headed toward Loznica and Mihailovich's headquarters. Nobody noticed the lone survivor crawl away into the darkness. He had faked his death as his comrades around were mowed down by the large machine guns. Unknown to anyone at that time, the lone survivor was one of Flosberg's Partisan Informants. Working undercover in the Ustaša unit was Sava Crntza himself. He would send a report on behalf of the Partisans that he was personally involved in an attack by Chetnik forces using Allied equipment. Most importantly, he witnessed the escape of two Allied agents along with their Chetnik collaborators. No one would be more delighted to hear his reports than the Soviet NKVD.

Once safely back at Rava Gora and Mihailovich's camp, Josef and Tess went inside the General's tent to give him a detailed debriefing. There was nothing more Team Hueron could do for him.

"I owe my life to you once again, my friend. If it wasn't for your assistance, Tess and I would be prisoners of the Gestapo."

"I suspected a trap from the beginning, so I had my big guns standing by, just in case you needed the support. When you didn't turn up for a couple of days, I knew something had gone wrong. As it turned out, they were in the right place at the right time."

"There is one final request I have for you before Tess and I leave. Could you arrange for a Serbian Orthodox priest? Tess and I would like to be married."

* * *

AT 2300 HOURS, two weeks later, in the rural countryside of France, the local BBC broadcast transmitted a coded message to Belgium resistance fighters working in France. The message indicated that a Lysander was scheduled to depart from England and pick up Penelope Walsh.

Peter Newman stayed behind to escort the new

inbound agents into Belgium. Unfortunately, Newman did not survive the war. Later that day, he was arrested by the Gestapo. Eventually he was executed at Sachsenhausen concentration camp along with five other British officers.

The scheduled pick up time was three-thirty in the morning at Compiegne Field. This was to be a double, Lysander operation. The first aircraft to land would pick up Penelope. The second was to pick up three aircrew evaders. The five of them traveled to the airfield in the back of a hearse supposedly for a funeral procession. They arrived at the airfield just after midnight and hid in a farmhouse nearby in the livestock barn. Penelope coordinated the pick up from her wireless set. None of the passengers scheduled to go out that night had anything to fear. Fifty French resistance fighters surrounded and protected the airfield. However, little did anyone on the reception committee know that the Gestapo had broken Penelope's wireless messages and had men in position monitoring the Lysander operation. They were to tail the *incoming* agents as they made their way into the French cities.

The Lysander came across the English Channel at five hundred feet and entered French airspace over the heavily defended coast of Pas de Calais. The black, cloud-covered skies protected the aircraft as no German night fighters would patrol the skies in these conditions. The Lysanders came in one-by-one after rendezvousing over Arras. They circled the airfield at five hundred feet. The agent in command of the operation flashed the proper Morse code signal to the Lysander pilot. The pilot acknowledged with his signal and began his approach to the airfield.

It was a simple maneuver. The pilot set up an orbit over the airfield and when he was satisfied the airfield was secure, turned the aircraft downwind, and squared the turn to final using the three flare pots in the shape of an inverted L as a reference. The pilot touched down at the first two pots, known as A and B, and then rolled to a stop at the last pot known as C. He then made an immediate 180-degree turn and headed back to flare pot A, and did another 180-degree turn to position the aircraft for an immediate takeoff into the wind. The agent in charge was at flare pot A. He went to the port side of the Lysander and facilitated the switch of passengers. When the outbound passengers were aboard and the cockpit roof slid shut, the agent in command gave a thumbs-up signal and shouted, "Okay!" This whole process took less than three minutes after which time the Lysander was off and then the next aircraft repeated the exact same maneuver.

When the first Lysander touched down and taxied back to flare pot A, the two inbound agents got off the aircraft. Penelope didn't waste any time climbing aboard the Lysander. Both inbound agents helped Penelope with her luggage as they got off, then they disappeared into the darkness.

A few hours later, Penelope was back at Tangmere Field. Waiting to meet them upon their arrival was the head of N section along with F section vice-commander, Vivian Tate, who greeted Penelope's Lysander. Once safely back at Tangmere cottage, everyone was treated to a hearty English breakfast at sunrise.

Vivian, smoking a cigarette, sat in front of Penelope while she devoured her breakfast, "You've done a remarkable job for N. Despite the stress of being in the field, every one of your wireless reports was clear, concise, and flawless. I wish all my girls could do the same job. Your hard work and dedication contributed to the revival of the Belgium resistance. They're back on track to assist the invasion force."

"Thank you, Miss Tate, I'm happy to be of service.

Like I told you, I'd be back before the end of the moon period and here I am."

"I want you to take some time off. Be with your family and loved ones. Don't bother coming back to Orchard Court anymore. I've successfully got you transferred to Yugoslav section. They're officially calling it Force 399 now. It's much safer in the Balkans than occupied France. They could use your language and wireless expertise. When the time comes, they'll let you know when to join them."

Vivian put out her cigarette and watched as Penelope finished the last of her breakfast. She didn't say another word to her. Vivian as always, was unemotional. Deep down, she was proud of her young protégé. She wanted to smile, but couldn't. Looking at Penelope, she saw herself six years earlier; a young intelligence operative coming back from a dangerous mission. There was still a long way to go before the war was over. Vivian also knew that Yugoslavia was not safe at all and in fact was a powder keg waiting to explode. She hoped all the best for Penelope. Then she finally said, "*Merde*" and cracked an ever so slight smile.

---

1. British radio operators were instructed by Home Station to carry their wireless radios with them at all times.
2. The word preacher in Serbo-Croatian.

Chapter 21

THE PROPOSAL

Harold Mattingly was officially assigned to General Eisenhower's staff working as a French interpreter. He would accompany all Allied officers and attend meetings dealing with French matters. In particular, he was assigned as the personal liaison officer for General de Gaulle's staff. He would shuffle back and forth between Haines Lodge and Duke Street on a daily basis. He was also privy to a host of classified information dealing with the Allied invasion of Europe.

It was the beginning of December, 1943. The upcoming holiday season was bleak in war-torn London. Many shops and stores were either closed or bombed to rubble. Hal Mattingly walked the streets near Trafalgar Square. He was looking for a special gift for Penelope. For three weeks, during the moon period in November, she had simply vanished into thin air. He was completely beside himself, as neither her parents nor the military knew anything about her whereabouts. Then on a cold, fall, night while he was at one of his daily visits to Penelope's flat, the doorbell rang. It was just before curfew. Everyone in the flat was reluctant to answer the door for fear it was someone from the war department with news about Penelope's death. Hal did the duty and answered the door. He was shocked to see his beloved Penelope dressed in her FANY uniform. She had returned safely from her mission to occupied France. Mr. and Mrs. Mitchell both sprang to their feet to greet their exhausted daughter. She came in and told everyone she had been overseas and that she had brought gifts for the whole family. For her mother, she brought a small case of powder. For her father, a pipe, for Sarah, a little pair of slippers, and for Hal Mattingly, a wool sweater.

Now it was his turn to return the gesture for the upcoming holiday season. He walked into a small jewelry shop on Whitcomb Street. The clerk, an elderly woman whose husband was killed during one of the London bombings in 1941, recognized Hal immediately as he walked in. She'd been holding his special gift for the last two weeks, waiting for his return after payday.

"Oh, it's good to see you, Corporal Mattingly. You're looking dashing as always."

Hal took off his cap and overcoat and hung them up on a hook, "Do you still have the ring?"

The old woman walked back behind the counter and took out a key ring with several keys attached. She fumbled through every one of them, building up suspense for the young man and found the one she was looking for. She looked around the store for added drama as if she were on the lookout for strangers. There was no one else inside the store except for Hal. Then she bent down below the display counter, unlocked and opened the small drawer, and withdrew the little case.

"It's still here as I promised. The day you came in with that lovely, young lady at your side is something I shall never forget. It was almost as if the sunlight was deliberately shinning on her face. She was a beautiful thing, and I must say, by the looks on her face, she is deeply in love with you."

"She singled the ring out almost at once. I would have never picked it out myself. But when you let her try it on and I saw the expression on her face, I knew I had to get it for her."

"My thoughts, too, that's why I'm giving it to you at cost. Here you go," she said as she handed the small case to Mattingly, who immediately opened it up to take a glance.

"A thing of this beauty should only belong to someone who can truly appreciate it."

"Yes, I know. I've saved a month's salary for it. Here you go, ma'am," he said as he handed her the small wad of cash.

"She'll be very pleased. I only wish I could be there when she opens the box for Christmas."

"Good day to you, madam, and Happy Holidays."

Hal left the jewelry shop and headed for the Embankment Tube station. There he caught a train back to Baker Street. He was to meet Penelope for dinner that evening. He thought how best to give her the ring. Would he ask her to marry him or should he wait until Christmas and ask then? These were all questions troubling his mind, let alone his new position working with the Office of Strategic Service. As he walked south, along the busy street, he saw Penelope. She had just gotten off from work and was walking to the Tube station. She caught sight of Hal and quickened her pace. Hal did the same and the couple embraced as they met. She was not dressed in her FANY uniform, but instead wore a skirt and jumper.

"I wasn't expecting you for another hour. I knew you'd

be at Trafalgar Square, so I was hoping to run into you there."

"It's a good thing you didn't because I was doing some shopping and that would have spoiled the lot. Where would you like to go for dinner this evening?"

"The usual—it's not too far and the crowds really haven't started yet."

"Let me formally escort you." The two lovers walked together as they made their way to Brompton Road. Hal was officially banned from the Studio Club. They were not allowing any guests to enter the club in preparation for the upcoming invasion of Europe. So, they had to find a different establishment to patronize. They had settled on a Yugoslavian restaurant that specialized in Serbian food located in South Kensington. Penelope had developed the taste for the cuisine while she was a student in Belgrade and the restaurant seemed to always have plenty of stock, despite the wartime rationing.

It was early for the dinner crowd. They were, in fact, the first customers for the evening, so they were seated right away. Hal asked for a table in the upstairs dining room, so they could be alone and away from anyone. Penelope asked for a glass of wine while Hal ordered his usual, the dark, local ale. Penelope knew Hal was an interpreter for the American officers and had a lot on his mind. When they were comfortably seated and enjoying their drinks Hal said, "The tempo has stepped up. I'm shuffling to and from Duke Street several times a day. In fact, I was lucky to get away for today."

"I'm afraid I've been quite busy as well. A lot's happening on the Continent. There's also a bit of a surprise tonight. A very dear friend of mine is in town. In fact, I've asked her to join us for dinner. She recently got back from an assignment overseas. She's also a wireless radio operator. I actually helped the head hunters from the war department find her. We were students together at Belgrade University before the war. My former roommate, she was recently married."

Penelope quickly told Hal the whole story about her friends, Dick Vojvoda, Josef, and now Celeste Kostinic. Then she added, "I'm anxious to hear all the details. She was on a special mission herself, if you know what I mean."

A few minutes later, a waiter ushered Celeste Kostinic upstairs to the dining room. Immediately upon seeing her dear friend, Tess practically sprinted to Penelope and gave her a hug, "I'm glad to see you, Penelope. There's so much I have to tell you. Is it safe to talk here?"

"Yes, by all means. Hal and I have been coming here for some time, plus the fact we've got the whole upstairs dining room to ourselves. Come on, have a seat, will you?"

Hal rose from the table and pulled the chair out for Tess. Penelope made all the introductions and then Hal ordered another wine for Tess.

"Let me be the first to congratulate you on your recent marriage," said Penelope.

"It was a quick ceremony because we had to get out of Yugoslavia right away. We were married in a barn in the Serbian countryside. We had an ox and pig as our wedding attendants." Tess looked around the empty room and switched to French so the Yugoslav staff would not understand their conversations completely, "Originally, I was supposed to go out by way of a British mission in Partisan territory and Josef by sea. However, he arranged for both of us to be picked up by a maritime unit. Josef insisted to his American superiors that he wasn't leaving unless I was with him on the PT boat. We had been through the experience of being separated before and he wasn't going to go through it again."

"I forgot to tell you, Tess. It's okay, Hal speaks excellent French. Go ahead, he understands everything."

Hal asked in his fluent French, "How was he able to do all that?"

"It was all arranged by S-phone. I'm afraid I can't talk about the details, but I can tell you that Josef was able to get through directly to his superiors in Bari."

When dinner and small talk were over, Tess switched to a more serious topic and continued in French, "Josef is back at Bari. He got a promotion with the Balkan Section Field Office. He'll be coordinating activities for the Americans in Partisan territory."

"What about you, Tess?" asked Penelope.

"My commander and I were officially disciplined for our behavior and breach of protocol as established by higher authorities. I can't really discuss the details, but at the moment, I'm still in the RAAF where I'll most likely be discharged. I'll wait out the remainder of the war. Hopefully, we'll win this damn war and Josef and I'll go back to the States where I'll be another war bride."

"How long were you over there?" asked Hal.

"I was there almost three months, sleeping in tents, barns with all the fleas, lice, and ticks, sometimes in a real bed. I also learned how to ride a horse and motorcycle as well as drive a truck and half-track."

Penelope raised her wine glass, "Love, I'm so glad you're home safe and sound. I've missed you terribly."

Hal took a swallow of beer. The Allied invasion of Europe was on his mind. He knew the plans and operations and thought about Penelope and the real possibility she would be sent overseas once again before the war was over. She might not be as fortunate as Tess. It was now or never. Besides, if he were to ask Penelope for her hand in marriage, she would probably want Tess as her maid of honor. He thought to himself, they might as well hear it all at the same time.

"Since I have both of you ladies here tonight, why don't I address the two of you?" He reached inside his pocket and pulled out the small case containing the ring, "I was going to wait until Christmas, but I can't wait any longer. Plus, there's the fact that your dear friend is here with us tonight to share in what I have to say." Hal stood up from the table, took the ring out from the box, and placed it on Penelope's finger. "Penelope, this is for you, my one and only, true love. Will you marry me?"

* * *

TWO MONTHS LATER, in January, 1944, at OSS Head-quarters Bari, Italy, Josef Kostinic and Howard O'Donnell were reading over a teletype message from signals staff in disbelief. The message said it was coming from Post Celeste. It went on to report that the American officer known as Alum had suffered a concussion and was hospitalized in Belgrade. The radio operator was now transmitting from a safe house outside Novi-Sad.

O'Donnell looked at Josef, "Can you believe this bullshit? The damn Krauts are actually playing back the goddamn radios, and the Brits are falling for it hook, line, and sinker."

"It's all disinformation now, possibly to keep all the Allies preoccupied from the landings at Palermo and Normandy."

"I don't give a shit now. They've pulled the plug on Mihailovich officially at the Teheran Conference. We're to give no and I mean *no* support to the Chetniks or

Mihailovich under any circumstances. It appears Churchill convinced Roosevelt that the Partisans were killing more Germans than the Chetniks, even though we personally provided the information to the contrary. It seems Roosevelt was not in the best of health during the conference. He was reported to have been aloof and incoherent. It was said that Stalin just sat there, with a little, shit-eating grin on his face, as if he knew something all along."

"What would you like me to do, sir?"

"We move on to the Partisans. We've got a war to win. OSS and SOE are now stepping up operations to Tito. We're sending in teams on every moon period from this day forward. Our objective is to tie down as many German units as we can, so they can't be redeployed to Western Europe. For the time being, I want you here in Bari. You are now the OSS expert on clandestine operations in Yugoslavia. No one has more experience in the field than you. When my team leaders start sending in their reports from the field, I want you to decipher something out of the mess. We'll go from there."

* * *

GERHERT WAS SITTING at his desk inside Gestapo headquarters at Jazak monastery. His wireless radio game came to a close in the Balkans with the escape of Josef and Tess. Though they did capture other agents and their sets, the SD was unable to exploit their efforts. All they could do was find a few ammunition dumps and round up some resisters who were committing acts of terrorism against German soldiers. Above all, they were unable to capture the elusive Celeste and her team, mainly because of the stupidity of the Abwehr and their agents who blotched the counterintelligence operation at Stremska-Mitrovica. SD

Chief Flosberg had the Abwehr agents arrested and sent back to Berlin for discipline by SS Reichsführer Himmler himself.

The only valuable intelligence Flosberg's SD detachment was able to get out of this particular radio game was the penetration of a communist cell that provided information about communist activities and in particular, their plans for the eventual victory in the Balkans by Soviet forces. For the time, it seemed the Allies had made up their minds and cast their support to Tito and his Partisan forces. The Chetniks, without Allied support, were no longer a threat to the German Twelfth Army. In fact, it was determined that the Partisans were now using their newly acquired weapons to wage attacks not upon the Germans, but rather upon the Chetniks. The focus of SD operations would now move to Tito and his whereabouts.

Flosberg considered himself a professional criminal investigator and not a soldier. It was on this chilly morning in January, 1944 that he received a cable from Gestapo Headquarters in Berlin. It stated that the Allies had pushed ahead, captured all of Italy, and were gearing up for an invasion on the Western front. Simultaneously, the Red Army had stopped the German advance at Stalingrad. Over fifteen thousand German soldiers were forced to surrender. The SS blamed the Abwehr for stupidity and faulty intelligence on Soviet capabilities. Himmler wanted all intelligence and counterintelligence matters consolidated into one party organization. There was a major cleansing operation going on at the highest levels. In particular, the SS wanted all captured Allied prisoners shipped back to Germany. Flosberg was looking at an order to have all twelve of his captured British and Canadian prisoners deported. He called Gerhert to his office. Upon entering Gerhert saw Flosberg, looking distraught and saddened. He was chain-smoking cigarettes and drinking heavily.

"Have a seat," Flosberg said as he offered Gerhert a cigarette. "You might as well have one of these, too," and he poured a tumble of Scotch for Gerhert.

"Tell me, what is it, Herr Flosberg?"

He handed Gerhert the cable, "Why don't you read it yourself?"

Gerhert took a seat in front of Flosberg and began to read the cable and then passed it back, "It's their death warrant; nobody survives this kind of deportation. You and I know what they're talking about. They'll send them all to death camps."

"I don't want any part of this. These men are soldiers. They should have sent them to a prisoner of war camp. They were doing their jobs. I'd have done the same thing if I was in their shoes."

"You can disregard the order."

"Are you out of your mind? They'd have us both in front of a firing squad by the end of the day. No, I want you as my witness; I'm signing this order in protest. If we lose this war and the Allies start inquiries for possible war crimes, I want it officially known that I didn't want to be part of it."

"I'll countersign the order; that should suffice."

"This won't stop them from going after you, too. No, I want a complete deposition and statement from *both* of us. We'll send it along with the prisoners and we'll keep a copy in my safe. If the Red Army succeeds in breaking through the Eastern front and invades the Balkans, then I want them to find it. You see, my friend, it's not the British or the Americans I'm worried about, it's the *Soviets* who worry me the most."

Part IV

THE FINAL PUSH

Chapter 22

OPERATION BROKEN ARROW

The Allies invaded Western Europe on the beaches of Normandy in June, 1944. The OSS Balkan section set up shop permanently in Bari, Italy and conducted routine missions inside Yugoslavia since the first of the year.

Penelope Walsh and her mission to northern France in support of N section were instrumental in revitalizing resistance networks in Belgium and Holland. These units conducted sabotage and counterinsurgency operations, slowing down crack German divisions from reinforcing the beaches at Normandy. F section operations into France were reduced to near nothing. They had Jedburogh and SAS teams taking the place of secret agents dropped into the field. Penelope's language skills, talents as a wireless radio operator, and courier were needed elsewhere. At Vivian Tate's demand, Penelope was officially reassigned to Yugoslav section and stationed at Brindisi Air Base. Before she left for Italy, she accepted Hal's proposal for marriage, but they agreed to put off the official wedding date until after the war, especially since there was a turn of events in favor of the Allies. They wanted Josef and Tess to be in the wedding and it would be easier for both to attend after the war. In this way, it would truly be a celebration.

Penelope's little daughter, Sarah, was becoming quite fond of Hal. He became the father to her that she never really had. Hal was also very busy working with SOE RF section because it now appeared the Americans would bypass Paris altogether and the city would be liberated by the Free French forces headed by General de Gaulle. That evening, in August of 1944, Hal dropped Penelope off at her parent's flat in the big, green, Ford sedan and parked around the corner. This was her last night in London. The next day, she would fly by Hudson aircraft to Algiers, Algeria and from there, continue on to Brindisi.

"Come in after you park. Mother has dinner for us," she told Hal.

It was a lovely supper. Mrs. Mitchell had cooked up a large pot of stew with plenty of meat, thanks to Penelope's extra ration coupons and Mr. Mitchell opened his best bottle of port for his daughter's last night in London. Everyone sat around the dinner table enjoying the evening.

"I hear Italy can get very hot this time of year," said Aleks Mitchell.

"Yes, but I'm looking forward to being by the coast. They have some lovely beaches, so it'll be a nice change from dreary England."

Hal spoke next, addressing the whole family, "You won't be alone, either, Josef Kostinic is stationed there."

"Yes and my other dear friend from school days at Belgrade University, we can't forget, Dick Vojvoda. Josef wrote Tess and said that he and Dick worked in the same office."

"Dick Vojvoda? Yes, that name rings a bell. You did mention his name once," said Hal.

"He reminds me a lot of you. He's tall, handsome, very

distinguished, but I'm afraid he's a bit of a lady's man—something you're not, but nonetheless, he does remind me a lot of you."

Aleks Mitchell drank some port from her glass, "Wasn't he the one who had the car that got you out of Belgrade?"

"He's the one. He was very resourceful come to think of it. Between him and Josef, I'm sure they'll make sure nothing happens to me."

After supper, Hal and Penelope stayed up and talked at the table. The Mitchells and little Sarah went to bed and left Hal and Penelope alone. Hal could only stay for a little while longer because he had to get the car back before midnight. They discussed all sorts of issues like their wedding plans, honeymoon, and where they would live after the war. They couldn't agree to stay in London or move to Palo Alto. There was one thing they did agree upon and that was the same as before her mission to France; if anything should happen to her, she wanted Hal to adopt Sarah and raise her as if she were his own.

"It's a lot safer in Italy than Nazi-occupied France, but could they use you for another type of mission like you did before, but this time into Yugoslavia?" asked Hal.

"Yes, I suppose they could, but at the moment, I'm not aware of anything going on that would need that kind of urgency like my last assignment."

"Please be careful. The war should be over by the first of the year. You'll have to hold out until then."

* * *

IN EARLY NOVEMBER OF 1944, Josef's job as an OSS analyst was routine and boring to say the least. He preferred operations in the field rather than sitting behind a desk and cubical. He was looking over maps and aerial photographs for possible amphibious landings when O'Donnell burst into the office and peeked over the partition, "Any idea where Vojvoda is?"

"He should be in his office."

"Well the son-of-a-bitch isn't there! Go find him and meet me back in my office, *pronto!*"

Fifteen minutes later, Josef and Dick reported to O'Donnell's office. They closed the door behind them as the two young officers stood at attention, something rarely done within the OSS.

"Gentlemen, I'll be blunt like always. Two events have been brought to my attention. First, we're getting all kinds of reports from the field that several American air crewmembers bailed out over Yugoslavia on their way back from Ploesti. One of my OG men confirms up to several hundred flyers, as many as four-hundred. They're being held primarily in Chetnik territory. Dick, you're the air movement's officer. I want you to find a way to get them all and I mean *all* of them out."

"Sir, if I might inquire," asked Josef. "I thought we were supposed to withhold all support for Mihailovich?"

"A few weeks ago, that was the case. However, we've come across this latest information from our agent in the field. He's been inserted in Chetnik territory at the request of the president. Mainly to keep the channel open, in case we had to deal with a situation just like this. I passed his report on to Donovan and he in turn passed it on to the president. Roosevelt's exact words were something to the effect of, 'Fuck the British, I'm the commander in chief. I want my boys back home.' I think that's all the authorization we need."

"Can I ask about the other event?" queried Dick.

O'Donnell lit a cigarette and continued, "This is the one that's troubling me the most. One of our teams embedded in Partisan territory has come across some startling intelligence. This information was provided by a Nazi party member who deserted to the Partisans. He told us of flying bombs being introduced into the Balkans, presumably to be used against Allied shipping lanes, or against the Soviets on the Eastern front."

"Mother of God, we're talking about more V-1 rockets," added Josef.

O'Donnell got up from his desk, walked over to the wall map of Yugoslavia, which he had posted with thumbtacks, "They're being moved from other parts of occupied Europe. This all comes at a time when the Allied command is launching a major attack against German rail and supply routes in northern Slovenia. The attack in Slovenia is to be part of a coordinated plan to destroy all lines of communication in the Balkans. They're trying to delay or prevent the withdrawal and redeployment of German forces to the major Anglo-American and Soviet battlefronts."

O'Donnell lit another cigarette and took a deep drag to gather his thoughts then continued, "This could all be disinformation by the party member deliberately planted by the Gestapo to lead us astray. We've got to find out, so I'm sending you back in. If they're V-1's, then the Krauts are probably moving them along the Ljubljana Gap. I want you to find them and blow the god-damn things up; it's as simple as that. I just got off the secure phone this morning with Donovan, and he wants a combined British and American operation in Slovenia under Force 399 command. Josef, I'm putting you in charge of the destruction of the V-1's and rail lines. It seems the Partisans did a shitty job of attacking some of the choke points along the Maribor-Ljubljana line. I want you to go back in and personally see to their destruction."

Josef stared at the wall map, trying to get his bearings on the locations O'Donnell was spitting out in rapid succession and made a remarkable discovery, "You're talking about penetrating *inside* the Third Reich itself?"

"That's the whole point. Now you can see the importance of this mission."

Josef took a seat on the hard, wooden chair and tried to remember what he could about Slovene geography from his studies at Belgrade University.

Then O'Donnell continued, "There are two safe areas the Partisans have secured in Slovenia. One is in Dolenjska and the other is in Stajerska. The safe area in Dolenjska is too far to the south and takes too long to get to the rail sites by courier line. Therefore, I'd like to drop you and your team directly into Stajerska in the Pohorje Mountains. The Partisans have secured a drop zone near Rogla and our OSS assets assure us the area is safe for live drops. The top has a flat, grassy meadow with several acres surrounded by large pine trees. It's the highest point for miles. Even on a dark night, the pilots should easily get in and out with no trouble. Now, along with all this comes added responsibility, so effective immediately, you've been promoted to the rank of Major."

O'Donnell picked up a folder on his desk and flung it to Josef. "I want you to review this file and pay particular attention to the field reports from "Popeye." He's our OSS asset in Slovenia right now. Every wireless message he's sent to Force 399 is there. The poor guy's been embedded for the last four months with the Partisans. God knows what he must smell like. They're constantly changing locations much like you did to prevent the Germans from fixing their location, and I might add, he's done a good job of that so far. I want you to get back to me within forty-eight hours with your operational plans. After that, we have a meeting scheduled for the following night with our British allies and Brigadier Maclean to finalize the operation. Force 399 is calling this mission, Broken Arrow."

"I'll get on it right away, sir," said Josef.

O'Donnell then looked squarely at Dick, "There's a reason Donovan wants a combined British and American operation. He wants to pacify the British while we work with Mihailovich. Dick, I want you to find a way to get me into Chetnik territory. I'm going back in personally and establish contact with Mihailovich. We screwed him in the ass once and I'm damn well not going to screw him in the ass again, especially if he helps bring our boys home. If he's harboring as many as they say, we're going to need all the help he can give us."

Later that night, Josef and Dick were inside the Vault at OSS headquarters in Bari. The Vault was nothing more than a broom closet in the basement, which housed all classified material in connection with OSS Balkan operations. Josef read over the reports from Popeye and learned that he was successful in knocking out one viaduct on the single-track line from Dravograd to Celje. However, the Partisan detail under his command was unsuccessful in totally knocking out the bridge at Zbelovo or the tunnel at Lipoglav. Rail traffic was only halted temporarily along the double-track line. Furthermore, the bridge at Tremerje, south of Celje, was in the open and heavily defended by at least one-hundred German troops and was therefore, unapproachable. Josef moved the aerial photograph closer to Dick and pointed to the bridges and tunnels along the Maribor line.

"It looks to me like the bridge at Zbelovo can be approached from the ravine below. There's plenty of cover with the thick willows and tall grasses along the waterway. Most importantly, the higher ground to the south of the bridges will give us the opportunity to hit and we can watch from the cover of the forests.

"Sounds simple in theory, but can you do it?"

"I'll need a demolition expert, radio operator, and some of the best Partisan fighters in the area."

"There's a Lieutenant who joined our unit just last week, his name is Milo Kovich. He's young,[1] only nineteen, but has excellent language skills and physically built. Above all, he was a Pennsylvania coal miner before the war with experience in demolitions and mining operations."

"Okay, if you think he's right for the job, then I'm all for it. What about a radio operator?"

"All of our operators are already out in the field. It will take several weeks to get one in from the States. O'Donnell wants one now." Dick lit a cigarette and blew the smoke out over their heads contemplating the next move.

"What about the Brits? Weren't they the ones who insisted on having all their own radio operators in the first place?" asked Josef.

Dick put out his cigarette, "First thing tomorrow morning, you and I need to make a trip to Brindisi. I do believe there's an old friend of ours down there who can possibly help us out."

BRITISH SOE HEADQUARTERS was located at Brindisi Air Base where they had a special air operations wing. Dick actually knew the area well as he made frequent trips to coordinate airmovements. Dick and Josef left Bari before dawn and traveled the distance by government Jeep. It was normally a two-hour trip, but they stopped along the way for coffee and breakfast and then continued on to Brindisi. SOE headquarters was located near the flight line of the bustling air base. The two men were dressed in their US army uniforms and showed the proper credentials to the sentry who escorted them into the building.

Josef looked out toward the Adriatic Sea, "Do you think we'll see McAdams?"

"For his sake, I hope we don't, otherwise I might take a swing at him."

"He covered up everything. They can't trace anything back to him. It'll take years to declassify all the files."

It was after ten in the morning and most of the meetings and briefings were complete. As the two men entered the office of Yugoslav section, a familiar face, Penelope Walsh, greeted them. She looked more beautiful and vibrant than ever. She even had a slight suntan from time on the beach, giving her a lucent glow, "This is a pleasant and unexpected surprise to see both of you," she said and embraced each of her two friends. "I received a message this morning saying that OSS was sending two representatives down today to discuss air movement options."

"You're just the person we need to talk to. Can we go somewhere secure?" asked Dick.

Penelope directed them to the briefing room at the opposite end of the building. Luckily for his sake, McAdams was nowhere in sight. The three companions entered and she closed the door behind. The briefing room had a large oak table and several chairs and the room had the smell of the all-too-familiar stale cigarettes and tobacco, "Your secrets are safe with me in this room. No one will bother us. All the briefings are done for the day."

Dick and Josef moved closer to the wall map of Yugoslavia, "Josef, why don't you ask her since you're in charge of the mission?"

Josef began, "We need your help. OSS is planning a joint British/American operation in Partisan territory. We're all out of radio operators. We thought we'd ask if you knew of anyone who we might be able to borrow who's already trained and ready to go in."

Penelope sat down on a chair, "Do you mind if I smoke? I'm afraid I've picked up this nasty little habit while I've been in Italy. It seems all the girls smoke like chimneys around here," then she lit a cigarette and took a long drag. "Is it a clandestine operation or will they be embedded?"

"Embedded, but all I can tell you is that we need a radio operator for a very important mission that could dramatically change the outcome of the war on the Eastern front and it's extremely dangerous."

"Aren't they all? I think the last wireless we sent in lasted a week and a half before the Gestapo killed him. His transmissions were the worst I'd ever seen. I'm afraid I don't know of anyone at the moment. We've got our manning request in to London for more help, but thus far, with the events in Western Europe moving quickly, they don't need wireless operators like they used to. Further-more, they're telling us they're having a difficult time finding ones who have any skills[2] at all. I'm sorry, boys, I wish I could help, but at the moment, we're fresh out of stock."

"It was a long shot. We thought we would ask anyway and it gave us a chance to come down and see you," said Dick. "You're looking beautiful as ever. I hear you're engaged, is that true?"

"Yes, he's a delightful and wonderful man, sort of reminds me a lot of you. We haven't set a date, but it will be sometime after the war."

"Lucky man. I wish you all the best."

"Thanks Dick, what about you, anyone, in particular?"

"You know there was only *one* I was ever interested in and I let her slip away," he said as he nudged her on the shoulder with his elbow.

"You mean like the time you left me at the train platform in Sebac?"

"Stop you two," interrupted Josef. "Penelope, we'll let you get back to work, but if something should come up within the next day or two, please let us know. We've got to get back to Bari. We have a lot to do before our meeting with Brigadier Maclean."

Penelope turned white as the blood drained from her face upon hearing this, "You mean all this has something in connection with *that* meeting?"

The two men looked at each other as if wanting either to speak. Josef finally said, "Why, yes, we're to give him the final brief of the operation, including our choices in personnel."

Penelope put out her cigarette, "Let me come right out and ask you something. Are either of you two boys going in?"

Josef calmly replied, "Yes, it's me. I'm the one going in. I'm the organizer and team leader for Operation Broken Arrow."

"Why didn't you say so in the first place? If that's the case, then I'm your man or should I say, your woman."

Josef interrupted, "It's out of the question. It's too dangerous. You did your part. You already went on a mission as a wireless. No one is asking you to go back in again."

"Seriously, I'll do it. Look, you said it yourself; there's a shortage of trained operators. I'm ready to go in tomorrow, if needed."

Now it was Dick's turn, "Penelope, we can't. It's way too dangerous. If you know what Broken Arrow is, then you know what we're up against."

"The penetration of the Third Reich and the destruction of V-1 rockets? My husband was killed by a German air attack and left my daughter fatherless. I know exactly what I'm up against. I'm going in with you as your wireless operator and that's final!"

Josef calmly placed his hand on her shoulder, "Are you sure, Penelope? We can give you some time to think it over."

"Yes, I'm sure. I'll let Yugoslav section know, they, in turn, will pass it on to Maclean at 399 headquarters. When do we leave?"

"In the next seventy-two hours. Dick has already coordinated with RAF Special Duties Squadron. We won't have to jump. The entire team will go in by Dakota[3] and land at a clandestine airstrip."

* * *

THE OSS wireless reports from the field were more serious than originally anticipated. The Germans were launching an offensive against Partisan positions in Strajerska and had driven the Fourth Partisan division south across the Sava River. Movements inside Stajerska would be more difficult than originally planned. The atmosphere inside the OSS briefing room at Bari was tense as Josef Kostinic and Howard O'Donnell pored over the reports and finalized their plans. Josef had not slept for two nights after Penelope agreed to go on the mission as wireless radio operator and courier. In a way, he welcomed her support for he could not or did not trust anyone else in this capacity. Under the circumstances, she was right; there was no one else. She was, as she said it herself, *his man*.

O'Donnell used a black marker and circled the area on the large map spread over the table, "The Partisans agreed to provide manpower support for the operation. I don't like this idea because it's more political than tactical. I'd rather have an entire OG team backed up by Rangers doing the job. But higher headquarters says they can't afford special teams outside the Western front; that's their priority."

"Don't forget the radio operator and courier. She's the best in the business; no one else, British or American, knows more about clandestine wireless radios than she does, and she's also fluent in German and Serbo-Croatian, which makes her my most valuable courier," said Josef.

"Yes, she's also a personal friend, if I remember?"

"We went to school together in Belgrade before the war. She and Tess were best friends."

"Then it's finalized. You'll go in on the next chock. Vojvoda has already coordinated the airfield landing with Popeye's team. They'll provide the reception committee."

"Dick wants to go with us to make sure the landing goes smoothly. He's also a personal friend and also knows about Penelope's background. He agrees with me. We don't want her to be exposed to any unwanted risk, which includes the landing. I'm okay with it, but it's up to you, sir."

"I see your point. Tell Vojvoda he's a wimp for not having the balls to ask me himself."

"I'll do that, sir."

"All right, take him along to secure the landing, but I want him back on that Dakota for the return flight, got that!"

---

1. It was not uncommon during WW II to have commissioned officers as young as nineteen, especially if they had language skills and were assigned to the OSS.
2. Tapping out Morse coded messages by skilled radio operators was rapidly becoming obsolete, paving the way for modern, secure, voice communications.
3. Dakotas/Gooney Birds were another name for the military version of the DC-3 (C-47).

Chapter 23

PENETRATING THE THIRD REICH

The area was called Pohorje, a small cluster of heavily forested hillside and mountain ranges just north of Celje. The area was guarded by some of the German 12th Army's crack troops from the battle of Stalingrad. Throughout the rest of Yugoslavia, German military strength was falsely inflated. Many of the units consisted of poorly trained conscripts with little or no combat experience or foreign nationals, mainly, Bulgarian and Romanian. This area was different. Everyone in the unit was in a heightened state of alert to be on the lookout for Partisan ambushes and especially commando teams from US and British intelligence units.

The Partisan reconnaissance team moved about with silence in the dense forests. It was after midnight local time. Most of the Germans were asleep. The Partisan commander, a young man in his early thirties with sandy hair and clean-shaven, motioned for two fighters to move forward and take a closer look. Sava Crntza moved forward from the shadows along with another, younger Partisan. Crntza, though a Major, disguised himself as a lowly private to better suit his cover as a German Informant. No one would question his loyalty, as long as he followed orders and did his job. The two men crawled on their hands and knees making as little noise as possible, just in case a German patrol was outside the compound. Crntza stopped at the top of a small hill overlooking the town of Pragersko and took out a set of field glasses. The nearly full moon and cloudless night provided excellent visibility. He adjusted his glasses and focused on the raised track jutting upward at an angle. There was a strange winged bomb attached to the top of the rails. Steam or some kind of vapor was emitting from the tail of the vehicle. Crntza could not be sure, but he thought the emission was some sort of fuel vapor. He turned to his partner and said, "We'd better shield our eyes just in case."

A few seconds later, the back of the vehicle glowed white, then a light-blue color at the same time they heard the noise. It sounded like a blast of thunder followed by a sudden rush of wind. Then the vehicle moved along the rail at lightning speed and flew into the air. The sound of the exhaust was now distinctly heard as the small flying bomb accelerated and disappeared into the darkness. The entire show was over before they knew it.

"What was that?" the young Partisan asked Crntza.

"I don't know, but it looked like some sort of flying bomb."

Crntza knew exactly what the device was because he was in constant contact with his Gestapo handlers back in Serbia. SS Obersturmbannführer Flosberg had briefed him, in particular, on what these devices were. Flosberg and his counterintelligence staff leaked out the information to the Allies that these weapons existed. His staff felt, since there was no military or strategic threat with these proto-type weapons, information should purposely be leaked to the Allies. They would send in another team to try to destroy them, effectively using the weapons as bait. This would be another trap to capture Allied agents. Flosberg felt sure that due to the preconceived importance of these weapons, the Americans would send in their best agents; someone who already had operational experience in the field. He was hoping they would send in the elusive, Alum, and his radio operator, Celeste.

* * *

THE DAKOTA AIRCRAFT from Royal Air Force Special Duties Squadron 148 left Bari, Italy at 0100 hours. The aircraft flew as a single ship across the Adriatic and arrived above the landing field on schedule, 8 nm northeast of Mislinje. There, OSS field operative, Major George Hamlin, the twenty-seven-year-old from Columbus, Ohio, codename, Popeye, was positioned by the A flare pot. He was in direct communications with the Dakota navigator via S-phone. There was no need to authenticate or use flash-coded light signals. Onboard the Dakota, Josef Kostinic, Milo Kovich, and Penelope Walsh were ready for landing. This was to be a moonlight landing on a prearranged airstrip. There was no need to wear parachute gear or overalls. All three were dressed in military clothing with Josef and Milo in their khakis and lightweight leather jackets. Penelope donned her green, army short coat and pants. All three wore their respective military ranks, including Penelope, who was now a Lieutenant in the British Army and not a FANY.

The Dakota touched down on the soft field and made a quick, 180 degree turn, back to the number-one flare pot. Hamlin walked over to the left side of the aircraft, making sure to avoid the propeller from the engine, which was still turning at idle power. The pilot opened his window and gave the thumbs-up signal. Hamlin, yelled, "We're ready. Everything is secure!"

The left rear door opened and out jumped the three passengers and their baggage. All three crouched down and moved away from the aircraft and propeller wash and over to Hamlin. He yelled, "Okay," and gave the thumbs-up signal. Three minutes after the Dakota landed, it was airborne once again and headed back to Bari with Dick Vojvoda onboard.

Hamlin, along with two more Partisan fighters, emerged from the shadows, converged, and secured the three passengers to the safety of the tall pines and poplars. Two more Partisans retrieved the luggage and supplies, including two Mark IIs and one SSTR-1 radio set. Then another aircraft could be heard approaching from the distance. It circled the drop zone to make sure it was still secure and then dropped several parachutes. Josef knew that this drop was the explosives needed to blow up the Liploglav tunnel and the rail bridge at Zbelovo. More Partisans emerged from the trees and recovered the canisters. Josef took a breath when everything went according to plan and composed himself, then made formal introductions, "I'm Major Kostinic; this is Lieutenant Walsh, my radio operator-courier and Lieutenant Kovich, my explosives expert."

Hamlin reached his hand out, "Major George Hamlin, pleased to meet all of you. Everyone around here calls me Popeye. I don't know what I did to deserve that name, but that's what they call me and the name stuck. My first task is to inform you that I received an urgent message to pass on to you. The message is from OSS Commander Mediterranean Theater. You've been officially assigned as the Assistant Chief of the Balkan

Field Section. A personal request from Donovan himself."

"Thanks for the great news. I'm sure that will come in handy out here in the field."

"I know, I'm just passing on what I was told. We best get you back to camp. I'm not sure what you were briefed on, but we don't have vehicles out here. We travel mostly on foot, or if we're lucky, on horseback or farm wagons."

"Not to worry. I spent three months in the field riding horseback."

"So, I've been briefed."

By seven in the morning, Josef and his Team Broken Arrow, made the journey to the OSS station located in the forested highlands. The station was cut deep into the side of a mountain overlooking the Zidani-Most to Ljubljana rail line. Here, they broke into their supplies, eating the rations that were just dropped in with them. They even shared the rations among the other Partisan officers present. The rations consisted of corn beef hash, Spam and powered eggs that Penelope couldn't stomach, along with real coffee. After breakfast, Josef briefed Hamlin on the latest intelligence from Bari and told him about blowing up the bridge at Zbelovo.

Hamlin added, "War materials come from the Third Reich along this rail line. The Partisan attacks haven't been successful anywhere on the line except for the viaduct I took out in Mislinje. Fourth Zone insists on doing the work themselves without any Allied supervision. I'm not sure if they don't trust us, or if they want all the credit themselves for post-war political gains."

"I've seen your reports. I think we can take the bridge at Zbelovo. It's the least guarded and we have plenty of cover to make our approaches."

"What would you like my men to do?"

"Get us to Zbelovo by courier line."

"We can do that, in fact, it's best to be on the move."

"What can you tell me about your sightings of V-1s?"

"My best unit is on patrol right now looking for more launch sites. In fact, we had reports last night of a launch. The rocket came down not far from here, apparently without a warhead and apparently, it landed like a regular airplane on a runway. They appear to be still testing the devices. It could be piloted or remotely controlled; we honestly don't know at this point."

"Any idea of where it could have been launched from?"

"Possibly near Pragersko. The team is due back later this afternoon with a report. I trust them more than some of the other Partisans I've come across during my mission. The Germans are monitoring our movements constantly. They track our wireless transmissions and they have informants everywhere. If word gets back to the Gestapo that an Allied patrol is holed up, they'll send in the mountain divisions. You can stay one step ahead of them by being mobile. To be on the safe side, it would be a good idea to leave your caps and insignias behind since traitors would likely disclose to the enemy your whereabouts."

Penelope put her coffee cup down and came up to Josef. She unpinned his collar rank and muskets then handed the devices to Major Hamlin. "We all speak Serbo-Croatian very well. If there's a traitor anywhere it will be difficult to identify our nationalities."

"Milo, hand Penelope your butter bars, too," said Josef, remembering his encounter with the Gestapo and his military issue jump boots. Then he addressed Hamlin, "Do you think we can get some German jackboots as well? I'll be more than happy to do some bartering."

"I'll see what I can do. The Partisans in this area are well-equipped. Leave me your sizes."

Josef rolled up his map, indicating he was finished with his briefings. "One last thing, what can you tell me about the escorts and the courier line?"

"There's a fellow by the name of Crntza. He seems to know the area the best. I'll let you have him and the remaining group of Partisans numbering about fifty men. You'll need every one of them to help carry your radios and explosives. The Partisans' mood changes daily around here. Sometimes, they're cooperative, other times they're distant. They take their orders on a daily basis from Fourth Zone headquarters. Tito calls the shots from there. Other than that, you have to trust them to get you from one safe location to the next."

"That doesn't sound very encouraging," said Penelope.

"I wish you the best on your mission. I'm sorry I can't stay and provide more assistance, but we've got our own tasking orders. I'll send for Crntza and activate your courier line."

"You've done enough already." Josef extended his hand, "See you back in Bari."

"There's one more thing I'll pass on to you. Call it advice or better yet, call it a warning. News travels fast within the Partisan ranks. The courier lines not only provide passage, but also transmission of information. News travels very quickly in Partisan territory. Adhere to strict security procedures."

Later that afternoon, Team Broken Arrow left the OSS station along with fifty heavily armed Partisans, two British Bren light machine guns, Sten guns, and captured German machine pistols. They moved along the Pohorje mountains via courier line. Young farm boys and sometimes girls, who were seldom over fourteen years old, operated these courier lines. One of the girls gave Penelope a locally manufactured peasant dress that she wore with her

German jackboots provided by Hamlin's Partisans. It was after midnight when the team arrived at a major road crossing. Josef sent a team of Partisans to scout the road ahead. Within the hour, the patrol came back with news that the Germans were all along the crossing. It would be difficult to cross that night. The team would have to wait for the patrol to move out the next day. The Broken Arrow team moved further back up the mountain to an alpine farm with a small barn. The team took refuge in the barn and Penelope was able to set up her radio and make her first radio transmission to Force 399 headquarters. This was a remarkable achievement in that she transmitted within forty-eight hours after being inserted directly into the Third Reich.

Chapter 24
MARIBOR-ZIDANI-MOST RAILROAD

At daybreak the next morning, Partisan scouts awakened them and reported the Germans had moved out of the area and the road was clear. The team would have to make a run for it before another patrol occupied the area. By nine in the morning, the courier line passed the main Maribor-Celje highway and was headed into the forested highlands above Zbelovo. It was here at this location that Josef met Crntza for the first time. Team Broken Arrow set up camp at a small Partisan farm. Once again, they used the family barn as sleeping quarters for the fifty-plus strike team. That night after dinner, Josef and Milo left with a Partisan patrol to scout the area around Zbelovo. Geographically, the city of Zebelovo was surrounded by low mountains thus affording the Partisans excellent opportunity for hiding. The Germans had a difficult time securing the entire area without committing massive troops to protect all the hills surrounding the rail yard. Josef was led by the Partisan known as Crntza. He was about the same age as Josef and spoke good English. Once they reached the outskirts of Zebelovo, Josef asked Crntza if he knew of any reports of flying bombs. To Josef's surprise, Crntza nodded his head.

"Tell me what you know."

"I don't know if it's true because I have not personally seen these flying bombs. I can tell you that some of the local railway officials who work along the line told me they have seen strange, torpedo-shaped objects being moved into the tunnel between Lipoglav and Zbelovo, mostly during the day to get away from Allied aircraft."

"So, you think the Germans could be using the tunnel as a storage facility for the weapons?"

"It's possible, but I have not seen the rockets myself."

"Let's go have a closer look and see what we're up against," said Josef.

As predicted, heavy German rail traffic was proceeding normally along the double-track railroad. The bridge that crossed the Dravinja River was smaller than expected. There would be more than enough explosives to destroy the bridge. There was also plenty of vegetation along the river to provide cover for their approach to set their charges. There was, however, a small detachment of German soldiers guarding the bridge.

"Just as I told you," said Crntza. "The local Partisans who lived in this area all their lives tell me the German patrol is always present, especially now after three unsuccessful attempts to knock out the bridge. Have a look?" he said as he handed Josef the set of binoculars.

Josef struggled to see through the binoculars and could see several guards moving along the double-track line and bridge, "Now, that's interesting. They have no lookout towers or watch towers. They're limited to line-of-sight vision from bridge level. Have a look, Milo."

Milo took the field glasses and focused the lenses. He scanned the area front and back and then forward and backwards. He moved several feet closer than to the side, occasionally mumbling something to himself. Finally, after several minutes looking through the field glasses he said, "On a dark night, we can easily move through the river bed and to the foot of the columns. From there, we can set the charges." He lowered the glasses and handed them back to Josef.

Josef leaned closer to Milo and said, "Come with me over here and I'll show you something." Josef looked at the Partisan known as Crntza, and said, "You stay here and watch." Crntza nodded his head.

Josef and Milo proceeded down the hill a few feet and then Josef sketched some markings on the ground with a stick, "I don't trust that guy. Did you notice every time we talked, he inched closer to us, so he could hear every word?"

"I think you're exaggerating, Major."

"No, it's true. I've been watching him since he joined our ranks. He speaks English very well, almost too well, and with an Oxford accent. He used words like, official, rocket, and torpedo-shaped. How does a Partisan peasant know what a torpedo looks like?"

"Do you think it's true what he said about the V-1s?"

"I know it's true because he specifically called them rockets instead of flying bombs. And yes, it does make sense about hiding the rockets inside the tunnel at night. By the way, how's your Russian?"

"I can get by. I know enough for casual conversation."

"All right, let's test the waters so to speak. Talk to me in Russian. If Crntza moves closer, we'll know he's up to something, but he won't be able to fully understand our conversation." The two men moved back up the hill closer to Crntza and then Josef and Milo continued conversing in their passable Russian.

"There are multiple columns. I counted at least four. There's no way we can set the charges and take them all out. We'll have to concentrate on the closest columns." He scratched a clear patch on the ground and began diagramming with his fingers in the soft dirt, creating a simple sketch. "I can set some chargers here and here," he said as he pointed to two of the columns.

"What about the possibilities the Germans are hiding their V-1s in the tunnel? Can we destroy them on the spot?" asked Josef.

Milo used the binoculars again and scanned the area, "We have a couple of options with our existing plastic supplies." He lowered the glasses and used his improvised map on the ground. "We hit the line here at the bridge and again at the mountain hillside *before* the tunnel," he said as he pointed to the two areas along the track. "We'll concentrate on the mountain hillside instead of the tunnel itself. This was probably the mistake the Partisans made earlier in trying to knock out the tunnel itself. If we can time it right, we can capture the rockets in the open. They'll have nowhere to hide them if we take out the bridge and the tunnel simultaneously. It's a perfect set up to trap them in the open. It will need to be followed up by an air strike at first light."

"Now you're talking!" said Josef.

"And it doesn't have to be a massive air assault. They could get the job done with a few Lightings or Thunderbolts. This also means we'll have to time our charges to go off just before daylight. The Germans won't have enough time to repair the lines and move the rockets to shelter. They'll be busy putting out the fires and repairing the lines. That's when our bombers have to hit them. It's our best chance to take them all out along with the tunnel."

The two men noticed Crntza moving closer and struggling to hear their words, but the two men continued in Russian as if were a natural occurrence.

"Any other options other than an air strike?" asked Josef.

"There's another option, but it won't guarantee total destruction. We could go up further on the line and hit them as they make their way in from Germany, possibly as far north as Maribor. There is a natural choke point up there, which divides war shipments to the rest of the Balkans. That's an option, but we'll have to get closer for a fuller assessment."

"I think we've got enough to go by for now. Let's get back to base and have Penelope send a message off. I'm with you on the first option; HQ will be delighted to hear our reports."

After they finished doing their recon work, Josef and Milo returned to their farmhouse base. Crntza left the group and returned to his home where he said his wife was waiting for him. Despite the German occupation, life went on. Business still had to be conducted and movement along the railroad was a priority in this area. So was the cover for Sava Crntza. After leaving the Partisan group and the OSS agents, he rode his horse down the mountain to a small town outside Celje called Vojnik. Most people who lived in this village were in some way connected to the rail line that passed through it. It was 0700 hours and the town's people were busy preparing for the day when Crntza rode his horse into the small stable at a nearby farmhouse. Once inside the barn, he closed the door and was greeted by a young man. He was in his mid-twenties with blond hair and blue eyes. He was, in fact, a member of the local railway Gestapo and one of the SD's counterintelligence operatives. He was there to debrief Crntza on the latest Partisan activities in the area.

Crntza dismounted his horse and tied the animal up in the stall.

"Good morning, Herr Crntza, how was your evening?" said the young man in German. Crntza did not even know his real name and did not want to know. He only knew him by his code name, Ivan.

Crntza replied in German, "Another night with those filthy peasants. I can't stand the smell of them. It would be nice if they took a bath once in a while." Crntza took out a handkerchief and wiped his face, "I have something for you, but it's going to cost you this time."

"I don't think you're in a position for demands Herr Crntza. We still have your wife and daughters in manacles." Then he pulled out a pistol from his jacket and held it at Crntza.

Crntza felt like striking the young man across the face, but withheld his anger for fear of getting a bullet between the eyes.

"You better listen up, you little shit, I've come across some new information that might interest you."

The young German did as requested, and took a seat on a milking stool, "So, what do you have that's so important to the Third Reich?"

"First of all, I want assurances that my family will never be harmed in any manner for the duration of the war."

"Go on."

"Second, I want them out of that wretched place and moved to a more comfortable setting."

"You've got to be out of your mind."

"All right, have it your way. You can tell Flosberg to find another man to infiltrate the latest OSS station in Slovenia."

The young German's bright blue eyes suddenly became

brilliant, "That *is* something. All right, I can pass your request to Flosberg, but I'm only the messenger. There's no guarantee your family will be released from that prison. Give me specifics."

"Now you listen to me carefully because I'm only going to say it once. You better not write any of this down because if the Partisans find it, they'll surely find me. First, there *is* another team that moved into the area. I've never seen them before. In fact, I can't even tell you if they're British, American, or Russian, because they all spoke English, Serbo-Croat, and Russian exclusively."

"So what, another enemy infiltration, in case you haven't noticed, we're losing the war. The Allies have complete air superiority over all Europe. They can drop in as many agents as they want."

"No, this is different. They're looking for the rocket facility. You know as much as I know that if the Third Reich is to have any chance against the Red Army, it's with these weapons."

"Give me specifics. Flosberg doesn't want generalizations."

"There is a two-man team operating independently from Team Popeye. One's my age, the other younger. The older one was obviously the team leader. Everyone took orders from him. He was short and stocky with thick, black hair. The other one looked like you; blond, blue eyes, but very muscular and fit. I think there was also another one they left back at their base. I didn't get to see him because we met at a rendezvous point away from their headquarters. It's probably their radio operator because they mentioned they needed to send an urgent message back to Italy."

"How did you know they were looking for the secret weapons?"

"The older one asked if I'd seen any, so I told him what I knew, which wasn't very much."

"Anything else?"

"They talked in detail about the rail lines. I showed them the bridge and tunnel at Zbelovo. They looked as if it would be a difficult target. Then they spoke in Russian. I didn't fully understand them, but they seemed to be detailing a plan."

"How did you know they were speaking in Russian?"

"I'm not that stupid, you fool. Don't you think I know the difference?"

"Sorry, I thought maybe you might know a little."

"No, it's quite different. Only the sounds and tones are similar. Other than that, they might as well be speaking Japanese."

"I'll pass what you told me to Flosberg by secure line. Meet me back here tomorrow at the same time. I should have a reply for your request . . . *your demands* by then."

When Josef and Milo returned from their recon, Team Broken Arrow spent the day at the farmhouse because it started to rain heavily. They had the place to themselves because the father and son joined the Partisans and left only his wife and young daughter. Penelope used the time to send another message via her Mark II wireless. The shelter provided an excellent location for wireless transmission. They had a 12-volt car battery, and a bicycle hand-crank accumulator courtesy of Team Popeye and Major Hamlin. In addition, she could fully extend her aerial outside the barn to get a clearer transmission. Josef gave her the details of their recon mission and told OSS/SOE they would stand by for further tasking orders. Once Penelope transmitted her message, she began to receive a routine transmission from OSS. She decoded the message and read it carefully again before letting Josef see it. She could not believe what she was reading.

"Josef, you better take a look at this."

Josef and Milo came over to Penelope's transmission station and Josef began to read the scribbled notes. The message was simple. It read as follows:

ADVISE ALUM HE IS NOW ACTING CHIEF OF BALKAN FIELD SECTION-STOP

ALUM WILL TAKE COMMAND AUTHORITY FROM COLONEL O'DONNELL WHO HAS BEEN RECALLED BY ORDER OF ROOSEVELT-STOP

The message went on to say the Allies were not happy with O'Donnell reestablishing contact with Credible Dagger despite direct orders from SHAEF Headquarters in London to break off all contact.

"Looks like you're the senior-ranking intelligence officer in the Balkans," said Penelope. "I don't know if this calls for a celebration or a condemnation."

"O'Donnell was warned to stay away from Mihailovich. Before we left, he knew the Chetniks were protecting downed American flyers. That's why he went to Chetnik territory—to oversee the rescue operation. Personally, I think the British were the ones who brought this upon the Americans. Nothing personal, it's just that Churchill put all his eggs in one basket, turning his back on Mihailovich. It's always been the policy of the United States to back both Tito and Mihailovich. We obviously underestimated the influence Stalin had over Churchill as well as Roosevelt."

Penelope replied, "I think it was more disinformation on behalf of the British missions, especially the ones operating in Partisan territory. Back at Baker Street, there were toughs in F Section who felt Yugoslav section was actually penetrated by communist forces and deliberately swayed their reports in Tito's favor."

"SOE Vice-Commander McAdams played a major role. I can't let my emotions get in the way of our mission. We'll proceed and wait for the response back from Force 399. I think it could take several days. O'Donnell was the strongest link to Donovan. With him out of the picture, they may want my response from the field. Did you establish a follow-on SCHED?"

"Tonight at twenty-one hundred hours, local time. I set it up after dark to be away from DF aircraft on patrol."

"Good work. Now let's all get some rest. We've been at it for almost two days straight, counting our time at Bari."

Chapter 25

KILO SIX

Team Broken Arrow moved to a more secure location. They called it a safe house, but in reality, it was a primitive barn cut into the hillside. The shelter was surprisingly habitable and everyone slept well with two Partisans guarding the front entrance. Around seven in the morning, the Partisan guards were awakened by the footsteps of three women clamoring up the hill. They brought with them their daily rations, which consisted of stale brown bread, sausage, dried fruit, hard-boiled eggs, and slivovitz, which was always in plentiful supply. Penelope was the first to wake up. They had given her the best place in the barn; a bed made from straw. Josef and Milo slept in their sleeping bags on the ground. She poured some water out of a canteen to wash her face then helped the two Partisan women unload the basket of rations. The two women seemed surprised to see a young, beautiful woman holed up with the roughed-up group.

Penelope said in Serbo-Croatian, "I know what you're thinking, but it's not like that. These men are working with me. We have a job to do. Please do not tell anyone you saw me. It will make it easier for all of us."

The older of the two women nodded her head, "We saw nothing. All we did is bring the basket to the entrance."

"That will be sufficient. Go now and remember what I told you. You did not see me here."

The women departed as stealthy as they had arrived. Penelope went back inside the barn where she started to make breakfast for the rest of the team. She fired up the small stove and put on a kettle of water. Josef woke up about the time the kettle steamed.

"Good morning, Penelope, you're up early."

"The Partisans have a personal delivery service. I don't like this arrangement. We could find ourselves waking up to a basket full of exploding hand grenades."

"Security does seem a little slack around here with people coming and going at odd hours of the day. You should know better. You didn't survive in occupied France without some regard to security."

"It's just an observation I noticed when the women approached the entrance. None of the Partisan guards asked questions or inspected the baskets before they brought it inside. Remember the bit of advice Hamlin gave us before he left?"

Josef also noticed the Partisan escorts were suddenly very distant ever since they'd established a camp on the hillside. The officers kept their distance and the enlisted men no longer had smiles on their faces. This was a stark contrast to his days with the Chetniks where each day he was greeted with friendly smiles and ever present and cooperative officers. When breakfast was over, Josef asked Penelope, "They seem more distant than on our first day. See if you can find out anything."

By mid-day, Penelope had found the reason for the Partisan's sudden change in behavior. She caught Josef shaving outside between rain showers, "I've probed around like you asked and I discovered something you might be interested in."

Josef wiped the soap from his face, exposing a clean-shaven face, something he never did while in Chetnik territory, "What did you find out?"

"It seems word does indeed spread very quickly in Partisan ranks, as Hamlin foretold. The reason for their sudden change in mood is because they found out you spent three months embedded with Mihailovich."

* * *

THAT SAME DAY, Hans Flosberg was busy going over his reports from the field. Flosberg's undercover operatives working inside Partisan territory had so far been unsuccessful in gaining new insight as to where Tito was organizing the resistance. All he knew was that the Partisans were getting stronger and better equipped by the day. They were now openly hitting German positions at will throughout occupied Yugoslavia. Along with that, the Allies had complete air superiority over the skies and they provided the Partisans with the all-important close air support to conduct these attacks. The outlook in the Balkans and in particular, Yugoslavia, did not look well for the Third Reich. It was all a matter of time.

Flosberg's thoughts of a German defeat were interrupted by the telephone. The ring came from the highly classified scrambler telephone reserved for important communications. This phone had not rung in several weeks. Flosberg answered the line, "Obersturmbannführer Flosberg." He listened intensely as the person on the other end spoke. When the conversation was finished Flosberg said, "That is most excellent! Tell Crntza his wife and daughters will be in custody here at Jazak monastery. They will be safer here than in Belgrade. He has my assurance that they will be well cared for, but he must proceed with our plan. I want the location and descriptions on my desk by noon." Then he hung up the phone.

Good police work was finally starting to pay off. Flosberg had been wise in planting Crntza with the Slovenian Partisan group in Stajerska. He had uncovered a new team of agents sent to blow up the V-1 rockets. All indications were that the Americans had sent in the best and most experienced agents. From Crntza's description, the agent could be none other than the elusive Alum himself. He called for Gerhert immediately.

IT WAS 2100 hours at night when Penelope came on the air. She tapped out her security checks and waited for the Mark II radio to respond and then she tapped out Josef's outgoing message. Milo Kovich was on the hand pedals charging the accumulators. The team's security was tight. Penelope strung the aerial herself and no one outside SOE except for Celeste Kostinic could tap out Morse coded messages quicker or more accuratly. Josef paced the floor inside the barn and waited in the dim lantern light.

"Something's coming across now," Penelope placed one hand over her left earpiece and with the other holding a wooden pencil, began to scribble out the Morse coded message. When she was finished, she opened up her code-book, and decoded the message, "Home Station says they can't support an air strike, not even a small package. Also, weather's a factor. They're forecasting a massive frontal system across all of Europe and the Eastern Mediterranean. Expect rain and snow at the higher elevations in the Karawanken Alps. They want you to proceed with the demolition yourself and emphasize that the work is to be done by your team and not with Partisan miners. What do you want me to say in the reply?"

"Acknowledge with my initials."

Then another message came in from OSS Headquarters, Bari, addressed to Josef personally. After the decoding procedures, Penelope handed the text to Josef:

OSS SWITZERLAND CHIEF, ALLEN DULLES, MADE CONTACT WITH A HIGH-RANKING GERMAN OFFICER, MAJOR GENERAL WILHEIM GLORE THROUGH AN AGENT KNOWN ONLY AS KILO SIX. REPORTS INDICATE THAT GLORE AND A NUMBER OF AUSTRIAN OFFICERS IN ZAGREB ARE READY TO COOPERATE WITH THE ALLIES. ACCORDING TO KILO SIX, HE BELIEVES GLORE IS PREPARED TO SURRENDER FOUR ENTIRE GERMAN COMBAT DIVISIONS OVER TO THE ALLIES, HOWEVER NOT TO TITO OR THE SOVIETS. KILO SIX RECOMMENDS THAT AN AMERICAN OFFICER BE SENT TO ZAGREB TO NEGOTIATE WITH GLORE. KILO SIX WILL MEET THE AGENT WITH RADIO OPERATOR IN THE NEXT WEEK TO COORDINATE THAT MEETING. BRING SUFFICIENT KUNAS, MARKS, LIRA, AND DINARS TO FACILITATE MEETINGS. KILO SIX SHOULD BE MET AT THE OFFICES OF THE DUBRAVA TEXTILE COMPANY, WIENERBAN BUILDING, ZAGREB. ASSUME YOU KNOW THE NAME, ASK FOR KILO SIX ANY TIME DURING THE DAY. USE PASSWORDS, REGARDS FROM

UTO. GLORE INSISTS ON SPEAKING ONLY TO AN AMERICAN ENVOY. THE PARTISANS, BRITISH, AND SOVIETS MUST NOT KNOW OF THE MEETING.

"Tell them I can't be in two places at the same time."

Penelope coded the message and sent if off. When she was finished, a reply came back immediately. It stated that the meeting with the German official was *critical* and the destruction of the rail facilities could not take place anyway because of the bad weather. OSS wanted to take advantage of this weather delay and politely asked Josef if he could attend the meeting in Zagreb.

Josef took out a map and spread it over the ground, "The Germans are, for all practical purposes, up against almost certain defeat and are desperate to save their own necks here in the Balkans. I can take three Partisan escorts, but it could take me well over a week to get there even by horseback." He stood up and came closer to Penelope and Milo, "This means I must leave you two to do the demolition yourselves. How do you feel about that?"

Penelope was the first to speak, "You're the senior-ranking American intelligence officer working in the Balkans. They wouldn't ask you to go to all the way to Zagreb if this wasn't important. It could mean shortening the war by several months. Milo and I can blow up the rail lines and V-1s. Besides, we've got plenty of help from the Partisans. We have almost a hundred and fifty men."

"Milo, what about you, how do you feel?"

"I'm with Lieutenant Walsh—all we really need are two people to blow the charges simultaneously. I can do one and she can do the other. The Partisans can cover our backs."

Josef stood up and scratched his head. "How much time do you have on the air?"

"I need to shut down in five minutes otherwise the DF units will be all over me."

"Let me do some thinking before you send your closing reply." Josef grabbed his coat and walked outside the barn. Two Slovenian Partisans were still outside guarding the entrance. He spoke quietly and said he would only be out for a few minutes. Josef walked up the hillside to the top overlooking the farm. It was a beautiful, fall night in late November of 1944. The skies overhead were partly cloudy covering the stars above. The war was almost over. He thought about the days past when he, Dick, Tess, and Penelope were carefree college students at the University of Belgrade and the Nazi attack on the city in April of 1941 that shook and changed their lives so suddenly. It seemed like a long time ago, yet here he was, almost four years later, as the senior-ranking US intelligence officer in Yugoslavia with a crucial decision to make. Should he ignore the order to go to Zagreb and be with his dear companions? Or, should he leave them alone to conduct possibly one of the most important sabotage missions of the entire war? He placed his hands over his face and rubbed his eyes. This meeting was too important to miss. The Nazi officer could indeed have more information about war plans on the Eastern front. His thoughts went out to General Mihailovich and his Chetnik forces. He wondered what they were going through at this very moment now that the Allies had turned their backs on him. Maybe the Germans wanted to split Yugoslavia into two separate countries, leaving the Eastern section to be run by the Chetniks and the Western half to the Partisans. No, there were too many far-reaching implications in this meeting. He had to go, despite leaving one of his dear friends behind. He knelt down on the soft earth, looked up, and prayed quietly hoping to make the right decision.

When he was finished, he stood up strongly and walked back down the hill. His decision was final. He'd go to Zagreb, but OSS would have to come up with another radio operator. He would insist on that in his closing reply. Penelope would stay with Milo.

At daybreak, Josef was packed and ready to go. The priority the night before was to develop a strategy for getting into Zagreb without tipping off the Partisans to their real motives. It was determined that the best way to proceed was to explain to the local Partisan officers that Josef had received redeployment orders from OSS Headquarters in Bari and he was being sent to Croatia to replace another officer recalled for disciplinary action. This seemed to suit the local Partisan officers just fine because they didn't feel comfortable with Josef leading the operation, especially since he had spent time with Mihailovich and the Chetniks. They were more than cooperative to provide for his departure.

The escorting team consisted of three Slovenian Partisans, four horses, plus one mule to carry their supplies and provisions. Josef was dressed as a simple peasant wearing local attire so as not to tip-off anyone along the courier line. His military uniforms and hardware were hidden in his pack. Milo and Penelope were waiting to see him off. Josef would use the standard courier lines for movement through occupied territories. As they would make their way into various Partisan zones, the escorts would establish contact with the local guides then ask for passage on to the next zone. According to OSS Bari, once inside Croatia he was to make his way to the town of Topusko. There he would meet up with a radio operator and be directed by American forces into Zagreb and hopefully to the meeting location.

"If the storm is as bad as they say it is, you'll have at

least a week before the operation. Use this time to make final preparations before you place your charges. When I get to Zagreb and the American station, I'll send word via wireless. Once I'm there, you can blow the charges. If, for some reason, I don't make it back, get yourselves to Semic and Fourth Partisan zone headquarters and wait there for your rescue flight home. If all goes according to plan and you blow your charges, go to Recica. There, you'll find a primitive airstrip. The Partisans will help you coordinate your flight back home. I'll join you when I can."

Penelope, holding her piping hot cup of tea said, "Good luck to you, Josef. It's nothing we can't handle; remember how it was when we fled Belgrade during the blitz? We shall celebrate together at my wedding."

He placed his arms around her, kissed her on both sides of the cheek Serbian style, "As my courier and my radio operator, during my absence you're in command of Operation Broken Arrow. Your decisions are final. What-ever you do, be safe. The Gestapo will be on your tails. Adhere to strict security procedures. There could be a traitor anywhere. This is not like occupied France. Up here, you're in the wilderness. People come and go. Moods change daily. Remember, there's a man who loves you very much waiting for you back in England."

Penelope handed Josef an envelope, "Speaking of that wonderful man, when you get to the American lines, please make sure this gets back to him."

"I'll do that, you have my word." Josef took the letter and then he and his escorts climbed into their saddles and rode away into the cover of the forest.

Part V

TOTAL VICTORY

Chapter 26

THE LIPOGLAV TUNNEL

Shortly after Josef departed for Zagreb, Sava Crntza met at the farmhouse in Vojnik with his Gestapo handler, Ivan. The young Gestapo man was dressed in a business suit and tie which was out of place in the peasant farmhouse. The two were discussing the latest orders from Flosberg's office. He wanted the entire OSS team arrested and shipped back to Jazak monastery, so he could conduct the interrogations personally. The only obstacle in making the arrests was the OSS team held the high ground at Zbelovo. It was presumed they would have lookouts and guards covering the approaches. Any attempt by the Gestapo to scale the hills and make the arrests would be met by a hail of gunfire. It was determined that their only chance of making the arrest was to get the team while they were away from the security of their hideouts and Partisan protectors.

Ivan asked, "Do you have any idea as to when they might strike the rails?"

"I have no idea. The weather is not cooperating and security is very tight. They send their requests for my assistance by messenger. For the last two nights, they have not left the safety of the mountainside."

"Our security forces are stretched too thin in this area. Foreigners provide most of our security. There is no way we can cover the entire twenty-five miles of track completely." The young Gestapo agent leaned closer to Crntza, looking at him directly in the eyes, "They'll trust you because you've come across as a loyal Partisan. You'll have to make the arrest yourself."

"Are you out of your mind? I'll be outgunned and outmanned."

"Then you'll have to do it when they're not expecting it."

Crntza stood up and walked over to the window. He looked across the Slovenian countryside and the surrounding hills. He could hear the sound of a train whistle in the distance. Then a thought occurred to him, "There is a way. If they do what I think they're going to do, they'll be separated from their Partisan guards either before or after their attack. I can surprise them and make the arrests then."

Ivan cracked a smile, "You see, I told you there was a way." Then he reached into his coat pocket and pulled out a slip of paper with a special telephone number, "Take this. When you have them in custody, call me at the Gestapo station at Celje. I'll have every available agent meet you wherever you shall be."

The fall German offensive in Slovenia recaptured many of the lost territories the Partisans occupied. Much of this territory was the area Penelope and Josef were trying to operate in. In addition, the weather system was one of the biggest of the year, raining or snowing for days on end. Josef had a difficult time on his courier line because of the weather. Some of the guides got lost in the snow-covered mountains, others never showed up, and the team had to wait until scouts were sent ahead or another guide showed up. Penelope and Milo had much better luck because the rain actually kept the Germans inside their encampments. The heavy rains covered up their boot steps, so they could set their charges under the Zebelovo bridge without detection. Milo and Penelope made more reconnaissance missions along the Celje-Maribor railway line. One night as the two were observing the southern entrance of the Lipoglav tunnel, they indeed noticed a freight train come out with several cars that had torpedo-shaped objects loaded on them. Penelope said, "I need to get closer so we can verify if they're V-1s."

"Don't be a fool, Penelope. We can't get within one-hundred yards of the line without someone noticing us."

Penelope raised her hand indicating she wanted her Partisan escorts to hold their positions and then she shoul-dered her Sten gun and made her way down the steep mountain slope; Milo followed behind automatically. They used the cover of the rainstorm to hide their movements and the heavy conifer forest to conceal themselves as they slid down the mountainside. When they were within several yards off the track, Penelope stopped and hid behind a large boulder. The locomotive was just passing her as she got a glimpse of the freight train. After the loco-motive and tender, a large troop car armed with soldiers came next. None of the soldiers were paying attention to the hillsides. They seemed to focus their attention down-ward and alongside of the tracks.

Penelope spoke in a whisper as Milo stopped behind the boulder next to her, "Those are definitely V-1s. You can see the little wings sticking out from the sides and if I'm not mistaken, there seems to be a little cockpit,[1] aft, next to the engine. Also, I can see the guards are not paying attention. They're all looking down toward the tracks." The two continued to watch as the seven-car freight train passed and disappeared around a bend. They also noticed that the tunnel itself was only lightly guarded.

"That's smart of them to move the rockets to the southern side. There seems to be more room to spread them out once they exit." Penelope then asked Milo, "Do you think we can hit the *inside* of the tunnel and trap the rockets in place?"

"Tunnels are normally not good targets for sabotage because the explosives simply enlarge the tunnel and become usable again once the debris and rocks are removed." Milo's words were interrupted when the two heard the sounds of another locomotive coming out from the tunnel. The two watched in horror as they saw a repair train, completely self-sustaining with a heavy crane, come rumbling by.

"I can't believe they have their own repair train tailing the V-1's. That thing can repair any track damage within hours, if not minutes," said Milo.

Penelope wiped the rain from her face, "We weren't expecting this. Let's get back to the Partisan Brigade up the hill. See if anyone knows something about the inside of that tunnel. We've got to find a way to blow it up, with everything inside."

Penelope met two of the Partisan officers at the top of the hill, "We need to come up with an alternate plan. Is there someplace we can talk in private? Just the officers and my assistant, Kovich?"

One of the Partisan officers nodded his head, "There's a small village on the other side of the hill. They have a couple of isolated farmhouses. We can use those for a short period of time."

The fifty-plus man unit relocated up the mountain and

took the northern slope away from view along the rail lines. The team took over one of the small alpine farmhouses. Two officers along with Penelope and Milo used the structure to warm and dry themselves from the torrential rain and sleet using the brick oven in the center of the room. Penelope spread a map on the table and addressed the Partisan officers.

"The Lipoglav tunnel is not that long, perhaps only seven or eight-hundred feet in total length. But it's fairly wide, with double-track lines inside. I'd like to try and blow the freight trains while they're *inside* the tunnel, but Milo thinks it's difficult. What do you know about the structure?"

The senior-ranking officer spoke first, "We have some miners in our group. Some of them have demolition experience, others worked on the construction of the tunnel itself. I can send for them. They'll be able to give us a better picture."

"Why didn't you tell us this before?" Penelope asked.

"I was told by Fourth Zone HQ that this was to be an Allied job. We were left out purposely by the Allies."

"Send for them by courier line. I want whoever they are here immediately!"

The Partisan leader sensed that Penelope was serious and a force to be reckoned with and motioned to his Lieutenant to move. The man left the farmhouse and quickly spread the order by messenger. Meanwhile, Penelope looked over the map with Milo and began to come up with a possible alternate strategy; one that would knock out both the rail lines and the V-1s at the same time.

Penelope turned to Milo, "What are your thoughts now?"

"The tunnel was lightly guarded. We outman the Germans in that category. We could gain access to the inside of the tunnel. Once inside, we'd have to set charges along the entire seven-hundred-foot length to be most effective, which would require a lot more explosives than the two thousand kilos we currently have. We might possibly even need drilling equipment."

"How much more are we talking about?"

"I'd need to do some calculations, but off the top of my head, I'd say at least another thousand kilos."

"There was one thing I learned working with the French resistance. You give the resistance leaders a certain amount of autonomy and they'll find a way to come up with the shortages. We blew a viaduct in France with explosives the resistance somehow managed to come up with. I suspect the same will hold true here. If we give them a job to do on their own, they'll find a way to come up with the explosives."

Just then, the farmhouse door opened and two men entered. One was the junior officer and the other, an older man in his late sixties. The junior officer said, "This man worked on the construction of the tunnel when it was built. He can help you."

Penelope said, "I'm Lieutenant Walsh, attached to the British mission. Can we blow the inside of that tunnel?"

To Penelope's and Milo's astonishment, the old man told them the Lipoglav tunnel had a lining over which there was sandy soil rather than solid bedrock. When the tunnel was originally built in the Hapsburg days, holes for explosives were placed at strategic intervals on both side-walls along the entire length of the tunnel. This was a design feature by the original architects in order to be able to block the rail line in the event of war. The old man went further to say that the Germans had overlooked the poten-tial danger and failed to block up the holes. They were ready-made for Team Broken Arrow to place their explosive charges without drilling.

"I can't believe the Germans are that stupid." She looked at the senior Partisan officer and asked, "If we let you and your team blow the bridge at Zebelovo, can you get us more explosives for the Lipoglav tunnel?"

Almost instantaneously, the officer nodded his head, "It will be difficult, but we can get you more. It might take a few days, but we have the sources."

Penelope gave him that sweet look that only she could do and then reached up and kissed the man gently on the cheek, "Get me one thousand more kilos of plastic and the job is yours."

"I'll get on it right way, Lieutenant. I'll meet you back at our headquarters in two night's time." He turned, spoke to his officer, and all three men left the farmhouse. Milo and Penelope were left alone, looking over the map by an oil lantern.

Penelope asked Milo, "I got you the explosives, now what?"

"You're on the right track using the Partisans at Zebelovo. In fact, we could stage a diversionary attack, focusing on the Zebelovo Bridge while you and I work on the Lipoglav tunnel. The German garrison will rush to the defense of the bridge and leave the back door open for us to work inside the tunnel. They won't be expecting this. We'll take one-hundred men from the Partisan Brigade and the rest can be used at Zebelovo."

Milo and Penelope spent the rest of the day and evening planning their attack on the tunnel. It was after sunset when they arrived back at the provincial headquarters and her radio sets. She sent Force 399 an update on their plans on the rail lines, but left out the role of the Partisans at Zebelovo.

Penelope also decided to use their Partisan escorts as sparingly as possible the days before their explosives arrived. She felt that a sizable force would be detrimental rather than beneficial, as the larger force would most likely alert the Germans out of their comfortable encampments during the storms. Crntza had not been called upon, so he too, was held at bay until the storms passed and the plastic arrived.

---

1. Later prototype versions of the V-1 were made to be piloted by man or remotely. They also took off and landed on runways much like a regular airplane.

Chapter 27

DISCUSSING SURRENDER

By the sixth day of his trip to Zagreb, Josef and his escorts finally reached the outskirts of Fourth Partisan Zone Headquarters near Semic. However, the Germans were launching counterattacks against Partisan positions in the mountains. Josef and his team had to move further up the mountains and *around* the city to get away from the attackers. On one of these treks up the mountains, the peasants who formed the protective screen around them adopted the practice of lighting little oil lamps in the Roman Catholic shrines. These oil lamps were only lit when the areas they passed were free of German patrols. This is how they made their way around Semic and into the liberated, Croatian village of Glina. It was now six days since he had left Penelope and Milo in Pohorje. The weather reports were favorable and there was to be a sizable break in the weather any day. Once inside Glina, Josef was led to a telephone line that connected directly to Topusko, which was the local Partisan headquarters. His escorts called to report their arrival and were told to wait in Glina for further orders.

Two hours later, an American Jeep with driver, drove up to their encampment with orders to bring Josef back to Topusko. This was a Partisan outpost only fifteen miles outside the city limits of Zagreb. Josef said his farewells to his Partisan escorts and jubilantly hopped on the Jeep. They then rode the last five miles into Topusko. They arrived in Partisan headquarters by nightfall. There, Josef discovered an OSS station was already established including a radio operator, Ed Harris, waiting for him. The young Jeep driver escorted Josef into the OSS command tent.

Once inside the tent, Josef was stunned to see his former commanding officer, Howard O'Donnell. Josef saluted O'Donnell, "This is a surprise to see you, sir. I can't believe we actually have a station this deep inside Croatia."

"There's a lot we're not being told in respect to Partisan activity. That's why they're sending me back to Washington. I'm on borrowed time as it is. In fact, if the Partisans actually knew who I was and where I'd been, they'd probably have me dangling from the end of a rope. I don't have a lot of time, so I need to get this to you right away." O'Donnell tossed a locked dossier to Josef, "Inside you'll find everything, including the cash requested by Kilo Six—the combination is 6722. You can read what's in there later tonight."

Josef took the case and placed it on the small table inside O'Donnell's tent. Then O'Donnell continued, "I'm supposed to be on my way back to Italy tomorrow morning on the first Gooney Bird out, but no one knows I'm actually here, so I'll keep a low profile for a few days. As you're fully aware by now, I've been recalled back to Washington. You'll be taking my place as the senior-ranking American intelligence officer here in the Balkans so there's a lot I need to brief you on before my departure.

That's the major reason OSS sent me here in the first place."

O'Donnell reached into his green army pack and pulled out a bottle of slivovitz, "I'm sorry I don't have any whiskey. I left Mihailovich's camp in a hurry and took only what I could grab. There seems to be plenty of this stuff around." He poured two, small shot glasses and handed one to Josef, "You're going to need this after what I'm about to tell you."

Josef nodded and gulped down the liquid as O'Donnell did the same, "Why don't you have a seat because this may take a few minutes?" O'Donnell grabbed a small stool and shoved it across the dirt floor to Josef. O'Donnell stayed on his feet, "First of all, I was the one who was to make contact with Kilo Six and find out what the Krauts are up to. But since the damn Brits went whining back to Churchill that I'd made contact with Mihailovich, he personally called Roosevelt and *demanded* my recall. So, here I am."

"I thought you were supposed to coordinate the rescue of Allied flyers out of Chetnik territory?"

"Yes, in theory that was my official cover story, but Donovan felt we needed to reestablish contact with Mihailovich before the end of the war. That's what I was doing in Loznica when a Dakota landed and two British MPs escorted me onboard the plane at gunpoint. I left the aircrew rescue unit intact with Captain Nick Lazic. He's coordinating the rescue unit until you officially take over."

"Who do they think I am, Superman? I can't possibly cover the entire country myself."

"Just relax. I'll get to that in a second. Let's start with your meeting with Kilo Six and hopefully Glore."

"All right, I'm listening."

"Here's what I know. You'll go into Zagreb and look

for the Dubrava Textile Company. You'll go in unescorted, disguised as a legitimate businessman looking to make contact with textile executives for a large purchase. We can't risk sending the radio operator in with you, it's too dangerous. I know, the Krauts wanted a radio operator, but this could be a trap to capture not only you, but more importantly, the radio operator as well. So, as a precaution, Harris will stay here with me until your return."

"What should I tell Kilo Six if he asks why I didn't show up with the radio operator as instructed?"

"Tell him what I just told you; we can't risk the Germans capturing the radio. He'll understand. You'll travel to Zagreb without the knowledge of the Partisans, so plan on leaving here at zero dark-thirty, before they wake up. You'll take the Jeep to the outskirts of Zagreb. Park it there at this safe house where they'll keep it until you return." O'Donnell handed him a slip of paper with the address to the safe house, "It's an automotive garage, I'm told. Next, go the rest of the way on foot or public transport if it still exists, to the Hotel Zagreb. You'll stay comfortably at the hotel. Rumor has it that Zagreb has been liberated by the Partisans and the Germans have pulled out. Unfortunately, you'll have to believe it when you see it. I'm guessing only pockets of the city are liberated."

"Okay, let's say I make it to the Hotel Zagreb, then what?"

"Wait until normal business hours and look for the Dubrava Textile Company. You have the address. When you get there, ask for Kilo Six and use your security codes."

"I was told once I got to the American lines, I would be briefed on the identity of Kilo Six."

"We're not totally sure who this guy is, but we believe

his name is Karla Sudovic, the Third Reich's Minister Plenipotentiary in Zagreb—hence the code name, Kilo Six. You'll find a picture of him in the dossier."

Josef poured himself another glass of slivovitz and gulped it down, "So, I set up the meeting with Glore through Sudovic and then what?"

"For Christ's sake, how am I supposed to know? Listen to what he has to offer and report back. That's all you can do."

"After my meeting with Kilo Six, what are my orders?"

"Meet back here for debriefing and Harris will transmit your report via wireless. He'll stay with me, so we can be in radio contact with Home Station in case something comes up. Luckily, the Partisans let him transmit and sometimes give him additional messages to send to Partisan sections. That's how I'm able to stay one step ahead of the British and my departure out of here. Anyway, after you report back to me on your meeting with Kilo Six, you'll go back into Chetnik territory and coordinate the movements of the Air Crew Rescue Unit (ACRU) as my replacement in Operation Halyard."

"Should I go in armed or unarmed to meet Kilo Six? This could all be an elaborate charade to ambush the team."

"Yes, that's a real possibility, so if I were you I'd take a Tommy gun and a .45 just in case."

"Okay, if it's a trap, I'll just start blazing."

"Now that's the spirit!" O'Donnell said as he slapped him across the back. "I knew there was a reason I recruited you out of boot camp. You've got spunk, not to mention a tremendous amount of experience for such a young man. By the way, you look like shit. When's the last time you took a bath? No, don't tell me, I don't want to know. Just make sure you leave tomorrow looking like a businessman.

See the quartermaster in the next tent over. He may have something more appropriate for you to wear. Now, go get some rest. They'll wake you at three. I'll be keeping a low profile here in my tent until you return."

Josef gathered the dossier and a last shot of slivovitz before retiring to bed. Then O'Donnell asked one final question as he walked out of the tent. "Did you ever find the V-1s?"

Josef nodded his head, "They're hiding them in the Lipoglav tunnel."

O'Donnell then cracked a smile. "Well I'll be god-damned, those sneaky sons-of-bitches."

BACK IN THE POHORJE MOUNTAINS, Team Broken Arrow had moved frequently during the last week in order for Penelope to broadcast her radio reports and get them away from German listening devices. They moved camp several times and each time took shelter in a peasant farmhouse or hut. Their Partisan guards camped in the fields while Milo and Penelope slept in the relative comfort of the barns and huts. Penelope transmitted her report informing Force 399 that they were ready for the operation. When she was off the air, her American SSTR-1 radio came on the air with a message from OSS Headquarters in Bari. The message was from the code name, Giant Killer. Penelope knew that was the code name for her long-time friend, Dick Vojvoda. The message stated that Alum had made it to Zagreb and was proceeding with his planned meeting. He also relayed to Penelope to keep the SSTR-1 radio on the air until they left for their mission, just in case he needed to pass on any last minute intel on the area. He wished her the best and signed off.

Penelope unplugged her headset, coiled up the aerial, looked at her wristwatch and told Milo, "Alert the Partisans officers to have their men ready to move out tonight. We'll need all available men for the mission. Tell them to meet here by one hundred hours."

"What about Crntza? Shall I send for him as well?" asked Milo.

"I don't think we have a choice. He's one of the best guides."

"Josef doesn't trust him. He thinks he's too suspicious. There's a lot about him that doesn't add up."

Penelope thought to herself for a moment then said, "All right, you and I'll blow the charges inside the tunnel as planned. We'll leave Crntza to watch the back door at Zbelovo. He can't do any harm from that distance."

Crntza by now was set up permanently at the farmhouse in Vojnik. Since he had not been called for by his Partisan commanders and there was a heavy storm in the area, he and his Gestapo handler, Ivan, decided to set up headquarters at the farmhouse. Ivan had a wireless radio and ENIGMA[1] machine brought in so they could be in direct communications with Flosberg's SD staff in Serbia. The German offensive in the area also depleted the supply of men at Ivan's disposal. He would have to rely on unskilled foreign fighters, mostly Hungarians. It was after ten that night, when the two men discussed strategy over lantern light, "Looks like there's a break in the weather pattern. I expect the Partisans to move out from their encampments and start hitting the rail lines."

"We've beefed up security at both ends of the Lipoglav tunnel as best we could, but many of the seasoned troops are being used for the offensive against the Partisans. The approaches are at least covered. If anyone tries to approach the entrances, they'll be met by machine gun fire."

"What about Zbelovo," asked Crntza.

"The same there, too. Although we've added a one hundred-man garrison, including four anti-aircraft guns and two mountain guns."

"Then there's nothing else I can do other than wait for my orders from Partisan headquarters."

"I'll leave you for the night then. I must get back before midnight. That's when the Partisans seem to be the most active in the area. I can't take the chance with this device." Ivan rose with his ENIGMA machine. He finished with Crntza and then proceeded to his vehicle for the return ride trip to Celje.

Penelope changed into a pair of black, camouflaged pants taken from a killed German commando along with a black sweater. The pants were modified by Partisan women to fit snug, and she showed off her shapely hips and body. She tied her hair back in a bun and placed a black beret over her blond hair. Despite living in remote and austere locations, she still demonstrated her beauty. She placed a backpack over her shoulders, which contained her alloca-tion of plastic explosives, detonators, and the detonation plunger. She and Milo would make sure that none of the Partisans had access to the actual demolition controls. There were only two plungers and Milo and Penelope were in possession of both. When they were finished packing, they joined the rest of the Partisans and marched into the cover of the forest.

---

1. Electro-mechanical rotor cipher machine used for encryption and decryption of secret messages.

Chapter 28

HITTING GERMANY'S RAILROADS

At three in the morning, the Eleventh Partisan Brigade with one hundred and forty-three men attacked the two entrances of the Lipoglav tunnel. Milo led the strike team on the southern side and Penelope the northern side. It was a cold, early December morning. Light snow fell over the course of the evening and there was a thin layer on the ground. This would make it difficult to cover their tracks, but they had surprise and numerical superiority. At the first sounds from the Thirteenth Brigade, which was to hit the Zbelovo Bridge in a diversionary tactic, Penelope and Milo would make their assaults on the tunnel. Penelope took seventy-five men and Milo the remaining elements of the Eleventh Brigade. They would assault the tunnel and set their charges inside, making their way toward each other, meeting up somewhere in the middle.

At the first sounds of explosions in the distance, as expected, the German defenders at Lipoglav rushed to the Zebelovo Bridge, leaving the Lipoglav tunnel open. Penelope gave the order for the attack to begin. As the first of the Partisan assault forces emerged from the slopes, they found no sentries at the entrances. Just to make it safe, the Partisans lobbed hand grenades into the tunnel, followed by a volley from their Sten guns. Only a few moans came from the tunnel, followed by more bursts from Partisan machine guns, and then there was silence.

Penelope shouted, "Move in, now!"

All seventy-five men entered the tunnel. Once inside, Penelope saw the repair train locomotive all steamed up and ready to go. She fired her Sten gun at the crew cab and two railroad workers came out with their hands up. The repair train consisted of locomotive, tender, and four cars carrying equipment and the crane.

Penelope held her Sten gun at the engineer, "How many men are with you?"

The engineer spoke exclusively in poor Slovenian, so she could not make out all of his conversation, but as near as she could tell, there were no soldiers on his train, only the engineer, fireman, and crane operator. He said all the soldiers had left to defend the bridges at Zbelovo. Penelope grabbed the Partisan Lieutenant who was responsible for the element and told him to take control of the train, "I've got an idea. Get your men on the train and we'll use it to set the charges instead of the ladders."

The holes were easy to spot on the ceiling of the well-lit tunnel. It was amazing the Germans hadn't noticed them because they were in plain sight. Penelope supervised the packing of the explosives in each hole and then she followed, placing the detonators in each charge and moved along to the next. At no time at all, they were halfway through the tunnel. That's when she noticed the rail cars containing the V-1s covered with netted camouflaged material, "How much more plastic do we have?" she yelled to her Partisan Lieutenant.

On one of the tracks of the double-track line, the

Germans placed six cars loaded with V-1 rockets in an attempt to hide them from Allied bombers and Partisan insurgents. Milo and his team moved in from the southern entrance of the tunnel and met halfway. They used the tops of the freight cars and ladders to reach the holes in the tunnel. The sounds of machine guns and grenade explosions in the distance indicated they didn't have much time. Milo came running toward Penelope just as the last charges were set. He also saw the V-1s loaded on the siding. He shouldered his Thompson submachine gun and came over to Penelope and her Partisan group, "How did it go?"

"I would say, light, almost too easy. I've got the charges set and ready to go, but I want to take out the Buzz bombs while we're at it. I've got several kilos of explosives left. How much do we need to take out the rockets?"

Milo called two of his Partisan Lieutenants and gathered all the plastic that was leftover, which was another twenty kilos.

"It's not much, but if I set the charges correctly, it should work. Give me another ten minutes to finish and I'll meet you at the entrance. We'll blow the charges together as planned." Penelope nodded her head and shouted for all the Partisans to leave the tunnel. It was up to Milo to finish the job now.

Twenty minutes later, the entire team met at the southern tunnel entrance on the slopes of the tracks concealed by trees. Milo connected his two leads to the plunger. Penelope had already connected her leads and the two waited for the final push, "Are you ready?" he asked.

"Let me do it. It's something I need to do."

"All right, go ahead." Milo gave the signal for everyone to duck. Penelope pushed down on both plungers simultaneously and a few seconds later, a loud thunder of consecutive explosions shook the ground, collapsing the tunnel from inside, then a final explosion, which sent fire and heat from the tunnel entrance indicating the V-1s had exploded inside.[1]

The Partisan officers ordered their men to move onto the higher slopes. Milo and Penelope followed in sheer exhilaration, as their plan seemed to have gone off successfully. When they reached the safety of the higher slopes, they could hear gunshots and small explosions from grenades and mortars. The fighting at Zbelovo was still going on heavily. The Partisans indicated that they needed to redeploy to assist their comrades. As the officers were preparing their men, a courier approached with an urgent message. The courier was none other than Sava Crntza. He was the best guide in the area and was dispatched by the Partisans at Zebelovo to send word that the Eleventh Brigade was urgently needed. When he was finished relaying his message to the officers, he came over to Milo and Penelope, "The fighting is still going on heavily down at Zbelovo. We're taking heavy casualties. The Germans were waiting for us. They outnumbered us with heavy machine guns and mortar fire. They've also encircled your encampment and are waiting your return. I wouldn't go back if I were you."

"What about our radios and equipment? If the Germans find my codes, they could use them against us."

Milo stepped in between the two, "It happens all the time in the rush for survival. I think our mission is over now. It's best we get to Partisans Zone Headquarters in Semic."

Penelope realized the retrieval of the radio set and codes was hopeless and let out a sigh. "All right, we'll leave now."

Crntza heard the words he was waiting for as he

planned, "I can escort you to Semic by courier line. I know this area well. We should have little resistance from the units."

Penelope shouldered her Sten gun, indicating she had made her decision and was ready to leave. She reached into her blouse, pulled out a silk map of the area, "Lead the way."

Crntza nodded and crouched down on his knees, "It's a long way off as you can see from the map. We'll need Partisan assistance the entire way. First, we need to get to Celje. The easiest and fastest way is to follow the rail lines."

"Are you out of your mind? We just blew the tunnel to pieces. The Germans will be all over this place!" shouted Milo.

"I've thought of that, but actually, they've redeployed their forces to the hills to try to encircle your encampment. They're stretched too thin along the tracks. If they want to go after the Partisans who damaged the railroads, they'll have to bring in reinforcements from Litja. That could take at least three to six hours this time of the morning."

"Then, let's do it now. I have a wedding to attend to."

Twenty minutes later, the three were back alongside the double-track railroad of the Maribor-Zidani-Most line. Several military freight trains were held along the tracks heading back to the Third Reich. Two trains were stopped, obviously stalled because of the damage and confusion along the line. The three came to an outcrop of trees when Milo saw a southbound locomotive sitting on a track all steamed up. This was the break he was waiting for. His OSS training, just like Josef's in preparation for deployment in the Balkans, consisted of learning to operate a steam locomotive. The locomotive had a tender and three, empty, flat cars.

"What a break!" he told the other two. "Get me to the cab and we've got our ride to Celje."

Penelope pulled the bolt back on her Sten gun and approached the crew cab. The engineer was nowhere in sight and the fireman was practically asleep at his station when Penelope jumped aboard the locomotive and shouted in Serbo-Croatian, "Get out of the cab, now!"

The fireman, seeing the Sten gun pointed at his head and fearing for his life, hopped down from the cab and ran for cover. Just to make sure, she fired a few rounds at the man's feet. Penelope waved her hand at the other two men, who then climbed aboard. Once the two men were inside the cab, Penelope jumped down and ran to the back of the tender. There, she released the three flat cars, leaving them unattended on the tracks. Fifteen minutes later, Milo was at the controls of the locomotive driving through the Slovenian countryside.

Crntza, was impressed with the improvisation and shouted into Milo's ear, "When we get to the outskirts of Celje, stop the train before the rail yard. We'll get off there and head for Vojnik. We can pick up the courier line from there."

Milo controlled the train for another twenty miles. There were no other encounters along the line by German patrols. When the train was seven miles outside of Celje, Crntza moved over in the cab from his spot as fireman and told Milo to pull the train to a stop.

"This is as far as we dare to go. It's almost sunrise and the Germans will be deploying their forces." Milo let out the steam and brought the locomotive to a stop. Penelope came down from the cab along with Crntza. Milo followed and dropped to the ground. Crntza wiped soot from his face with a handkerchief, "There's a small town up the road. I know of a place where we can rest and get something to eat. Once we've rested, I'll escort you to the back roads and the courier line. The Partisans in this area work predominantly at night." Crntza showed them a small switching house used to control the line along the railroad, "This is a good place to stay until nightfall. If you're like me, you two must be completely exhausted."

At this time, both Milo and Penelope couldn't agree more. They both had been up for over thirty-six hours. They needed some time to rest, eat, and collect their thoughts. Crntza continued, but this time addressed Penelope, in particular, "Before we go any further, I need to get you a different set of clothes and food. We won't get far with you dressed in black, especially if we come across a German patrol."

"All right, what did you have in mind? We're not exactly near a department store."

"Yes, I know. I can get you some clothes here in the local area. I have a few friends who could lend us something more concealing than the black outfit you have on, but I need to leave you two here for a couple of hours."

Milo and Penelope, now completely exhausted, took Crntza up on his offer and decided to use the place to get some rest. The switching house had a dirt floor, but was an adequate and safe shelter for a few hours. They found some canvas tarps and spread them out on the floor while Crntza readied for his journey into the local area, "If I'm not back by nightfall, assume that I ran into trouble. You'll have to move out on your own. Head south for Zidani-Most. Stay in the highlands where you'll most likely run into a Partisan line. Good luck to both of you." With that, Crntza left the structure and disappeared into the Slovenian countryside.

Milo said, "There's still something about him I don't like. He's a little too sneaky."

"Under the circumstances, I don't think we have a choice. If he's not back by nightfall, we'll leave without him."

The two made themselves as comfortable as they could using the canvas tarps and had no trouble falling fast asleep. After a few short hours of some well-deserved sleep, the two were awakened suddenly by a young man dressed in a civilian suit holding a machine pistol. There were two other German soldiers backing him up with machine guns as well. Milo didn't even have a chance to reach for his Thompson. The man spoke in broken English, "Get up! You're under arrest!"

Neither of them could fake or talk their way out of this one, especially with Thompson and Sten guns and dressed in dark clothing. Milo shouted obscenities, accusing Crntza of the double-cross. Penelope raised her hands into the air, "It's no use, Milo."

---

1. To this day, satellite imagery still shows the extensive surface damage along the entire length of the Lipoglav tunnel caused by the explosions inside the tunnel.

Chapter 29

STRATEGIC DECEPTION

After twelve in the afternoon on December 6, 1944, Josef checked into the Hotel Zagreb. As O'Donnell suggested, the city was only partially liberated. He had to make his way around several German checkpoints, but finally arrived at the hotel. He took a small room with a single bed on the top floor overlooking the streets below. Josef took another bath and changed into the clothing he'd gotten from the quartermaster's tent, which did nothing to suggest he was a legitimate businessman wanting to make a large textile purchase. Therefore, he made another trip into town and bought a business suit, overcoat, and hat from a local clothing store and returned to his hotel room. He once again took the stock off the Thompson so it could fit under his overcoat and tucked the .45 behind his back belt. He looked just like a Chicago gangster instead of an OSS operator.

Later that afternoon, Josef found the office building in Zagreb that was the headquarters for the Dubrava Textile Company. It was located on the top floor of an office building. As he entered the office, a secretary greeted him.

She was in her fifties wearing loose clothes that hung on her lean figure, indicating the people of Zagreb had suffered during the occupation. She was busy shuffling papers in a file cabinet. Josef did as instructed from his dossier.

"Good afternoon, madam, I'm here to meet with Mr. Sudovic, with regards from cousin Uto."

The secretary stopped in the middle of her tasks as Josef spoke the words. She contemplated her response as she kept her back to him. When she was satisfied with her response, she turned around from her duties and looked at Josef, "We were expecting a much older man. Shouldn't you be fighting with the Partisans?"

"If you know who sent me, then it doesn't matter. When can I expect Mr. Sudovic?"

The woman moved over to her desk and picked up the intercom and waited for the connection. Then she spoke softly into the receiver, "Your cousin Uto is here. Should I send him in?" The woman hung up the receiver, "You can go right in. He's expecting you. I cleared all appointments and activity for the day. You can stay as long as you need to."

Josef entered Sudovic's office and was about to place his hat on the hat rack next to the door when two men grabbed him from behind from both sides and took the Thompson and .45. These men are professionals, thought Josef, as they frisked him and found the money belt stuffed with cash. A man was standing with his back to Josef, looking out the window of his office and smoking an ebony pipe. He was of medium height and age and wore a tattered, brown suit. Josef said nothing and waited for the agent known as Kilo Six to turn around and face him. The man cautiously turned around and faced the American intelligence officer who had come to meet him. At first glance, he probably thought the same thing as his secretary in seeing the young man. Josef recognized him from the pictures in O'Donnell's dossier.

"I was expecting two of you and someone much older. So, how is my cousin Uto?"

Josef, convinced the correct code words were exchanged, relaxed, and introduced himself, "Major Josef Kostinic, Office of Strategic Service—the senior-ranking American intelligence officer here in Croatia and for all of Yugoslavia, for that matter. Are you Mr. Sudovic?"

The man switched to English with an Oxford accent, "It's not important who I am at this point. In fact, it's probably best you don't, because the less you know, the better. Have a seat, young man."

Josef moved closer to a hard wooden chair and Kilo Six continued, "I'm sorry for the uncomfortable surroundings and the two bodyguards, but as I'm sure you're fully aware, we didn't know if you came here to assassinate me. Judging by your hardware, that was a real possibility."

"I thought the same thing from you. I didn't know if I'd take a bullet between the eyes as I walked through your front door."

"You brought the cash, but we were expecting two people. You were told to bring a radio operator. Where is he?"

"We couldn't take the chance of a Gestapo ambush to capture our radioman and ciphers."

The two bodyguards and Kilo Six burst out laughing.

"I don't see the humor in it. I just wanted to stay alive."

"Rest assured, young man, we're not with the Gestapo. Before I begin, I need to ask you something. Are the Partisans aware of this meeting?"

Josef took a seat on the very hard and uncomfortable wooden chair situated in front of Kilo Six's desk, "To my knowledge, no. We took care in making sure this meeting was conducted without the knowledge of anyone in the Partisan ranks."

"What about the British?"

"Especially the British, probably more so than the Partisans."

"And the Soviets?"

"I wouldn't be here if the Soviets knew. The NKVD would have killed me before I entered the city limits."

Kilo Six took a seat behind his desk and placed his pipe in the ashtray. His face changed to that of despair, "The war for the Third Reich is almost over. It's only a matter of time. Germany is run by lunatics, destined to turn the Rhineland into wasteland, and kill millions more for their cause. There are some who want to bring an end to this madness with some sort of humility and dignity. That is why I am here discussing this matter with you. The persons involved in this matter are also at great risk. There is not much time. The internal security service is on our tails as well as the Partisans. We only have a small window of opportunity. After that, the door will shut and Germany and the rest of the world will have to deal with the aftermath."

"If you're not with the Gestapo, then you must be with the Abwehr?" asked Josef.

"Your intuition serves you well. I take my orders from what's left of that organization."

Josef continued, "Let me assure you that I have the fullest authority to discuss any matters that Glore so desires. In addition, I'm prepared to go anywhere to discuss these matters in person with the persons concerned. Before we go any further, tell me, what your connection is and what is it you want in return?"

"I'm a simple businessman with ties to industry here in

the Balkans. I was approached by members of the German high command with the idea of surrendering all forces in the Balkans directly to the Americans. You see, they and I, fear what the Soviets will do after the war."

"All right, how can we help you?"

"General Glore is prepared to surrender the entire German, Twelfth Army and the XVI Panzer Corp. under his command. In addition, he has the fullest support from two other Generals commanding the other divisions in the Balkans. All total, three-quarters of a million men and equipment. But, there are certain conditions. First, Glore wants to surrender only to the Americans, not the British, or especially the Soviets. Second, he wants assurances from your government that all Axis military personally surrendering to the Americans be offered the fullest support as specified under the Geneva Convention. Finally, he wants assurance from the Allies, the Americans, in particular, that no invasion of Istria will take place, cutting off the southern flank."

"That's a tall order, anything else?"

"That is all."

"Are they prepared for any flexible response from the Allies?"

"That, I do not know. This is all they passed on to me and thus, I'm passing it on to you."

"I can tell you this, Mr. Sudovic; I think that's your real name. Your people are in no position to bargain. I must remind you that I have my orders as well. First on the list is unconditional surrender. Under the terms of our alliance, unconditional surrender must be made to the occupying forces in the area. Here in Croatia and Serbia, that means surrendering to the Partisans."

Kilo Six moved to a different topic, "Well, I can see

you are a man of indeed stature and more mature for someone your age. How old are you Mr. Kostinic?"

"For the record, I'm twenty-six. Now, let's get down to business. I was sent here with two specific tasks. One, to find out *who* you are and you haven't confirmed that to me. Second, I'm to set up a face-to-face meeting with General Glore himself, no one else. So, before we move to the second task, tell me about yourself? How did you come in contact with the Switzerland station?"

Kilo Six proceeded to tell Josef the story of how he had made contact with Allen Dulles in Zurich. He had disguised himself as a member of the clergy with forged papers and documents. He traveled through Croatia and Slovenia and into Istria as a Roman Catholic priest wearing a cassock.

"There's more, Major Kostinic. In early 1943, Glore secretly negotiated with high Partisan officials on a possible deal to stop fighting each other." Josef fidgeted in his chair, as he understood this to mean Tito or members of his staff. Kilo Six swung his chair around to look out his office window again and continued, "During these meetings, the Partisan delegation proposed an accommodation in which the Germans would cease their attacks against the Partisans in return for cessation of attacks against the railroads and mines on which the Germans depended. Glore told me himself that these Partisan officials made it clear they regarded the Chetniks as their first enemy and wanted to be free to turn their entire strengths against them, not the Germans."

"So, this so-called accommodation allowed the Germans to have protection of their rail lines and mines and gave the Partisans what they wanted more than anything else, freedom to devote all their efforts to defeating Draza Mihailovich and the Chetniks?"

"That is my understanding of this matter. As you can see, this is extremely sensitive information and is why General Glore asked to speak directly with the Americans instead of the Partisans."

"If word should leak out about this matter, it would prove to the world that the Partisans had direct collaboration with the Germans well before the allegations against Mihailovich for collaborating with the enemy."

"That is one way of looking at it. That is why I asked you if the Partisans knew anything about this meeting. If they did, they could jeopardize the entire operation." Kilo Six reached for his pipe, lit a match, and slowly applied the fire to the remnants of the tobacco, "Where is your radio operator? Did you come to Zagreb as requested with the radio and operator?"

"I left him back at our mission at Zone headquarters outside the city limits. He's waiting my return."

Kilo Six reached into his coat pocket and handed Josef the first of two small 3 x 5 index cards. "Then I'd like you to send this message. Its specific information on units willing to surrender and commanders who have already committed." He then handed Josef the second card, "On this card are instructions on how to get to divisional headquarters at Sremska-Mitrovica. This is where Glore set up his temporary headquarters. As you know, the Soviets are within artillery range of Belgrade and have forced the Wehrmacht to redeploy to a safer area."

"Sremska-Mitrovica is deep inside Chetnik territory. It may be difficult."

"It's all difficult. I am equally at an imposition. How do I know you won't leave this meeting and have a regiment of Partisans waiting to arrest me?"

"The truth is, you don't. You'll have to take everything at face value. Remember, *you* were the one who approached *us*. And you're right, I could have a squad of Partisans or GIs waiting outside. You are, in fact, a Nazi collaborator and under wartime conditions, you are guilty by association."

"Then, I'll await my fate." Kilo Six rose, indicating the meeting was over. "We'll keep your weapons so you won't try anything foolish. Please transmit my message to your people in Italy, when you have something, contact me here at my office. We'll go from there. Also, use the utmost care and follow strict security protocol. The Gestapo has penetrated not only Partisan intelligence units but also the Allies, including the Soviets. They have their spies everywhere. We are on borrowed time as it is."

Josef left the textile company in disarray. His orders were to make contact with Kilo Six and find his identity and then schedule a meeting with General Glore to discuss the terms. What he found out instead was that the Allied Strategic Deception campaign had worked. The Germans were expecting an Allied invasion of Istria and second, almost by default, he discovered the Partisans were more guilty of collaborating with the enemy than the Chetniks. He contemplated a few options for getting to Stremska-Mitrovica by himself, but none of the options would guarantee non-Partisan involvement. He would have to report back to Bari and await further instructions. He decided to wander the streets of Zagreb for a few hours before heading back. In a way, he felt semi-civilized once again. He had spent weeks in the field behind enemy lines living in remote areas. Food was still not plentiful in the cities, but there were a few taverns open that served meals. He decided to get a hot meal and a cold beer.

Chapter 30

PRISONERS OF THE GESTAPO

Penelope and Milo were taken to local Gestapo Headquarters in Celje. There, they underwent many interrogation sessions conducted by Ivan. They also received extensive coverage by the local German media. Photos were taken of the captured *saboteurs* as the Gestapo took great pride in capturing them. The press went further to post flyers on public places warning other potential saboteurs of the outcome of committing such acts. The posters read: These two enemy saboteurs will be punished to the fullest extent.

The Gestapo separated Milo from Penelope and transported each of them to a military rail car destined for Gestapo Headquarters in Serbia. Milo was placed in a maximum-security prison car with other captured combatants and political prisoners. Each man was chained to another, making any attempts at escape impossible. Penelope had slightly more comfort in that she was transported in a regular coach with another female prisoner shackled next to her. The other prisoner was *supposedly* a Partisan operative charged with acts of terrorism. She was dressed in a simple dress, high boots, and a blue, Italian tunic.

Penelope still had on her dark pants, now with holes in the knees and overcoat, but her boots were confiscated back at Celje as a precaution, so she wouldn't make an escape attempt. All she had on her feet were a pair of wool socks.

The military train pulled out from the Celje station just after six in the evening, late enough to get away from possible Allied bombers and Partisan attacks. In addition to prisoners, the train carried vital military supplies to the meager forces on the Eastern front that were in desperate need. Thus, the train would have priority on the double-track line to Eastern Croatia and into Serbia. The young, railway Gestapo agent known as Ivan and his plainclothes SS guard, assigned to guard over them, sat opposite Penelope and the Partisan woman. They allowed them to smoke, but not to speak until given authorization. It would be at least two hours before the train was safely out of Partisan territory and far enough away from liberated Zagreb. The train would travel south of the Croatian city where the Germans still held territory along the rail lines.

Two hours later, Ivan and the SS guard rose to stretch their legs and have a cigarette. Ivan informed the two women they could talk, but to keep their voices down. He told them they would be in the corridor having a smoke and then the two men stepped out of the compartment.

Since her arrest, Penelope had spoken exclusively in English, emphasizing her position as a British officer. The Partisan woman was the first to speak up in the compartment. She spoke in a Croatian dialect with a slight German accent. Penelope was immediately suspicious. "My name is Semona, what's yours?" she asked.

Penelope paid no attention to her as if she didn't understand, but continued to look at Semona from the corner of her eye. Semona appeared to have been recently captured or was allowed to change and bath before her journey. Her face and hair were clean, and she even had a slight fragrance. Penelope also noticed her knees and elbows were not scraped like hers. If the woman had just been captured, then she must not have been subjected to the harsh treatment that Penelope had gone through at the hands of Ivan and his henchmen. Penelope was still not convinced of safe conversation. She remembered her training back at SOE. She recalled Vivian Tate telling her, "Should you be captured, be particularly cautious of the ruthless methods of the Gestapo. They will use any methods at their disposal to acquire information. Sometimes, they insert a friendly imposter to gather that information."

Penelope smiled and turned her head away from Semona who continued, "Don't be afraid. If they sense fear, they'll stop at nothing to try and extract information." The woman took out a pack of German cigarettes the guards gave her from her coat and placed one in her mouth, "You wouldn't have a light would you?" she asked. Penelope remained speechless, but the woman persisted, "You know we still have a long way to go. It might make the journey easier if we could talk. Sooner or later the guards will cut us off and we won't be able to speak."

Penelope, convinced now that the woman was an imposter, spoke in English, "Be fearful for what lies ahead." The Partisan woman, obviously not familiar with English, pulled herself back after she realized she would not get anything more out of Penelope.

* * *

JOSEF SPENT the night in Zagreb and left the next morning at sunrise. He returned to the OSS station later that morning and reported directly to O'Donnell's tent.

O'Donnell looked as if he hadn't slept the entire night. His hair was a mess, and it looked like he hadn't shaved in several days. He looked surprised to see Josef walk into his tent.

"I can't believe you're still alive. I was certain it was an ambush and I had sent you to your death. I hope it was worth it. What do you have?"

"It wasn't a Gestapo trap, thank God. I met with Kilo Six and his two bodyguards, though I never confirmed Mr. Sudovic's identity. I was frisked as soon as I walked into the place. Naturally, they took the money and weapons. As near as I can tell, Kilo Six was not a Gestapo agent but rather Abwehr. I must also assume after meeting with him that Glore is acting on their behalf as well, not the Gestapo's. Kilo Six told me he took his orders directly from the remnants of the Abwehr, whatever that means. They didn't kill me, so I assume they are serious about surrender terms. I did pass on to him what you told me with respect to unconditional surrender. It seemed a moot point. He was more interested in asking me if the Partisans or the British were involved in these discussions. I told them they were not, as instructed, and no one knows about the meeting except the American OSS. Next, he asked if the Russians knew anything. I told him we never discussed anything with the Soviets as well. Finally, he told me to be careful, that the Gestapo knows everything. He gave me a startling revelation, that the Gestapo penetrated not only the Allied networks, but also the Partisans and Soviets. They have their spies everywhere."

O'Donnell still paced the ground with his head down in thought. "We suspected a rivalry between the Gestapo and Abwehr from the very beginning, but this is the first I've heard about the penetrations. It does explain some of what I'm about to tell you." O'Donnell stopped pacing the ground and continued, "The Partisans are furious! News does indeed travel fast around here.

They found out that you left for Zagreb to meet with a German agent to discuss surrender terms and that you spent time with Mihailovich. So, you're right, that information had to come from somewhere. It looks like the Gestapo, through their informants, could have passed that information to them. As a result, the Partisans want you and me out of Fourth Zone immediately. Our time is very short here."

"I got back as soon as I could, sir. I didn't want to travel at night for fear some renegades would steal the Jeep."

"There's something else that's come up during your absence. You may want to sit down before I tell you."

Josef took a seat on one of the chairs and reached for the bottle of slivovitz on the table.

"While you were away, Harris and I received several urgent messages from his wireless. The first one stated that the Sicherheitsdienst, Berlin arrested Glore and shipped him back to Germany to face charges of high treason. Home Station wants us to break off all ties with Glore and his agents. So much for the surrender terms. The second message came from OSS Team Popeye and Major George Hamlin in Starjerska by way of Bari. They reported the two members of your team you left in Slovenia were arrested by the Gestapo in connection with the bombing of the Zidani-Most railroad. Evidently, they were successful because all rail traffic has come to a complete halt along the line. The third message was transmitted from Partisan Fourth Zone headquarters. They confirmed that an American and British agent were arrested and sent by prison rail car to SS Headquarters in Serbia for further interrogation."

Josef was shocked and beside himself. His worst nightmare had come true. He poured himself a glass of slivovitz and gulped it down and then had another. He shook his head and said to O'Donnell, "I should have never left them. They were too inexperienced in the field." Josef poured himself another shot and drank it down, "I felt I had to go to this meeting. It was a chance to end the war. Now I realize that I should have turned down the request from 399." He slammed the shot glass down abruptly on the small table. "Is there anything else?"

"Harris has been monitoring his radio constantly since you left. He's been getting reports almost every hour. So far, nothing's changed."

"Did you tell Vojvoda?"

"I made contact with him immediately via wireless. Naturally, he shares your concern. He's arranged for both you and me to fly out. Tomorrow morning, two Gooney Birds will land at the clandestine airstrip. One will take me back to Brindisi, the other will supposedly take you to Salerno. The British 148th Special Duties Squadron was supposed to fly both aircraft, but Vojvoda got yours to be flown by 15th Air Force crews. The two aircraft will be flown as a flight of two and land in fifteen-minute intervals. I'll leave with the Brits on the first one, you'll go on the second one, flown by the Americans. Except, you're not going to Salerno. You're going back to Mihailovich's camp and resume my position with Team Halyard. Vojvoda stuck his neck out for you. He felt you'd be more useful there, instead of flying back with me for debriefing. Remember, officially you're going into Chetnik territory to help Halyard and the aircrew rescue operation, but while you're there, do what you can as far as Kovich and Walsh."

Josef reached into his coat pocket and pulled out the index cards given to him by Kilo Six, "What would you like me to do with this message from Kilo Six?"

"If the Gestapo has penetrated OSS and SOE, let's go ahead and transmit the message. Give the Krauts something to think about."

Josef added, "I'm not leaving this country until I find them."

O'Donnell asked curiously, "Why *did* she go on the mission in the first place? Didn't she already go into occupied France once before as a wireless?"

"Yes, but she insisted on going back in with me on Broken Arrow. Vojvoda and I went to the British because at the time we were all out of radio operators. Harris was in country, so we had no choice. She was already a fully trained operator with one clandestine mission under her belt."

"Still, you should have never let her come."

"You don't know her like I do. I couldn't stop her if I had put her in chains. Once she found out about our mission and the possibility of blowing up V-1 rockets, she insisted on going back in. Her husband was killed by a German air raid early in the war."

"If it's any consolation, it appears she did in fact destroy both the tunnel and the V-1s. So, what can you do if she's being held prisoner of the Gestapo?"

"I'll ask for a rescue operation."

"Nothing wrong with trying. What do you have in mind?" asked O'Donnell.

"The political situation here is on the brink of all-out civil war. The only thing holding the country together is the German occupation. It goes back to the enemy of my enemy is my friend. I found out from Kilo Six the Partisans made a pack with the Germans as early as 1943. The *accommodation* was an agreement for the Partisans to stop their terrorist attacks against the supply lines in exchange for nonaggression on Partisan activity. This would give the

Germans the supply routes into and out of Germany and give the Partisans what they wanted; complete devotion to crushing Mihailovich and his Chetnik forces."

O'Donnell spoke silently, "So, you think Mihailovich and his forces can help?"

"If I'm going to Chetnik territory, I'll be within striking distance from Gestapo Headquarters."

Chapter 31

THE RESCUE ATTEMPT

The next morning at exactly 1100 hours as planned, Howard O'Donnell left on the first Dakota for Brandisi Air Base. The second C-47 touched down at the clandestine airstrip outside Glima. This C-47 was scheduled for a one-hour turn and then to continue on to its final destination into Serbia. The rear door of the C-47 opened, a crewmember dropped several bundles of supplies for the OSS station, and one passenger jumped off. That person was Dick Vojvoda, dressed in his army greens. Josef helped him with his personal bag and together they rode a Jeep back to the OSS station for the short break. Dick's face was ashen. He also looked like he hadn't slept in several days. When the two arrived back at the OSS camp, Josef told Dick about his meeting with Kilo Six and the warning that both the Communists and Germans had penetrated OSS. Dick gave Josef the latest information on what OSS could gather from the captured agents.

Dick produced a silk map from his pocket and continued, "In all likelihood, they took them to Jazak monastery located here," he said as he pointed to a remote area in the Fruska Gora hills. "The SS and the Gestapo have moved out of the Hotel Palace in Belgrade to a more secure location. It seems an imminent counterattack by the Soviets to retake Belgrade is in the works. They want to occupy the city before winter sets in. The monastery is like a fortress, but is lightly guarded, mostly by non-Germans."

* * *

THE MILITARY TRAIN Penelope was traveling on was taking an unusually long time to reach eastern Croatia. The train stopped several times for air raids by Allied aircraft. Each time the train stopped, the two women had to get off the train, still shackled together, and make their way to a safe location, usually a ditch or low spot along the tracks. This gave Penelope an idea. She thought to herself that the best chance for escape was immediately before or after each air raid. During these maneuvers, the Germans let their guard down for a fraction of a second to save their own necks, leaving the prisoners to find cover on the ground. Ivan and his SS guard would make their way to the safe area first and then come and fetch the prisoners. In this manner, Penelope and her companion were left unattended for a few minutes. The only catch was if the other female prisoner was a member of the Gestapo or Abwehr, who could possibly warn the guards of her escape. Penelope decided to investigate the matter for herself. She knew the woman spoke no English and her Serbo-Croatian was that of a native speaker, but she could be an agent working for the Gestapo and have knowledge of German. She used the cigarettes as a possible indicator. As soon as the guards were out of the compartment for their cigarette break, Penelope reached into her pocket and pulled out the cigarette given to her earlier and placed it between her lips. Without looking at Semona, she said in a quiet voice, speaking in German, "I can use that light now."

Semona reached into her pocket and pulled out a lighter. This lighter had never appeared before and would not be in possession of someone being held as a prisoner of the Gestapo. As she was trained by her SOE hand-to-hand combat specialists, Penelope, using her unshackled hand swung at Semona, hitting her on the side of the head. She fell instantly unconscious. Penelope searched inside her dress and found another pack of cigarettes, which she immediately tore apart. Inside the cigarette pack, she found an identity card showing the woman was a member of the German Abwehr. This was a remarkable piece of information because she thought she was a prisoner of Gestapo and not the Abwehr. Perhaps her SS and Gestapo escorts were also unaware that Semona was a German intelligent agent working against the Gestapo. She had to come up with a different plan now.

Penelope searched the woman further and found a small key hidden inside her underwear. The small key was universal that fit any set of handcuffs. Penelope quickly unlocked her cuffs and freed herself. The train was scheduled to make a routine stop in the next fifteen minutes. She estimated she was somewhere in eastern Croatia. She cracked open the compartment door and saw her two escorts at the far end of the corridor, smoking and laughing, not paying much attention. Like a cat, she slid out of the compartment and worked her way to the exit where she opened the door between coaches and found she was on the last coach. The train was moving at full speed, still too fast to make a jump without injuring herself. She had to get off the train at any cost, even if it meant injuring herself. She decided the risk was worth taking. The tracks were slightly elevated on the rail lines as it passed mostly agricultural areas. It was now or never. She saw a patch of recently plowed fields and jumped. She made a parachute-landing fall and rolled down the embankment, scraping her arms and legs. She came to a stop at the edge of the fields, but not before one of the guards on top of the train saw her jump. He whistled for the train to stop and fired his rifle at Penelope, hitting the rocks and dirt under her feet. She could not move because it felt like every bone in her body was broken. She could not be sure if her arms, legs or wrists were all broken as well. The train continued to roll down the tracks for another quarter of a mile before it came to a stop; then a swarm of SS soldiers came after her. She tried to crawl away on the soft earth, but it was no use. They were on top of her before she could make a get-a-way.

* * *

JOSEF AND DICK met with the rest of the ACRU team at Mihailovich's camp. Nick Lazic was the on-site commander and Josef told him to continue his normal duties, rescuing the downed airmen, "We want you to go about your business with regards to the airmen. Dick and I are here on an SI mission to gather intelligence on German troop movements. We'll conduct deep penetration operations near Fruska Gora. Please do not mention our mission in any of your wireless transmissions. There are two reasons for this. First, I received confirmation the Gestapo has already cracked OSS coded messages from the field. They've been using captured radios and key pads and have become extremely efficient in their endeavor. Second, Force 399 doesn't know Dick and I have landed in Chetnik territory. If they should discover additional American operatives have been dropped in the area, they might raise a stink over it. We can't jeopardize your rescue mission or endanger American lives so please, don't mention us over your radio links."

"I understand, we can do that," said Lazic.

Now it was Dick's turn to talk, "Major Kostinic already discussed our mission with Mihailovich. He's agreed to let us take several Chetnik fighters to help with our mission so you won't be cut short on manpower. It's best we don't give you any more details than we already have. As far as you know, OSS inserted Kostinic in place of O'Donnell to take overall command of the station and you've never seen or heard of me. Our intelligence mission should last no more than three days. There is no need to go looking for us. We'll get our own transportation out when the time comes." Dick reached out and shook Lazic's hand. "Good luck with your rescue mission. See you back at Bari."

After briefing Lazic and the ACRU, Dick and Josef met with Mihailovich one final time before they left on their mission. Mihailovich had his headquarters set up in a tent alongside the Drine River and the town of Loznica. Josef saw in Mihailovich an entirely different man than the one he had originally met at this same location almost four years earlier. The civil war and the war against the Axis had taken its toll on this once vibrant man. He was lean and gaunt and his clothes seemed to hang from his thin body. His round, wire-rimmed glasses were bent on one side, and he looked as if he hadn't slept for days. Josef introduced Vojvoda to Mihailovich.

"This is Richard Vojvoda. He's the one I told you about who helped me escape from the country back in forty-one. He was waiting for me as I negotiated my way through the no-man's land in Bulgaria."

Mihailovich lit a cigarette from the small lantern in his tent, "She must mean a great deal to you to go through this much trouble."

Dick bent over with a cigarette from his lip and took a light from the lantern as well, "She's a gem. Not to mention one of the brightest individuals I've ever known. I'm risking court martial, but I'm not leaving the country until I find her."

Mihailovich blew cigarette smoke above his head and then continued, "My sources tell me that in all likelihood, they've taken the two agents to Gestapo headquarters now located at Jazak monastery in Fruska Gora. The place is like a fortress. Let me show you." Mihailovich pulled out a picture of the monastery and pointed to the general location in the hills, "We can get you within two or three kilometers of the monastery. After that, you'll be on your own. The good news is that since the place is built like a fortress, it is lightly guarded plus the fact, the Germans can't spare a whole garrison of troops to protect it. It's mostly guarded by a small contingent of SS or Gestapo bodyguards. You can probably take out their entire defenses with the Chetnik force you'll have with you. We can back them up with a 50 caliber machine gun mounted on a truck."

Josef asked, "Any idea if they're already held captive or are they still en route?"

"I have one reliable source who has provided us with good information. He's a Partisan defector who has joined ranks with our forces. If anybody knows anything, it's him. He has contacts with people who work with the Gestapo."

"What sort of contacts?" asked Dick.

"Mostly with the people providing food and supplies for the Germans. My men can get you in contact with him once you're inside his sector, which is currently located on the north side of the Sava River."

"How soon can we move out?"

"My people are saddled up and ready to leave on my orders. You'll have to go on horseback through the mountains, I'm afraid. We don't have any vehicles, plus you'll want to stay off the roads. Allied aircraft patrols are hitting retreating Germans along the main road. It turns into what you Americans call a turkey shoot. In addition, when the Allied aircraft leave, Partisan snipers hit any units left on the roads, Chetnik or German. Needless to say, it's very dangerous between here and the Sava."

"You have been most helpful. If we get the two officers out of the monastery, we'll work our way back here. There's something else I want to pass on to you, in case I don't make it back. When I was in Zagreb, I made contact with a German agent who wished to make arrangements to discuss surrender terms to the Americans and Chetniks and not the Partisans and Soviets. The agent told me that Tito secretly held discussions with the German high command as far back as 1942 to work out some sort of pact to protect German rail supply lines. The pact was supposedly an agreement between the German high command and Tito to stop all sabotage activity along the rail lines in exchange for Germans not attacking Partisan units. The result would allow the Partisans to concentrate their full efforts on defeating the Chetniks who Tito considers to be their number-one enemy and not the Germans. I know all this is based on hearsay, but it's something I think you should know about."

"It is true. I've known about this so-called accommodation for some time. But what can I do about it now that the Allies have turned their backs on me?"

Josef responded, "You'll be known throughout history

as a man who truly was credible and one whom we could trust. I'm sorry Churchill and Stalin didn't see it the same way as I do. I can promise you that I will do everything in my power to let the world know what you have done for freedom."

Chapter 32

JAZAK MONASTERY

The military train pulled into Sremska-Mitrovica station with several Abwehr agents waiting to board the train the moment it came to a complete stop. Penelope was back onboard, bruised and skinned, with a possible broken arm. Semona, the Abwehr agent was nowhere in sight. Penelope's Gestapo escort, Ivan, and his SS back up man yanked Penelope to her feet as the train came to a stop. Abwehr agents met them on the platform as they got off the train. It was obvious that some sort of a power struggle between the Gestapo and the Abwehr was going on as to who was to take custody of the prisoners. In addition, they were looking for their female agent, sent to try to extract information from Penelope, but she had vanished like a ghost.

Sremska-Mitrovica was as far to the east as the German supply network ran. Flosberg and Gerhert, along with twelve SS soldiers, arrived at on the platform. Flosberg had been informed of Penelope's escape attempt and wanted to make sure she did not try the same maneuver again. He took all available SS guards from the monastery.

Penelope came out first, as her Gestapo escorts carried her off the train, and placed her on a gurney. Milo came next from the male prisoner car. He, too, was unable to walk and had to be assisted off the train and onto the platform. Penelope could not see him because she was lying on the gurney, but Milo showed signs of a harsh interrogation. He was severely beaten with multiple bruises, cuts, and lashers all over his body. His face was swollen with a broken nose and two black eyes. Flosberg was stunned at the sight of the two. He approached the two Gestapo men, Ivan, and his SS guard, "This is an outrage! Your orders were to arrest the two and bring them to me, not to interrogate and torture them."

Ivan said, "These two are terrorists, subject to the Kommando Order."

"I don't care about the Kommando Order. I'm in charge of all security forces in Yugoslavia. You will follow *my* orders!" Flosberg waved his hand at Gerhert, who immediately motioned to the SS guards to take possession of the prisoners. Flosberg continued, "These are extremely important prisoners. They have vital information about the security of the Third Reich. They're part of an investigation and dragnet we've spent months working on. We've already had one attempt by the Abwehr to botch this investigation, and I'm not going to stand by and watch the Gestapo ruin all our work as well. Take the prisoners to my headquarters immediately!" Flosberg shouted to Gerhert and everyone else who was watching on the platform.

Milo and Penelope were immediately transported back to Jazak monastery where they were taken to the infirmary. Both were treated for their wounds and injuries and placed in separate holding cells. Milo mostly suffered from cuts and bruises. Penelope had not fractured her right arm, but it was badly sprained. After sleeping in their cells for the night, Gerhert awakened and summoned Milo at five in the morning. It was still dark outside when two SS guards brought him to Gerhert's office located on the east wing of the monastery. He was drinking a strong cup of fresh coffee and the aroma filled the air as Milo was escorted in.

"Close the door and leave us alone. I'll call when I'm finished," he said to the two SS men. "Please have a seat, Lieutenant," he said in very good English.

Milo extended a swollen hand, grabbed the back of the chair, and sat down. He did not say a word. Gerhert poured another cup of coffee from the pot and offered it to Milo, "Do you take cream and sugar?" he asked. Milo did not say anything and kept his mouth closed. "Come now Milo, this is real coffee. In fact, it's American coffee from one of your supply drops. You see Milo, it is Milo?" he asked as he continued to hold the coffee cup. "We've been on your tail for some time now. In fact, we know almost everything." Gerhert pointed at a map of Yugoslavia posted on the wall in front of Milo to see. The map was marked with all the areas that had OSS or SOE missions with their code names. Milo could see some of the names he was familiar with like Hayward, Ranger, and Alum, but displayed no emotion. "As I was saying, we know almost everything. The one thing we have not managed to acquire is the OSS agent known as Alum and his radio operator. Just tell us what you know about him and his radio operator, Celeste?"

Milo still sat motionless in the chair. "You're better off talking, Lieutenant Kovich, because through the goodness of the SD, we are treating you respectfully. We can classify you as a terrorist insurgent instead of a military officer and have you immediately executed. So, why don't you just tell us what you know about Alum and his radio operator?"

Again, Milo sat motionless and expressionless in the

chair. Then Gerhert spoke, "Have it your way then. Since you are not cooperating, I'll have to send you immediately to a labor camp. I have a vehicle ready to take you to Jasenovic." Gerhert placed the coffee down and left the room. Immediately, two SS guards entered the room, placed handcuffs over Milo's arms, and escorted him out the door.

* * *

JOSEF AND DICK left Mihailovich's camp at sunrise. It was a cold, early December morning with a heavy overcast. This cloud layer was a blessing in disguise because it prevented Allied aircraft patrols searching for German troop movements along the main road that paralleled the Drina River. Josef showed Dick how to ride the horse. Josef decided to ride as far as Sremska-Mitrovica. From there, the Chetniks had contacts with a local farmer who had access to a utility truck that he used to transport hay and alfalfa to stock animals at Jazak. The team had to avoid three Partisan ambushes along the way and on two occasions, they had fierce firefights lasting several minutes until the Partisans ran out of ammunition. The team made it to Sremska-Mitrovica by nightfall. The Germans, having nothing to fear from a rag-tag team of Chetniks[1] on horseback, let them pass at the river crossing at Sremska-Mitrovica. Once safely in the city limits, they found the safe house and waited. Josef and Dick used this time to plan their next move.

Josef took out his map of the area, "I've been told there is a single road with one, possibly three roadblocks that lead up the hill to Jazak. We'll never make it through every one of them. Therefore, we have to go up the side of the hill on horseback. There is no way the Germans can cover all approaches to the monastery with the forces they have. Once we get to within a few kilometers of the monastery, and past the last checkpoint, we'll split up, and make our approaches."

"Then what do you expect us to do? Shoot our way in and look for Penelope and Milo?"

"The best way is to disguise ourselves as monks. I remember when we were studying here at Belgrade, Tess and I made a picnic trip out here. We even visited several of the monasteries. On one of my visits to Jazak, I noticed a small stable located not far from the main compound. The stable had a room for the monks to change clothes after they worked with the animals. If my hunch is correct, that facility is still there, and the monks are probably still using it."

"I'm still not following you."

"They have clean robes that we could change into. All we need are two, one for you and one for me. We'll wait for nightfall when everyone is asleep and make our way inside. Once inside, there is a side entrance right off the kitchen. I'll have the rest of the strike team meet there and we'll let them in. Once the entire team is inside, we can search for the agents and overpower the guards. Hopefully, Mihailovich's intelligence is correct and the facility is lightly guarded."

"What happens if we're too late, and they're not there —worst yet, what if they're killed?"

"Then, at least we'll know their fate. I'm prepared to cross that hurdle when the time comes. How do you feel?"

Dick thought for a moment then said, "I didn't come all this way for nothing. I owe the world to Penelope. I'm in."

* * *

GERHERT WALKED outside his office and approached Flosberg in the hall, "He's not saying a word."

"I knew this was going to happen. The female is down in the infirmary recovering from her injuries. All the Gestapo could get out of her was that she is a British agent using the codename, Penelope. Evidently, she tried to jump from a moving train. I'll say one thing for her, she's got guts for trying. We need to try a different approach. I just received a little piece of information that might get her to talk. As far as the male prisoner, I've got no choice but to send him to Jasenovic. Orders are coming in direct from Berlin and SS counterintelligence Chief Krupke himself to move the prisoners if they don't talk."

Flosberg and Gerhert walked into the monastery infirmary, which was nothing more than a small room. Inside they saw in person for the first time, the woman they thought had eluded them for so long. She was dressed in a hospital gown and her left arm was wrapped in a bandage.

Flosberg was dressed in a civilian, brown business suit rather than his SD uniform. He and Gerhert were not the sinister-looking figures so depicted by her SOE trainers. It was now after seven in the morning. Penelope refused to eat the small breakfast of oatmeal, English tea, and dry toast set before her. She had a look of pure evil in her eyes as she looked upon the two SD men as they entered. Flosberg spoke first and in perfect English, "Miss Celeste, I'm Hans Flosberg, Chief of State Security for all Yugoslavia. This is my technical assistant and interpreter, Ernst Gerhert."

Penelope was surprised to be addressed by that name because the only name she gave the Gestapo under interrogation was, Penelope. She immediately thought about Tess and Josef's mission into Serbia the previous year. She decided to speak and move the interrogation in a different direction, "Did you kill him? I heard the screams early this morning."

Flosberg glanced at Gerhert with a concerned look and said, "This facility has many tenants, one of which is the local Gestapo. What you heard were the screams of one of *their* interrogators working on a Partisan resister. My department's responsibility is only with captured Allied agents. Your fellow agent is safely in his cell awaiting deportation. We never harmed him in any manner. However, once he leaves the facility and is deported to a labor camp, I cannot guarantee that safety or his life, for that matter. He has refused to talk, so therefore we pass him on to other security services."

"You're lying. Why should I believe a word you say?"

Flosberg pulled up a chair and moved closer to Penelope, "Since you're feeling much better now, let us be frank. You have been caught conducting sabotage operations and terrorist activities against the Third Reich. You are directly responsible for the murder of several Wehrmacht officers and soldiers. By direct orders from the Führer himself, you fall under his Kommando Order and will be treated accordingly." Flosberg got up from his chair, walked over to the window, and looked out. "On the other hand, if you cooperate with us and tell us *certain* things, I can forestall or even postpone your inevitable situation. The choice is up to you. Your comrade made his choice and so he will be leaving our custody."

Penelope, still in pain, managed to move her mouth and give off a shrewd remark. "Are you out of your mine? I'd be collaborating with the enemy."

Flosberg gave Gerhert a nod and he left the room. A few minutes later he reappeared with a wheelchair and moved it next to Penelope's bed. "Very well, young lady, we'll conduct this session somewhere more appropriate." Gerhert picked her up from the bed and placed her on the wheelchair.

The three left the infirmary and went straight to Flosberg's office on the north wing. Gerhert pushed Penelope behind Flosberg and the three entered the small office. Penelope couldn't escape if she wanted to. Once inside, they went through another door into a much larger room and closed the door behind them. Inside this room was a showcase for the SD. There were maps on the wall of all Europe showing SOE and OSS missions. Some had red X's scratched across them; others were left intact, such as the one in Yugoslavia known as Alum. Penelope saw several Mark II radio sets with pictures of men behind them. There were other pieces of clothing and uniforms stacked up next to them. She was stunned to see the effectiveness of the Gestapo.

Flosberg spoke, "Miss Celeste, everything you see in this room has been taken from captured agents. We even have official photographs of these individuals from SOE headquarters on Baker Street. We are not the enemy, young lady. You have a traitor back in London, who has provided us with most of the information you see before you. He or she is the enemy, not us."

Flosberg moved over to a British Mark II wireless radio set placed on the table. This radio did not have any photographs attached to it. There were also the codebook and one-time key pads associated with the set and several crystals. Flosberg continued, "We have been in contact with SOE using these sets for some time now. The traitor is in a very high position and the country sections don't even know about this. Yugoslav section, in particular, has provided us with almost everything we have requested through the playback of these radio sets."

Penelope could not believe the words he was saying, but it was impossible to be anything but the truth. He was too accurate in his descriptions of SOE cryptography. "Let me be very frank again with you, young lady. The war is almost over. The British and Americans are a few weeks away from the streets of Berlin! The Russians are closing in from the east with over two million men! It is *they* who are the enemy now. If they should come across the information we know, they will use it against the Western Allies after the war. Our job is to find everything we can about your intelligence operations and *keep it* from the Russians."

Gerhert turned the wheelchair around to face him. "As you can see from this room, there is only one agent we have not managed to capture. Just tell us what you know about the American OSS agent known as Alum and his radio operator. Are you Celeste?"

"You must think I'm some stupid bimbo. That may have worked with some of the girls in France or Belgium, but it's not going to work on me. You'll just have to put a bullet through my head."

"I'm afraid it's not that simple. You have already seen too much into our operation. As much as I would like to do just that, I'm under *direct orders* to gather information for counterintelligence operations. If I cannot gather that information, then you're to be sent off to a labor camp where you will die a slow, painful death rather than fall into the hands of the Soviets."

"I'm not saying another word!"

"Miss Celeste, I could bring in the Gestapo and their

henchmen and have them gang-rape you until you provide us the information about Alum and his radio operator, but we're not going to do that. I've got something more effective." Flosberg walked over to the table with the radio sets and picked up a file.

"This just came in from one of our Partisan Informants in Stremska-Mitrovica. There are two American agents preparing an assault on this facility to secure your release. Their information led them to believe that the monastery was only lightly guarded. That was the case a day or so ago, but with this latest information, I've called in a team of reinforcements. The entire Twelfth SS Mountain Division has taken up positions surrounding the monastery. If anyone is foolish enough to attack this facility, they will be met by overwhelming firepower placed in strategic locations, effectively cutting the assault team into pieces. They won't be recognized as human beings."

"No, that's impossible!"

Gerhert said, "I'm afraid it *is* possible. We've received information that one American fits the description of your organizer, Alum himself. That information was verified by me because I was nearly killed by one of the grenades he tossed under my vehicle, but not before I got a good look at his face. The other agent is tall, muscular, with premature gray hair. He fits the description of one of your classmates who attended Belgrade University with you before the war."

Flosberg reached for a cigarette and placed one between his lips, "Just tell us what you know about Alum and his mission and I'll call off the Mountain Division. You have my word that no harm will come to either of the two men or yourself. You will stay in my custody, until the war is over."

Penelope could not believe the amount of information the Gestapo had amassed about her and her companions. "I'll never parley with any of your filth."

"Very well, have it your way. We'll take you back to the infirmary, sit you in front of the window. From there you'll have a bird's eye view of the assault. You'll hear their screams as the Mountain Division cuts them to pieces."

The Chetnik team waited until nightfall to make the assault on the monastery. Josef and Dick each took seven men on horseback and rode up the mountainside until they could not go any further. They secured the animals and proceded the rest of the way on foot. They straddled their way along both sides of the road leading up to the monastery to the rendezvous point which was the stable shed used by the monks. Dick and Josef met the rest of their teams and planned their next move. Just as Josef predicted, several clean cassocks were hanging on hooks. He took two off the hooks and sized them up. One of the cassocks appeared to be large enough for Dick so Josef threw it toward him, "This should fit. It might be a little short, but I think it will get the job done. Now, let's take a look at our next move." Josef took out a small sketch of the monastery that included the latest intelligence from Mihailovich's sources and spread it on the ground. One of the Chetniks lit a candle to provide light.

"This is where we have to split company. According to Mihailovich, Penelope, in all likelihood, is held in one of the cells located on the second floor. These cells are unlike the ones the Gestapo use for interrogating other resistance fighters in the basement. The SD has taken over the western wing of the monastery that faces our approach. The SD uses different interrogating techniques than the Gestapo. The windows are not barred and doors to the rooms are lightly guarded, if guarded at all. We can expect the doors might not be closed or locked. Our challenge once we get inside the monastery is to get to the second floor and search each room one by one until we find the right one. This sounds difficult, but the SD probably only has one or two rooms that they can spare for this task."

"Tell us, how can we get up to the second floor?" asked Dick.

"As I told you before, we'll use the service entrance on the far side, next to the kitchen. Dressed as monks, we'll enter there. Once you and I clear the area, we'll signal for the rest of the men. At that point, there is a stairway leading up to the second floor directly from the kitchen. This is how food is delivered. We go up that stairway to minimize exposure for the rest of the team. Then we make our way to the west wing. Once we find Penelope and Milo, we can go out the window and rope down to the first floor from there and run for the cover of the trees. Once we get Penelope and Milo out, we'll make our way back here, get on the horses, and use the cover of the Fruska Gora to get back to Stremska-Mitrovica."

"Nothing goes according to plan. If the guards should be alerted to our presence, they could call for reinforcements. I think we should split up and make two assault approaches. One from the kitchen, the other from the west side, that way we'll have help from a different flank, should the guards start shooting from inside."

Josef thought for a moment and then said, "All right, since I'm most familiar with the monastery, I'll take seven men and enter through the kitchen."

"No, that's precisely the point. If something should happen and you're killed or captured, we won't have the knowledge or experience to try a second attempt. *I'll* take the kitchen; you stay on the west side in the trees and wait for my signal from one of the windows."

Josef knew this was the most logical strategy and nodded his head in agreement. "All right, but you'll probably have to kill a few guards in the process. You've never been in the field before. This is not like training back at the Farm. Are you sure you want to do it?"

"I'm sure."

"That's it then, let's take stock of our equipment and supplies. I want to begin the assault by two in the morning."

Each member of the team had six grenades, a .45 caliber pistol with silencer, an automatic weapon of some sort, either a Sten or Merlin submachine gun, and sufficient ammunition. In addition, each team carried a fifty-foot coil of rope. All the Chetnik fighters were dressed in either dark grey or black clothing. Unfortunately, Dick and Josef did not have dark clothing, but they did wear their olive green US Army uniforms under their cassocks. Each man had their faces darkened with a charcoal stick that one of the Chetniks had brought along for just such an occasion. With final preparations complete, the team split up into two groups. Just before the men separated, Dick reached his hand out to Josef.

"You know, Penelope was the one who contacted me by telephone and gave me advance notice that the Germans were about to launch an airstrike on Belgrade. Her contacts inside the GSI intercepted coded messages that indicated Göring's Air Forces were about to attack the city. I owe my life to her. If she hadn't notified me, I would've still been in bed when the bombs fell. My apartment was one of the first buildings struck that morning. She was the one who told me we had to escape the city, not me. That's why she was with me when we drove up to Tess's apartment that day. See you back in Bari."

Dick shook Josef's hand and then vanished into the darkness. Josef took his seven men and worked their way toward the west side of the monastery. It was exactly 0200 hours.

Penelope was awakened very early by the sound of keys unlocking her cell. The light was turned on from a switch on the outside of the door, giving the guards control of light into her cell. The cell had an iron bed with a thin mattress, a single chair, and one tiny window that looked out to the forests of Fruska Gora. Gerhert walked into the cell. He looked as if he just woken up. His hair was a mess and he still hadn't shaved or washed his face nor was he dressed in his usual business attire that he normally wore. She suspected it was very early in the morning, probably before three or four o'clock. She had not slept well that night thinking about her daughter, Sarah, and Hal Mattingly. She was also troubled about the words her Gestapo captors said to her about two men leading an assault on the compound. She wondered if Josef and Dick were crazy enough to be pulling off a stunt like this.

Then Gerhert spoke and interrupted her thought. "It's time, young lady. Herr Flosberg will be here shortly for the little show that is about to get under way." He moved the chair closer to the window, "Get up and have a seat here by the window. I want you to see what's about to unfold."

Gerhert moved Penelope out of bed and placed her in a chair by the open window. Flosberg then walked into the cell with two other uniformed SS men. Flosberg was in full uniform. Penelope saw for the first time that he wore the SS equivalent rank of a Lieutenant Colonel. The three men entered the cell and then closed the door behind them.

Flosberg continued, "You needn't worry about any torture sessions this morning. What I'm about to show you should get you to talk. As I've been saying all along, what we want most is information about Alum and his network. You see, we believe the Allies are planning on another invasion somewhere in the Balkans; possibly in Istria to cut off our flanks and prevent our forces from retreating through the Maribor Pass, leaving us exposed to the Red Army from the east. We need information vital to the survival of thousands of men stationed in the Balkans. We don't want any more bloodshed. We want you to help us. If you agree to work for us and play the radios back and can gather information about these possible invasions, then I'll guarantee the safety of not only you, but your two friends as well. These friends of yours are about to make a suicidal attempt at assaulting the monastery."

"You woke me up for this? You should know me better than that. You people started this war, not us. I'm not betraying my country so a few of your people can save their necks. I hope the Red Army comes swooping in and slaughters every last one of you."

"Talk is tough, young lady. Let me show you something." He moved Penelope closer to the window. "Have a look there, though the darkness on the side of the road. Can you see them?"

She struggled in the moonlight, but she could make out several machine gun emplacements, and German soldiers dug into the side of the mountain, waiting.

"The two American agents have no idea what they're about to face. I just received word a few minutes ago that a team of twenty or so guerrilla fighters has started to make their way to the monastery. My men will cut them down to pieces before they know what hit them. Just give me your word that you'll work for us and I'll call off the Mountain Division."

Penelope shook her head, "How can I believe you? How do I know you're even telling me the truth? You could have made up this whole charade."

"Does the name Dick Vojvoda mean anything to you? How about Josef Kostinic or Vivian Tate? We have our sources. Trust me, young lady, these men are making a foolish mistake trying to rescue you."

Penelope was surprised to hear the names, especially Vivian Tate's. "I don't believe you. You can't guarantee that kind of cooperation. It's all a trick."

Flosberg gave one of the SS men a nod and he left the cell and returned with a telephone line. "The Twelfth commander is waiting for my orders. If I don't call by the time the assault team comes in range, his orders are to open fire."

Penelope responded by spitting at the men in the face.

Dick Vojvoda and his strike force used the cover of the forest and came as close as they could to the main road. The final approach to the monastery would have to be made using this road because it led directly to the back entrance near the kitchen. If they scaled the slopes away from the road, they would still have to come back eventually to the road. Dick decided to minimize the exposure and take the chance using the slopes. Unknowingly, this gave Penelope more time to contemplate her decision. Dick spoke in Serbo-Croatian to the men, "Let's stay in the trees until the last minute."

On the western side, Josef and his team stayed in the cover of the trees the entire time because they did not have to worry about being spotted. They made better time in reaching the objective. They came to within a hundred feet of the west side of the building. Josef saw for the first time the location and windows where the SD held their prisoners. Penelope could be in any one of the rooms on the second floor. He would wait there until Dick gave him a signal, "Relax for a few minutes. We can't do anything more than wait."

One of the Chetnik officers came up to Josef, "There is only one road leading up to the monastery. We have a machine gunner in position with a B-17 50-caliber hidden in a hay truck should they need it for support. He's ready to take out anything that moves on that road."

Josef thought for a moment to himself, *this could be our means of escape.* His thoughts were interrupted by the sound of automatic gunfire and explosions coming from the direction of Vojvoda. It was an intense firefight not coming from eight men engaging a small force. The Chetnik officer looked at Josef as they heard the screams of men in pain and agony.

"We've got to help them. They're in serious trouble!" he shouted. Without acknowledging him, the Chetnik officer took all his men and headed toward the sounds of gunfire, leaving Josef behind alone. More gunfire and explosions erupted as he could hear mortar rounds drop on Dick's position. This was not the work of a ragtag band of Hungarian and Bulgarian bodyguards, but the sound of well-trained Special Forces. Someone must have tipped them off on their presence. All Josef could do was wait.

Tears started to fall from her cheeks as she heard the sounds and explosions outside and knew if Flosberg was telling the truth, Dick and Josef were caught in the trap and fighting for their lives.

"There is still time. I can make the call, put an end to this senseless madness, and your friends' lives will be spared."

"I still don't believe you. You could be shooting into thin air, for all I know."

"Then give me your word, I'll stop the shooting, and the three of us will walk down, and you can tell your friends to surrender peacefully. Your lives will be spared."

Penelope continued to resist, "No, I'm not doing it! Ever!"

Flosberg, now showing signs of frustration, stood her up and pushed her closer to the window. "See it! Feel it! Your friends are being mowed down to pieces. Is this what you want?"

Josef glanced at the monastery and could see plainly in the window a figure that looked like Penelope with Gestapo men all around her. He could not stand it any longer. The mission appeared a failure. Now it was a matter of survival. He took out his Merlin submachine gun and ran down the hill toward Dick and the rest of the team. As he crashed through the trees and bushes, the gunfire subsided. However, it sounded as if it were an eternity, the battle only lasted a few minutes. It was all over. The assault force was no match for the SS division. His only thought was to get close enough to see if there were any survivors. He fell to his knees as he approached the battle zone. He saw bodies everywhere; mostly Chetniks, but no sign of Dick. Then the unthinkable came into his view. Several of the SS soldiers dragged a body from a ditch by the feet and dropped him to the ground. They wrapped the rope used to escape down the windows around the feet of the body and tied the other end to the back of a motorcycle sidecar then drove away with the body at the end of the rope, but not before Josef saw the dark robe of the monk's cassock. His friend, Dick Vojvoda, was dead. Rage and hatred took over all his emotions. He stood up from cover and fired his Merlin at the SS men dragging the body, hitting several. He continued to fire and yell obscenities until he emptied the magazine. He slapped in another and continued to fire. The SS men, now alerted to a survivor, turned their attention on to Josef. They fired at him from all sides. Bullets flew by his head and body, hitting nearby trees, splintering fragments, hitting him in the face. More bullets hit the ground around him. Then the mortar crews lobbed a round over his head missing their mark by one-hundred feet. The explosion knocked him to the ground, but also knocked some sense into him. He dropped the empty Merlin machine gun and began running down the hill toward the main road. His instincts and training now took over. If the Chetniks were right, the machine gunner would be waiting at the bottom of the hill in a hay truck. Josef drew their fire and continued down the mountainside. The SS soldiers ran in pursuit, as Josef made his way to the hidden 50-caliber.

The telephone rang and Flosberg picked it up. It was now quiet outside except for a few sporadic shots. Flosberg grunted something into the receiver then hung the phone up, "It's all over. All the bandits are dead, including your friends. I tried to reason with you, but you left me with no choice. Now I cannot guarantee your safety or your life, for that matter. You are a terrorist insurgent subject to the Kommando Order. Expect to be deported to a concentration camp by mid-afternoon. Good day, young lady. It was a pleasure meeting you." He placed his hat on his head, turned, and left the room.

Josef moved down the hillside back to their initial staging area. He saw one of the horses left behind that got away, probably awakened during the shootout. Josef stopped the horse and immediately hopped on the animal and got back on the road and rode down the hill to a safer area. The maneuver put more distance between him and the SS detachment. As he came around the corner, he noticed the hay truck parked off to the side of the road. Josef started yelling in Serbo-Croat. "Get the gun out!" A young man leaped from the driver's seat and headed to the back of the truck. Josef approached the truck and saw a young man he recognized. It was the same young man who had fired on the Ustaša unit as he and Tess were fleeing Sremska-Mitrovica many months earlier. It was young Propovjednik, Aleksander Radivich, with his captured 50-caliber machine gun, "Propovjeknik, get the gun ready and fire when I say so!" Josef said as he jumped off the horse.

Young Radivich understood his instructions and recognized the man issuing them. He said, "It's good to see a familiar face. I didn't know who to expect."

"We were ambushed by the SS. They've killed everyone. I'm the only one to survive. I'll drive the truck. You stay on the machine gun. If anyone comes around the corner, open fire!"

Josef got into the driver seat and turned the truck around just as Radivich uncovered the machine gun. Two SS soldiers riding in a motorcycle sidecar came into view. Propovjednik opened fire. The sidecar exploded with human body pieces flying in all directions. He continued to fire as Josef sped down the road to Sremska-Mitrovica and safety.

* * *

THREE WEEKS LATER, Josef Kostinic, the only remaining OSS member of Operation Halyard, Rudko, Stefan, and Aleksander "Propovjednik" Radivich, along with several thousand Chetnik fighters stood at attention on the makeshift airfield in Bosnia-Herzegovina as General Draza Mihailovich paid tribute to his fallen Chetniks and Captain

Richard Vojvoda whose body was never recovered. They were all waiting for the last American C-47 to land in Chetnik territory and take them back to Italy.

This was the final journey for Josef Kostinic. His mission to Yugoslavia to establish the credibility of a worthy ally was over. Three days before, General Mihailovich said farewell to Captain Nick Lazic and the last of five hundred American airmen rescued inside Nazi-occupied territory. Mihailovich provided safe haven for all these Americans at great cost in human lives and suffering by the Serbian people. In all, not a single American flyer lost their life thanks to Mihailovich and his support. Josef made one final plea for Mihailovich to get on that plane with him and go back to Italy. Mihailovich refused.

The US Army Air Corp. C-47 touched down on the makeshift airfield just after nine in the morning. The plane made two 180 degree turns then came to a stop. With engines still running, the rear door opened, and a crew member motioned Josef to come forward. Josef saluted Mihailovich one last time then gave him a hug, "Thank you for all you've done for the people of the United States. The parents and families of five hundred airmen will be eternally grateful you returned their loved ones to them. I have no use for this. Why don't you take it?" Josef un-shouldered his Merlin submachine gun and handed it to the General.

Mihailovich took the weapon and said, "You are welcome. You will always be remembered as a friend of the Serbian people. There is something I want to give you in return." Mihailovich reached into his belt and pulled out a dagger, "This *is* the Credible Dagger. I want you to have it. Pass this on to the next generation of warriors who protect freedom."

The bearded man mounted his horse and raised a

sword in the air. The entire Chetnik force numbering in the thousands came to attention. Josef boarded the C-47, took one final look at his friend, and saluted him. The General rode off up the mountain, proud and soldierly on his horse. Josef knew that he was leading his army, the tattered remnants of the hundreds of thousands who had once punished Hitler's Reich to his last stand. It was a moving sight that Josef would carry for the rest of his life.

---

1. By this time in the war, the Chetniks were classified as Allies with the Nazis, instead of enemy combatants.

Epilogue

Josef Kostinic took a sip from his now cold cup of tea and placed it down on the small coffee table, "My good friend, Chetnik leader Draza Mihailovich, was executed by a firing squad on July 17 of this year, less than forty-eight hours after a Yugoslav military court found him guilty of treason and collaboration with the Nazis. All this despite the fact he helped rescue over five hundred American airmen, trapped behind enemy lines. I even volunteered to testify at his trial—of course, I was refused by the Tito government."

It was late in the afternoon when Josef and Tess finish telling Mattingly the whole story. "Now that I've told you the whole story about credible dagger and my mission, I want to share with you the latest information we have on Penelope."

Hal addressed both Josef and Tess, "I stayed in London with Penelope's parents for one year, after the war, waiting for her to come home. She was officially listed as missing. We'd thought maybe she'd worked her way to the Soviet or Norwegian sectors. Everyone was hoping she'd come knocking at the door like she'd done so many times during the war. I finally gave up and moved here."

Josef continued, "When the war was over, I was assigned to the Allied Control Commission in Bulgaria. One of my jobs was tracking down Nazi war criminals and bringing them to justice. During the investigation and interrogations, the Soviets came in contact with a civil servant who survived the war and worked for the Gestapo in Yugoslavia. It was Ernst Gerhert. He gave me his complete deposition."

Tess added, "Up until this point in the war, the SD still did not know the true identity of Penelope Walsh. They were under the impression that she was *me* because our radio fists were very similar and we were about the same age. Because of this uncertainty, her identity was never fully determined. That was a major reason why the British government was unable to find any traces of her after the war. We found out otherwise."

"What I discovered after interrogating Gerhert was that Penelope held out and did not give away any information about our network or her radio checks. In fact, Gerhert testified that she performed her job admirably. Not one British or American operative was compromised by her capture and Gerhert told me she gave the SD absolutely nothing. Something he was quite disturbed about because all the previously arrested agents gave away information or cooperated."

"She's a British officer, so, why *did* she end up at Jasenovic concentration camp and not a prisoner of war camp?"

"After our failed rescue attempt and Penelope's resistance to cooperate, Flosberg was *forced* to send her to Jasenovic. According to Gerhert, Flosberg didn't want to send her, but he had direct orders from SS counterintelligence chief, Otto Krupke in Berlin. If he didn't go through with the deportation, he and Gerhert would face a firing squad that afternoon. So, she was deported that afternoon, just as young Propovjednik and I were making our escape across the Sava River. In fact, it's safe to say that one of the reasons why I was allowed to escape was because the Gestapo had all their resources tied up transferring this dangerous prisoner known as Penelope Walsh."

"What else can you tell me?"

Tess spoke now, "She was my best friend, so I'll be the one to tell you. Gerhert testified that approximately three weeks after Penelope was transferred to Jasenovic, the Allies crossed the Rhine River into the heart of the Third Reich, and the SS wanted no traces left of any of their counterintelligence activities and treatment of captured Allied agents. So, the SS was ordered to execute both Penelope and Lieutenant Kovich, the American OSS agent on Josef's team. I'm sorry to tell you this, but our beloved Penelope was actually murdered by the Croatian Ustaša and their Nazis masters, her body was cremated. There was nothing to recover. Because of her heroic efforts at Lipoglav, she will almost certainly be awarded the George Cross."

Hal was deeply crushed as he finally heard the inevitable. Tears began to fall from his cheek. Tess handed him a tissue then added, "In 1946, there was a mysterious fire at F section's Orchard Court location, and many of the SOE records were lost or destroyed. However, Penelope's former supervisor, Vivian Tate, managed to make copies of all her female agent's records. I found out about this one evening when I confronted Tate at the war department. I introduced myself as Penelope's best friend and former SOE operative. She then gave me a complete set of Penelope's records. I thought you should have them." Tess reached into her handbag, pulled out a large folder with the letters REGDOD stenciled on it, and handed it to Hal Mattingly.

"What do the letters mean?"

"I have no idea. Maybe some sort of code used by Miss Tate to help keep track of all her agents who were lost or captured during the war. There were several of them. You may want to look through this in private. She was quite a uniquely amazing and wonderful woman."

"If it's any consolation, Hal, I discovered Flosberg did, in fact, treat Penelope with respect. No harm or mistreatment came to her while she was held captive in his custody. The SD admired her beauty as well as her courage. Flosberg himself was not as fortunate. The Red Army captured him shortly after the Germans surrendered in April of 1945. When the Soviets saw the atrocities committed by the Nazis and their puppet Ustaša, they summarily executed him. Not before, however, he was stripped, beaten, and hung alive on a meat hook for several days, then shot in the back of the head with a shotgun. He obviously didn't deserve it, but he was responsible for all security matters inside Yugoslavia. The Soviets made him accountable."

"So, that's how it all ended?"

"I'm afraid so," continued Josef. "Prior to his arrest and capture by the Soviets, Gerhert kept in his possession something that belongs to you." Josef reached into his pocket and pulled out the diamond engagement ring Hal had given Penelope the night he proposed to her.

"I didn't even know she had this on her when we were in the field. She must have felt that in an emergency, the diamond could be of some value. Gerhert gave it to me during his incarceration, so I'm giving it back to you." Josef placed the ring in Hal's hand. "There is one *last* piece of information I need to pass on to you." He reached into his coat pocket again and pulled out the letter, "I promised Penelope I'd deliver this to you."

Penelope had given this same letter to him to mail back in 1944 as he left for Zagreb to meet with Kilo Six. He had never gotten the chance to mail it. Hal took the envelope, opened it immediately, and began to read. When he was finished, he placed the ring and letter back in the envelope.

"That's everything we brought with us today. Is there anything else we can do for you, Hal?" asked Tess.

Hal thought for a moment and then called out in French to his housekeeper. "Sonia, bring the child here, please."

As they were waiting for Sonia to arrive, Hal said to Tess, "There is someone I'd like you to meet. I do believe you already know her."

A few minutes later, the woman appeared with the child. Tess recognized her immediately. She saw the blue eyes and dark hair. She was six years old now and growing up into a beautiful young child.

"Papa, Papa!" the young girl cried. Mattingly swooped her up in his arms and placed her on his lap, "This is Sarah Walsh. I made a promise to Penelope as well. If anything happened to her, she wanted me to look after her."

May 9, 2005

The surviving, rescued airmen from Operation Halyard, along with former, aging OSS operatives, gathered at the White House for a special presentation by President George W. Bush. They were there to present the "Legion of Merit" to Gordana Mihailovich, daughter of the late Draza Mihailovich.

In April of 1948, President Harry Truman posthumously awarded Draza Mihailovich this citation as official recognition for his aid in the rescue of five hundred US and Allied airmen trapped behind enemy lines. This award, however, was kept secret for political reasons until the fall of the Iron Curtain, when many OSS records were declassified. Below is the full text of the citation.

"LEGION OF MERIT - CHIEF COMMANDER: General Dragoljub Mihailovich distinguished himself in an outstanding manner as commander-in-chief of the Yugoslavian Army Forces and later as Minister of War by organizing and leading important resistance forces against the

enemy which occupied Yugoslavia, from December 1941 to December 1944. Through the undaunted efforts of his troops, many United States airmen were rescued and returned safely to friendly control. General Mihailovich and his forces, although lacking adequate supplies, and fighting under extreme hardships, contributed materially to the Allied cause, and were instrumental in obtaining a final Allied victory.

- Harry S. Truman, March 29, 1948."

Acknowledgments

First, I would like to thank the United States National Achieves in College Park, Maryland for their help and assistance in researching for this book, especially material related to OSS operations conducted during World War II (many of which were only recently declassified in 2002) and the concept of strategic deception. I was able to read maps, aerial photographs, drawings and messages written by agents in the field. There was evidence that many of these brave individuals suffered or were under stress as evident by bloodstains still on the documents.

Next, I would like to thank the Imperial War Museum in London, England, especially for the information on the Marconi Mark II wireless radio, code usage, and SOE organization. In addition, they gave me valuable information on Westland Lysander operations (Moon Flights) and clandestine landings. From a pilot's perspective, the 'Lizzie' was a remarkable aircraft and well ahead of it's time for a high-winged, single-engine, monoplane.

I would also like to thank the Hoover Library at Stanford University in Palo Alto, California. They have an additional and quite extensive archive of material on OSS operations in the former Yugoslavia related to Partisan activity. This saved me a tremendous amount of time as I did not have to fly back and forth to Washington D.C., from the West Coast.

Speaking of the West Coast, I can't leave out my undergraduate geography teacher at UCLA, the late Professor, Emeritus, H. L. Kostanick, a one-time member of the OSS. Professor Kostanick, who operated in Yugoslavia during World War II, inspired me to write my original, Cold War version of *The Balkan Network*, over thirty-four years ago and was the inspiration for the character, Josef. He was also the first person to disclose to me the extensive clandestine, insurgency operations behind enemy lines by U.S. and British forces during the war.

Finally, I would like to thank my family, especially my wife Mary, who allowed me to write and pursue my ambitions of becoming a novelist. She put up with me being another "fixture" in the house while I was busy typing away on my computer. Without her support and dedication, as well as reading several manuscripts, none of my stories would be in print.

About the Author

Gregory M. Acuña is an emerging author. *Credible Dagger* is the second book in a series and the prequel to *The Balkan Network*. He is currently writing his fifth book, another Cold War Thriller about a US Army officer who tries to sell Pershing II Missile deploy- ment information to the Soviets.  However, his beautiful East German contact is also a double agent working for the Americans and East German intelligence.

Gregory M. Acuña is a former USAF pilot and current B-777 Captain for a major U.S. air carrier.

Also by Gregory M. Acuña

As a way of saying thank you, for purchasing this book, I am offering a free copy of my book, The *Balkan Network* when you join my Reader's Group at:

WWW.GMACUNA.COM

More books by Gregory M. Acuña

Available in ebook, print and audio formats.

Credible Dagger

The Balkan Network

Nimble Dodger

author@gmacuna.com